Valerie Woods was born in Yorkshire and now lives in a village near the east coast. She is the author of *The Hungry Tide*, winner of the Catherine Cookson Prize for Fiction, *Annie*, *Children of the Tide*, *The Romany Girl*, *Emily*, *Going Home*, *Rosa's Island*, *The Doorstep Girls* and *Far From Home*, all available in Corgi paperback.

Find our more about Valerie Wood's novels by visiting her website on www.valeriewood.co.uk

Also by Valerie Wood

THE HUNGRY TIDE
ANNIE
CHILDREN OF THE TIDE
THE ROMANY GIRL
EMILY
ROSA'S ISLAND
THE DOORSTEP GIRLS
FAR FROM HOME

and published by Corgi Books

GOING HOME

Valerie Wood

CORGI BOOKS

GOING HOME
A CORGI BOOK : 978 0 552 14845 0

Originally published in Great Britain by Bantam Press,
a division of Transworld Publishers

PRINTING HISTORY
Bantam Press edition published 2000
Corgi edition published 2001

3 5 7 9 10 8 6 4

Set in 11/12½pt New Baskerville by
Kestrel Data, Exeter, Devon

Corgi Books are published by Transworld Publishers,
61–63 Uxbridge Road, London W5 5SA,
a division of The Random House Group Ltd,
in Australia by Random House Australia (Pty) Ltd,
20 Alfred Street, Milsons Point, Sydney, NSW 2061, Australia,
in New Zealand by Random House New Zealand Ltd,
18 Poland Road, Glenfield, Auckland 10, New Zealand
and in South Africa by Random House (Pty) Ltd,
Endulini, 5a Jubilee Road, Parktown 2193, South Africa.

Printed and bound by
Clays Ltd, St Ives plc

Papers used by Transworld Publishers are natural, recyclable
products made from wood grown in sustainable forests.
The manufacturing processes conform to the environmental
regulations of the country of origin.

For my family with love

Acknowledgements

With thanks to Harry Buck for the loan of old farm books and sayings.

To Catherine for reading the manuscript.

General reading sources:

A Secret Country by John Pilger (Jonathan Cape, London, 1989).

Archaeology of the Dreamtime by Josephine Flood (William Collins, Sydney–London, 1983).

GOING HOME

Chapter One

'My father says your mother was a whore!'

Ralph Hawkins hesitated for only a second, then crunched up his fist and directed it towards the conveyor of the insulting remark. It found its mark on Edwin Boyle's chubby chin and knocked him to the ground.

'Don't ever say that again or it'll be the worse for you.' Ralph rubbed his knuckles with his other hand. The blow had hurt him too but he didn't mind that, he'd been wanting to hit the little toad for some time and even though he wasn't completely sure what his adversary had meant by his statement, it had been made with such gleeful venom that it was obviously not complimentary.

Edwin started to blubber and their teacher, Miss Henderson, came hurrying towards them, her movements restricted by her old-fashioned, overlong black gown. The ribbons on her bonnet swung around her neck and her slippered feet pitter-pattered on the school yard. She was followed in less haste by Edwin's sister Phoebe.

'No fighting boys,' the teacher twittered. 'It is not gentlemanly! Now get up Edwin, and Ralph, say you are sorry to Edwin for hitting him.'

'But I'm not sorry!' Ralph glared down at Edwin and was gratified to see that a hole had been torn in Edwin's striped stockings just below the knee of his knickerbockers. 'He insulted my mother.'

Miss Henderson's face turned pink but she stammered, 'I'm sure he didn't mean to. Now come along and make up, there's good fellows.'

'They're not good fellows,' Phoebe interrupted. 'Not either of them. They're both horrible and Edwin's just a cry-baby.'

'And you're horrible too, Phoebe Boyle. You'll never be a lady,' her brother retaliated as he scrambled to his feet. 'Father says you won't.'

Ralph turned his back on them and walked towards the gate where he knew his mother would be waiting in the trap if she hadn't sent one of the Aboriginal boys to meet him, as sometimes she did if she was busy. But today she was there already with his young sister Peggy. Next to their trap was another, with Mrs Boyle sitting in it waiting for Edwin and Phoebe.

Both women had their backs to him and appeared to be talking together, though they were not close friends. His mother and father didn't have many friends, only people like Ralph's godfather Ralph Clavell and Benne and

Daisy Mungo, the parents of Jack, his best friend. Few people from Sydney visited their farm socially. It was set high up in the hills overlooking Sydney Cove. The best view in all the area, his father boasted, he could sell it for a fortune if he wanted to, but he wouldn't.

His mother, Meg, turned to greet him, but her smile faded and she raised her dark eyebrows as she saw the sullen expression on his face. 'In trouble again, Ralph? What have you been up to this time?'

'Ralph and Edwin have been fighting, Mrs Hawkins,' Phoebe broke in from behind him before Ralph could offer an explanation, and he gave her a withering look. 'Edwin was rude.'

'Edwin!' Lucinda Boyle turned to her son. The difference between her and Meg Hawkins was immediately apparent. Her demeanour was ladylike, her manner gentle and cultivated. She had the fair translucent skin and soft blond hair of an Englishwoman, and was dressed too in the manner of the ladies of the mother country in her sprigged sheath dress with its ruched bodice and draped skirt, though today, because she was driving her trap, she wore no bustle. Meg was weather-browned, her hair dark and unruly beneath her wide hat, and she wore a plain, though good-quality bleached cotton gown. Nevertheless she was a handsome woman with a proud, strong and defiant look about her.

Ralph caught his mother's glance and in-tuitively she didn't question further but told him to get into the trap. 'Boys will fight, Mrs Boyle,' she said, and shook the reins. 'Don't worry about it. They'll be friends again by 'morning.'

Mrs Boyle smiled in agreement and wishing each other goodbye they moved off in different directions, with the two boys glaring at each other and Phoebe looking smug and twirling a blond ringlet around her finger.

'Want to tell me about it?' Ralph's mother asked as they pulled up the steep dusty road towards home.

He glanced at his sister sitting next to him and shook his head. 'No,' he muttered. 'It was nothing. Edwin Boyle is a dirty toad that's all.'

'Toads are not dirty.' Peggy, with all the assurance of a ten-year-old, defied her brother's wisdom. 'It's only because they live in mud that people think they are.'

'Oh, shut up Peggy,' he said irritably. 'I'm trying to think.'

He would ask Jack, he decided, he would surely know what it meant. Even though Jack was younger than Ralph, he knew the answers to so many things. He had had a different upbringing from Ralph. He knew the names of animals which roamed the bush, he could fish, he knew how to dig out lizards or frogs from the ground and could climb the highest trees without fear of falling. He could arm-wrestle better than anyone else Ralph knew, and he was allowed to wander over the hills alone; he went into Sydney by himself, often walking all the way if he couldn't get anyone to take him, and he had a private tutor who came to teach him four days a week at his home on land above Creek Farm where Ralph and his family lived.

Jack was sitting on the veranda steps waiting for him as they trotted up the steep drive. His chest was bare and he wore a pair of ragged trousers. His hair was a mass of tight dark curls, he had a huge grin on his face and his dark eyes gleamed with mischief.

Meg sighed when she saw Jack. 'Get changed out of those clothes, Ralph, before you go anywhere and be back here for supper at six o'clock.'

Ralph jumped down from the trap and raced inside, tearing off his belted tunic. He reappeared a few minutes later wearing an old shirt and an even older pair of trousers. 'And you'll feed the pigs before either of you get any supper,' she shouted after them as they ran towards the creek.

The water of the creek was cool and refreshing and after they had pushed and splashed each other, they ran down the hill to the pond which Joe, Ralph's father, had dug many years ago when first arriving at Creek Farm. This water was warmer, being still, and they dived in simultaneously and swam the width of it before emerging on the other bank.

'Race you to the other side,' Jack shouted and whooped as he dived again, and Ralph knew that he wouldn't catch him. Jack was as fast-moving in water as he was on the land.

'I want to ask you something,' Ralph said, as they lay in the warm grass and felt the heat of the evening sun drying them; two young and slim bodies, one brown-skinned, one fair and bronzed by the sun. 'Something you might know.'

'Hmm?' Jack said sleepily, his eyes closed. 'Ask your teacher.'

'Can't,' Ralph said shortly.

Jack turned towards him. 'Why not?'

Ralph felt his cheeks burn and he turned over onto his stomach so that Jack wouldn't see his face. 'I think it's something not very nice.'

Jack laughed. 'Hey, I already told you about babies!' He had a curious accent, English, but clipped and slightly nasal.

'No, it's not that, stupid! It's – it's – Do you know what a whore is?'

Jack whistled. 'Hey! You don't want to know about them. They're *bad* women!'

Ralph turned to face him. 'Why are they? How do you know?'

Jack shrugged. 'My father says I can go anywhere in Sydney except to the Rocks, because that's where the bad white women are. The whores.'

'I'll kill that Edwin Boyle – and his father.' Ralph curled up his fists as he had done earlier when he had hit Edwin, but next time, he vowed, he would make him bleed.

Jack shook his head after Ralph told him what Edwin had said about his mother. 'It don't make it true, just because that's what he said, and it won't make it better if you hit him.'

For all his mischief, Jack had a peaceable merry nature, always turning away from aggravation and confrontation. In his short life he had been called all manner of names by white men who thought they were superior, but he had been taught by his parents to know that he was as good, if not better than these usurpers of his country, but that he needn't necessarily tell them so; better by far, they advised, to let them remain in ignorance.

Jack was of mixed blood. His father, Benne, was an Aborigine, as was his mother's mother. She had married a white farmer, and Jack's mother had been the result of that union. She and Jack were lighter in skin colour than his father. Both had the same dark glossy hair, deep brown eyes and high cheekbones of the true Aborigine, but with the straight nose of their English ancestor.

Jack's father, Benne, and Ralph's father, Joe, had formed a lasting friendship twelve years ago, before the convict, Joe Hawkins, had obtained his pardon and freedom, and when Benne had led him towards the gold seam at the top of the creek. Benne hadn't wanted gold – as an Aborigine he wouldn't have been allowed to keep it. What he wanted was sheep and some land which he wouldn't be turned off, and now he had both, bought in Joe Hawkins's name but belonging to Benne and his family.

'Your mother's calling, we'd better go.' Jack jumped to his feet and pulled on his trousers. 'And I've got to feed the dogs, so I won't stay for supper. See you tomorrow.'

He loped up the hill towards his home and Ralph watched him before he too rose to his feet. He thought that Jack had a most enviable life. He didn't have to go to school and be taught by a prissy schoolmarm, as he did. Jack had been taken away from the mission school by Ralph's mother when she saw how bright he was. Through Mrs Boyle she had arranged for him to have a tutor, an Englishman, a former convict, with little money and no prejudices about teaching a native Australian boy. Jack already knew more about English history than Ralph; his reading ability wasn't as good though his understanding of mathematics was better, and he knew more about wild creatures and the wonders of nature than Ralph could ever expect to know.

Ralph fed the pigs, his chore for the day, and reminded his sister to feed the hens, then went inside and greeted his godfather, Ralph Clavell, who had come to supper. Ralph Clavell and his father were somehow involved in the business of gold and sheep, but Ralph didn't understand how or why. His godfather had formerly been a ship's surgeon and had decided to stay in Australia after making several voyages with the convict ships. It was on one of these that he had met Ralph's parents.

After a supper of chicken soup and mutton pie, Clavell and Joe went outside to smoke and Ralph hung around, idly listening to their conversation about the price of sheep at market, then as his father went to make sure the outbuildings were secured for the night, he joined his godfather on the veranda.

'Uncle Ralph?' he said nervously. 'Can I ask you something?'

'Fire away, young man. What do you want to know?' Ralph Clavell was tall and thin with a laconic sense of humour, and he always seemed well disposed towards his youthful namesake.

'I had a fight with Edwin Boyle today,' Ralph began.

'Did you, by Jove! Well, that doesn't surprise me. If he's anything like his father he'll bring out the worst in anybody. I remember Captain Boyle very well and so do your parents.'

'He said – that his father had said that my mother was a whore. So I hit him.'

Clavell pursed his lips, though he didn't appear to be shocked. 'Good for you! Never let a man, or boy, for that matter, insult a woman, no matter who or what she is.'

'So is it true?' His voice was low, he was aware of his mother and Peggy just beyond the veranda wall. 'Was she, I mean? Is that why she was a convict and sent to Australia?'

'Women were not transported because of

making their living on the streets,' Clavell responded with a frown. 'That wasn't a transportable offence, and I can tell you, young Ralph,' he shook a finger at him, 'that for some women that was the only way they could put food into their mouths.' He took a deep breath. 'But to your question. No, your mother was not a whore.'

He gazed out into the gathering darkness. Ralph, following his gaze, saw his father returning. Clavell's voice dropped. 'Meg was accused of slandering a magistrate and of theft, and transported for seven years. Both cases were subsequently proved to be untrue and she was pardoned. Your parents were not allowed to go back to England, but they wouldn't have chosen to anyway. They knew that there was a better life here.'

Ralph nodded. That much he knew. His father was fond of saying that if he had stayed in England he would be either starving in the gutter or dead from hanging, instead of being one of the richest men in New South Wales.

When his father rejoined them Ralph went inside to his room and sat on the deep window sill and looked out over the land. Land which was covered with thousands of sheep. Land and sheep whch would one day be his. Or at least, his and Peggy's. His father insisted that everything they had would be shared equally. 'We'll have none of this English business where the son gets everything and 'daughter gets nowt but a dowry on her marriage,' he said time and time again. 'Peggy will get her fair share and she can choose what she wants to do with it.'

He could see the curls of smoke drifting up from his father's pipe and Uncle Ralph's cigar and hear the murmur of their voices, then unmistakably he heard his godfather say, 'You're going to have to tell the boy something soon, Joe. That unprincipled wretch Boyle's been stirring up trouble again. Ralph's just been asking questions about his mother.'

Chapter Two

'If I were a boy I could go to sea like Papa does,' Amelia muttered, and tossed her thick brown hair out of her eyes as the wind caught it and flew it streaming flag-like about her head. She and her mother and father, brother Roger and younger sister May were picnicking on the sands at Spurn Point, the low-lying narrow finger of sand and shingle which ran between the mouth of the Humber and the German Ocean.

Amelia had run up the dunes for a better sight of a sailing ship leaving the pilot boat in the river and heading out on its own to greet the swirling waters of the sea. 'It's not fair. Girls have such boring lives.'

Her father, Philip Linton, coming up after her, heard her last remark and said jovially, 'Not at all true. Just ask your mother.'

'Oh no, Papa! Not like that. Not like poor Mama! But I would like to sail a ship.'

'When you are older, in a couple of years or so, then you can come on a voyage with me.

Your mother would like to do that too.' He smiled at his nine-year-old tomboy daughter. She should have been the boy instead of Roger. Roger was happy with his farming studies and wandering over the land, observing the wildlife and poring over his books on birds and animals. Even now he had wandered off in the hope of finding some rarity. Amelia wanted adventure and only a year ago had cut off her hair and squeezed her plump little bottom into a pair of her brother's trousers and announced that she was going to run away and join a fishing smack at the Hull docks.

Her father had volunteered to take her down to the docks to watch the fishermen bringing in their catch from the trawlers. She saw the ragged, barefoot, barechested apprentice lads hauling on the heavy fish baskets, and this and the stench of fish and the squirming slippery cod and haddock had so turned Amelia's stomach that she had changed her mind, for the present, she'd said, and would take a merchant ship when she was older.

'I'd like to go to Australia to meet my cousins,' she pouted. 'I'm sure they have more fun than we do here. England is so stuffy!' and she kicked out at the spiky marram grass with her neatly laced boots.

'You've been spoilt, Amelia.' Her father's tone was impatient and she looked up at him anxiously. He didn't often get cross. 'You don't know how lucky you are to live the life you do.

To have plenty to eat, a warm bed to sleep in, everything you could possibly want!'

She hung her head. 'I'm sorry, Papa. I do know really and I'm not unhappy, it's just that I want to *do* something. Something exciting.'

Roger called to them. He was crouching over something on the shingle. 'Here! Come and look. I've found a yellow horned poppy!'

Amelia raised her eyebrows and sighed, and was relieved to hear her mother and Ginny, their housekeeper, who had prepared the food and accompanied them, call to them to come and eat.

Later in the day they tramped back along the rough track of the peninsula with their wicker baskets, hampers and blankets towards the carriage which was waiting for them at Kilnsea. Amelia walked at her mother's side whilst her father carried five-year-old May on his back and Roger still searched along the banks for rare plants or looked into the hedges for birds' nests.

'It's been a nice day, Mama, I'm sorry I was such a crosspatch this morning.'

Her mother looked down at her and then stopped to take a breath and Ginny tutted and took a basket from her, muttering that Mrs Linton shouldn't be exerting herself or walking so far in her condition. A baby was due in three months' time, but Emily Linton was strong physically and mentally. Not for her a proper ladylike kind of life; she had been through too much to let a natural event deter her from being with her family.

Emily Linton looked after the management of the estate with her relative Samuel, who supervised the physical side, but she also drove out in her trap every week to visit the farms and smallholdings and talk over any problems with the tenant farmers. She had built up a respect from the workers on her land and from the neighbouring landowners, though not always from their wives, who tittle-tattled amongst themselves about her past life. But she cared not for their regard, she had the love of her husband Philip and her children and the devotion of her house staff in whose eyes she could do no wrong.

'You must try to learn patience, Amelia,' she said gently. 'We are so lucky with what we have. People are starving all over the country, they have no work and nowhere to live. Think of them next time you are feeling grumpy.'

'I do try, Mama,' Amelia sighed. 'I think perhaps I'm not a very nice person.'

'You're a very nice person.' Her mother took her hand. 'You're just growing up, that's all, and it's difficult, no matter who you are.'

'Papa says we can go with him on a voyage when I'm older. Could we go to Australia to see Ralph and Peggy and Uncle Joe and Aunt Meg?'

Her mother laughed. 'Australia is much too far away. You've forgotten about the new baby! I wouldn't want to take a young baby on such a long voyage.' She grew thoughtful, and then added softly, 'Though there were many who did, and survived.'

'If I went to Australia I should look for rare plants like Sir Joseph Banks did when he went with Captain Cook.' Roger cradled a pale blue egg in his hand and showed it to his mother. 'I only took one,' he said, 'there were others.'

'Sam says you shouldn't take any,' his mother admonished him. 'You know how cross he gets when you steal birds' eggs.'

'I shall go on an adventure into the bush when I'm there,' Amelia broke in, 'or else go digging for gold. I'll bring you a nugget back if you like, Ginny,' she added. 'Then you'll have a piece of your own to polish.'

Emily Linton and Ginny exchanged glances and smiled. Only Ginny of all the servants knew the worth of the small rough chunk of brown and yellow mud-like substance which lay on the mantelpiece in the drawing room and which she wiped reverently every morning with a soft cloth.

'Shall we go soon?' May piped up from her father's back, 'and will it be a big ship like you sail in, Papa?'

'It would have to be a big ship, May,' her father said, 'and no, it won't be soon. It will be years and years and years, if in fact at all.'

He glanced across at his wife. She badly wanted to see her brother again and his wife, Meg, and their children. But whether she would dare to make the voyage to the other side of the world, remembering, as she was bound to, the first time she had sailed to Australia, was another matter altogether. But she would have to, if family ties ran strong within her. For her brother could never visit her. In spite of his wealth, Joe was banished from England for ever.

Chapter Three

'I can't tell him about his mother,' Joe Hawkins had said to Ralph Clavell all those years before, as they'd smoked on the veranda. 'Meg will have to.'

But Meg couldn't either. She couldn't bring herself to discuss the matter with her much loved son. So it was never mentioned again, though it hung silently as a shadow between them all. Not until over ten years later, when Ralph had quarrelled with his father about staying out carousing all the night and, as his father said, not doing his fair share of work on the estate.

'We could afford to get more paid help,' Ralph grumbled defiantly. His head ached and he would have liked to go back to bed. 'We don't have to work all the hours of the day and night! We're supposed to be rich but what good does it do us?'

Joe grabbed him by his shirt. Meg had said something similar when she'd complained of him never being at home except for meal times and bed. 'We're not born wealthy like those "Exclusives,"' he said. 'We're from working stock! It's how I was brought up by my da and he by his. It's in my blood. Where I come from if tha doesn't work, starvation stares thee in 'face.'

Sometimes, when he was angry, his Yorkshire dialect came to the fore. Ralph could see and hear that he was angry now and he backed off. 'I'm sorry, Da. I know that's how it was in the old country. But it's not like that here. You can afford to take time off. You could take Ma out sometimes. You could visit other places. See something of the country. She'd like that. And I could take over, if only you'd let me.'

Joe stared at him. 'I couldn't ever explain to you how it is. There's a compulsion inside of me that says I have to work.' His voice dropped. 'You could never know, never having experienced it, but I have this terrible fear, deep inside of me, that if I don't work I might lose everything and finish up back in 'gutter.'

'But you won't,' Ralph insisted. 'You can't possibly spend all the money you've got.'

His father shook his head. 'I've just said! You'd never understand. You've never been without. You ask your ma. She'll tell you 'same.'

'Your father won't change,' his mother said when he spoke to her later. 'I keep trying to persuade him to take some time off. It was hard in the old days, Ralph. No-one who hasn't experienced those times could possibly

29

understand. There were those of us who were so low we were trailing our chins in 'gutter.'

'Ma,' he said in a low voice as the memory of an old insult returned. 'What did you do to survive? Before you were sent to Australia, I mean?'

He wished he hadn't asked. He saw the misery and shame on her face before she turned her head away and answered. 'I never thought I'd have to tell you. I allus hoped that it would stay hidden.'

'Then don't!' He faltered and reached for her hand. 'It doesn't matter. I'm sorry!'

'No!' She lifted her head and there was a proud, defiant look in her eyes. 'I'll tell you. You're a grown man, it's time you knew. I wanted to survive and there was onny one way for women like me who had come from nothing. I never knew my father and I went 'same way as my mother. I worked 'streets of Hull, my home town. I was a street woman!'

He felt cold all over and he swallowed hard. So it was true. Edwin Boyle and his father hadn't been lying all that time ago, but Uncle Ralph had. 'And – and so, is Da my real father?' He could hardly bring himself to ask the question. He suddenly felt dirty and vulnerable. 'Or don't you know who he was?' He didn't mean to sneer but it seemed to him that that was how it must have sounded.

Meg answered slowly. 'I never wanted you to know, though your father – Joe, he always said we should tell you. But there never seemed to be a right time.'

'So he isn't my father!' He felt as if he had been punched. I'm a bastard! And I thought I was so grand.

'No, he isn't your father.' She took a deep breath and her eyes filled with tears. 'And neither am I your mother.'

He was more shocked by the revelation that Meg wasn't his mother than he was over anything else. This was something quite unexpected and he ran from the room like a child and was physically sick. Meg came after him and cradled his head in her lap and told him that she couldn't have loved him more even if she had given birth to him. 'But Peggy is yours,' he said jealously. 'I can remember her being born.'

'Yes,' she said. 'She is, but we've never treated you any different. You were my son, mine from 'very beginning.'

'But my – real mother! Who was she?'

'I don't know,' she whispered. 'There was so much confusion on the ship. There was a violent storm one day and we were put below deck. It was dark and we were packed inside 'lower decks so tight there was no air – and she was very sick, your mother, I mean. She had no milk to feed you and she asked me to hold you to try and pacify you. You sucked on my finger.' She smiled and wiped away a tear. 'I knew then how it felt to love somebody and I'd never felt it afore. Then – ' She hesitated. 'Later we were let out and brought up on deck. I was still holding you and I couldn't see her. There were so many women. Then there was a cry of man overboard.'

She put her hand across her mouth and closed her eyes and for a moment she couldn't speak. When she did her voice was choked. 'Onny, it wasn't a man. It was her. It was your mother.'

He felt a cold shiver run through him. 'Who else knows?' he asked. 'Apart from Da, I mean? Does anyone else know who she was?'

She shook her head. 'We never knew her name – at least, Emily – your aunt Emily and I didn't. Maybe Philip Linton did, though he never said. He always went along with 'story that you were born to me on 'ship.'

'He was an officer on board, wasn't he?' Ralph blew his nose. He knew the story of his father's sister Emily, and of how Philip Linton had cleared her name and then taken her back to England where they had married.

'Yes, he was 'surgeon's mate, though he should have had a higher rank. Ralph Clavell was 'ship's surgeon. He delivered you.'

'So might Uncle Ralph know who she was?' Suddenly it was important to know her name. Even though she was dead he wanted to know who she was and why she was on a convict ship.

'He might,' she agreed. 'Ask him.'

That afternoon he rode towards the town of Parramatta where his godfather lived. His head was aching, his body felt sluggish and his legs felt as if they didn't belong to him. He had consumed a vast quantity of wine the night before, after he and Jack had been turned away from every club they visited as they toured Sydney. They had been turned away, not because they were intoxicated, but because Jack's skin was the wrong colour and he was the wrong race. And although Jack insisted that he didn't want to join these clubs anyway, Ralph persisted in trying with unfailing regularity and always with the same result.

'Mr Hawkins, sir,' the doormen would patiently say. 'You are very welcome to join us, but I'm afraid your friend is not.' They would glance sneeringly at Jack in his expensive European suit, white shirt and cravat, and Ralph would be like a bull at a gate and have to be restrained.

'You make it worse,' Jack had said to him last night. 'Don't you realize? I must be the best dressed, best educated native in New South Wales, better than those ignorant doormen, so how do you think I feel being turned away every time? I don't want to join your lousy clubs! Why would I?' He'd turned and walked away and left Ralph standing there with a grinning doorman whose smile was wiped off his face as Ralph hit him.

'Don't come back here.' The doorman's voice was muffled as he put a hand over his bleeding nose and shouted after Ralph. 'I'll make sure you're banned from now on.'

'Keep your damned club,' Ralph had bellowed belligerently and as he turned the corner he almost bumped into Captain and Mrs Boyle, who, with Phoebe, were on their way to the theatre. He'd made a bow to Mrs Boyle and Phoebe and inclined his head to Captain Boyle who did the same.

'Where are you off to, Ralph?' Pheobe was never formal and her father frowned at her. 'If you're looking for Jack you've just missed him.' Her eyes sparkled. She knew of their long friendship and she knew also of her father's dislike of the two young men. 'Why don't you join us for coffee after the theatre?'

'Why yes, do, Mr Hawkins,' Mrs Boyle agreed. 'Edwin is joining us later. That would be so nice.'

'You have forgotten, my dear,' interrupted Captain Boyle in a tight pompous voice, 'that we have arranged to meet the Simpkins. We cannot take along other – uninvited guests!'

Mrs Boyle looked confused but Ralph broke in to save her any embarrassment. 'It's kind of you, ma'am, but I have made other arrangements for the evening. Perhaps some other time?'

He bowed again and Phoebe smiled wickedly and said, 'Yes, do call – and bring Jack with you. If he will come!'

He hadn't been able to find Jack anywhere and so he'd dined and wined alone, and cursed Jack for leaving and thought about how fine a woman Phoebe Boyle was, and did she really mean for him to call on her? It wasn't the thing

34

to do, but then Phoebe Boyle wasn't the sort to follow convention. Her father would have something to say to her for inviting him and an Aborigine to call. And the more wine he drank, the more attractive the controversial Phoebe became.

A woman like her would make a fine wife, he'd deliberated over his glass. She's beautiful and fashionable. She'd never be boring. She would always have something to say and she would be very happy to have my friends around, no matter what race or colour. I don't know how I would put up with her father, though, or her brother. His dislike of Edwin Boyle had diminished slightly. They were civil to each other but could never have been friends and he often thought that Edwin avoided his company.

He had drunk a bottle of wine, a glass of ale and two brandies before being politely asked to leave the restaurant, and had walked all the way home. Too intoxicated to mount, his horse had led the way as he'd held him by the reins.

As he rode now towards Parramatta he kept turning his head. He thought he could hear a rustle behind him, there was always the possibility of bushrangers even on this well-trodden track, but he could see no-one. He had almost reached the crossing which dropped down towards the main Sydney-Parramatta road, when a figure jumped out in front of his horse and caught hold of the snaffle. His hair was dark and curly and he had a scarf covering the bottom half of his face.

'You idiot, Jack! You scared the living daylights out of me. You might have had me off too,' Ralph said huffily. 'You know how temperamental Star is.'

'Rubbish,' Jack grinned, pulling off the scarf. 'He knew I was there all the time. Unlike you who didn't! I've been running alongside you ever since you left home.'

Ralph grunted. He was still mad at Jack for going off and leaving him to drink alone the previous evening. 'I was concentrating,' he muttered. 'I've a lot on my mind just now.'

'So why are you going to Parramatta? Especially at this time of day. Too hot for you white man,' he parodied in pidgin English.

Ralph dismounted and led the horse to a grassy sheltered area. If he could talk to anyone, he could talk to Jack. 'Because . . .' He swallowed. 'I've just had some news. Because I've been told that Ma and Da are not my real parents.' He sat down on the grass and took off his hat and fanned his face. 'I'm staggered, Jack. I just can't believe it.'

'That's incredible!' Jack sat down beside him and put his chin in his hands. 'It's a shock I suppose, but does it make any difference?'

'Well of course it makes a difference! I don't know who I am! I'm not Ralph Hawkins, I'm somebody else!'

'You look exactly the same to me,' Jack said

laconically. 'You look the same as you did when I left you last night, except for having drunk too well. You sound just the same!'

'But I'm not!' he replied angrily. 'I've just found out that I'm not who I thought I was. My parents are not my parents. Peggy isn't my sister. And my real mother was drowned when she fell overboard from the convict ship! I don't know what to do,' he said, with desperation in his voice.

'But you don't have to do anything,' Jack said patiently. 'If your real mother is dead, there is nothing to be done, she has gone to her ancestors. If she'd been alive then you could have gone and looked for her. But as she isn't – !'

Ralph stared at his friend. 'I need to know who she was and why she was on a convict ship! I need to know what crime she committed to be sent to Australia.' He got to his feet. 'I'm going to Parramatta to see Ralph Clavell. He might know. He might have some answers for me.'

'Do you want me to come?' Jack squinted up at him.

Ralph shook his head. 'No. I want to go alone.'

Jack nodded. 'I'll wait here then,' and as Ralph turned away and remounted, he called after him, 'I hope I recognize you when you come back!'

I should have known better than to tell him, Ralph pondered as he rode towards Clavell's house. It won't seem important to him. The Aborigines swap wives and sisters and they look after each other's children, or at least they used to before the missionaries converted them, and they seem to be no worse for it. Jack's extended family lived around Benne's land. They drifted in and built their bark *mia-mias* or shelters where they stayed for a while before moving off to explore the dubious joys of Sydney.

Times were changing fast for the native Australians. They no longer hunted for their food as their ancestors did, but were encouraged to give up their nomadic existence and work as labourers in exchange for food, shelter and clothing. They were being influenced by a civilization which covered their innocent nakedness, provided them with Christian beliefs and gave them alcohol which dulled their senses. They were being wiped out by despair at the loss of their land and the diseases which the conquering authority had brought with them.

'You've ridden in this heat? You're out of your senses, young man.' Clavell had just woken from an afternoon sleep. 'Have you fallen out with your father again?'

Ralph grinned sheepishly. 'Not exactly, though he thinks I don't do enough work around the farm.'

'Well, you probably don't. Not many young men do, especially not rich young men like you. If you'd been poor you'd have had to work a lot harder.'

'Yes, sir,' he replied, anticipating yet another lecture. 'So my father says.'

'Ah!' Clavell rang a bell and asked a maid to bring some iced lemonade. 'So you have had a few words?'

'Yes, but that's not why I'm here, sir.' He sat down in a cane chair and stretched his long legs. 'I've come to ask you a question.'

'Yes?'

'About my mother.'

'Can't you ask her?' Clavell's eyes narrowed and his thick grey eyebrows beetled together.

'About my real mother.'

'Ah,' he said again. 'Has someone been saying something?'

Ralph nodded. 'Ma told me. She told me this morning that she wasn't my real mother.' He felt his eyes prickle. Damn! I hope I'm not going to make a fool of myself again.

'She *is* your real mother!' Clavell barked at him. 'You wouldn't find a better mother than Meg. What you mean is that she isn't your *natural* mother. The one who gave birth to you!'

'Yes, sir,' he agreed meekly. 'That's what I meant.'

'All over the world there are women bringing up children that they didn't give birth to,' Clavell continued in the same harsh tone. 'It doesn't mean they're not making a good job of it. It's the easiest thing on earth to conceive a child, far harder to bring one up!'

Ralph remained silent. Better to let him rant

on for a while, then he could ask him the question.

'So I suppose you want to ask me if I knew who she was?' Clavell said at length. 'I delivered you, you know. That's why you were given my name.'

Ralph nodded. 'Yes, Ma said – that you'd delivered me on board ship, and that, that my – natural mother had drowned.' He hesitated, then said in a low voice, 'I would like to know who she was and why she was on board a convict ship.'

Clavell stared him in the face. 'And then I suppose you'll want to be off on a wild goose chase to England to find your other family?'

Ralph stared back at him. 'My other family?' That hadn't crossed his mind. But yes! There must be people in England who were related to him. Blood relations. 'Yes,' he said. 'That's exactly what I would like to do!'

Chapter Four

'Her name was Scott.' Clavell poured two glasses of lemonade and handed one to Ralph. 'Rose Elizabeth Scott. I checked the lists after we had landed and I particularly remembered her name because Scott was also my grandmother's name.' He took a deep drink, and then added, 'She came from York. At least, she was sent from York County Gaol.'

Ralph licked his lips. 'And – did it say on the list why she had been transported?'

Clavell nodded. 'It did.' He took another drink. 'Are you sure you want to know all of this? It's finished, you know. It was another lifetime.'

'I have to know,' Ralph replied. 'I can't just leave it now that I've started.'

'I suppose not.' Clavell looked at him. 'But be careful how you handle this. Don't hurt Meg. She's loved you as a mother loves a son, and Joe has brought you up as his own.'

'I won't, sir. It won't affect my feelings for them. But I would like to know.'

'It said on her file – attempted murder. She was sentenced to ten years' transportation. Of course what that really meant was a lifetime's banishment. Women never went back. Well, hardly ever,' Clavell gave a small smile, 'except in exceptional circumstances, such as your aunt Emily's.'

Ralph sat stunned. This was worse than he had anticipated. He thought it would have been a crime of stealing, but nothing more than that. Of all the young people he knew who were the sons and daughters of convicts – 'currency lads and lasses' they were called if they had been born in Australia – none of their parents had committed worse than theft. And all, they protested, had been innocent of the charges brought against them.

But attempted murder! That was a real crime, especially for a woman! Far worse than becoming a street woman in order to eat. The lemonade fizzed inside him and he felt sick. Had she been wicked, then, to commit such a crime?

'She seemed a pleasant young woman,' Clavell was saying. 'Gentle, quietly spoken. Not high born, you know, but from good stock I would imagine.' He paused momentarily. 'She obviously couldn't cope with what was in front of her. The voyage was bad enough, especially for a pregnant woman, but she would have needed to be strong to withstand the rigours of Parramatta Female Gaol, which is where she would have gone if she couldn't find a place as housekeeper;

and she would have had to give up her child.'

He glanced at Ralph. 'Your mother – Meg, she was strong. She organized the women on the ship; she was the one who complained about the conditions or asked for extra rations and blankets, and I expect your mother saw that and that's why she handed you over to her. She must have known you'd be safe with her.'

'What are you saying, sir?' Ralph was bewildered. 'Are you saying she deliberately gave me up?'

'I'm only guessing of course, I didn't know what was going on in that hellhole below decks. But she handed you over to Meg and then when they came up on deck—' He hesitated. 'You said you wanted to know, so I'm telling you. She didn't fall overboard. She jumped. She committed suicide.'

Ma didn't tell me that. Ralph sat quietly, just staring into space. She only said that the woman who was my mother had drowned; she was trying to protect me from that knowledge. A warmth spread over him and he knew that he must comfort her, tell her that it didn't matter that she hadn't given birth to him. She was his mother in every other sense.

Yet he felt sad that a woman should be so desperate as to take her own life. Rose Elizabeth Scott. What had driven her to that final act? Was it guilt? Who had she tried to kill? Who had been his father and where was he? Was he dead or still living in England?

His mind was full of confused thoughts and imaginings as he rode out of Parramatta towards home and he was startled as Jack rose up in front of him from his same position on the ground where he had left him.

'Did you find out about your mother?' Jack loped alongside him.

'I found out more than I wanted to know,' he said morosely. 'I found out her name – '

Jack put up both hands and protested. 'Aborigine custom forbids the mentioning of dead people's names!'

'But you don't follow native custom,' Ralph argued, 'except when you used to go walkabout and miss your school lessons!'

'Sometimes I do,' Jack retaliated.

'All right, I won't mention her name to you. But I can tell you that she came from the same part of northern England as my parents did.'

'So they must have known of her or her family! I've seen a map of England. It's a very small place.'

Ralph shook his head. 'I don't think so. It might be small compared to Australia but it's full of people.'

Jack sighed. 'Yes. That's why they sent so many here and turned my people out.'

'I think I shall go to England, Jack. To try to find out what happened.'

'You can't change anything. You have only known Meg and Joe as your parents.'

'I need to know,' he said. 'You know about

44

your ancestors. You can trace your family back since – what is it? Since Dream Time?'

Jack nodded. 'Since Dream Time. But those are our ancestral spirits who were there when the world began.' He was silent for a while as he ran by Ralph's side. Then he said, 'Yes. I can see it is important to you. Come with me tonight. We'll find a quiet place where you can think.'

The supper Ralph shared with his parents and Peggy that night was eaten under a strained attempt at normality. Peggy had been crying, her eyes were red-rimmed and she kept sniffing into a handkerchief; his mother was pale-faced and his father ate hurriedly, saying there were dingoes about so he would have to go out again.

'I'll come with you, Da,' Ralph offered, but his father refused, saying that Benne and some of the hired boys were going with him.

'Stay with your ma,' he said gruffly. 'Don't go raking around Sydney. She could do wi' some company.'

'I'm all right, Ralph,' his mother said after his father had picked up his rifle and gone out. 'You don't have to stay. You could have gone instead of your father.'

'He won't take time off, Ma. You know that. I could manage the sheep station, I know how, but he won't let me. He has to do it all himself!'

'It makes him feel good.' Meg smiled. 'He's so proud of what he's achieved.'

Ralph wasn't convinced and a sudden thought occurred to him. 'Are you sure it's not because

I'm not his real son? If Peggy had been a boy instead of a girl would she be allowed to take charge?'

'That's a dreadful thing to say.' His mother was angry and rose from the table. 'You've both always been treated 'same!'

'But there can't be many farmers in this country who share the land and stock between their sons and daughters!' he insisted. 'Everybody I know, the sons get the farm and the daughters get a dowry!'

'Peggy might not want to get married,' his mother said sharply, 'and if she didn't then she would always be dependent on you to take care of her. Your da doesn't want that. He wants her to be independent and so do I!'

Ralph excused himself and got up from the table. He was behaving abominably, he knew, but he couldn't help himself. He was so very confused. 'I'm going out,' he said brusquely. 'I'll see you in the morning.'

'Don't get drunk!' his mother called after him as he went through the door. 'That's how trouble starts!'

He came back and planted a kiss on her forehead. 'I won't,' he said softly. 'I'm not going into Sydney. I'm going walkabout with Jack.'

He took a blanket, which he put over one shoulder and secured with a belt around his waist; he wore his oldest trousers and thick shirt and carried a stout stick. He had sturdy boots on his feet, whilst Jack was barefoot and carried no blanket but had draped a strip of wide cotton cloth around his bare chest which partly covered his cut-down trousers and bare legs. He too carried a stick.

'Where are we going?' Ralph asked as they strode out away from the farm and towards the hills.

'Who knows?' Jack replied. 'We'll go where our feet and dreams take us.'

Dusk was settling as they climbed and although the civilization of Sydney with newly built stone houses and white cottages was encroaching upon the hills above the harbour, it hadn't yet reached the bush high above Creek Farm. As he looked down, Ralph could see the grazing flocks of sheep belonging to his father and Jack's father, Benne. They could hear the occasional shot of rifle fire which told them of the crusade against the wild dog of Australia, the dingo.

Up here on this higher ground the hazy blur of the distant Blue Mountains made them seem approachable. They could hear the incessant croak of cicadas and the cacophony of birdsong all around them, the raucous cry of the cockatoo and parrot and the squeak and rustle of nocturnal animals coming out for their nightly forage. As they walked, they disturbed sleeping lizards and reptiles, their feet crackling on the carpet of dry grey leaves of the eucalyptus and gum trees which swayed above them.

'Here,' Jack said after two hours' walking,

when with Ralph stumbling in the gloom and relying on his stick to probe the rough ground, they came to a small clearing, a grassy area surrounded by sweet-smelling bushes and ferns. A faint light from the sky showed through the grey-barked, ever-present eucalyptus trees, which rustled their top branches in the evening air. Jack looked around him. In the gathering darkness he seemed to have become more native than when they had set out. 'This will do.'

Ralph sat down with some relief. It had been a hard climb, even though he thought himself to be fit. Jack searched around amongst the trees until he found what he was looking for: an old tree with its grey bark hanging off in strips. He sought for a foothold in its trunk and, reaching as high as he could and taking a loose edge of the bark, he tore it until it hung down in sheets. Then he moved out of the clearing and Ralph lost sight of him for a few minutes until he reappeared dragging a thin branch from a sapling and two forked branches from a larger tree.

Ralph started to get to his feet to help him. 'No. I'll do it,' Jack insisted. 'I shall forget the knowledge like so many of my people have done. We are becoming lazy and getting used to walls and windows. We shall forget our ancestry, those of us who are left.'

Ralph sat down again. He understood Jack's needs. They had known each other since childhood. Their parents had been friends ever since Benne had brought his new wife Daisy, pregnant with Jack, to meet Meg and Joe. Daisy had lived all of her life in a stone house. Her white father had thought that he was doing the right thing by bringing her up in the European manner, although her Aborigine mother had taught her the ways of her forebears. Daisy had taken favourably to Meg, who treated her as an equal, and when she gave birth to Jack the two women had called their sons brothers.

Now Jack was attempting for a few short hours to live as the Aborigines had once done: to walk upon his own territorial land which was his by right, or so his father had told him, as he in turn had been told by his father and grandfather. He had come to commune with his spiritual ancestors in whom, in his role as part white man, he only half believed.

He placed the forked branches together and held them fast by the branch of the sapling, then draped the torn sheets of bark over them to make a rough shelter. 'You will need your blanket in the *mia-mia*, white man,' he grinned, his teeth showing white in his face, and he took off his own cotton cloth and threw it on the ground.

Suddenly he sprang into the middle of the clearing and with his feet apart he adopted a confrontational stance, his arms held wide, his hands held low and his fingers stretched in a challenge.

Ralph pulled off his boots and jumped to his

feet and, pulling his shirt over his head, threw it on the ground next to Jack's discarded garment. He stood opposite Jack and he too lifted his arms but with his hands held high in a passive manner.

Jack took two steps forward and bending towards him grabbed Ralph about his lower hips. They stayed locked as Ralph stood perfectly still, offering no resistance, his arms still held high, until he felt himself being lifted up and thrown into the clearing where he landed on both feet. 'Huh,' he grunted and now he took the confrontational stance whilst Jack took the passive.

Jack's body was firm and muscular and Ralph had difficulty in gaining a grip around him but he did and with a great effort swung Jack off his feet and threw him as he had been thrown, into the middle of the clearing, where he dropped lightly on his feet.

Now it was Jack's turn again and Ralph forced his strength down into his legs and feet, making himself heavy so that he was awkward to lift, but Jack's strength was phenomenal and once more Ralph felt himself lifted and thrown. Again he landed on his feet and became the challenger but he knew who would eventually be the winner, and after several more rounds, Jack threw him and he finally failed to land on his feet and sprawled in the grass.

'I give in,' he panted. 'You're too good for me.'

'I am,' Jack agreed and went off to find water which he had heard gurgling nearby. He drank from a stream and came back with water cupped in a large leaf, and with a handful of berries and nuts which he offered to Ralph.

'I ate supper.' Ralph refused the offering. 'But I'll have a sup of water.'

The darkness gathered and although it wasn't cold Ralph pulled his blanket around his shoulders. 'I wish we'd brought a tot of rum,' he said.

Jack shook his head. 'As from tonight I'm giving up alcohol. When I left you in Sydney last night, I went into one of the native reserves. The place was appalling, it was filthy and just falling apart. The men had been drinking rum all day and were sitting around in a drunken stupor, and the women were almost as bad.'

Ralph protested, 'but you're not like that!'

'No, I'm not,' he answered quietly. 'But the settlers think that the Aborigines are no good. They don't realize that the white man's rule has destroyed them. Our forefathers didn't know of alcohol or money before the white settlers came. We exchanged goods with our fellow tribesmen and if we had a quarrel, then we fought each other. Life was very simple then.'

He sat quietly for a few moments, then said, 'If only I could teach them, black and white, that there could be a better life.' He turned and looked at Ralph. 'A life such as you and I enjoy as brothers; as our fathers, yours and mine do, who respect each other's traditions and don't interfere but live harmoniously together.'

'But Jack.' Ralph leaned towards him. 'You're different. Because of your white grandfather and your mother's influence, you have had an education and can think of these things.'

'And are you saying that without my English background I would still be an ignorant savage?' His voice was scornful.

'I'm not saying that, but you might have been if you hadn't been shown another way! But those natives down in the reserves don't know any better. Right or wrong, some other nation would have come to this continent and changed their lives. It's a question of power. Your people have been uprooted from all they believed in and now they don't know which way to go.'

'I know.' Jack lay down on the ground. 'Quiet now,' he said, abruptly ending the discussion. 'I'm going to commune with my ancestors,' and Ralph couldn't tell if he was serious or not.

Ralph lay down beside him and closed his eyes. He needed to think of what to do. Should he go to England to find his relatives, if he had any, even if it meant upsetting Ma? His da, he thought, wouldn't mind too much. He might even be pleased, especially if he promised to visit Aunt Emily. I think I will go, he mused, it would be a great adventure if nothing else.

He felt himself drifting off into sleep and as he relaxed he dreamt he could see the great ocean before him, the turbulent white crests and the crashing waves sweeping across the decks of the ship which carried him: the ship with white sails which moved like a huge swan. 'The *Flying Swan*,' he murmured, and he could hear Jack moaning in his sleep, only in his own dream it wasn't Jack, but a woman who was crying as she stood by the bulwarks of the ship looking back at him, as if saying goodbye.

Jack was carried on a gentle wind, up and up until he reached a high plateau where he was carefully laid down. He was naked and alone in a vast area of scorched earth which was devoid of trees or vegetation. Then his eyes opened wide as a horde of huge animals approached him, their feet moving stealthily and their claws extended. He lifted his spear in warning but still they came. They were unlike any other animals he had ever seen, with huge heads and grinning teeth. Crocodiles opened their massive jaws and winged goats with dainty feet flew about him. Giant kangaroos sprang over him, furry wombats nuzzled against him and enormous snakes slithered up his legs and wrapped themselves about his body. Yet strangely he did not feel threatened or afraid. They were telling him something, weaving a story which he did not quite understand.

As he watched them he lowered his spear which was now a firestick. The clearing was becoming cultivated, grass was growing and trees and bushes sprouted from the ground, their bare branches now covered with unfolding leaves. Mimosa bushes were opening up bright yellow flowers which smothered him with their perfume. Tall trees shed silver-grey leaves down on him, and on the slim branches koala bears were hunched, chewing on tender gum-tree leaves. He could hear the hum of bees and he felt the sweetness of honey on his lips and as he looked up, cascades of waterfalls rushed down high escarpments and fell into crystal-clear streams and rivers.

He opened his eyes. Daylight was filtering through the treetops and Ralph was stirring beneath his blanket. Jack sat up and stared into space. Who am I? Am I a black man living in a white man's world or a mixed breed belonging to neither? What part of my ancestry is the stronger?

Ralph sat up too and blinked. 'I've had the strangest dream,' he croaked. 'But I know now what I am going to do. I'm going to England to find out who I am and where I came from.'

Jack nodded. His mind was still hazy from his own dream-filled night, yet he knew that he had to cross the long bridge between black and white. 'Yes,' he murmured. 'And I am coming with you.'

Chapter Five

'Let's go home, Ginny! I'm bored and I'm cold.' Amelia pulled her fur collar up around her neck.

'You'll have to be patient, Miss Amelia.' Ginny's tone was sharp. 'You were bored at home and wanted to come. You didn't have to. Besides, Miss May still has to choose the material for her winter dresses, and we need more buttons and thread.'

Amelia sighed. 'I hate shopping. Do be quick, May, and make up your mind.'

They had visited drapers, mercers and haberdashers in the town of Hull, but sixteen-year-old May could not decide whether to choose a rich dark red velvet which she thought looked so grown-up and Amelia said looked like curtains, or a pretty shade of green. 'I wish Mama had come,' she complained. 'She would have helped me to decide. Amelia, you are of no help at all!'

'Your mother doesn't like to visit Hull, you

know that.' Ginny now became cross with May. 'The crowds make her nervous.'

'The green is lovely. No really, May, I mean it. Have the green, it's very pretty with your fair colouring.' Amelia smiled sweetly at her sister. Anything, she groaned inwardly. Just choose anything and let's go home!

'It's time you were married with a house full of children,' Ginny grumbled at Amelia as they trundled home in the carriage. 'That would stop you being bored.'

'You never did, Ginny! Why inflict marriage on me? Anyway, I haven't met anyone I want to marry.'

'Your time in Switzerland hasn't improved you, Miss, and anyway I've been too busy looking after all of you to think of getting married myself,' Ginny retaliated and Amelia pondered that they must be the only family in the whole of the country who were put in their place and ruled so firmly by their housekeeper; even herself at nearly nineteen when she was supposed to be considered grown-up.

Then she relented as she always did and smiled mischievously at Ginny. 'Poor old Ginny. What a lot you have to put up with. Six of us! It's a wonder you and Mama are not white-haired.'

'I comb cold tea on my hair,' Ginny retorted. 'Otherwise I would be.'

It was dark by the time they arrived home. The lamps were lit and the fires burning in all of the rooms and the two sisters asked if they could have their supper from a tray by the fire in the sitting room. Ten-year-old Lily was curled up in a chair reading a book and blinked sleepily as they entered, and the eight-year-old twins Joseph and Hannah were stretched out on the floor drawing pictures.

'Did you bring us a present,' they chorused without even looking up.

'Certainly not! Why would we do that?' Amelia gave a secret smile at Ginny who had her arms full of parcels and placed them on a side table before leaving the room.

'You did. You did!' The twins jumped up immediately and Lily put down her book and looked up with interest.

'No. I brought something for Lily, because she never asks.' Amelia gave her young sister a box of chocolates and was rewarded with a kiss. 'But as for you two, have you done anything to deserve a present?'

'We've been very good today,' Hannah said seriously. 'And we haven't made a lot of noise,' added Joseph. 'Well, not too much.'

'Well, all right then.' Amelia relented and picking up two more parcels handed them to the twins, a wooden engine for Joseph and a Russian doll for Hannah.

'You indulge them, Amelia,' her mother remonstrated as she entered the room.

'I know,' she agreed. 'Ginny says I should get married and have a house full of children of my own.'

'Not yet,' her mother disagreed. Marrying off her daughters was not a priority in her eyes. 'You're not ready yet!'

'I'm not,' she allowed. 'And besides, no man would have me! I'm far too controversial and self-opinionated. Most men that I've come across want a pretty little lady to adore them and agree with whatever they do or say.'

'And how many young men have you met who are looking for those requirements?' Her mother poured the tea from a flowered china pot.

'Well, not so many I admit! But when I was in Switzerland, young men were invited to the Academy just so that we could practise the lessons we had been taught; the art of polite conversation and so on.' She sighed. 'I'm afraid you and Papa wasted your money, Mama. I never was commended. I was told time and again that I was far too outspoken.'

Her mother laughed. 'I might have known. But you wanted to travel. It seemed for the best.'

Amelia dropped her voice so that the younger children couldn't hear. 'I have to do something, Mama! I need an occupation!'

'Your father and I have been discussing that. We know that you have been restless since you returned home, and we wondered if you would like to stay with Aunt Anna for a while?'

'Aunt Anna! But how would that help?' One of

her father's sisters was married to a businessman and lived in York.

'Well, you are not fully occupied here, and I thought that as York is such a busy city and Anna is involved in so many things, there would be more for you to do than there is in Holderness. There would be concerts to attend, and the theatre and the chance to meet people; and you would be perfectly safe under their roof.'

Amelia lifted her head and looked thoughtful. 'Aunt Anna does *good works* doesn't she?'

'She does.' Her mother smiled. 'But she isn't pious. Quite the contrary. She stirs up authority and people's consciences.'

'So what is she doing now?'

Her mother shook her head. 'I don't know. Why don't you write and ask her?'

'Perhaps I'll write and ask if I might visit. I'll go before winter really sets in and the weather's too cold.'

It was agreed she should visit and her father took her to the Hull railway station the following week acompanied by Nancy, one of the maids. Amelia had wanted to travel alone but her father, and also her mother, had refused to allow it. 'It's not fair,' she'd complained. 'I'm perfectly capable of finding my own way there. Why should I have someone with me the whole time? You never did, Mama, when you were young!'

Her mother had shaken her head at her. 'It

was different for me, as you very well know, Amelia. Our lives were not the same. And you may think I had more freedom than you, but I hadn't. I had much less.'

Amelia was contrite. What a pig I am, she'd thought. I am so inconsiderate. 'I'm sorry, Mama. Of course you are right to be worried.' But she still railed against what she thought of as the restraints of womanhood.

'I'll write when I'm returning, Papa,' she said, kissing him goodbye at the station. 'Just one or two weeks, that's all. Aunt Anna will have had a sufficiency of my company by then.'

She felt sooty, cold and crumpled when she left the train at York and on arriving at her relatives' house was pleased to be shown to a pleasant room, which in daylight overlooked the Knavesmire. There was a bright fire burning and a brass kettle of hot water waiting, which Nancy poured into a bowl so that Amelia could wash and change before going down to supper.

Aunt Anna and her husband Albert hadn't any children of their own, but Anna made up for this deficiency by looking after everyone else she came into contact with, and she fussed over Amelia, making sure she had the best seat by the fire and a footstool for her feet, and a fire screen just by her so that the heat of the flames didn't spoil her complexion.

'I'm perfectly comfortable, Aunt, thank you,' Amelia insisted as her aunt plumped up a cushion behind her. 'Really I am.'

'Do you follow the racing, Amelia?' Albert boomed. 'Lots of ladies do nowadays. Grand sport, you know.'

Amelia smiled. Her uncle had chosen this house especially for its close proximity to the racecourse on the Knavesmire. 'I have been to Beverley once or twice with some friends and their parents,' she said.

'Then you must come with us some time,' he said, 'though your aunt isn't very keen.'

'Phww,' his wife snorted. 'I have other things to do with my time; besides, the ladies who do go are only interested in what everyone is wearing. They're not in the least interested in the horses!'

'So, what is occupying you at the moment, Aunt? Have you taken up a cause?'

'I have, and you may well be interested, my dear. We could do with someone like you. Young and unmarried with time on her hands.'

Amelia raised her eyebrows. Aunt Anna was forthright to say the least, but it was a trait she admired, particularly in women. 'Tell me about it,' she invited. 'Although of course I won't be imposing my company on you for long, I must be home in time to prepare for Christmas.'

They were interrupted by the sound of the supper bell but as they entered the dining room and took their places at the table which was set with fine silver and fragrant bowls of flowers, Anna discoursed on her latest pet project. The plight of the Irish immigrants in York.

'You see, most of them came over to England years ago, when the railways began. There was no work in Ireland but plenty here in England. The Irish navvies came in their thousands and the women and children followed. Now, of course, there is no work for any of them, and in any case the inhabitants of this country resent them. They say there isn't enough work for our own people, let alone the Irish.'

She toyed with her soup, then pushed her dish away. 'And of course they are perfectly right. But they can't go back to their own country. There's nothing for them there either.'

Her husband grunted. 'Lazy good-for-nothings most of 'em! All they seem to do is sing about how good it was in Ireland and how they wish they were back. They should go, that's what I say!'

Amelia ignored his remark and asked her aunt, 'So how are you able to help them?'

'Well, it's the children really that I want to help. I would like to think that they have a chance even if their parents haven't. So I'm trying to get them into school. The boys are most unwilling and don't stay more than a day or two, and some of the children are Catholic and their mothers will only let them go to a Catholic school, if they will agree to them going at all.'

She sighed and looked down at her plate

which had been served with cold beef and ham. 'You see, Amelia, most of these people are so poor that they need the children to work to bring in some money, but there are one or two families who do want their children to have an education, and so I am able to place them into school.'

'And who pays for the children's education?' Amelia asked and glanced at her uncle as he gave a snort.

'Various benefactors.' He answered for his wife. 'Your aunt has amazing powers of persuasion.' He nodded his head sagely. 'Believe me, Amelia. She could charm the tail off a donkey!'

Amelia glanced from one to the other; she believed he was right. 'But how do you think I can help? I don't have any money of my own.'

'Oh, I don't want your money, my dear.' Aunt Anna was aghast. 'No, that wasn't my intention at all. But we do need some practical help. Well, here you are, heaven sent. An intelligent, well-educated young woman.'

Well-educated! Amelia laughed and thought of the two schools who had asked her parents to remove her as they said she was disruptive and was leading the other children astray.

'You're just the person,' her aunt continued. 'You can help the Misses Fielding – if you will,' she added. 'They would be so pleased!'

'But,' asked Amelia, slightly bemused, 'who

are the Misses Fielding? And help them in what?'

'Oh! Didn't I say? Two sisters. They run a small school in York for poor children.' Anna beamed at her. 'You can be a teacher!'

Chapter Six

'Goodness, it's so hot down in Sydney. There are people fainting in the streets!' Phoebe came into the drawing room and flung herself onto a sofa, kicking off her shoes as she did so. 'And guess what everyone is talking about, Mama! I met Josephine Challis and she had heard it from Louise Mortimer.'

Mrs Boyle smiled and stood back to admire her flower arrangement, which she then placed on a corner table. 'Those two young women are becoming regular gossips!' she murmured. 'Whose character are they dissecting now?'

'No. No.' Phoebe protested. 'Not who – what! Louise heard it directly from Ralph himself.'

'Ralph?' Her mother raised her eyebrows. 'I suppose you mean Mr Ralph Hawkins? You young people do not concern yourselves with the niceties of manners any more!'

'Oh, Mama! I have known Ralph Hawkins since we were at dame school! He wouldn't expect me to call him *Mr* Hawkins any more

than I would expect him to call me Miss Boyle.
Unless you or Papa were present, of course, and
then he would!'

Her mother sighed; her strong-willed
daughter always seemed to win arguments. 'So
what is it that you heard? Though if it is something disreputable I do not wish to know!'

'Oh, nothing disagreeable. Quite the contrary
and I am *so* envious.' Phoebe got up and walked
across to the open window. She looked out at the
small neat garden and the view of the harbour
below, which was filled with sailing ships and
steamers. 'He's going to England!'

'Oh!' Her mother took a deep breath. 'Really?
Going home. How wonderful! How wonderful,'
she repeated. 'Is anyone else going with him?
His mother?'

Phoebe glanced at her and then looked away.
'Erm, I don't think so. His mother can't, can
she? I mean, would she be allowed?'

'I'm not sure. Perhaps not. Although the rules
have been relaxed a little for former convicts.
Particularly if they have been pardoned. But it is
not something anyone discusses with the persons
concerned,' she added.

'Not considered well-mannered!' Phoebe remarked, a trifle cynically.

'Indeed not,' her mother rebuked. 'I wouldn't
dream of mentioning the subject.'

Phoebe chose discretion. She knew that her
mother visited Meg Hawkins at Creek Farm
whenever her father was away on a voyage.

Captain Boyle, for some reason which she couldn't fathom, disliked Meg and Joe Hawkins intensely and she was sure it wasn't simply because they were ex-convicts, for the Hawkins were hard-working people who had made a success of their lives in Australia. Perhaps it's because they are rich, she pondered. They are much much richer than we are, thousands of acres of land, thousands of sheep, a magnificent house and I've heard rumours of gold. Father wouldn't like that. She knew with certainty that her father had an avaricious, jealous nature.

'I wonder why he has decided to go?' her mother was saying. 'Mr Joe Hawkins has a sister there, I understand, perhaps he will visit her.'

'Oh, but yes! Did you not know, Mama? Joe Hawkins's sister was a convict too, only wrongly convicted, and a handsome young naval officer obtained her pardon and took her back to England. So romantic,' she bantered. 'And of course they then married!'

'I suppose Louise Mortimer told you all of this too?' Her mother's tone was ironic.

'I can't remember who told me,' Phoebe replied. 'But the story has been around for years. I'm surprised you didn't know, Mama. Papa must know. They came over on the *Flying Swan*. You remember, Papa said he'd sailed on it. He used to refer to it as a creaky old tub!'

Lucinda Boyle nodded her head vaguely, then as if pulling herself together, said briskly, 'It was before I came to Australia. I didn't come out until Edwin was two.'

'Wouldn't you love to go back, Mama?' Phoebe led her mother on gently. 'Wouldn't you like to see your own mother again before it's too late?'

'I would.' She swallowed nervously. 'But it isn't possible. Your father would never agree. Besides, he rarely sails to England now.'

'But Papa needn't come— I mean, he wouldn't have to go,' she corrected herself hastily.

'Whatever do you mean, Phoebe? I couldn't possibly travel alone. It would be unthinkable!'

'Not alone, Mama! I would come with you and we'd take a maid. Oh, and,' she said in a flurry of excitement as if she had suddenly thought of the idea, 'if we went on the same ship as Ralph— Mr Hawkins,' she added mischievously, 'he could escort us.'

'But then, everyone would assume that you and he – !' She stard at Phoebe. 'You're not – he hasn't – ! Phoebe, is there something you haven't told me? Your father would never agree to it!'

Phoebe lowered her eyes. 'He does like me, I think,' she said demurely. 'He has a very large fortune, Mama, all of my friends are quite set upon him.' Then she stopped her playfulness and continued in her normal manner. 'Of course,' she said, 'although he is very handsome, everyone agrees on that, he is rather cocksure and he does not always behave as he should, and he often drinks too much wine.'

'Like most young men. But you like him,

do you?' Her mother's tone was anxious. 'You must be careful not to have your heart broken, Phoebe, men are not always what they seem.'

'And neither are women,' Phoebe answered flatly. 'But yes, I like him well enough.' But not well enough to marry him, she mused. She turned again to the window. An Aborigine boy was tending the garden and when he saw her watching he scuttled out of view. A shadow settled on her. No, not enough to marry. I won't be marrying anyone, she thought. Not unless I can have the one I really want.

'What do you mean, you'd like to go to England?' Captain Boyle stared at his wife. His face was flushed and his eyes bleary and she was sure he had been drinking before he came home. Before she could reply, he continued. 'For God's sake, Lucinda. I've just got back from China and you want me to be off again?'

'I didn't mean immediately,' she explained diffidently. 'I meant some time in the future. I'd like to see my mother again, she's a good age now, she may not live very much longer.'

'Humph. She's good for a few years yet, I'll be bound. She'll live as long as she can just to spite us so we have to wait for her money!'

'That's unfair,' Lucinda protested. 'She was always generous when you were just a lieutenant.'

He didn't reply immediately, but sipped on a brandy. 'I'll think about it,' he said eventually. 'I suppose the old girl might look on you more favourably if you did visit her.'

'That wasn't my intention,' she murmured. 'Blood ties are strong, and she has never seen Phoebe.'

'Phoebe! You'd take Phoebe?' His eyes narrowed. 'Well, I suppose that would be a good idea. Maybe some finesse might rub off on her if she was in England. She wouldn't be consorting with convicts' offspring if she was over there!' He snorted. 'Currency bastards!'

He saw the distaste on her face. 'Well, it's true. The whole country is overrun with them.' He put down his glass. 'I'm going up to change, then I'm off to my club.'

'But you've only just come home – and what about supper?'

'Supper?' He turned from the door which he was about to open. 'I'll eat out. Don't wait up for me.'

Though she was hurt that her husband should prefer the company of the gentlemen in his club to her own, she felt a sense of relief wash over her. The same relief that she felt whenever he announced that he was going on a voyage. She rang the bell. 'Hetty,' she said to the maid who answered her summons. 'Tell Cook that only Miss Phoebe and I will be in for supper.'

Captain Boyle slept in his own room that night; at least, his wife thought that he had, and he didn't appear for breakfast but came in for luncheon looking heavy-eyed and haggard. He glowered at her from across the table and then glanced at Phoebe. 'So what are you looking at, miss? Why are you looking so smug?'

'I hadn't realized that I was, Father,' Phoebe answered coolly. 'I certainly don't have anything to be smug about.' She turned to her mother. 'Mama, did I tell you that some people I know are going to England?'

Her mother hesitated, then shook her head. 'Really? How exciting!'

'It will cost them a fortune.' Phoebe sighed. 'It must be nice to be able to afford the journey.'

Her father frowned. 'Who's going?'

'Well, Ralph Hawkins for one,' she said calmly. 'I'm told he's booked a berth already. He'll be in England for their spring.'

Captain Boyle pushed his chair from the table, scraping the legs noisily on the polished floor. 'Damned convicts,' he muttered, rising from the table.

'He's not a convict, dear,' his wife chided nervously. 'His parents might have been but he is not.'

He shook a finger at her. 'Don't tell me what he is or isn't! I know more about that family than you think. His mother is a liar and a whore and his father is a thief.'

'Was, Father!' Phoebe interceded as she saw her mother stiffen at the coarse language. 'Not any more. They are the richest farmers this side of Sydney.' She gave him a derisive smile as she taunted, 'You don't have to feel bad about it just because they can afford to send their son to England.'

Captain Boyle flushed. 'I don't feel bad about it,' he bellowed. 'But they were sent here to be punished, not to make a fortune!' He picked up a handbell and rang it furiously. 'Fetch me my brandy,' he demanded of the young mulatto maid who answered. 'And be quick about it. And you, young woman,' he said, pointing a finger at Phoebe. 'Get out, I want to talk to your mother.'

Phoebe looked down at her half-eaten meal, but dared not protest. I've gone too far this time, she considered and felt remorse as she glanced at her mother's ashen face. 'I beg your pardon, Papa,' she ventured. 'I didn't intend to be rude.'

He didn't answer but flourished his hand that she should leave immediately. She closed the door quietly behind her and leaned against it, pressing her ear to it in an attempt to hear the conversation within.

The maid came back with the brandy decanter and looked at Phoebe in a frightened manner. 'He's not angry with you,' Phoebe whispered, moving away from the door. 'He's got a touch of gout, that's all.'

Captain Boyle poured himself a brandy whilst his wife stared at the mutton on the serving salver. The meat was growing cold, and fat was congealing around its edges. Her appetite was quite gone and she made a mental note to tell Cook to send the joint down to one of the Aboriginal reserves.

'That young woman,' her husband was saying. 'She's quite spoilt my surprise. Completely ruined it!'

Lucinda looked up. 'Surprise? What surprise?'

Captain Boyle leaned over the table and pulled off a piece of pink meat from the joint. He put it in his mouth and chewed. 'Why, what we were talking about last night.'

She waited. His humour seemed to be returning.

'I said I'd think about this trip to England that you mentioned, to see your mother, you know.' He eased a piece of meat from his teeth with his fingernail and she turned her eyes away. 'Well, I did think about it. Last night at the club, and I decided that perhaps you should go.'

She looked up, hoping. Hoping that he wasn't just playing a cruel joke on her.

'And now that young minx has spoilt it.'

'She wasn't to know what you were planning, dear,' she pleaded, and knew now that he was going to change his mind, if he had ever made it up in the first place.

'No, I suppose not,' he conceded. 'She's a thorn in my side, that young woman. I don't know what will become of her. No man will have her, that's for sure, in spite of her fine looks. I can't think of one family with sons who would welcome her as a daughter.'

If she had a fortune they would, Lucinda mused. But she hasn't. At least not until my own mother dies.

He stood in front of the unlit fireplace which was filled with fresh flowers. 'So what I had decided was that you should go to England; and now, when I think again about it, whilst you are there you can try and marry Phoebe off to some rich gentry or other. Your mother knows the best families, she'll know of somebody. They like eccentrics in England and Phoebe is certainly one of those.'

Lucinda felt herself grow hot. Her face was burning. Did he mean it? Would he change his mind?

'I shan't go of course. I've no wish to go back. Damned cold, wet country that it is, and I've plenty to do here. I can't take the time off. No, you go, my dear.' He smiled with an unaccustomed show of affection which made her uneasy. 'Take as long as you want, I shall be all right on my own, just me and Edwin.'

'You mean that we are to go alone? Without an escort?' she stammered. 'But how will we manage, with baggage and everything?'

'I'll book you on a ship where I know the captain; you'll be all right. Why dammit, Luce! Women are travelling on their own all the time these days. Where's your spirit of adventure?'

His eyes ran over her and she shivered. He wanted rid of her and she knew the reason why.

'Just make sure, before you return, that you marry off your daughter and that your old mother leaves you plenty in her will.'

She swallowed and smiled. 'I'll do my best,' she said quietly. The journey would be hard for a woman such as her, she had hardly travelled anywhere since coming to Australia. But it would be worth any kind of hardship just to go home. Any hardship at all.

The next morning after her husband had gone out, she dressed in a sprigged muslin day dress and put on her large straw hat, for the day promised to be very hot. Already there was a heat haze shimmering over the land. She called for the trap to be brought round to the door.

'You want me to come, Mrs Boyle?' The Aborigine who looked after the two horses, one which her husband rode and the other which was used for the trap, tipped his hat.

'No, thank you, Smith. I'm not going far.' She shook the reins and set off towards the Sydney road, then when she was out of sight of the house she turned, cutting back up a side avenue which would take her up towards the rough climb which eventually led to Creek Farm.

She was hot and sticky by the time she arrived nearly an hour later. She was nervous as always, for the road wasn't used much and it was not wise for a woman to ride alone. It wasn't her first time, however, and she knew that Meg Hawkins drove down it regularly whenever she came into Sydney. But then Meg Hawkins was a different type of woman from her. Strong, wise and braver. Much braver.

Pulling in through the gate, she drew up

by the veranda and gave the reins to a dark-skinned boy who came to greet her. 'Is your mistress at home?' she asked.

'Oh, yes,' he grinned. 'Missy Meg always at home. She cooking good dinner.'

The house had been extended considerably since Meg and Joe Hawkins had first come to live there. Though the front façade retained its simplicity with its open veranda which commanded a view over Sydney, two wings had been added to increase the size of the rooms and the rear extended to make a large kitchen, which Meg still supervised, and to include a dairy and a laundry room.

Lucinda Boyle climbed the steps and knocked on the open wooden door, then called. 'Meg. Meg! Are you there?'

Meg came through from the kitchen into the cool hall. Her hands were floury and there was a smell of beef cooking. 'Mrs Boyle!' she greeted her. 'This is nice. Come in.' She noted her visitor's flushed face and that her fair hair was wet beneath her hat. 'It's far too hot for you to be out! There's nothing wrong, is there?'

'Oh, no,' Lucinda breathed, and gratefully took the chair which Meg offered. 'Nothing is wrong. But I had to tell somebody my good news.'

'And you chose to tell me?' Meg said with pleasure in her voice.

'Why yes, because I knew you would be

pleased for me. Some ladies would not be as happy for me as I know you will be.'

Theirs was a strange friendship; one, born a lady, wrenched from her homeland on her husband's decision. The other, from the most wretched of backgrounds, torn from it on the decision of the law. They had an affinity born originally of loneliness and the need of another woman to talk to, which they had recognized years before as they waited for their children outside school.

But theirs was a secret friendship. Lucinda Boyle knew that should her husband find out, he would immediately ban her from calling on Meg. Today was the first time she had dared to visit whilst the Captain was at home and not at sea.

Meg smiled and sat beside her. 'So what have you to tell me, Mrs Boyle?' She was always formal. She could never bring herself to call her friend, who was undoubtedly a proper lady, by her first name.

Lucinda took hold of her hand. 'I'm going home,' she said softly. 'I'm going home – to England.'

Meg squeezed her hand. 'Oh, I'm so glad.' Sudden tears wet her eyes. 'Oh, so glad for you! But I'll miss you.'

Lucinda nodded. 'I shall miss you too, Meg. I heard', she said, 'that Ralph was travelling to England too. Phoebe heard it from some of her friends.'

77

'Did she tell you why?' Meg asked softly. 'Do you know why he's going?'

'To see his aunt? Your husband's sister?'

Meg shook her head. 'No, that's not 'real reason, though he'll visit Emily and her family whilst he's there. He doesn't remember her of course, he was very young when she went home.' She looked pensively into the middle distance for a moment, then got to her feet. 'But I'm forgetting myself. You must be parched. I'll get us some tea.'

'In a moment.' Lucinda stayed her. 'Tell me why he's going. You're upset, Meg. Don't you want him to go?'

'I'm afraid he won't come back,' Meg said in a low voice. 'I'm afraid of what he'll find when he gets back to his roots.'

'I don't understand,' she questioned. 'To his roots?'

'I mean that he's going to search for his real family, if he has one.' Meg turned to her friend. 'I have never told anyone this before, but I know that I can trust you. Ralph is not my son. His mother died on board ship when we were being transported. I didn't give birth to him.' She gave a small involuntary sob. 'He is my son,' she said fiercely. 'But now he needs to find out about his real mother, the women who gave birth to him.'

'And no-one else knows?' Lucinda asked softly.

'Only Ralph Clavell and two others, and,' she added bitterly, 'Captain Boyle has always suspected.'

'But it doesn't matter any more, surely?' Lucinda asked. 'Ralph is an adult.'

'No, it doesn't matter to anyone but me,' Meg whispered. 'But it proves that I've been acting a lie all of these years and now I've been found out.' She lowered her head. 'I've tried so hard to change my life. To prove that I'm as good as anyone else. But I'm not.'

'But you are! There is no-one perfect. Not a single one of us. If you knew the thoughts I had sometimes, you would know that I am a very wicked lady!'

Meg gave a shaky laugh. 'I do know one perfect lady,' she said, wiping her eyes. 'Joe's sister. She always was an angel even though terrible things happened to her.'

'I'd like to meet this perfect lady.' Lucinda smiled. 'For I don't believe in her!'

Meg gave a gasp. 'Would you? Oh would you, Mrs Boyle? Would you see her and take a message from us? I know that Ralph will visit but he might forget what I want him to say.'

'Of course I will,' Lucinda assured her. 'I would be delighted to.'

Meg grew thoughtful and hesitated before saying, 'But no, I couldn't ask you. It would be too difficult for you. Captain Boyle wouldn't like it if you visited Emily. She was once a convict.'

'Captain Boyle is not coming with me,' Lucinda assured her, 'and I shall tell him only what I want him to know.' Her lips turned down. 'My husband has his secrets, or he thinks he has,' she added. 'I have a reason for asking about your son, Meg. Can you tell me when he will be travelling and on which ship? You see, Phoebe and I will be travelling without an escort and I would be grateful for some help on the voyage.'

'He'd be glad to help, I'm sure of it. I'll find out 'details.'

'One other thing, Meg.' Lucinda Boyle's expression was anxious. 'I rather think that your son Ralph is fond of Phoebe. What do you think of that?'

Chapter Seven

'Dearest Mama and Papa,' Amelia wrote. 'I can't think how I came to be involved in one of Aunt Anna's mad schemes. She wants me to be a schoolteacher! I have insisted that I would be no good at all as I haven't the patience, but she is so persuasive and persistent, rather like you are, Papa, and I am to meet the Misses Fielding tomorrow.

'They cannot afford any help apparently, they are on their "uppers", as Aunt Anna says, and lead very frugal lives. I suppose I can stay for a couple of weeks, but I shall insist on being home for Christmas.

'From your ever loving daughter,
Amelia.'

The house in which the Misses Fielding lived and taught was tucked away in Back Swinegate, a narrow lane off St Sampson's Square, the busy market area which was lined with old inns, shops and houses. Amelia and her aunt were welcomed at the door by Miss Harriet, whilst Miss Fielding, the elder of the two sisters, was making tea.

'We have a girl comes in to help each morning,' Harriet explained as she ushered them into the parlour, a cosy, crowded room with a piano, a desk, table and sideboard, shabby chairs and a bright cheerful fire burning in the grate. 'But otherwise we manage very well on our own,' she added. 'Of course we have always had to, since we were very young.'

'Have you no living parents, Miss Harriet?' Amelia asked boldly. Harriet Fielding was perhaps five or six years older than herself and as her sister Elizabeth came into the room carrying a tea tray, she saw that she was in her early thirties.

Introductions were made again and Miss Fielding poured the tea and handed round a plate of dainty cakes. Amelia took one for she guessed that they had been baked especially for their visit. They chatted politely for a while and then Harriet answered Amelia's previous question.

'Our parents died when we were very young, Miss Linton,' she said. 'I don't remember my father at all and my mother only slightly. But you remember her, don't you Elizabeth?'

'I do.' She inclined her head. Like her sister she was fair with blue eyes and a slight, fragile frame. Perhaps they don't eat enough, Amelia thought as she sipped her tea and observed them.

'Our father died when Harriet was a baby and I was about four. Our mother died when I was eight.' She glanced at her sister. 'We have looked after each other since then.'

But who else took care of them, Amelia pondered, and how sad, having no other family; she thought of her own boisterous, happy family, but asked no more questions, it didn't seem fair to pry into such a sensitive issue.

'As we have only a small inheritance, we have to make our own living, so we decided to open a school,' Harriet explained. 'Elizabeth is very clever, she takes after our father. He was a schoolmaster and ran his own school.'

'Mother was clever too,' Elizabeth broke in. 'She had her own confectionery shop after Father died and was very successful.' Her face suddenly took on a frozen look and her lips tightened. 'Would you care for more tea, Mrs Gregory? Miss Linton?'

Amelia was shown the schoolroom, which was across the tiny hall from the parlour. It was not a large room and was divided by a curtain. 'As you see, Miss Linton,' said Miss Fielding, 'we do not have a great deal of room but we manage to take eight pupils. Two of them are fee-paying, which pays the rent, and the other pupils are paid for out of the generosity of benefactors such as Mrs Gregory.'

'But if you have just the one room, Miss Fielding, will it not be rather crowded with another teacher?'

'We need three more pupils to make the school pay its way, Miss Linton,' she replied. 'Harriet suggested that we could use the parlour for older pupils if we had another teacher, and we could also give piano lessons in there.' She hesitated. 'We cannot afford to pay very much, Miss Linton, perhaps expenses and a small salary.'

Amelia glanced at her aunt who raised her eyebrows and gave an imperceptible nod of her head.

'I realize that there are few teachers who can afford to take such a position as this. Young women who teach for a living are generally quite poor, but I understand that earning your own living is not your prime consideration?'

'No, it isn't,' Amelia said slowly, wondering what tale her aunt had spun. 'I haven't taught before and I'm not sure that I would be a very good teacher.'

'Well we could try each other out! If you could take the new pupils,' Harriet said eagerly. 'Read to them, teach them to write and add up simple numbers? Nothing too difficult!'

'I suppose so,' she said reluctantly. 'Perhaps for a week or two until you find someone more suitable. I did tell Mama I would be home to help with Christmas.'

The two Misses Fielding looked wistful. 'You're from a large family, Miss Linton?' Harriet asked. 'I suppose it is always very merry?'

'Yes indeed.' Amelia felt almost ashamed to

admit it. 'I have two brothers and three sisters, my parents of course and other relatives who live near. We are always a houseful.'

'Then of course you must go home,' Miss Fielding said softly. 'You mustn't worry about us.'

Amelia pondered as they drove home. 'Aunt Anna,' she said, 'how did that happen? I had no intention of agreeing. And I did not wish to be paid a salary!'

Her aunt smiled. 'They would not have wanted you to work for nothing. They have their pride. I had told them that you wished to try out your independence, that you were a young woman with modern ideas! That's right isn't it? And your inherent good nature took over when you discovered that they could not afford anyone else. But you will find that not only are you giving something to those dear sisters and their pupils, but will gain great satisfaction for yourself in doing so.'

I hope she's right, Amelia thought the next morning as she prepared herself. She dressed in a plain gown and fastened her thick hair into a coil in the nape of her neck. But I am determined that I will not be persuaded to stay for longer than I said.

'What time do we go, Aunt?' she asked as they finished an early breakfast. 'I forgot to ask.'

'The pupils arrive at nine,' her aunt replied. 'But I am not coming. I have other business to attend to. Patrick will take you as near to St Sampson's Square as he can get and then come back for me as I need the carriage this morning. You can find your own way from there, can you not?'

Amelia looked at her blankly. She could hardly take her maid Nancy to accompany her, what would she do all day? She swallowed. She had wanted freedom and now it seemed that she was about to get it.

'Look for the Roman bathhouse, dear,' her aunt advised, 'then Finkle Street and Back Swinegate is just behind. It's quite easy to find.'

So unused to travelling alone, Amelia immediately became lost within the alleyways and lanes surrounding the market; but to her delight, rather than feeling perturbed at being alone for the first time in a strange place, she actually revelled in it. She dawdled her way past the shops, but hurried past the taverns and through the alleyways, though they were so thronged with hurrying people she didn't feel nervous, and quite by chance, rather than design, she found herself outside the door of the Misses Fieldings' house.

She could hear chanting coming from inside the door as she knocked with the shiny brass knocker, and realized that the pupils were learning their numbers tables by rote. She smiled to herself as she remembered doing the same thing with her governess at home in Holderness.

'Oh, Miss Linton,' Miss Harriet greeted her. 'We had quite given you up and thought you had changed your mind about coming.'

'I'm so sorry I'm late,' Amelia began guiltily. 'I'm afraid I got lost.'

'It doesn't matter in the least,' Miss Harriet assured her. 'Just so long as you are here now. It's very easy to become lost within York if you don't know it. But it won't take you long to find your way around.'

The day passed quickly. She was introduced to the children, a mixed class of three boys and five girls. Two of the girls were the fee-paying pupils and Amelia sat with them and Miss Harriet behind the curtain and listened to them read, and then gave them a subject for a story which she asked them to write in their own words and which she would comment on the next day. Then she sat with Miss Fielding whilst she taught the remaining children simple arithmetic.

She watched the children as they chanted. Apart from the fee-paying pupils they were poorly dressed and two of them, a boy and a girl, were in very thin clothes and not wearing shoes, even though the day was cold. The little girl kept curling and uncurling her toes and Amelia resolved to ask Ginny if she had kept any of Lily's old shoes or if she had already given them away to the village children. Rarely was anything wasted in the Linton family. Their mother said she remembered well enough about hard times and so any spare clothing, blankets or shoes were given to the poor.

Amelia beckoned to the girl when the lesson was finished and Miss Fielding had gone out of the room for a moment. 'What is your name?' she asked.

'Moira, miss.' She had pale gingery-coloured hair which looked as if it hadn't ever been brushed.

'And how old are you, Moira?'

'I'm nine, miss. Ten in two weeks.'

'I'm ten already.' The barefoot boy spoke up. His hair was very dark and he had deep blue eyes. 'Nearly eleven. And our Eamon is only seven so he can't come to school yet, but when he does I shall leave.'

Both children had strong Irish accents and both had pinched looks about their faces.

'Are you brother and sister?' Amelia asked.

They nodded. 'This is Kieran,' Moira piped up. 'He doesn't like coming to school, but Ma says he has to. We have to learn to read and write so that we can get work.'

Amelia thought of her younger brother and sisters who had a governess at home. Joseph too grumbled at having to learn lessons. He would rather be out on the estate with Roger and Uncle Sam, and Hannah would rather play with her dolls. Lily was the only one with any aptitude for learning, but there was no prospect of them ever having to look for work to earn their living.

'How would it be if I helped you with your

reading and writing, Kieran, along with Miss Fielding and Miss Harriet? We'd get on very quickly then, and you could leave sooner than you expected and try for work.'

The little boy put his head on one side and thought about it. 'Sure,' he agreed. 'We could give it a try.'

Moira looked at her eagerly. 'Would you be helping me too, Miss Linton? Ma says I need a bit of a push on me backside to get me going.'

Amelia laughed. 'Why not? Shall we try to have you both reading by Christmas?'

It was decided that Amelia should give the two children extra lessons on their own, and after Patrick, the coachman, had collected her and escorted her back to her aunt's in the carriage that evening, she reflected that it had been a very satisfying day. She worried though that she was being a nuisance to her aunt and uncle by requiring Patrick to escort her to and fro every day. But there was nothing else for it. The days were short, the weather was damp and foggy and she could not journey home alone in the darkness.

In the cosy parlour with the fire warming them, Kieran and Moira soon began to improve in their writing and arithmetic, but their Irish accent was so strong that although Amelia was sure they were reading the words correctly, she couldn't always understand what they were saying. Again and again she corrected their

English until at last she thought there was some improvement.

Then came the day when there was a hammering on the door and a giant of an Irishman stood there with a pack on his back. He asked particularly for Miss Linton and in some trepidation, Harriet brought him through into the parlour where Amelia was sitting with Kieran and Moira and two other children. The lamps were lit and the children were grouped around a chenille-covered table with their books in their hands.

'Mr Mahoney wants to speak to you, Miss Linton,' Harriet said nervously. 'I'll just get Miss Fielding.'

'I don't want Miss Fielding,' the man said brusquely. 'It's this young woman that I want. She's the one who's teaching my bairns to give up their Irish tongue and speak the English.'

Amelia stood up, as did the children. Kieran and Moira stared apprehensively at their father. 'Shall we go out into the hall, Mr Mahoney?' she said in a braver tone than she felt. 'Then the children can get on with their lessons.'

'I'll say what I have to say right here, miss. I never wanted them to come to school. They should be earning their own bread by now, same as I did at their age. Not sitting with a book in their hands in front of a warm fire as if they were grand folk! It was their mammy's idea that they should come and I gave into her in a weak moment.' He stared hard at Amelia and she saw that his eyes were as blue as Kieran's. 'But I'll not have them forgetting their roots. Irish we are and proud of it.'

'And quite right too, Mr Mahoney.' Amelia spoke up, for she guessed that he was mostly bluster. 'I am in complete agreement with you. It's most important that we know our own historical background, and as soon as the children can read and write sufficiently well, we shall be teaching them, in a simple form, the history of both England and Ireland.'

She smiled at him. 'I'm sure you will do the same. But as far as teaching them English, if they are to stay in England they will have more chance of obtaining work if their accent can be understood, and they will never lose it completely, I can assure you of that. And why should they want to, it is charming!'

Mr Mahoney stood open-mouthed, then said, 'Charming? To be sure, nobody has ever said that before.'

'Well I'm saying it. And they are delightful, intelligent children. They need every opportunity they can get.'

He backed away to the door. 'Well, as long as it's understood.' He waved a finger half-heartedly. 'They keep their Irish tongue!'

'I understand completely, you need have no doubts on that. Good day, Mr Mahoney. Thank you for coming.'

She heaved a sigh as the door was closed behind him and the children, all but Moira, sat down again. 'Sorry, miss,' she said, hanging her head. 'It was my fault.'

'How was it your fault, Moira?'

'It was our Eamon, he was babbling on something terrible last night and I screeched at him, "you eejit, speak English for God's sake," and Dada was just coming in the door and heard me. He fetched me a clout and said we were getting above ourselves and he'd take us away from school.'

'And I said we wanted to stay, miss,' Kieran butted in. 'I told him that you said we'd be reading by Christmas.'

Amelia gave a huge smile. 'And so you will. That's a promise.'

Chapter Eight

'So what shall we do? How shall we get round it?' Ralph looked anxiously at Jack. 'The clerk was definite about it.'

Jack put his chin in his hands and gazed down from the Hawkins's veranda towards the creek. 'He wouldn't take a bribe?'

'No, I tried that too. He said he would be out of a job if he did.'

'There's only one thing for it then. I'll have to come as your manservant!'

Ralph roared with laughter and slapped Jack on the shoulder. 'Brilliant! Does that mean you'll press my trousers?'

'No sir, it don't! You press your own damned trousers, white man.'

'What's going on out here?' Meg came out, followed by Joe. 'Can we share in the joke?'

'It's no joke, Ma.' A sudden gloom came into Ralph's voice. 'We can't get Jack on board ship as a passenger. When I went to book they asked if he was a native Australian and when I said yes, same as me, they asked what colour he was. Then the clerk said all the cabins were taken.'

'And were they?' his father frowned.

'No, I saw the list. There was plenty of space.'

'Mrs Boyle and her daughter are travelling on 'same ship,' Meg said. 'I understood 'ship was only half full.'

'I'll wear my white tunic and travel as Ralph's servant.' Jack grinned as he spoke but there was anger in his eyes. 'I'm determined to go.'

'Why do you want to go, Jack?' Meg asked. 'What is there for you in England?'

Jack shook his head. 'Don't know, Missus Meg.' He used the name that he had given her when he was a child. 'I just feel the need to go. I dreamt that I should. There's something waiting for me.'

'I'll go in,' Joe said vehemently. 'They'll not argue wi' me.'

'No, sir,' Jack protested. 'Book me in as Ralph's manservant. We can have some fun with that, hey Ralph? I'll buy some new clothes and expensive luggage and no-one will know what to make of it.'

'What does your father think of you going to England?' Joe asked.

'He thinks I'm crazy, sir,' he grinned. 'And I probably am!'

'Ma says we'll need warm clothes even though it'll be spring when we get there.' Ralph and

Jack walked towards the tailor's shop to collect the suits that were ready. The two men were roughly the same size, though Jack was stockier, and Ralph had ordered four woollen suits, two for him and two for Jack, though Jack had specified his colour preference. He had also ordered shirts and cravats and two greatcoats.

'You will surely not require two greatcoats, sir?' the tailor had remarked. 'One will be sufficient.'

'Make it two,' Ralph insisted. 'And two top hats, two bowlers and don't forget the gloves.'

'Yes, sir. How many pairs?'

'Four!'

The doorbell jangled as they went into the shop and Mrs Boyle and Phoebe, who had just been attended to, turned towards them. Mrs Boyle carried a small parcel.

'Mrs Boyle! Miss Boyle!' Ralph bowed, as did Jack. 'How very nice to see you.'

They exchanged greetings and Mrs Boyle commented, 'I understand you are travelling to England on the same ship as we are, Mr Hawkins.'

'Really?' Ralph expressed astonishment although his mother had already told him. 'That is good news! Perhaps we can be of assistance to you whilst on board? Jack is also travelling with me.' He glanced at the tailor hovering by the counter. 'It makes it easier, does it not, to have one's servants on a voyage!'

Phoebe laughed merrily. 'I don't know how

95

you would ever manage without him. Jack must be your right hand.'

'Oh indeed he is.' Ralph took a step back away from Jack's malevolent glare. 'I couldn't possibly travel without him.'

They collected all their parcels and walked back to the trap in which they had driven to town. Presently they caught up with Phoebe who was waiting for her mother outside a florist's shop. She held a parasol over her head for the day was very hot.

'What was all that about?' Phoebe asked bluntly. 'What are you two up to?'

'Nothing, Miss Boyle.' Ralph doffed his hat. 'It's true. Jack has to come as a servant otherwise he can't have a cabin.'

'Why ever not?'

'In case you haven't noticed, Miss Boyle,' Jack said softly, 'I have a dark skin.'

She gazed at him steadily for a moment, then with a faint blush on her cheeks, said, 'So you have! I hadn't noticed.'

'Isn't she absolutely adorable?' Ralph murmured as they walked away towards the Haymarket where they were soon absorbed into the noisy bustle of market trading, the ring of the hammer in the blacksmith's forge and the cheerful laughter and pungent smell of ale and tobacco emanating from the inns and taprooms. 'She epitomizes the perfect Englishwoman. Fair hair, fair skin, but with a glow about her that can only come from the Australian sun.'

'Wrong. Quite wrong!' Jack said. 'She is nothing like the average Englishwoman. Her mother, Mrs Boyle, is, she's gentle and calm and ladylike. Miss Boyle is nothing like that. She might look like an English rose but beneath that fine skin she is pure Australian.'

'You of all people can say that?' Ralph said in astonishment. 'I thought you were of the opinion that only the Aborigine was pure Australian!'

'I am an observer of people,' Jack said calmly, 'and there are some who adapt to whatever culture or climate they happen to live in. Miss Boyle is one of those.'

'Well, thank God she doesn't take after her father or behave like her brother,' Ralph said brusquely. 'She would be unbearable if she did.' He gave a sigh. 'As it is, I find her delightful. She's merry and charming and – '

'And if it were not for her father disliking you, you would be out to capture her?' Jack commented drily.

'I'd not let him put me off,' Ralph protested. 'I'm very taken with her, Jack. There is no-one else who makes me feel the way I do.'

'Take care, my friend, that you don't get hurt,' Jack said softly as they climbed into the trap and he took the reins. 'Miss Boyle is not the one for you.'

The ship was due to sail the week after Christmas and the next few weeks were spent in a flurry of Christmas preparations and packing for the voyage. Peggy decorated the veranda with branches of eucalyptus and sweet-smelling jasmine and twined red ribbon around the top of the veranda posts.

'When I was a bairn in Hull,' Meg watched her from the doorway, 'I used to stand shivering outside 'windows of 'big houses in the High Street or Albion Street and wish and wish that I could go inside. Some of the merchants' houses had fir trees with flickering candles and presents hanging on the branches, like they did in foreign countries, and coloured boxes tied up with ribbon round 'bottom of 'tree and always a log fire burning in 'grate.'

'So what did you do, Ma?' Peggy was concentrating on arranging sprigs of mimosa through the ribbon and forgot for a moment about her mother's past.

'We did nothing,' Meg said bluntly. 'Sat on a doorstep if we didn't have a room, or went down to 'soup kitchen in 'Market Place and warmed ourselves by 'brazier.'

Peggy turned around, stricken that she had been so unfeeling as to forget, but her mother was smiling. 'We are so lucky,' she said. 'Your da and me. So very, very lucky.'

Peggy put her arms around her mother and squeezed her. 'So are we,' she said huskily. 'Ralph and I, lucky to have you and Da.'

Joe came up the veranda steps and complimented Peggy on the decorations.

'Did you have a tree at Christmas when you were a boy, Da?' she asked.

'No, Ma said it was pagan and wouldn't let us have one in the house, but Da would bring in a branch from a tree and Emily and me used to decorate it wi' coloured paper, though I doubt she would remember, she was onny a bairn. And we had chicken for Christmas dinner! Ma allus fattened one up specially and would put it to cook while we were at church on Christmas morning, oh, aye, and mistress from 'big house allus brought us a plum pudding and give us a sixpenny piece.'

'What riches, Joe.' Meg smiled. 'You'll be telling us you were given presents as well.'

Joe's eyes clouded over. 'Aye, a nearly new scarf one year and a wooden whistle that my da made, and a handkerchief for Emily with her initial on it.'

Meg put out her arms and Joe stumbled into them. 'So much harder for you than me, Joe,' she whispered into his bristly beard. 'I know how you miss Emily.'

He shook his head. 'Not so much now,' he said. 'Not now that I've got you and my own family. I don't know what I'd have done without you, Meg. It's just – it's just with Ralph going away it brings all 'memories flooding back.'

He drew away from her and took a deep breath. 'Anyway, I've got a surprise for all of you, you and me, Peggy and Ralph.' Meg and Peggy waited expectantly. 'On Christmas Eve,' he said, 'we're going to drive into Sydney, and we're spending 'night at best hotel that money can buy, Royal Hotel – and we're having our Christmas dinner there as well.'

They both stared at him. 'It's booked already so you'd better get yourselves off to buy a new frock or two.' He drew himself up. 'And I've ordered a new suit, because while we're there we're going to have our pictures took so that Ralph can take them to England and show to Emily and Philip and their bairns, so that they'll know what their Australian family looks like all these years on.'

Meg and Joe were ill at ease at the hotel, unused to such luxury and attention, but Ralph and Peggy were very merry and on the photographs they were smiling into the camera, whilst Joe and Meg looked as if they were carved from stone.

They were photographed with Joe seated and dressed in an unaccustomed frock coat and narrow trousers, with a cravat at his neck and holding a pair of gloves in his hands. Meg in a dark red silk dress stood beside him in a sideways position to show off the padded bustle in her pleated and tucked long-trained skirt, the close-fitting bodice boned to emphasize her neat waist and trimmed with lace frills on the shoulders and wrists. Her still dark, unruly hair had been caught in a chignon with a dainty beribboned hat set on top of her head.

'Ma, how elegant you look!' Ralph exclaimed when he saw her. 'You outdo all the ladies of Sydney.'

'But it's not me, is it?' she laughed, though a flush on her cheeks showed how pleased she was at his compliment. 'And Emily won't know me.'

'Well, no doubt they will have changed too,' Joe said and gazed at his wife admiringly. 'We're all older and living a different life.' Then he said with a sheepish grin, 'I reckon you'll have to get some use out of those clothes, Meg. Maybe we'll take some time off and do a bit of travelling.'

'Now?' Ralph blurted out. 'But I'm going away! Who'll look after the station?'

'Oh, onny for a few days!' Joe exclaimed. 'And Benne will keep an eye on things. I didn't mean longer than a week.'

Meg smiled at her son and husband. It was enough. A concession such as this from Joe was a great step forward.

The day of departure was scorching hot and Meg wore a new muslin gown and a large hat to wave goodbye to Ralph from the quayside. Daisy and Benne were there to see Jack off, and Captain Boyle escorted his wife and daughter on board though he didn't wait to see the ship sail. He ignored Joe who returned the compliment by staring straight through him, though Meg felt his eyes linger over her and he gave her a slight bow as he passed.

Joe took her arm and led her to the waiting trap. 'I'll buy you something a bit smarter than this, Meg,' he said. 'A barouche maybe, something more fitting for my lady wife.' A gleam came into his eyes. 'And that'll give Captain Boyle summat else to lust after.'

Meg held her hand to her forehead to shield her eyes from the sun and looked down at the shimmering waters of the harbour as they climbed the hill. The sight of the ship had revived so many memories. 'Will he come back, Joe?' she said softly. 'I'm so afraid that he won't.'

'Don't worry, Ma,' Peggy interrupted. 'He'll be back.'

Joe said nothing for a moment, then he too turned his head to see the ship as it headed towards the harbour mouth. 'I don't know, Meg. It's fate. He might. He might not. It all depends on what and who he finds.'

Chapter Nine

'Alone, Mr Hawkins? Where is your servant?' Phoebe and her mother stopped their perambulating around the deck when they saw Ralph leaning on the ship rail.

'Sick, Miss Boyle.' Ralph grinned. 'As soon as we hauled anchor. He's flat out on his bunk moaning and groaning.'

'Sick as a dog, I am,' Jack had said when Ralph went to look for him.

'But we're not out of harbour yet.' Ralph laughed. 'You can't be sick!'

'I can and I am,' Jack groaned from his bunk. 'Just go away and leave me.'

Ralph opened the cabin door. 'No lunch then? No lamb cutlet or steamed pudding?'

Jack had picked up a book and thrown it at him. 'Get out, I'm dying.'

'He'll be all right when we reach open sea and are under sail,' Mrs Boyle said. 'I remember I was the same when I left Portsmouth to come to Australia.'

'Are you a good sailor, Miss Boyle?' Ralph turned his attention to Phoebe. 'Have you much experience?'

'None whatsoever, and for heaven's sake stop calling me Miss Boyle. No, my father was never willing to take us to sea with him.'

'My husband didn't believe in mixing his professional life with his family life,' Mrs Boyle said hastily with a warning glance at Phoebe. 'And yes, I think whilst we are on board for this long voyage we could perhaps drop some formality, though I must confess I do not know how to behave towards your friend Jack. Of course he is not your servant!'

'Indeed not, ma'am. He is more than my equal. More intelligent, more of a gentleman than I could ever hope to be, but please don't tell him I said so, Mrs Boyle,' he insisted, 'or I shall never live it down.'

'I wonder if I have something to relieve his suffering?' Mrs Boyle said thoughtfully. 'I know I have sal volatile, but I don't think that would be effective. If you will excuse me I will have a look in my medicine box.'

'I'll go, Mama,' Phoebe offered.

'No, no! You won't be able to find it. I know exactly where it is. I will only be a moment.'

She scurried away and Phoebe leaned on the rail at the side of Ralph. 'Amazing!' she said.

'What is?' Ralph turned to look at her. She was very close and the effect made him feel quite heady.

'Mama. How she's changed within just a few hours of leaving home. Leaving me alone with a man – agreeing to using your first name! We're travelling alone, you know. Father wouldn't agree to us bringing a maid. He said he wasn't going to pay the extra fare and that he was the one who needed looking after whilst we were away enjoying ourselves. Mother has never been without a servant in the whole of her life, yet she seems to be revelling in the freedom.'

'She is a charming lady,' Ralph said softly, 'and you obviously favour her.'

Phoebe looked at him frankly. She seemed to be amused by his remark. 'Don't be misled, Ralph. I don't have my mother's charm, only her looks. I'm more likely to have inherited my father's tenacity.' She turned and looked down into the churning water. 'Believe me, Ralph. I'm very clever at getting what I want.'

He leant forward so that his lips were near her cheek. 'So am I,' he whispered, but pulled away quickly when he saw Mrs Boyle heading back down the deck towards them.

'I almost kissed her, Jack,' he said later, when he took in the oil of peppermint that Mrs Boyle had supplied. 'And she didn't take offence. I can't believe my nerve. I must have been mad!'

'She didn't object?' Jack sat up and leant against the bulkhead.

Ralph shook his head. 'I don't think so,' then added truthfully, 'she seemed to be rather amused.'

The first half of the voyage passed pleasantly enough and when the weather was suitable the young people played skittles on deck whilst the older travellers played chess. Ralph and Jack entertained everyone when they demonstrated Aborigine wrestling, and some of the crew members requested a turn, but none could out-throw Jack. He was undoubtedly the champion and whereas some of the crew had previously treated him in a surly manner, this was now tinged with some respect. He behaved impeccably, being neither subservient nor proud. Every evening he dressed immaculately for dinner, even though he ate alone in his cabin, and crew and passengers were obviously non-plussed over his standing.

'He is a charming person,' Mrs Boyle commented to Phoebe as they undressed for bed. They shared a cabin, another of Captain Boyle's savings. Ralph had offered to let them have his and he would share with Jack but Mrs Boyle would not hear of it. 'Such fine manners. I wonder where he learned them?'

'From his parents, I suppose.' Phoebe stood in her underdrawers and stretched her arms, touching the ceiling with her fingertips. 'Schooling doesn't necessarily teach manners as we well know.' She gave a cynical laugh 'Father always said he had wasted his money in sending me to the School for Young Ladies in Parramatta!'

'You know that I have to look out for a suitable husband for you whilst we are in England?' Her mother climbed awkwardly into her bunk. 'Your father insists.'

Phoebe slipped her nightshift over her head. 'I don't wish to marry, Mama, but if I did,' she said in that determined manner which her mother knew so well, 'I would choose a husband for myself.'

'Elizabeth,' Amelia said to Miss Fielding a week before Christmas, 'I have something to ask you – two things in fact.'

Elizabeth Fielding looked up from her sewing. There were only the two fee-paying pupils attending school at the moment and they had left early. Amelia was travelling home the next day. 'Yes?'

'Would you and Harriet come to Holderness and spend Christmas with me and my family? I would so like you to and I have already asked Mama and she said they would be delighted if you would come.'

Elizabeth flushed with pleasure. 'That is the nicest thing anyone has ever said to us. How very kind. But, but we can't, I'm afraid,' she said regretfully. 'The expense of the journey you know, and besides we always entertain a friend of Harriet's, and his father. They would be so disappointed if they were not able to come.'

'Oh,' Amelia said. 'Oh, what a pity. I was so looking forward to it. This friend of Harriet's,' she continued, 'is he a suitor?'

'He would be if he had any money.' Elizabeth

lowered her voice. 'Thomas is a clerk for a manufacturing confectioner. He doesn't earn a very big salary and he has to keep his father as well as himself.' She sighed. 'I'm afraid Harriet will have to wait a long time for the married state. Mr Thacker is unable to work, but is otherwise set for a long life.'

'Poor Harriet,' Amelia murmured as she thought of Harriet's youth slipping by. For herself she was not worried. With no gentleman that she was fond of and her new-found independence firmly in her grasp she was quite happy with her solitary state.

'And the other thing?' Elizabeth's voice intruded into her thoughts.

'Er – oh, yes!' Amelia smiled and sat down next to her. 'If you would like me to, I will continue after Christmas. Kieran and Moira are reading quite nicely. Kieran said that he will leave to start work, but that his younger brother will come. So encouraging,' she said enthusiastically, 'that the two children have persuaded Eamon to come to school.'

'Oh, I'm so pleased,' Elizabeth's face lit up with happiness. 'So very pleased.'

'Just one thing though Elizabeth. I hate to inconvenience my aunt unduly and although she doesn't complain that her coachman has to bring me in and out each day, I thought how much more satisfactory it would be if I lived nearer.'

'But that would mean you taking lodgings

in York and I'm sure your parents wouldn't approve, and also,' Elizabeth added, 'you would be out of pocket, my dear, your salary would hardly cover extra living expenses.'

'That is why I have a suggestion to make and I do hope you and Harriet will approve.' Amelia pointed up to the ceiling. 'You remember that day when there was a leak in the roof and I went up to investigate?'

Elizabeth nodded but looked puzzled.

'Well, I didn't realize that there was another room up there.'

'A room!' Elizabeth exclaimed. 'It's barely a cupboard. You're surely not suggesting that you live up there!'

'I am. It is small I agree, but I need little space just for sleeping. I can have a truckle bed brought from home and a small chest of drawers, perhaps a rug for the floor. I shall need no more than that.'

'But you will freeze under the roof, there's no fireplace up there!'

'I don't feel the cold,' Amelia insisted. 'Please say that I can try it. If it is not convenient then I will give it up and go back to my aunt's house.'

She saw the hesitation on her companion's face. Elizabeth, she knew, would not want anyone to be inconvenienced for her sake, and Amelia's aunt had been more than generous to them already.

'I will keep myself of course, if I might have

the use of the kitchen.' Which will be amusing to say the least, she mused, as I am no cook. I will have to take lessons in the kitchen whilst I am at home.

So it was agreed and Amelia set out on her train journey the following day. She had posted a letter to her parents in time for them to meet her at Hull railway station but not soon enough for them to arrange for someone to accompany her from York. She had sent Nancy home some weeks before, for she had no need for a maid and besides, the girl was unused to having so much time on her hands.

Her uncle saw her off at the station and made sure she joined a ladies-only compartment. 'Goodbye, Amelia. It's been very nice having you with us, your aunt has enjoyed your company I know. We shall see you again soon, I expect?'

'Indeed you will, Uncle.' How very kind they are, she thought, and waved to him as with a great spurt of steam the train pulled out of the station.

'Amelia! You have travelled alone!' Her father wasn't cross, just startled as she alighted without a companion.

'I have had a very good journey, Papa, and two very pleasant travelling companions. Two ladies who have been all the way to India and back on their own! Travelling from York to Hull was no hardship, I assure you, after hearing of their adventures.'

She took his arm as he led her out towards

the carriage. 'I told them of Mama being transported to Australia when she was young,' she said. 'They were most intrigued.'

'I'm not sure that your mother would approve of your telling her story to strangers,' her father objected.

'It was because they were strangers that I did,' she explained. 'They have lived such adventurous lives that I knew they would be interested. I don't tell everyone! Not the two Miss Fieldings for instance, they live such quiet genteel lives that I think they might be shocked!'

It was dark when they arrived home and the house was lit with lamps and candles and roaring fires in all the rooms. 'It's so good to be home, Mama!' Amelia hugged her mother and all her family in turn. 'I didn't realize how much I was missing you all and how lucky I am to have all of you.'

'It's good to have you home, Amelia. We've missed you too.' Her mother's cheeks were flushed a soft pink, pleased to have all of her brood under her roof once more. 'Now we can really think about Christmas. Did the Miss Fieldings agree to come?' she added.

Amelia shook her head. 'They had to decline, although I think they would have liked to come. They always entertain friends at Christmas. Perhaps they would come at Easter. I would like to repay their kindness; they're such good people, Mama, always thinking of others, especially the poor children. It would be nice for them to be cosseted; they live such frugal lives, yet they don't complain.'

'Then ask them,' her mother agreed. 'They might prefer the spring, not everyone enjoys our harsh winters in the Holderness plain!'

As they sat down for supper, Amelia's father asked, 'Have you told Amelia the news?'

'No, not yet.' Her mother smiled, her eyes sparkling. 'I wanted to get our greetings over first.'

'Oh, what news?' Amelia looked around the table. Her brothers and sisters were obviously waiting in anticipation too. 'I know!' She gazed at the twins. 'Father Christmas is coming early!'

'I hope not,' said her mother solemnly, 'for we're not yet ready for him. No,' she said. 'Something even better than that. I've had a letter from Aunt Meg. Your cousin Ralph is setting sail from Sydney just after Christmas. He will be here to visit us in the spring.'

Chapter Ten

Elizabeth Fielding had put the finishing touches to the Christmas goose ready for cooking the next morning. It was a poor specimen, so she had filled its cavities with chestnut stuffing and pieces of pork and a whole onion, in an attempt to plump it out. She washed her hands to remove the grease and took off her apron and was about to put another log on the parlour fire when there was a knock on the door.

'Now who's this?' she murmured. Harriet was out doing last-minute shopping, but she had her key. 'Christmas revellers perhaps?' The knock came again. Harder this time and somehow more determined. She gave a sudden shudder. Surely not? Not on Christmas Eve?

She turned the iron key in the lock and slowly opened the door. Her heart sank as she saw who was standing there.

'Well, Lizzie! Aren't you going to let your dear papa in? Are you going to keep us standing on the doorstep?'

Reluctantly she opened the door wider to admit a tall grey-haired thickset man, and then stood back to let the woman behind him enter also.

'Well come along. Let's go in by the fire. We're frozen, aren't we, Dolly? You have got a fire I suppose?'

She led them through the small hall and opened the door into the parlour, glad that the fire was burning low and that she hadn't built it up. Perhaps if they were cold they wouldn't stay long.

'We were doing some Christmas shopping,' the man said. 'Thought we'd drop by to see how you were. Where's Harriet?'

'We are quite well, thank you. Harriet is out.' She didn't ask them to sit down, nor did she ask how they were. She could see for herself that they were healthy and prosperous. He wore a warm wool cape and hat which he didn't remove and Dolly had a fur cape around her shoulders, a fur hat on her straw-coloured hair and a very pronounced bustle beneath her winter dress.

'Haven't you got a kiss for me then Lizzie?' Dolly's voice was high-pitched and without inflection. Elizabeth's lips brushed her proffered powdered cheek and she smelt the aroma of stale perfume.

'How's the school business then?' The visitor lowered himself into a chair. 'Making money, are you?'

'A living, thank you. We manage.'

'Mmm.' He glanced around the small room. 'Looks the same. Nothing new.' He leaned back in the chair and smiled complacently at Lizzie. 'If you need anything you only have to ask.'

And there are always conditions, she reflected bitterly. A leopard doesn't change its spots. But she simply inclined her head and repeated, 'We manage, thank you.'

She heard Harriet's key in the door and her sister's voice calling from the hall. 'Elizabeth! The carollers are coming, do we have a mince pie for them?'

She burst through the door, her cheeks red from the cold air. She stopped short when she saw the visitors. 'Oh. Hello – ! This is a surprise.'

'Well, yes it has been some time since we called, but I'm always busy you know.' He sighed. 'And then there was the tragedy, which meant I couldn't socialize.'

'Tragedy?' Harriet asked. 'What tragedy?'

'My poor dear wife – you didn't hear?'

Elizabeth felt a sinking despair come over her. 'We live very quiet lives,' she began.

He shook his head. 'I don't know how I survive; so much to happen to one man.' He gave another, deeper sigh. 'My wife – so little time together. She died. Drowned. Found her body in the Ouse!'

Elizabeth sat down abruptly and Harriet clutched the arm of the chair.

'A dreadful accident,' said Dolly.

'How?' Elizabeth asked in a low voice. 'How did it happen?'

'I don't know,' he answered, shaking his head again. 'I had turned my back for only a moment to admire the sunset when I heard her cry out. She must have slipped. I rushed to get help, but too late.' He took out his handkerchief and blew his nose.

'We're so sorry,' Harriet murmured. 'Aren't we, Elizabeth?'

'Very sorry.' Elizabeth licked her suddenly dry lips. 'We never met your wife of course, but yes, very sorry. When did this happen?'

'Oh, must be seven – eight months ago,' he said. 'I'm only just getting over it.'

'You didn't think to tell us before?' Elizabeth asked.

'Well, as you say, you had never met my wife,' he replied testily.

'He has so many commitments,' Dolly cut in. 'He's always in demand, aren't you, Eddy? This committee or that.' She sniffed and put her gloved hand to her nose. 'I don't suppose there's a cup o' tea is there?'

Elizabeth hesitated, but Harriet interrupted. 'Oh, dear. No, so sorry! We must be off. Elizabeth are you not ready? The service at the Minster starts in half an hour and there's sure to be a crowd. Perhaps you would like to join us?' she asked the visitors.

'No, no.' He pulled himself out of the chair. 'Can't be doing with all that religious rubbish.'

'It is Christmas,' Elizabeth said quietly. 'Or had you forgotten?'

'Forgotten! Can hardly forget with Dolly here to remind me.' He gave his companion a pinch on her cheek. 'Wanting this and that! Can we give you a ride to the Minster?' he added. 'There's a cabby waiting in the square.'

'No thank you.' They chorused a refusal of his offer. 'We like to walk,' said Harriet. 'We're used to walking,' added a grim-faced Elizabeth.

'We'll be off then.' He looked down on them both. His joviality seemed to have disappeared and distaste appeared on his face. 'You get more like your mother every time I see you, Lizzie. Hope you haven't inherited her wicked temper?'

She took a deep breath. 'Only when I am provoked,' she answered quietly. 'When I am ill-used.'

His eyes narrowed. 'Glad to hear the school is prospering. You'll be building up a good reputation. Take care that you don't lose it.'

As she closed the door after them, Elizabeth leant her head against it and tried to quell her angry tears.

'Come and sit down, Elizabeth. I'll make you a cup of tea.' Harriet led her to the fire and sat her down, then put a dry log and a few pieces of coal on the fire. Soon the flames were dancing high.

'Why do you think he came?' she asked as she poured the tea. 'It must be eighteen months

117

since he was last here. He came then to tell us that he was marrying again.'

Elizabeth rubbed her forehead. A dull headache was hovering over her eyes. 'A wicked whim,' she said. 'And also to remind us – as if we needed reminding. His wife,' she added. 'Poor woman. They were not married for very long. Do you think she slipped or – ?'

'Don't think about it,' Harriet said hastily. 'It was most unfortunate, as it was with Bella.' But she shivered and drew nearer to the fire.

'Dolly is still with him,' she said after a moment or two. 'At least she is constant.'

'Yes, she's always there. Always has been.' Elizabeth sipped her tea. 'Are we missing the service?' she asked.

Harriet shook her head. 'I told a fib. It starts in an hour. Do you feel like going now?'

'Oh, yes.' Elizabeth pulled herself together. 'I need to go now more than ever. I need to get rid of this hatred that's gnawing away at me.'

'Listen!' Harriet put her head up. 'There are the carol-singers. Let's invite them in and then we'll get ready.'

At the Minster, Elizabeth folded her hands together and bent her head. The majesty of the great cathedral always calmed her. We are nothing in the whole scheme of things, she pondered. We have so little time on this earth, so why is it that there are some people who go out of their way to make others unhappy, and who do their best to exert power over them?

Such a one is Edward Scott. I should pray for his enlightenment that he might see the error of his ways. But I can't. I hate him with such intensity that it threatens to ruin me.

She bent her head lower in contrition, yet still she couldn't forgive him for ruining her life and that of her sister, her mother and his other wives who had suffered at his hands. Dear God, she prayed. Forgive me for my anger and give me peace. Bless the soul of my dear departed father and bless my mother, wherever she is, in this life or the next.

On Christmas Day, Thomas Thacker and his father arrived for luncheon. Thomas had brought a bunch of violets for Elizabeth and a pretty scarf for Harriet. Mr Thacker, who leaned heavily on two sticks with his twisted and gnarled hands, had brought a bottle of sherry. 'To toast your health, dear ladies, and your good fortune.'

They each drank a glass of sherry before luncheon and afterwards, as Harriet and Thomas, who had offered his help, cleared away and washed the dishes, Elizabeth and Mr Thacker sat by the fire and drank another.

'You are looking a little peaky, my dear. You could do with a brisk walk to bring some roses to your cheeks. I would offer,' he said with a fleeting smile, 'but I fear I cannot walk far.'

'Harriet and I have said we will take a walk by the river tomorrow. We like to do that on Boxing Day. But for the moment I am quite content to sit by the fire and enjoy your company.'

She paused. He was a good friend to her and Harriet, they had known him a long time. 'We had a visitor on Christmas Eve,' she told him. 'Edward Scott. He brought bad news, as he so often does when he visits.'

Mr Thacker looked across at her and his eyes were suddenly wary. 'What news?'

'Of his wife, the last Mrs Scott. It seems she drowned in the River Ouse.'

'He is very careless with his wives,' he murmured. 'That makes three who have not lived to a ripe old age.'

A look of anguish crossed Elizabeth's face and he added quickly, 'You will not find peace, Elizabeth, if you do not accept that your mother is dead.'

'I can't,' she whispered. 'Not until there is proof.'

'She would have contacted you, or me, or someone she could trust if she were still alive. She would not have deliberately left you not knowing.' He sighed. 'I blame myself constantly, even after all these years. I was the one who introduced her to Scott.'

'You were not to know.' She reached out and touched his hand. 'It's Christmas,' she said, trying to smile. 'We must not be unhappy, Mama would not want that. We must look forward to another, better year.'

In the tiny kitchen as Harriet and Thomas washed and dried the dishes, she told him of Edward Scott's visit. 'He has upset Elizabeth,' she said. 'I think sometimes that he comes purposely to remind us of what happened, so that we can never forget or put it behind us.'

Thomas, who was very tall and thin, bent low and kissed her cheek. 'If only we could marry, Harriet, I would help you forget. But then you hardly remember, do you?'

She put down her drying cloth. 'I remember nothing of what happened, only what Elizabeth has told me,' she said quietly. 'But I remember the scent of my mother and the softness of her face when she bent over my cot.'

'Father says she was the kindest, sweetest woman he has ever met, after my own mother. He also said that he would have asked her to marry him except that he was penniless, and she had a legacy left to her from your father. My father was too proud to ask her because of that,' he said. 'But Scott wasn't and he got it all in the end.'

'Poor Mama,' she said softly. 'Poor, poor Mama.'

Chapter Eleven

'Brr, it's so cold!' Jack turned up his coat collar against the rain and shivered. He and Ralph were watching the progress of their ship into Portsmouth harbour. On the quayside they could see knots of people, seamen, porters and others waiting to greet the passengers as the ship eased its way in.

Ralph agreed. 'It's supposed to be spring,' he said. 'But it's so grey. Where's the sun?'

'Mr Hawkins. Mr Hawkins! Oh, isn't it so exciting?' Mrs Boyle joined them. 'We're all packed. Phoebe is just fastening up our trunks.'

'It's so cold, Mrs Boyle,' Ralph complained. 'I hope you won't catch a chill.'

Mrs Boyle was dressed in a plain grey fitted gown with long sleeves and short train, and over it a matching wool jacket. 'Indeed I won't,' she smiled. 'I have my old mantle which I took out with me to Australia. I never wore it there, but I shall wear it now. My daughter laughs at me because it is so old-fashioned, but I shall be glad of it on the journey to Southampton.'

She gave a deep satisfied sigh. 'It is so good to be almost home.'

'Will your brother be there to meet you, Mrs Boyle?' Ralph began. 'If not we shall be glad – '

'Oh, I'm sure he will be. I wrote to tell him of the ship and when we would be likely to arrive.' She was in a dither of excitement. 'Will I know him, I wonder? Will he recognize me after so many years? And my mother, I expect she will have aged considerably! My poor father.' She had a catch in her voice. 'He died not long after I left England.'

Ralph and Jack said nothing, but let her talk on, of how she was looking forward to seeing her old home again. Of her brother who had taken over the estate after their father's death, and of their mother who still lived with him and his wife.

'Now, Mama. I'm sure that Ralph and Jack don't want to be bored with our family history.' Phoebe appeared behind her.

'On the contrary,' Ralph replied, thinking that Phoebe had often been sharp with her mother over the last few days, 'I am intrigued by it. I am very pleased for you, Mrs Boyle, that you are seeing your family again.'

She smiled at him. 'I hope that you too will find whom you are seeking, Mr Hawkins.'

He raised his eyebrows. So Ma had told her why he was here.

'Your aunt will be glad to see you,' her eyes

held his, 'but you will not forget those at home, will you? Your mother and father will be anxious for news of you.'

'I won't forget, Mrs Boyle, and you will visit us in Yorkshire?'

'Yes, indeed. After a month or so, when my family and I have exchanged all of our news and events, then Phoebe and I shall travel and visit old friends and hopefully make new ones.'

Phoebe turned to Jack. 'And what about you, Jack? What do you hope to find in England that isn't in Australia?' Her voice was rather tight and irritable.

He gazed at her and said quietly, 'I shan't know until I find it, Miss Boyle. Perhaps nothing. Perhaps what I am seeking, I have already found.'

'Huh,' she muttered. 'I hate riddles.' She shivered. 'It's cold, I'm going back to the cabin.'

'Allow me to walk with you?' Jack said. 'I must look for my gloves.'

Ralph and Mrs Boyle watched their progress back along the deck. 'I'm worried about her,' Mrs Boyle murmured. 'I don't think she will settle in England. There will be too many restrictions.'

'Settle?' he said in surprise and dismay. 'But it is for a short time only, surely? Six, nine months? Will you stay longer than that?'

She turned away to look at the approaching harbour. 'I don't really know, Ralph. I don't know if I can tear myself away a second time.'

*   *   *

Ralph and Jack watched as the carriage carrying Mrs Boyle and Phoebe moved off from the quayside. They had been introduced to Mrs Boyle's brother and his wife, and Ralph had noted the look of anger on Phoebe's face when her uncle had drawn back in astonishment from Jack's presence and inclusion in the party.

'Are we going to come across trouble, I wonder,' he murmured, half to himself.

'Of course,' Jack replied, his eyes on the carriage vanishing into the distance. 'At least I am. But it is what I am used to, so we won't worry about it. If there is trouble you must try to disappear. I can look after myself.'

Their next destination was London, to visit the bank on behalf of Ralph's father. Joe had arranged that Ralph could draw money from an account whilst he was in England, so they tried to negotiate for a hire carriage to take them there.

'You'll have to pay up front, sir,' the cabby said, 'and yon black fellow will have to travel outside.'

'No,' Ralph said firmly. 'He travels inside or we take our business elsewhere.'

'Sorry, sir. Can't do that. My other passengers would object if they thought a blackie had been sitting on the seat.'

Ralph clenched his fists and made to answer, but Jack interrupted. 'All right, cabby. Don't worry yourself about it. But perhaps you can tell me where I can buy a chaise? That'll be the thing to do. What about it?' He turned towards Ralph. 'Do you fancy a ride to London in a nice fast buggy?'

'Why not?' Ralph relaxed and grinned. 'Do you have sufficient money about you?'

'Enough for half a dozen or so, and change enough for supper.' The two young men walked away side by side, leaving the cabby with his mouth wide open.

At the bank the commissionaire put his hand on Jack's shoulder to prevent his entry. 'What is your business here?' he growled.

Jack wrapped his fingers around the man's wrist and his other hand he put on his chest, easing him away. 'None of yours,' he said quietly and tightened his finger grip.

The commissionaire winced. 'Beg pardon,' he muttered through clenched teeth.

'I didn't quite catch – ?' Jack stared him in the eyes.

'Beg pardon, *sir*.'

Jack nodded and dropped his hold and followed Ralph towards the desk where the tellers were watching. Ralph concluded his business and then said, 'My friend wishes to open an account here.'

'I, er, I'll have to get the manager, sir,' the teller stammered and hurried away.

The manager bowed respectfully to Ralph. 'So pleased to meet you, Mr Hawkins. Your father has given us the satisfaction of his custom for many years now, though we have not had the pleasure of meeting him.'

'You're not likely to,' Ralph said lazily. 'He can't come back to England. He's an ex-convict, you know. Sent out for punishment and made his fortune.' He smiled thinly at the unfortunate man's discomfort. 'Look after my companion will you? We're getting a little tired of waiting.'

'Of course, of course.' The bank manager glanced condescendingly at Jack. 'Now how much would you like to deposit? And shall I put it in your own name or in your master's?'

Jack looked at him coldly and took a small leather drawstring purse from his coat pocket. He slowly undid the cord and opened the purse, then threw it onto the desk in front of the startled teller. A small shower of gold dust fell out onto the mahogany. 'Weigh it first,' he said softly, 'and tell me how much there is. You know we black fellahs can't read or write or add up.'

The teller looked up at the manager who hastily said, 'Perhaps if you would come into my office sir, we can be private there.'

Jack crooked his finger at the clerk to give back the purse, then smiled. 'Wouldn't want to lose any, would we? I should have to go back home and dig up some more!'

'Snivelling, mealy-mouthed dingo,' Ralph griped as they came out of the bank and walked towards their chaise.

'We know it's what happens,' Jack said in a matter-of-fact manner and took the driving seat. 'And no amount of gold dust will make a difference.'

Ralph glanced at his friend as they moved off. Somehow, in this ancient city of London, Jack seemed out of place. Even in his fine clothes, he looked more native than ever he did in Sydney where he blended with the landscape. That is his land, Ralph thought. He belongs there. Why did he want to come here, to England?

'Many years ago,' Jack said, and it was as if he had been listening to Ralph's thoughts, 'an Aborigine, Bennelong, learned the English language and wore English clothes. He was befriended by the Governor and brought to England. He was taken to parties and functions and displayed as an object of curiosity for people to look at and marvel at.'

'How do you know this?'

'There are many stories about him that have passed down the years,' Jack replied. 'But I was also told about him by my tutor. He told me that although I would have an education, because I was of mixed blood I would be like Bennelong was at the end of his life, belonging to neither one race or another.' He clicked his tongue to move the mare along. The streets were crowded with traffic. 'Where are we going?' he asked.

'We'll look for an inn.' Ralph glanced about him. 'We'll probably be turned away from the hotels.'

'He also said', Jack continued, 'that I must find a native woman to marry if I wanted the

Aborigine race to continue, otherwise we would be wiped out.'

'Is that what you will do?' Ralph asked, and then grinned. 'You won't find an Englishman willing to give his pale-faced daughter to you anyway.'

'That's true,' Jack agreed. 'But perhaps I will marry an Englishwoman who needs my wealth and I can still father children with an Aborigine woman. We are not bound to one woman as you Englishmen are.'

'Here, try this place.' Ralph pointed to a small inn on a corner of a street. 'It looks all right. But,' he said as he climbed down, 'I still say you'll never find an Englishwoman to marry you under those terms. Besides, she'd be ostracized. It's accepted if a white man takes a native woman, but never a white woman marrying a black native.'

'He also said – my teacher,' Jack continued as they walked to the inn door, 'that I should come to England and then go back home to teach my native brothers about another way of life.'

'So that's why you have come?'

Jack grinned and opened the door, inviting Ralph to enter first. 'No, sir, I just knows you can't manage widdout your faithful Jack!'

Chapter Twelve

They were given comfortable accommodation at the inn and the landlord made no fuss about Jack, though they had to pay in advance for their rooms. The other guests were a mixed crowd ranging from seamen to travellers in merchandise and passengers of public transport who were stopping overnight on their journeys.

After a good supper, they retired early to bed, with Ralph intent on starting his search for details of his mother the next day.

All night Jack tossed and turned, disturbed by the sounds of the constant traffic which passed the inn. As dawn slid through the thin curtains with silver-grey fingers, he got out of bed and taking a blanket, he lay down on the floor by the fire. He gazed with a fixed stare into the flickering flames until his eyes closed and he entered his dreaming world.

He was in a narrow boat with other natives, all of them naked except for their loincloths. In his hands he gripped a pair of oars and he pulled in unison with his fellows across a vast expanse of water where there was no sign of land.

There was sweat on his brow and blisters on the palms of his hands and he grunted and chanted in unison with the other rowers. Then he looked up. A great wall of water barred their way, higher than twenty men standing on each other's shoulders. No, more: higher than forty, fifty men, and their boat was rapidly approaching the heart of it. Harder they pulled and it was as if the wall was sucking them in, and as Jack looked upwards, the crest of the wave broke and avalanched towards them.

He was washed out of the boat and plunged into a tunnel of blue-green water which led him to the bottom of the ocean. There he saw all manner of wondrous fishes and shiny red coral, before being tossed upwards on a foaming white crest and carried towards a white sandy shore. As he lay exhausted and panting he felt the relentless sea slapping his face and shoulders.

'Jack. Wake up.' Someone was gently slapping his face. 'Wake up, we've overslept.'

He sat up. The fire was almost out and Ralph was standing over him, shaking his arm. 'You were dead to the world,' he said.

Jack ran his hand across his forehead. 'I was,' he said. 'To this one, anyway.'

After breakfast they went to the Home Office to enquire about lists of female convicts. They were sent to look at the transportation register books and then at the Assize agenda books. They found the name of Rose Elizabeth Scott and brief details that she had been found guilty at York Crown Court of attempted murder.

Ralph stared down at the page. There she was. No longer just a name he had been given, but proof that she had been living and had committed, or tried to commit, a horrendous crime. Why? he asked himself. Why did she do it? And who did she try to kill?

'Where can I find out more?' he asked the clerk.

'What do you wish to know, sir? The indictment?'

'Yes. Who accused her. Who she tried to kill, and the names of witnesses.'

They waited whilst the clerk trawled through various record books, until finally he said, 'Unfortunately there is nothing more than I have already given you. There were so many convicts, and not all the records survived.' He closed up his book. 'You will have to go to York, sir, if you need more information.' He gazed at Ralph. 'Is it important that you find out about this woman? She may be dead, you know, women didn't always survive the journey.'

'It is important,' Ralph replied grimly, 'and I know that she didn't survive.'

'Let's sell the chaise,' Jack said as they climbed aboard. 'We'll buy two good horses and ride to York.' He knew intuitively that Ralph was downcast and guessed that an invigorating ride would dispel his despondency.

'We could go by train,' Ralph replied. 'It wouldn't take so long.'

'No,' Jack said. 'We shall see the country better by horse. I may never come again.' He was anxious to get away from this noisy bustling city. His head was bursting from the shouts of tradesmen, the clamour of wheels, the clatter of carriages and barking of dogs. This city was far busier then Sydney ever was and he felt hemmed in. He wanted to look towards the horizon, to see space and sky. 'I want to go home and tell my brothers what this country is like.'

Ralph was in no mood to argue. But what was he going to find in York that he didn't already know? That his mother had tried to kill someone and to atone for her sins had committed the ultimate sin of suicide.

'I need a driver,' said the merchant who was interested in buying the chaise and the mare. He looked towards Jack. 'Does the blackie need another job?'

'No, he doesn't,' Ralph said sourly. 'He stays with me.' And he gained ultimate satisfaction in handing over to Jack the cash for the sale in front of the merchant.

Ralph's temper improved as they set out on their journey north. They took their time and stayed overnight at inns on the way. In the small towns and villages they were treated with respectful curiosity and as they clattered into the cobbled streets of York on the afternoon of the fourth day, were immediately charmed by it.

The bells of the Minster were pealing as if in welcome and the sun glinted on the waters of the River Ouse. The streets were narrow and buildings were close together, many houses were half-timbered with oversailing top storeys, and there was a sweet aroma in the air.

They found an inn for the night where they were given a good supper of meat pie. Ralph drank a glass of ale but Jack asked for water, keeping to his promise of never again drinking alcohol. The next day whilst Jack took himself off to explore the city, Ralph, in some trepidation, went to the Law Courts to search the repositories for the deposition in the case of Rose Elizabeth Scott.

'Here it is, sir.' The clerk handed him a dusty volume with his finger marking the entry. 'Rose Elizabeth Scott,' he read out, 'the accused, charged with attempted murder of her husband, Edward Scott, man of business. Witness, Mrs Dorothy West. Accused found guilty, sentenced to ten years transportation.'

Ralph's face flushed and he felt his heart beat faster. Her husband! His father? Was he still alive and if he was, would he want to see his son?

He went outside and sat down on the stone steps wondering what to do next. He could attempt to find Edward Scott, that wouldn't be too difficult if he was living in or around York. But would he want to see a son who suddenly turned up from the other side of the world? And did Rose and Edward Scott have any other children?

Rose and Edward Scott. He tried the names several times in his head, then his own name, Ralph Scott. Ralph Hawkins. Which would it be?

'Hey! Are you going to sit there all day?' Jack called to him from across the street.

Ralph got to his feet and crossed over to join him. 'Let's go to Holderness,' he said. 'I need to talk to Aunt Emily.'

'Do you think the children are ill, Elizabeth?' Amelia asked. 'This is the third day that they haven't come to school. They were rather quiet at the beginning of the week, not themselves at all.'

'Possibly,' Elizabeth answered vaguely. She didn't seem to be really listening.

There was a knock on the door and Amelia said, 'I'll go. It's maybe the postman.'

But it wasn't. It was a small barefoot girl wearing a man's jacket over a tattered dress and sacking apron, who handed her a scrap of paper and said in a broad Irish accent, 'Will you be giving this to Miss Linton? It's from Moira.'

Amelia took the paper. 'Is she ill? And what about Eamon? He hasn't been at school.'

'They've gone, miss. All of 'em. They'll not be coming back.'

'Gone! Gone where?' She unfolded the scrap of paper and saw Moira's careful hand.

'To look for work, miss.' The little girl turned away and then came back. She clutched at the checked shawl which was draped around her head. 'Would you be throwing away any scraps o' bread, miss?'

Amelia looked down at her and then said, 'Yes. Wait a moment.' She hurried into the kitchen and picked up a loaf, barely begun, from the bread crock, then reaching for her purse she took sixpence from it and handed bread and money to the little girl.

'God bless you, miss.' The little girl put the sixpence in her pocket and took a huge bite from the loaf.

Amelia slowly closed the door and read the note as she walked into the parlour. 'It's from Moira,' she said. 'She says that they are moving to Hull. Her father is going to look for work on the docks.'

Elizabeth's face crumpled and tears rushed to her eyes. 'That's the final straw,' she choked. 'I can't go on.'

Amelia looked quickly at her. 'Whatever do you mean, Elizabeth? What is it?'

'I heard the other day that the two private pupils are leaving. Their parents are moving from the district, and now with the Irish children gone – !'

'But we'll get other pupils,' Amelia began.

'No.' Elizabeth shook her head. 'It will be too late. The fees for Moira and Eamon will be withdrawn. I can't expect the benefactors to pay when the children are not here. We are working on a shoestring Amelia,' she said. 'This is a new term, there will be no more pupils.'

Amelia sank down on a chair. 'So what shall we do?'

Elizabeth took a deep breath. 'Harriet and I will manage as best as we can with the pupils who are left, but I'm very much afraid, my dear, that we can no longer afford to pay your salary, small though it is.'

'But I don't need—'

'I know that the salary isn't of paramount importance to you, Amelia. But I cannot justify you working for nothing, especially when there are no extra pupils to teach. I am so sorry,' she added. 'We have enjoyed having your company here. You have been such an asset.'

'You would let me know if things improve?' Amelia coaxed. 'I could come at very short notice.' They are so proud and independent, she thought. They would be offended if I suggested a loan.

'Of course.' Elizabeth gave a sad smile. 'What we need is a small miracle, Amelia. Not too big. Just enough pupils to make a living so that we don't have to scrimp and save constantly. We are willing to work, but there are many private schools opening now and free schools too for the poor children. It is going to get even harder.'

Amelia packed her bag and prepared to depart for home the next day. She would leave some of her belongings on the chance that she might return. Then she went to shop in the market. She bought fresh fish and beef, vegetables and fruit, and chose delicacies and confectionery that she knew the Fielding sisters never bought. She arranged to have them delivered and walked back towards the little house tucked away in a corner.

As she crossed Sampson's Square she caught sight of a man. A broad-set man, whose skin colour was dark, with hair that was black and thick and curly and who walked with a regal step. As he approached her he tipped his hat with his gloved hand and she smiled in return. By his manner of dress, a grey double-breasted frock coat and slightly flared checked trousers, he looked every inch a gentleman, and yet there was a natural simplicity beneath his elegant and expensive apparel. She couldn't begin to guess at his origins. Not African or Arab. He stopped. 'I beg your pardon, ma'am. I am looking for the County Court. Could you direct me?'

She explained the directions and once more he tipped his hat as he moved away. She pondered that no English gentleman would have had the temerity to stop a lone gentle-woman in the street. She permitted herself to look over her shoulder. He was, she decided, the most beautiful man she had ever seen.

'I'm going to prepare us a special supper,' she told the sisters. 'Now you are not to laugh at my attempts, but I thought as I am going home, that we should make this an occasion.'

'But it is not a celebration,' Elizabeth began. 'We don't want you to go.'

'I know,' Amelia smiled, 'but you have been so kind to me that I wanted to do something in return.' She also knew that she had bought far too much food, and that it would last the sisters for at least another week.

'I think I shall try to find the Mahoney children when I next visit Hull,' she said as they sat to eat their supper. 'I don't like to think that they might be destitute like the child who came to the door. Poor little girl,' she said softly. 'Her clothes were in rags.' She paused, then said, 'Such a contrast: when I went out earlier I saw an elegantly dressed man in the square, a foreign gentleman, dark-skinned. The cost of his gloves alone would have kept the child in food for a month. He was,' she added, 'the most beautiful man I have ever seen.'

Harriet laughed. 'You mean handsome, surely, Amelia?' Not beautiful!'

'No,' Amelia said slowly and described him. 'Not just handsome, although he was that too, but he had a gentle beauty radiating from him. It was as if there was no anger, no aggression in him and yet there was a surety, a firmness about him that wouldn't stand any nonsense.'

'My goodness, Amelia.' Elizabeth smiled. 'Don't say that you have fallen in love with a total stranger?'

'Oh, she has. She has!' Harriet, who was

inclined to a romantic disposition, clapped her hands enthusiastically. 'I wonder who he is?'

Amelia laughed with them. 'How silly we are! There, I knew we would have fun tonight!'

Chapter Thirteen

'Mama. Mama. Quickly. Come and look! Ginny! There's someone coming.' Hannah and Joseph almost fell into the hall in their excitement. 'There's a man – two men,' said Joseph. 'And one of them has a black face,' said Hannah, 'and they're riding beautiful horses.'

Ginny ushered them into the drawing room. 'Now where are your manners?' she said severely. 'Why are you behaving in such a way? It's not the first time we have had visitors!'

'No! But Ginny, one of them might be Cousin Ralph, but the other—'

'Might also be a guest,' said their mother as she came into the room. 'So remember your manners, please, or you go upstairs instantly. In fact,' she looked down at them, 'I think perhaps you had better do that, you both have very dirty faces.'

'Oh, Mama, no. There isn't time,' they chorused. 'They're here.'

Ginny raised a finger and they became silent.

'We'll be good,' Hannah whispered. 'Really we will, we won't say a word if we can stay.'

Their mother smiled. Hearing the doorbell and the sound of voices, she went into the hallway to greet the guests.

'Is it really you, Ralph?' Emily put out both her hands to him. 'I can't believe it after all these years.' Her eyes became wet with emotion. 'It's so good to see you.'

Ralph bowed, then leaning forward kissed her on both cheeks. 'Aunt Emily. I don't think I remember you, yet my mother and father have spoken of you so often it is as if I know you so well. And I have had a picture of you in my head.'

She is as beautiful as they said, he thought. So serene. He turned to his companion standing behind him. 'Aunt Emily, may I please present my good friend Jack Mungo, he's—'

'Benne's son!' Emily smiled and put out her hand. 'How very pleased I am to meet you. I remember your father so well. He was instrumental in our good fortune, as was your great-grandfather, but you won't remember him?'

Jack also bowed and bent over her hand. 'I don't, Mrs Linton. He went walkabout before I was born and never came back, but my father often talks about him.'

'Come in, come in. Oh it's so good to see you. This is Ginny, my good friend and housekeeper, and these two rascals are Joseph and Hannah.

Joseph is called after your father, Ralph, and he's just as much trouble as Joe ever was when he was young.'

His aunt put her hand to her mouth and her lips quivered when she spoke of her brother Joe. 'Are they well, Joe and Meg? I do so miss them.'

'They are very well. At least they were when we left Sydney. There are so many messages and things to tell you that I had to write everything down so that I wouldn't forget!'

They sat down and presently Ginny brought in tea and cakes. Hannah tugged at her mother's skirt. 'What is it, Hannah?' her mother said. 'You are not to whisper, you know it's rude.'

Hannah cleared her throat. 'I only wanted to ask if Mr Mungo was a prince?' she said. 'And also to ask why it is that Cousin Ralph hasn't got a black skin too if he lives in a hot country?'

'I am not a prince,' Jack answered solemnly. 'My people don't have kings or princes; and your cousin Ralph is trying very hard to get a skin colour like mine, but no matter how long he stays in the sun, he only turns red and blotchy!'

'We get freckles,' the twins cried in unison, 'and so does Amelia if she doesn't wear a hat.'

'Run along now,' their mother laughed, 'and don't get into mischief. You can ask questions later.' She turned to her guests. 'Amelia is in York at present. May is staying with friends for a few days and Roger is out on the estate with his father. Lily is studying in the library and will be in for tea. But you will meet them all eventually.'

They chatted for a while, exchanging news and catching up on over two decades of events, for it was that length of time since Emily Linton had come home from her exile.

'You should come out on a visit, Aunt Emily,' Ralph said. 'Ma and Da would love that. Da does miss England, although he says he doesn't.'

Emily nodded. 'I have been so busy all these years,' she said. 'Rearing children, running the estate, then I have Aunt Mary and Deborah and Sam to look after, and I'm not sure how I would feel about going back. That journey!' She shook her head. 'It was so very hard.'

'I know,' Ralph said. 'Da says it was, especially for the women. But my mother hardly ever talks about it. Do you know why I came over, Aunt Emily?' he said abruptly. 'Did Ma tell you?'

'She did,' she answered quietly. 'Meg wrote to me and explained that you wanted to find your roots, to find out about your natural mother. She was sad, I think.'

'It doesn't alter my feelings for Ma,' he said quickly. 'I just need to know about my past.'

'Meg needs the reassurance that you care. She is vulnerable, your mother, although you might not think so.'

Ralph laughed. 'No. Not Ma! She's so resilient, so steadfast.'

'And brave,' Emily added. 'Without Meg I wouldn't have survived.'

'Aunt Emily, I hope you don't mind, but I took the liberty of inviting a friend and her mother to visit whilst we were here. They came over on the ship with us. A Mrs Boyle and her daughter, Miss Phoebe Boyle.'

'Meg wrote to tell me,' Emily replied in a puzzled manner. 'But this cannot be the wife of Lieutenant Boyle? It is surely a coincidence of name?'

'Captain Boyle,' he corrected. 'The same. He apparently was an officer on the *Flying Swan*. Mrs Boyle is a friend of Ma's.'

'I can't believe it,' she said softly. 'Not the wife of that man.'

'Mrs Boyle is a very gentle lady,' Ralph replied. 'But her husband is—'

'Not a gentleman, Mrs Linton,' Jack broke in. 'He is not liked. He is arrogant and he is a bully.'

She nodded. 'He always was. Yet his daughter is a friend of yours? A good friend?' She raised her eyebrows questioningly.

'I would like to think she might be more than that one day,' Ralph admitted.

'Oh,' she demurred. 'I don't think Meg or Joe would approve of that match.' She looked at Jack for confirmation, but his face was non-committal.

They heard an excited cry of voices and a scraping of feet on the gravel outside the window and Emily shook her head in amused exasperation. 'The children's governess is not well,' she explained, 'and has given them the day off, which is why they are in such high spirits. They would normally be working at their lessons.' She got up from her chair and moved to the window. 'Oh,' she exclaimed. 'Here's Amelia come home!'

The two young men also rose and followed her gaze down the drive. Amelia, flanked by her brother and sister, was standing with her bag by her feet as she listened to them. Then she glanced towards the window and pushed a stray lock of hair beneath her hat. Joseph grabbed the handle of her bag to help her and Hannah raced inside.

'Mama,' she gasped. 'You'll never guess. Amelia is here and she walked all the way from Thorngumbald! She took the carrier from Hull. Wasn't that an exciting thing to do?'

'Indeed,' her mother murmured. 'I wonder why she didn't tell us she was coming?'

She turned to her visitors. 'I'm afraid you will think this is a mad household, gentlemen. We are not at all conventional, Amelia least of all. She does cherish her independence,' and she wondered at the half smile on the face of Jack as he gazed out of the window at the rather dishevelled figure of her eldest daughter.

'Oh, I'm so sorry,' Amelia said breathlessly as she came in. 'If I had known – please forgive my appearance.' She smoothed down her travelling clothes and fiddled with her hair. 'But I am so pleased to meet you at last.' She gave her hand to Ralph and made a slight curtsey. She turned to Jack and her face, already pink, flushed a little more.

He bowed. 'We have met, Miss Linton,' he said softly. 'But have not been introduced.'

She extended her hand and he took it and held it. 'Indeed, we have!' she said. 'What a coincidence.'

'Met?' Ralph exclaimed. 'When? Where? You never said, Jack.'

'In York.' Jack kept hold of Amelia's hand and looked steadily at her. 'Quite by chance. I had lost my way and Miss Linton directed me. And of course I didn't tell you.' He smiled at Amelia and his eyes danced with mischief. 'A man must have some secrets, even from his best friend.'

Amelia was so cross with herself. She had decided that she would travel by carrier from Hull to the village of Thorngumbald and then ask if the driver would take her on towards home. But he was of a surly disposition and said he hadn't the time. He obviously didn't recognize her as Miss Linton from Elmswell Manor and perversely she didn't inform him, otherwise she was sure he would have been much more obliging.

She had been quite confident that the walk would be a mere nothing. But she had not reckoned on the weight of her bag or on her unsuitable shoes and before she was halfway home her feet were aching, her arms were stiff from carrying the bag and a breeze had got up, blowing off her hat several times and untidying her hair. Had she thought for one moment that guests had arrived, she would have crept in by the back door and up the stairs to make herself presentable.

As it was, she knew that her face was flushed, her hat was askew, her chignon had fallen down and her shoes were muddy. I don't care, she grouched, whilst keeping a polite smile on her face. They must take me as I am. But she was astounded to meet the dark-skinned man she had imprudently described as beautiful to the Misses Fielding, standing next to Cousin Ralph.

Presently she excused herself and went upstairs to change and her mother rang for Ginny to show the visitors to their rooms.

'Mrs Linton,' Jack began. 'Is it convenient for me to stay? I know that you didn't expect me.'

'Oh but we did!' Emily Linton replied. 'Meg wrote to us and said that you were travelling with Ralph. Your room has been ready for the last week. We expected you sooner.'

'We went first to London then to York, Aunt Emily.' Ralph explained. 'I have started looking for details of my mother already. But I wanted to ask your advice and that of Uncle Philip. I have discovered that the charge of attempted murder was brought by my mother's husband, who presumably is my natural father.' A look of pain crossed his face. 'He may not wish to see me – if he is still alive. Does he even know if I exist? And why did he not plead for clemency for my mother?'

His aunt turned her gaze towards the window. Rooks were cawing and thrushes and blackbirds were flying past, trailing pieces of straw in their beaks. 'There are no whys or wherefores in reasoning why men or women act the way they do,' she replied in a whisper. 'I know that better than most. I was transported because of a man's antagonism towards me. He was a man with hate in his heart, a man without remorse.'

'Where is he now?' Ralph ventured. He had heard of this man from his mother.

'He spent time in gaol and then we paid off his debts to free him, to give him another chance.' Her face was pale as she spoke of the man who had blighted her life. 'He is dead now. He made nothing of his life afterwards and became involved with men even more wicked than he. He betrayed them and was killed, so we heard.'

She glanced towards Ralph and he saw sadness written on her face. 'If you want peace of mind and answers to your questions, Ralph, then you must seek your father out. He might well have been a good man and your mother a wicked woman. Or perhaps the other way around. My husband will help you, he has had experience in these matters.'

She gave a sudden smile which lit up her face,

and he could see that she had eventually found peace. 'I was very lucky. Philip never gave in until he proved my innocence. Perhaps you will do the same for your mother.'

Chapter Fourteen

I'm not sure what to make of Cousin Ralph,
Amelia thought as she took off her hat and threw
it onto a chair in her bedroom. He seems very
sure of himself, that square jaw shows confidence
and self-will. But Mr Mungo is charming. How
strange that we should have met in York. She
felt a warm surge of pleasure. I haven't changed
my opinion of him. He *is* beautiful. And handsome. A smile rose to her lips and she glanced in
the mirror. Her smile disappeared. Oh, what a
fright I look!

All but May appeared for supper and the
two guests, after resting and changing their
travelling clothes, took their places at the dining
table.

'I will come with you to York, if you wish,
Ralph,' Philip Linton said, having been primed
of the situation by his wife, 'and to visit your
father if you find him.'

'That's good of you, sir,' Ralph acknowledged.
'I would appreciate some help in going through

the records. I'm not much good at that kind of thing. Too impatient, you know. Jack has offered to come with me if we find my father's whereabouts but we haven't decided whether it's a good idea or not. Because of Jack's colour, you see.'

How churlish! Amelia was shocked. How can he say such a thing in front of Mr Mungo? And he's supposed to be a friend! She glanced at Jack Mungo to see his reaction but he was chatting to the twins and didn't appear to have heard Ralph's remark. Then he turned towards her and she determined to give him her full attention to make up for Ralph Hawkins's rudeness.

'Did you enjoy your stay in York, Miss Linton?' Jack asked. 'I found it charming. So ancient.'

She agreed. 'I love it. Although I wouldn't wish to live there permanently. I love the countryside, you see. I'm happier in the wide landscape, and below the vast skies which are here in Holderness.'

'I must admit that I am most impressed by the vista,' he smiled. 'I was glad to escape from London for that very reason. Here, I'm sure that I can smell the sea. It isn't very far, I think?'

'A few miles only,' she replied. 'And the River Humber isn't too far.'

'Then I will go,' he said. 'Perhaps tomorrow, unless there is anything planned?' He turned to Amelia's mother. 'Would you have any objections, Mrs Linton? I can be up early and be back for luncheon.'

'Perhaps we could all go,' Amelia said eagerly. 'Could we take the carriage, Papa, and go to Spurn?'

'I was going to walk,' Jack broke in. 'I don't wish to inconvenience anyone.'

'It's too far to walk!' she exclaimed and thought of her enforced walk from Thorngumbald and the blister on her heel.

Her mother gave a sudden laugh. 'No, it isn't,' she said. 'I've walked to the river from here. Many years ago, of course. I wouldn't like to do it now!'

'Jack walks for miles,' Ralph revealed. 'Or rather, he runs. When I ride on horseback he runs alongside and always keeps up.'

Like a little dog, I suppose, Amelia griped, as she saw her plans disintegrating.

'I'm afraid I shall need the carriage tomorrow,' her father interrupted. 'But perhaps the next day?'

So it was decided. Jack would go off on his walkabout; to get to know the countryside, he explained. Ralph would go over with Philip the details which he had gathered, before he left for the day's business. Amelia could see her day being boring. It appeared that everyone but her would be occupied.

But, to her delight, as she looked out of her window at noon she saw Jack running up the drive and across the lawn, and she hurried down the stairs and into the garden to greet him. He had risen before dawn and set off before anyone else, even the servants, was awake. 'I went towards a place called Waxholme,' he said. 'But it was falling into the sea. Then I ran down the coast towards a small town they called Withernsea. It was very cold!'

Amelia gazed at him. He was most improperly dressed for the climate, wearing only a pair of cotton trousers rolled halfway up his calves, and a white linen shirt. She lowered her eyes and saw that his feet were bare, his toes were brown and firm and she wondered if his soles showed pale as he ran. He must have caused quite a stir amongst the locals, she thought.

'How did you know which way to go?' she asked.

'I have seen a map,' he explained. 'I had a tutor when I was a boy, who taught me about England. He was an ex-convict', he added, 'who had once been a teacher. My schooling was excellent, as good as Ralph's.'

'Oh, yes, I didn't mean to imply—' she broke off in confusion.

'Please, don't upset yourself, Miss Linton,' he said. 'It's just that sometimes people think that I am an ignorant native.' Before she could think of a suitable reply, he went on, 'When I asked a man in Withernsea what was the name of the place, he stared at me for so long that I thought he had no tongue or that he was deaf. Then he started to shout at me as though *I* were deaf!'

'You'll be the talk of Withernsea and all of Holderness,' she pronounced.

'Yes, I think so. The man I spoke to will be a celebrity and the story of the black savage will expand. I will grow to eight feet tall and be covered in hair!'

His skin was dark gold, she decided. The colour of honey. 'But – you are not black,' she stammered.

He reached for her hand and held it. 'I am black, Miss Linton, in spite of my light skin. Don't be embarrassed,' he said softly. 'It is what I am used to and I don't mind. In Australia the Aborigines are considered to be an inferior race compared with the English. In Britain, blind eyes were turned away from the convicts, so too in my country, white faces turn away from the Aborigines. We are not there, we are as nothing. But I know who and what I am. One day perhaps we will be seen as we really are.'

She withdrew her hand. 'I hope so.' She lowered her eyes from his. She felt that he could see into her soul and she didn't want him to. She didn't want him to because she knew that she would be found wanting.

At luncheon, Sam and his mother Mary Edwards and his half-sister Deborah Francis appeared. They all lived together at the gatehouse but often joined the Lintons for luncheon or dinner.

Deborah, a middle-aged lady with childlike behaviour, stifled a scream when she saw Jack, then she carefully circled him, her eyes wide and her mouth slightly open. She darted forward and touched him and as swiftly drew away and stood at Sam's side. 'Who are you?' she asked. 'Why do you look as you do?'

Amelia thought she would die of embarrassment. They were all used to Deborah's peculiar ways but strangers found her odd.

Jack smiled. 'I am from another country.' His voice was soft and encouraging as if he was talking to a child, which he was. Deborah had never properly grown up. 'I am from Australia.'

'Emily has been to Australia,' Deborah declared. 'But she doesn't look like you!' She glanced at Ralph. 'Are you from Australia too?'

Ralph nodded. 'I am, Miss Francis,' he replied and anticipated her next question. 'But my family have not lived there as long as Jack's have.'

'My family have lived here for hundreds and hundreds of years,' Deborah declared with an encompassing sweep of her arms. 'And now Emily is looking after it for us, aren't you, Emily? For me and for Sam.'

'That's right, Deborah.' Emily smiled at her. 'Of course I am. Now, would you like to come and sit here beside me?'

Deborah shook her head. 'No thank you. I will sit by Sam and Mary so that I can watch them.' She nodded towards Jack and Ralph.

'Our relationship is a little difficult to explain,' began Mary Edwards. 'I am Sam's mother, and his father was also Deborah's father. And now we all live together as one happy family, don't we Deborah?' Deborah nodded and tucked her arm contentedly into Mary's.

'And am I right in thinking that you are also related to my father and Aunt Emily?' Ralph asked.

'Indeed,' Mary replied. 'Emily and Joe's father, your grandfather, was my cousin, so even you and I, Mr Hawkins, are relations of a sort.'

Ralph pondered and glanced at Aunt Emily, then said, 'I fear not, Mrs Edwards. My family relationship is also difficult to explain, but I am not Joe and Meg's son. They adopted me, and that is why I am in England, to try to find out about my natural parents.'

A letter came from Mrs Boyle the next day thanking the Lintons for the invitation to visit them, and saying that she and her daughter would be travelling north the following week. 'We shall travel by railway train,' she wrote. 'Phoebe has worked out that we shall arrive at the Hull station at four o'clock on the Friday afternoon. If Mr Hawkins and Mr Mungo are available to meet us we should be most grateful, but if it is not convenient, then we shall hire a carriage to bring us to your home. I am so looking forward to meeting you, Mrs Linton, and passing on greetings from my dear friend, Meg Hawkins.'

'I don't understand at all,' Emily said to Philip

when they were alone. 'She sounds so nice. How can she be married to that dreadful man?'

'Everyone makes mistakes,' Philip smiled. 'Perhaps she made one when she married Boyle. We shall find out, won't we? Anyway, we must meet her at the railway station.'

In the days before the Boyles' arrival, Philip took Ralph to York to search through the court records of Rose Elizabeth Scott and to try to find Edward Scott's present address, if he was still alive.

They found his name in a directory of business, trade and professional inhabitants of York, where he was listed as a confectioner with an address in Coney Street. They sought out the shop but over the door the name read Brown and Son.

Philip went into the shop to enquire. 'Oh, Scott's been long gone,' said the shopkeeper as he weighed out a bag of honeycomb toffee for a small boy. 'Four years I've been here. I bought the business from him, paid top price as well I don't mind telling you. He's a sharp one is that fellow. He used to have another shop down in Stonegate which his wife ran.'

He took payment from the child and then, lowering his voice, added, 'He'd an eye for the ladies, that one. Had a fancy woman for years even when he was married. His wife died and then I believe he married again a couple of years ago. I heard they went to live out Nunthorpe way.'

'It can't be the same person,' Ralph said as they walked towards Stonegate. 'The shopkeeper said that Scott's wife had died.'

'He may have put that story about,' Philip replied, frowning, 'unless of course it was a different wife, not your mother!'

'There's been a few owners since Scott,' the next confectioner revealed. The shop smelt of spun sugar and chocolate. Large glass bottles filled with coloured sweets lined the walls and trays of toffees and bonbons were laid out on the counter in front of them. 'His first wife owned this shop before he married her. I'm going back a long time of course. There was some kind of scandal, I believe, or so my mother told me, I was only a lad at the time.'

'A scandal!' Ralph murmured as they came out. 'Maybe that was the start of the trouble.'

His mind raced. If his mother was Scott's first wife and she had been married before, then the scandal could have been about the break-up of a marriage, but why would his mother attempt to kill her new husband? He voiced his musings to Philip Linton.

'No use surmising,' Philip replied. 'We are working in the dark here. Come on,' he said. 'We've done enough for today. Let's go home.'

'I'm beginning to wish I'd never started this,' Ralph confided to Jack later that evening. 'I've a feeling I'm going to uncover something nasty.'

'I told you that your mother has gone to her

ancestors. You should not disturb her. Let her rest.'

'I can't,' Ralph muttered. 'I have to know.'

At supper, Aunt Emily asked how he had fared. Had he found out anything more?

'Not really,' he answered. 'Except that Edward Scott kept a confectioner's shop, two in fact, and that his wife had died and he remarried.' He chewed on his lip. 'But whether it was my mother, I don't know.'

'Take some time off to think about it, Ralph,' Aunt Emily advised. 'Your friends, Mrs Boyle and her daughter, will be here tomorrow.'

Ralph and Philip Linton drove into Hull to meet Mrs Boyle and Phoebe at the railway station. Ralph had carefully dressed in a dark brown tweed sack jacket, yellow waistcoat and brown and yellow checked trousers and a string tie, and Jack caustically commented on his attire. 'You're not trying to impress anyone, by any chance?' he asked. 'Do you think that Miss Boyle will be swayed by your fashionable clothes?'

'She might be.' Ralph fastened the top button of his jacket. 'She'll see me in a different light anyway, away from home.'

'That's true,' Jack nodded. 'And she too, how will she be, away from her native country?'

'I have a feeling her mother won't want to go back home,' Ralph glanced in the mirror and flicked away a stray hair from his collar, then stroked his side whiskers. 'So will Phoebe go back without her? Will I be able to persuade her?'

Jack was silent, then said quietly, 'Go softly, friend. Tread carefully for fear of pitfalls.'

Ralph laughed and turned towards him. He picked up his round billycock felt hat which he had newly purchased in York and twirled it around his finger. 'What nonsense, Jack! Look at me! How can she possibly resist?'

Phoebe put on all her charm on being introduced to Captain Linton, but to Ralph she appeared tired and irritable as they followed her mother and Philip into the Station Hotel for refreshments before continuing their journey to Holderness.

'So kind of you to meet us, Captain Linton.' Mrs Boyle gratefully accepted a cup of tea. She seemed noticeably more lively than her daughter.

'An interminable journey,' Phoebe grumbled. 'I declare it seemed longer than from coming from Australia.'

'But so worthwhile.' Mrs Boyle shot a warning glance at her for her unintentional rudeness.

'Oh, indeed.' Phoebe perked up. 'We are so looking forward to meeting everyone: Mrs Linton and Amelia and – '

'Roger, May, Lily and the twins, Joseph and Hannah,' Ralph finished for her.

'And how is Jack?' Phoebe asked nonchalantly. 'How is he coping with the different climate? I must say I felt very cold whilst in Hampshire.'

'My brother's home is large and draughty, I'm afraid,' Mrs Boyle remarked. 'It always was, but I had forgotten.'

'Jack is well, he's looking forward to seeing you again, as we both were,' Ralph added meaningfully, but Phoebe merely sipped at her tea.

'Is it good to be back in England, Mrs Boyle?' Philip Linton asked. 'Are you renewing old acquaintanceships?'

'Oh, yes. It is so wonderful to be back with old friends and familiar faces.' She sighed. 'I have never felt completely at home in Sydney, I regret to say, Captain Linton.'

He nodded. 'You are like my wife, Mrs Boyle; although there were great opportunities in Australia, she couldn't wait to come home to England.'

Mrs Boyle seemed slightly embarrassed. 'Has it been difficult for her to adjust?'

'No,' he shook his head. 'Perhaps more difficult for some others, people who don't understand the circumstances, and of course rumours did circulate about us at first. But not any more, we are accepted for what we are.' He paused and then asked courteously, 'And how was Captain Boyle when you left Sydney? Keeping well, I trust.'

'Yes, thank you.' Mrs Boyle gave a brief résumé of her husband's activities and his state of health and the voyages he embarked upon, and then Philip said that if they had finished their tea it was time they were leaving. They had an hour's journey ahead of them.

'What are they like, Ralph? The Lintons?' Phoebe whispered as they went out. 'Are they pompous and strait-laced like my uncle's family are? I shan't abide it if they are.'

Chapter Fifteen

Phoebe discovered the Lintons were not stuffy or strait-laced, neither was the house cold and draughty, but warm and welcoming. Their beds had hot bricks in them and a maid ran the warming-pan over the sheets before Phoebe climbed in to have her best night's sleep since arriving in England.

She slept late the next morning and breakfast was brought up to her. The maid opened the curtains and the sun streamed in through the window. 'It's a lovely morning, Miss Boyle,' she said. 'It smells of summer and all the daffys are nodding their heads.' Phoebe looked at her in some surprise. At her uncle's house the servants had been subservient and uncommunicative.

'Is my mother up?' She stretched and surveyed the tray on the bedside table. It had boiled eggs, toast and marmalade and piping hot coffee and a small posy of primroses on it.

'Yes, miss. She had breakfast with Mrs Linton

and now she's walking in the garden with Miss Amelia and Mr Hawkins.'

She breakfasted, then washed and dressed and looked out of the window. The trees were in full leaf and there was a cherry tree on the lawn which had shed blossom into a pink carpet below it. A honey bee buzzed around a flowering clematis which clung to the walls beneath her window.

She heard voices in the drawing room as she went down the stairs, and through the open doorway she saw Jack in conversation with Roger. Roger was a shy young man and had had little to say to her during last night's supper, but now he was talking animatedly to Jack.

'Miss Boyle!' Jack greeted her. 'How are you this morning?'

'I'm well, thank you. I slept very well.'

'We're just talking about the flora in Australia. Master Roger knows as much about it as I do.'

'Not really,' Roger protested. 'But I have always been interested in nature and wildlife, both in this country and abroad.'

'Then you would love Australia,' Phoebe declared, 'it is so colourful and vibrant, the skies are full of chattering budgerigars and cockatoos, and there are lizards and snakes, wombats and kangaroos!'

He looked rather crestfallen. 'I'd like to see them, but I doubt that I ever will. I'm needed here on the estate.' Then he excused himself and Jack proposed to Phoebe that they join the others outside. 'It's been suggested that we visit Spurn Point. It's a strip of land which divides the river and the sea, perhaps we could go tomorrow after you and your mother are rested.'

She sighed and said that she hoped that the Lintons didn't feel obliged to entertain them.

'I don't think so,' Jack replied. 'They are very hospitable, but also very busy people, they will go about their own business once you are settled in.'

'I'm such a crosspatch, aren't I, Jack?' She looked up at him. 'Always finding fault. Never happy.'

He nodded and gazed back at her. 'What will make you content, Miss Boyle? What will settle your impatient heart?'

She blinked and swallowed. 'For the moment, for you not to keep calling me Miss Boyle, or do you feel you have to whilst we're in company?'

'Yes,' he said. 'I do. Whilst we are in England we must follow English convention. It is only right. We are guests here.'

She sighed again. 'Yes, I suppose so. Come along then, let's go out and make polite conversation.'

'Miss Boyle is so pretty, isn't she?' May said to Amelia later when they were alone. 'She looks more English than you do, Amelia.'

'That's only because she's fair-haired with blue eyes. She takes after her mother. I'm dark because I'm like our father. A Linton.'

May tossed her own fair curls. She was glad

that her colouring was like their mother's and that she hadn't thick unruly dark hair like Amelia's. Not that Amelia wasn't handsome. She was. She had good bone structure and a fine figure, but she wasn't dainty and pretty like Miss Boyle.

'Is she going to marry Cousin Ralph, do you think, Amelia? They would make a striking pair, he's very handsome.'

'All you think about is how people look, May, and who they are going to marry!' Amelia said irritably. 'Can you not look more closely than that? It is what they do and think that is important!'

'So what are you thinking about that is so important?' May asked pertinently.

'I'm thinking that you are the most tiresome girl ever, with your sillly questioning!' Amelia cast a withering look at her sister and marched off to her room.

Miss Boyle's appearance had in fact surprised her. She hadn't expected her to be small and fair or dainty, but somehow to be hardier, as befitting a resident of a comparatively new country and all she had heard of it. Ralph Hawkins was broad-shouldered and bronzed, and casual in his manner, but then, she mused, the Hawkins live in the country whereas the Boyles live in Sydney, which Mama and Papa say is a very modern town.

The next day Amelia, Phoebe, May and Lily and one of the maids all piled into the carriage with hampers and blankets. Mrs Boyle elected to stay behind on this occasion. Ralph and Jack each rode a mare, and they all set off for Kilnsea, where they would leave the carriage and walk to Spurn Point. The day was bright but breezy and Amelia passed Phoebe an extra shawl, which she had brought knowing that someone would complain of the cold.

'What is special about this place, Miss Linton?' Phoebe asked.

'It's unique,' Amelia replied. 'It's a narrow bank of land, sand and shingle, which the sea has carried down from the coast and tipped into the Humber mouth. But it is constantly altering shape, its point moves southwards and westwards and sometimes if the tides are high, it is breached.'

Phoebe stifled a yawn. 'Really?'

'Also,' Amelia glanced at her and continued, 'it's a place where migratory birds fly in in their thousands; but the magic is standing right on the edge of the Point between the river and the sea and watching the waters converge. You have to see it to understand the atmosphere,' she added, guessing that her companion was bored. 'It's impossible to explain the sense of isolation – the mystery of Spurn.'

'And you can run up to the top of the sand dunes,' said Lily who had been listening, 'and pretend that you can see the roofs of the houses of Ravenser-Odd which drowned hundreds of years ago.'

Phoebe raised her eyebrows at this and said, 'I long to see it.'

When they arrived at Kilnsea, Amelia explained that it was a long walk to the tip of Spurn. 'Perhaps you would prefer to ride, Miss Boyle?' she said. 'I'm sure that one of the gentlemen would walk instead.'

'Come up behind me, Phoebe,' Ralph suggested. 'There's no-one to see us.'

'Oh, can I too?' May asked. 'Mr Mungo? Could I come up behind you? Could I, Amelia?'

'I don't see why not,' Amelia said, thinking that as May was not yet quite grown-up, it would not be considered unseemly. But as for Miss Boyle, well, the decision was up to her.

Phoebe hesitated, then said, 'I think it would be preferable if you rode and carried a hamper and the blankets, Ralph, they are quite heavy. I will walk.'

Ralph looked crestfallen but agreed and the men set off, Ralph with blankets and a hamper, and Jack with a smug May behind him on his mare, her arms around his waist and a blanket over her shoulder.

'Miss Boyle,' Amelia began. 'I notice that you address Cousin Ralph and Mr Mungo informally by their first names. If we are to be friends, may I suggest that we do the same? Here in the country, we do not stand on ceremony. We behave formally only when the occasion arises, when we are with strangers or those who we know would expect conventional behaviour!'

Phoebe tucked her arm through Amelia's. 'Thank goodness for that, Amelia,' she said. 'My friends and I all use our first names, though we are careful when our parents are around, they expect us to behave with gentility and follow protocol! But the young generation of Australians are much freer, we don't adhere to the old ways. Not with each other anyway.'

She laughed. 'Even my mother, who is so very English in her manner, actually called Ralph and Jack by their first names when we were on board ship. She seemed to shrug off her shackles once we were away from my father.' She stopped abruptly. 'I shouldn't have said that, I suppose,' she muttered, 'although it's true.'

Amelia made no comment. She would not have dreamed of discussing her father in such a manner, though, she mused, I gather that Captain Boyle is not a gentleman.

'How does Captain Boyle view Jack Mungo?' she asked tentatively. 'I find Ralph's attitude strange and rather patronizing towards him, even though he is a friend and not a servant.'

Phoebe stared at her. 'A servant! Never that, though they had to pretend that he was to get him a passage. No,' she said emphatically. 'I have known them both since we were children. They are like brothers. One black. One white.'

Then I have got it wrong, Amelia pondered. Which means that we are different. That great gulf of sea divides us in more ways than distance.

'But my father', Phoebe continued, 'hates

Jack, hates Ralph, hates Ralph's parents, and my mother says that if I should write to Papa, then I am not to mention that we are visiting your mother and father. Not that I am likely to,' she said. 'Write to him, I mean.' She gave a dry laugh without humour. 'The day that I write to Papa he will get a very big surprise.'

By the time Amelia and Phoebe reached them, May and Jack had found a sheltered spot on the sea side of the promontory, tethered the horses to a stake in the ground and laid out the blankets and unpacked the hamper. The maid, Prue, laid out a white cloth and unpacked the other basket, bringing out meat pies and pasties, boiled eggs, cold ham, a bottle of lemonade, curd-cheese cake and sweet apple tart.

They ate immediately as they were all hungry after the walk and the fresh air. When they had finished Phoebe rose to her feet and said, 'I'm going to view this magical place.' She picked up her skirts and ran up the dunes, disappearing over the other side.

Ralph was lying on his back, already half asleep, but Jack rose to his feet. 'Perhaps I'd better follow her?'

'She'll come to no harm,' Amelia began, but he was already halfway up the dunes to the top. She looked around. May was paddling in the water and Lily had disappeared, to look for her lost town, I suppose, she thought, and continued to help Prue to clear away.

Lily stood in a concealed hollow looking towards the entrance of the estuary. If she tried very hard she could imagine the island which had been thrown up by the sea, had become a township, had had a thriving shipping and fishing industry and sent MPs to Parliament in medieval times; and had then succumbed to the waves, drowning its inhabitants, its animals, houses, churches and inns, until there was nothing to be seen but the heavy swell of the waters.

A sudden movement startled her. She had thought that she was alone, but no, there was Miss Boyle running down the undulation towards the river shore. Lily started forward to join her, to tell of what she knew, but she stepped back as another figure ran down in front of her: a man, lithe, swift and dark-skinned. He caught up with Miss Boyle, who had looked back and slowed as she saw him. Lily saw her smile and hold out both her hands which he took into his and put to his lips.

Lily sank down into the hollow so that she could no longer see the two figures. She was grown-up enough to know that she had witnessed something she wasn't supposed to, and child enough not to understand the significance. She pondered, thinking of her two elder sisters: May, who sighed and mooned over Mr Mungo, and Amelia, who having had much earnest conversation with him, was becoming, Lily imagined, rather attached to him.

I had better pretend that I have not seen anything, she decided. Grown-ups are such odd people, they do and say very strange things and make life most complicated. Books are so much easier to understand. She sighed and rose to her feet. There was no sign of Miss Boyle or Mr Mungo on the shore and no sound of voices, only the sigh of the sea and the rush of the river and the rustle and whisper of the marram grass beneath her feet.

Chapter Sixteen

Roger took Ralph and Jack on a tour of the estate, whilst Amelia escorted Mrs Boyle and Phoebe into the town of Hull to do some shopping.

'I'm impressed by your efficiency, Roger,' Ralph remarked. 'The hedges are neat, the crops are thriving, the farms are in very good order.'

Roger nodded. 'Uncle Sam keeps everything up to scratch and I liaise with the farm bailiff. Uncle Sam isn't good with book work, so Mother looks after that with the farm manager.'

'Is that usual in England?' Ralph queried, 'for a woman to run an estate?'

'Not really,' Roger said. 'But Sam's father, Roger Francis, bequeathed the estate to him on condition that Mother ran it with him. He's not able to,' he added, 'not by himself.'

Ralph nodded. He'd noticed that Sam was rather ponderous and slow, though he was not thick-witted or even as odd as his half-sister

Deborah. But there's something missing, he pondered. It must be a family trait.

'The estate is a good size to handle, not running to the acreage that we have back home. It takes us a week to ride over our land,' he said.

'Do you farm, Jack?' Roger asked.

'Yes, we have land, only not in our own name. And sheep.' He grinned. 'And gold!'

'Mother has a gold nugget on the mantelpiece in the drawing room,' Roger said. 'It was given to her by an old Aborigine when she was in Australia.'

'I know,' Jack nodded. 'He was my great-grandfather. It was the first gold to be found near Creek Farm. Your mother had been kind to him, giving him food and not turning him off the land as so many white people did.'

'Then Jack's father took my father to look for more,' Ralph added. 'And they found a rich seam.'

'It must be such an exciting country to live in,' Roger said rather wistfully. 'I wish I could see it.'

'Come back with us when we go,' Jack said. 'Surely you can be spared for a year or two? Everything seems to run very well here.'

'I'd like to,' Roger sighed. 'But I'm not sure if I could.'

Amelia showed Mrs Boyle and Phoebe the sights of Hull, the fine buildings, the old inns, the river and the docks. They stopped for lunch before they started the important business of shopping.

Amelia sipped her coffee and looked out through the window into the market-place. There was the usual busy activity of traders and shoppers, carriers' carts and carriages and as she looked across, she saw a familiar figure on the footpath at the other side. It was a young girl dressed in a thin skirt and shawl who was begging from passers-by.

'Excuse me just a moment.' She rose to her feet and went to the door of the café and looked out. A carriage went by, obscuring her view, and then a horse and cart and by the time they had passed, the girl had gone.

'I beg your pardon,' she said to her companions as she returned to the table. 'But I thought I saw someone I knew. Someone I met in York.'

'What a pity,' said Mrs Boyle. 'Had she seen you, your friend could have joined us.'

'She wasn't a friend, Mrs Boyle,' Amelia corrected. 'It was a young girl. A poor girl, one I taught when I was living in York.'

'You were a teacher!' Phoebe exclaimed. 'Not for a living, surely? As a philanthropist?'

'Not either of those reasons,' Amelia explained. 'I was helping two sisters who run a school in York for poor children. My aunt, who knows the Misses Fielding, asked if I would be willing to assist them, so I did. I found it very fulfilling,' she smiled. 'Very satisfying.'

'So why is the young girl in Hull?' Mrs Boyle asked. 'Has she left York?'

'Yes. Her father was going to look for work in

Hull.' Amelia paused. 'If it was her, I'm almost sure she was begging.'

Whilst Phoebe and her mother looked in the shop windows and then went inside to make their purchases, Amelia took a turn a short way up and down the streets near by. But there was no sign of Moira and she was convinced that the girl she had seen had been her. I must come back another day, she pondered, and make enquiries. There will surely be an Irish community here in Hull. Someone must know of the Mahoney family.

It was decided that Amelia and her father, Phoebe, Jack and Ralph would set off early the next day for York. Amelia's mother had arranged for several ladies in the neighbourhood to come to Elmswell Manor for luncheon. The ladies were keen to meet Mrs Boyle and learn of life in Australia, and, Emily suspected, to learn more of her own background, but if this was the case then they were disappointed. Mrs Boyle spoke of the bush and wildlife, of highly cultured Sydney, of the foreign ships which frequented the harbour, and said nothing of the controversial beginnings of the country.

Jack insisted on travelling on top of the carriage with the coachman to make more room for the others inside. 'I can see the countryside better too,' he insisted. 'I must take memories home with me to tell my countrymen.'

Ralph was fairly quiet on the journey. Worried, Amelia suspected, about a possible meeting with his father, if, in fact, Edward Scott was his father. Perhaps Ralph's self-assured manner covers doubts and uncertainties, she mused, and glanced at him as he gazed out of the window. His expression was inscrutable. It must be deplorable to discover that you are not who you thought you were. Better by far to know of your parents' background, convicts though they might be, than to have no knowledge at all.

Her own mother's background had been explained very fully and Amelia, far from being ashamed of it, had decided that her mother had been very brave to overcome such adversities and was now living a successful and fulfilled life.

Phoebe was chatting to Amelia's father about voyages which her father had made. 'I believe you knew him, Captain Linton? You have made voyages together?'

'Yes, we first met on the *Flying Swan*, and then on one or two other voyages over the years. But I made only short trips whereas your father preferred longer voyages, and I make very few now. I don't like to leave my wife and family for too long,' he smiled.

How kind and considerate he is, she thought. She compared him with her own father who had never given her or her brother Edwin any affection throughout their childhood, but had always expected them to conform to his ideals, particularly that of mixing with the right kind of people in order to improve their 'livelihood'. How very irked Papa is going to be with both of us, she pondered. Can we stand up to him, I wonder? Well, I can, she determined. But I'm not sure of Edwin. He is not as strong-willed as I am.

As they clattered through the gates of York, Phoebe marvelled at the antiquities, at the towers and turrets along the city walls and the half-timbered shops and inns with their upper-floor jetties overhanging the lower. 'It is amazing that these old buildings are still standing,' she exclaimed, 'and that they haven't rebuilt.'

'Public opinion has always been against demolition,' Captain Linton explained. 'And although there has been some destruction of the walls, and some rebuilding, I don't think there was money to spare for new development. It is just as well for us, for now we can enjoy all the treasures of the past. More and more discoveries are being made so that York will one day have an even richer heritage than it has today.'

'It's wonderful,' she said, and wound down the window to call up to Jack. 'Jack! Isn't it wonderful?'

How odd, Amelia thought, that she should share her delight with Jack and not with Ralph when I thought that they were almost affianced. But then she changed her mind again as Phoebe gave Ralph a wide smile and allowed him to hand her out of the carriage as they arrived at an inn. They have known each other for so long, she acknowledged. It is just the familiarity of old friends and different customs from the one we are accustomed to in England.

After discussion over morning coffee it was decided that Captain Linton and Ralph would hire horses and ride over to Nunthorpe to call on Edward Scott, and that Jack, Phoebe and Amelia would walk across town to visit the Fielding sisters. They would all meet back at the inn later in the day.

How surprised they will be to see me, Amelia thought as she knocked on the sisters' door with pleasurable anticipation at meeting her friends again, but her smile became fixed when she saw how pale and thin Elizabeth had become.

'Oh, please come in,' Elizabeth said. 'How lovely to see you.'

'I'm sorry not to give you notice of our visit, Elizabeth,' Amelia kissed her on the cheek, 'but our arrangements were only made yesterday and I did so want you to meet our friends.'

Elizabeth dropped a curtsey to Phoebe and then Jack and invited them to sit down. 'It doesn't matter at all,' she insisted. 'We have so few visitors that I am delighted that you should call. Harriet is out at the moment but will be back shortly. She has gone for an interview, Amelia. She is hoping to obtain the position of governess in a household in the city.'

Amelia murmured that that would be most convenient as she could still live at home, but was inwardly dismayed at the thought that the school must be failing if Harriet was having to resort to outside teaching.

'Miss Boyle and Mr Mungo are visiting from Australia,' she explained. 'Mr Hawkins, who is a distant cousin of mine, is also with them, but today is on business elsewhere in York. I hope to have the opportunity to introduce you on another day.'

She saw a nervous swallow in Elizabeth's throat as she said, 'Australia! What a long way to come. Are you – are you visiting relatives?' She glanced at Jack Mungo. 'Or friends?'

'I have come with my mother, Miss Fielding,' said Phoebe. 'Her brother lives in the family home in Southampton, as does my grand-mother, whom I had never met before coming to England.'

'And I am accompanying Miss Linton's cousin,' said Jack. 'He is searching out relatives in this country and thinks he has found them here in York.'

'Ah! How interesting.' Elizabeth folded her hands in her lap and for a moment there was a strained silence, then they heard the front door open and Harriet call from the hall.

'I'll put the kettle on,' said Elizabeth. 'You'll take a cup of tea, Miss Boyle, Mr Mungo?'

There was a murmur of voices as Elizabeth greeted her sister in the hall and then Harriet came in. 'How lovely to see you, Amelia. We have missed you so.'

Introductions were made and Amelia saw

Harriet's eyes widen when she was introduced to Jack, and decided that an explanation was necessary.

'Do you remember, Harriet, on the day before I left York, that I mentioned that I had met – er, a foreign gentleman who asked for directions? Wasn't it strange that he should turn up at our home with our cousin Ralph Hawkins?'

'Indeed I do remember,' and Amelia caught a look of mischief in Harriet's eyes. 'I remember the conversation very well! How do you do, Mr Mungo. I am very pleased to meet you.'

She sat down on the arm of a chair, leaving the seat free for Elizabeth when she returned. 'I believe you have travelled from Australia?'

'We have never met anyone from Australia before.' Elizabeth came into the room with a tea tray. 'We know nothing at all about the country. Do we, Harriet?' She glanced down at her sister.

'No,' Harriet said. 'Absolutely nothing. Except what we have read in books.'

Elizabeth nodded and returned to the kitchen for the teapot, bringing it back wrapped in a quilted cosy to keep the tea hot. 'Are you a born and bred Australian, Miss Boyle?' she asked, 'or an immigrant?'

'I am a native Australian,' Phoebe replied in a positive manner. 'As native as Mr Mungo, though he wouldn't agree with that. But my roots are very firmly set there, even though my parents were born in England.'

'And what do you think of England, now that you are here?' Harriet asked. 'I expect you find it cold and damp compared with the climate of Australia!'

'Yes, I do, I must admit, although the warmth of hospitality more than makes up for it. The Linton family are very welcoming,' and she said it with such sincerity that Amelia felt very amiable towards her.

'Holderness is a wonderful place,' Jack added. 'I hadn't expected to find such wide open spaces as there are there, but the sea is very cold!'

'We have never been,' said Harriet, 'although Amelia has invited us.'

'Come soon,' Amelia urged. 'The weather is warmer now and it would be so nice if you would come whilst we have our friends still with us.'

Elizabeth started to demur, but Harriet interrupted her. 'That would be nice, Amelia – and Elizabeth, I am to start as governess in three weeks, so we could go before I start. There will be little time off after that.'

They gave their congratulations on her success and it was agreed that the sisters should come the following weekend. 'Papa will insist on sending the carriage for you,' Amelia said. 'So all you have to do is pack a valise. Oh, I am so pleased, and Elizabeth, the country air will bring back some colour to your cheeks.'

'Perhaps we could visit Spurn Point again,' Phoebe said eagerly. 'That would be quite a tonic for Miss Fielding.' She turned to her. 'It is such a magical place.'

Ralph and Philip Linton devised a plan on their way to Edward Scott's house. Ralph was to say that he was in England on personal business, and that whilst he was here, he was looking into the possibility of starting up a confectionery business in Sydney, and that he had been told that York was the place to make enquiries. Philip would say he had introduced Ralph to his brother-in-law who lived in York and that he in turn had mentioned Edward Scott's name.

'We must keep it simple, Ralph, otherwise we shall get found out.' Philip looked up the drive of the moderate house which they were now approaching. 'He might not see us today of course.'

Ralph was exceedingly apprehensive. He had had a nervous tension in his stomach ever since setting off this morning. What if he didn't like Scott? How was he to find out if he was his father? How would he bring up the subject of his mother? A million questions ran through his head and he didn't have an answer to any one of them.

'Bear up, young fellow.' Philip dismounted and tied the reins to a rail. There was no groom scurrying round to take care of the horses, so obviously Scott didn't keep a stable. He mounted the steps and noted that the paint on the door was faded and peeling in places. So he's not rich, unless he puts his money into something other than property. He put his finger on the bell and turned to Ralph who was slowly following him. 'Come on,' he encouraged. 'He's not going to eat you.'

Chapter Seventeen

'Mr Scott will see you now, Captain Linton.' The maid, who had answered the door and taken his card, invited them in.

'So kind,' Philip murmured and on being taken through to the small library, said to the man standing to greet him, 'I do hope we are not disturbing you, Mr Scott? May I introduce you to Mr Ralph Hawkins, a relative of my wife, who is visiting us from Australia.'

Scott's eyes narrowed. 'Australia! You're not a convict's offspring are you? Or a poor farmer's lad? I hear they went out in their thousands to try and make a living when they couldn't make one here.'

Ralph bristled. This was an abrupt beginning. He didn't care for Scott's attitude towards a stranger, but he replied politely. 'Yes sir, my parents were convicts. They stayed on in Australia and settled there.'

Scott grunted, but said no more and listened as Philip outlined their business and how they had come across his name. 'I understand you have been in the confectionery business for a good many years, Mr Scott, and are therefore experienced in the setting up of small shops.'

'Yes,' Scott agreed rather cautiously. 'I've had one or two. There's not a fortune to be made from them though, so if you are expecting instant riches, young man, then you'd have to look into something else – or get yourself a rich wife,' he added with a guffaw.

He scanned Ralph up and down and Ralph was pleased that he had dressed in a plain jacket and trousers. I don't appear as if I'm worth a fortune, he thought, but rather as if I need to make one.

'Where did you say I'd met this relative of yours, Captain Linton?' Scott asked Philip suddenly. 'Albert – ?'

'Gregory. At the racecourse, I think he said,' Philip answered vaguely. 'He seems to conduct most of his business there.'

'Gregory! Yes, I've heard the name. Can't remember meeting him though.'

'He remembers you,' Philip said firmly. 'Said you had had two or three shops in York at one time – was one of them in your wife's name?'

Scott's lips set in a firm line. 'My first wife, yes. You know how ladies get set about things, you have to pander to them occasionally.'

'I do beg your pardon,' Philip apologized. 'I didn't mean to intrude into your personal affairs.'

Scott waved his hand in an air of dismissal. 'It was a long time ago. My wife died rather tragically and I sold the shop and bought another. I don't talk about it.'

Philip nodded, but Ralph murmured sympathetically, 'I trust you had the comfort of sons or daughters to sustain you, sir.'

'No, I didn't as a matter of fact,' he grunted. 'Never wanted any myself. Well, gentlemen.' He changed the subject. 'Shall we discuss business?'

As they rode back into York, Ralph asked, 'What do you think, sir? Do I have a look of him? Could he be my father?'

Philip glanced at him. 'You want me to say no, don't you? That you are not in the least like that insufferable man?'

'I do rather,' Ralph agreed. 'I can't say that I took to him at all, but maybe he'll improve on a second meeting.'

'I doubt that very much. But as for you looking like him, I can't honestly say. His colouring is different from yours, his hair is grey now but he has been dark. Your build is different too. Perhaps you are like your mother's side. There's no accounting for family likenesses, just look at my family. May and Roger are like their mother, Amelia is like me and the others are a mixture of the two.'

Yes, Ralph thought. Amelia is her father's daughter, the same thick dark hair, the same dark eyes and his determined manner. Not soft and gentle like her mother. Yet, he surmised,

Aunt Emily must have had a strong backbone to have survived her former life. Perhaps Amelia is like her after all. We cannot judge by appearances.

He found himself looking at Amelia and her father, analysing their appearance, and then at Phoebe and comparing her with her parents. Phoebe looks so much like her mother, yet has none of her characteristics. I hope, he thought uneasily, that she has none of her father's. Her brother, Edwin, I had always thought was like Captain Boyle, pretentious and conceited, but he is quieter now that he is older and seems less confident than he was when we were young. What a mixture we are. I'm beginning to wish I had never started this caper. It would have been better to remain in ignorance. I really don't want Scott to be my father.

The Fielding sisters came to Holderness the following weekend. The weather was cold and blustery with some rain showers, so that they were not able to venture far, but Elizabeth said she was quite happy to stay indoors and enjoy the comfort of the beautiful house. She was pampered by both Amelia and her mother who perceived that she was not well and insisted that she had breakfast in bed each morning and that she had a rest during the afternoon.

'You are spoiling me, Mrs Linton,' she said, awaking from a nap by the fire in the sitting room as her hostess had tea brought in to her.

'Not at all, my dear. Everyone else is busy doing something. Your sister and Amelia have gone for a walk, the men are riding around the estate, I don't know where Miss Boyle is, but Mrs Boyle, believe it or not, is talking to Cook and Ginny in the kitchen.' She laughed. 'I do believe that she was quite amazed at our behaviour towards our staff, but now that she is used to us she can see that there is respect on both sides.'

'It is a most unusual situation, Mrs Linton, although of course I have never had the experience of such a quantity of servants as you have, only a girl to help out; but their loyalty towards you is obvious, especially that of your housekeeper.'

'Ginny. Ah, well, Ginny is very special. She is my friend as well as my housekeeper. We have known each other a long time.'

'Most unusual though?' Elizabeth repeated as she drank her tea.

'Not really,' said Mrs Linton. 'You see, we were both servant girls. I haven't always owned such a grand house. In fact, Miss Fielding, I worked here as a servant. But Ginny helped me such a lot when I was young and in trouble. I can never repay her for that.'

'I didn't know.' Elizabeth put down her cup and saucer. 'Amelia never said.' Then she smiled and she seemed to lose her wanness. 'So it is true,' she said, 'that gentlefolk are born and not made, for I would always have taken you for a true lady, Mrs Linton.'

The door opened as she was speaking and Mrs Boyle came in. 'I can vouch for that,' she said. 'For I have met many so-called "ladies" at my brother's house who have no breeding whatsoever, even though they profess to be high-born. And I have also met convict women in Australia, one in particular, who have the edge on them every time.'

'Convict women, Mrs Boyle?' Elizabeth Fielding's voice was hushed.

'You speak of Meg?' Mrs Linton interrupted. 'My dearest friend Meg whom I miss so much, even after so many years.'

'And my friend too,' said Mrs Boyle. 'Although my husband would disapprove if he knew of our friendship.'

Elizabeth looked from one to another. 'I don't understand! How can you possibly have a friendship with a convict woman, Mrs Boyle? Did she not do something terribly wicked to be sent out as a convict?'

'No more than I,' Emily Linton replied softly. 'For I was sent out too.'

Then the two older women looked at each other in concern as Elizabeth Fielding put her pale face in her shaking hands and wept as if her heart would break.

'She is under a great strain, Harriet,' Amelia said later after they had sat by her sister's bedside. Mrs Linton had despatched Elizabeth there and sent for the doctor.

'It is because we have only one pupil left, Amelia, and her fee won't pay the bills. That is why I am going to work as a governess; but Elizabeth worries so.'

'Then I have a suggestion to make,' Amelia said firmly. 'Elizabeth can stay here with Mama until she is feeling better, and I will come back to York with you and teach that one pupil.'

'But you have guests, Amelia! You can't leave them to their own devices.'

'Cousin Ralph is going back to York anyway and Mrs Boyle and Phoebe are travelling to Harrogate in a day or so to visit acquaintances, so that just leaves Jack, and he will probably go with Ralph. It will only be for a few days, Harriet, until Elizabeth has recovered.'

She viewed Harriet anxiously. 'Are you sure there is nothing more that is worrying Elizabeth? Her troubles seem so very deep-seated.'

Harriet shook her head. 'Have you ever had financial worries, Amelia? Is there anything more worrying than losing the roof over your head?'

'Perhaps not,' agreed Amelia who never had had those problems, but she was not wholly convinced and neither, she knew, was her mother. 'But I am quite sure that there is something more.'

'Miss Fielding is in some kind of crisis,' the doctor reported to Emily Linton. 'Perhaps there is something worrying her that she is not telling us. Keep her in bed for a few days, give her eggs, milk and cream to build up her stamina, and then bring her downstairs for short periods. Don't let her be disturbed by loud noises or excitement.'

Elizabeth, however, insisted that there was nothing wrong with her, she had simply become overtired. 'We have been very short of money all our lives, Mrs Linton,' she admitted. 'But we have always managed. Lately, however, it has been more difficult to make ends meet.' Then she rallied and put on a brave smile. 'I feel so much better having been here and now that Harriet is to be settled in her new position, things are looking so much brighter.'

'If you wish to talk anything over, Miss Fielding, do please feel assured that you would have my confidence. I do know so well that sometimes we need to share our problems.'

Elizabeth insisted that she had no further worries. She said that she would stay for a few more days and that perhaps she could make herself useful in helping Lily with her studies. Lily, she had observed, was an intelligent girl with an academic brain. 'She could go far in any profession, Mrs Linton, if you and Captain Linton would permit it. Please don't allow her talents to be wasted because she is a female.'

Amelia, Harriet, Ralph and Jack travelled to York by train and Amelia was embarrassed by the scrutiny which Jack was subjected to by the other passengers. How does he bear it? she wondered. Yet he seems not to notice or else not to care.

'Will you visit Mr Scott again, Ralph?' she asked later as the two men escorted her and Harriet to the Fielding house.

'I must,' Ralph said. 'And I shall take Jack with me this time. He is going to assume the role of my servant. I want Scott's reaction to the possibility of my having wealth.'

'But why?' Amelia puzzled. 'I thought the object was to find out if he is your father.'

'So it is,' Ralph said swiftly. 'But there's something about the man I can't quite fathom. He also said his first wife had died tragically. That could have been my mother. Presumably the authorities notified him when she died on board ship. And he has apparently been married again since then.'

'Well that would be natural, surely?' she said sharply. 'It doesn't make him a villain because he took another wife!'

Ralph didn't answer this and was certainly not going to tell her what the confectioner in Coney Street had told him on his previous visit to York, that Scott had been a man for the ladies and had been having a liaison with a woman whilst still married.

Ralph and Jack stayed overnight in an inn and the next morning hired horses to take them to Edward Scott's house. 'We have been observed,' Jack remarked as they rode up the short drive. 'I saw the curtains twitch.'

'Must be a woman there, then,' Ralph said with dour humour. 'Men hardly ever look out of windows.'

The maid admitted them but seemed to be at a loss to know what to do with Jack. She observed him nervously, but when Ralph casually handed Jack his hat and scarf, she whispered to him to wait in the hall, and then scurried out of sight.

'You're not alone, Mr Hawkins,' Scott remarked when he appeared. 'Who is the fellow with you?'

'My manservant,' Ralph replied briefly. 'I brought him over with me.'

'Manservant, eh? What is he, an Abo?'

'He is an Aborigine, yes. Of mixed race. His maternal grandfather was English.'

'Does he speak any English?'

'He does.'

'Hmm,' said Scott. 'So, your parents must have made a spot of money if they can afford to let you have a servant come with you?'

'They have made some,' Ralph said as if reluctantly. 'They're sheep farmers.'

'They haven't found gold then?' Scott seemed more inclined to ask pertinent questions now that Ralph was alone without the presence of Captain Linton.

Ralph didn't reply directly, best to leave some questions unanswered. 'As a matter of fact, sir, another reason why I am in England, apart from the confectionery business which I am looking into – I'm sick of sheep, to be honest sir,' he added confidentially, 'is that they are not my real parents. I was adopted by them when I was a child. My *natural* mother died on board the convict ship which was taking her out to Australia, and I thought I'd try to find out if I had any relations still alive whilst I am over here.'

He saw the sudden startled flinch of Scott's body and the flush which touched his cheeks, and knew with a surety which appalled him that his remark had hit home. Scott, he was now almost sure, was his father.

Chapter Eighteen

'He's charming, isn't he?' said Harriet after she and Amelia had been escorted home by the two young men, and were eating a cold supper in the parlour.

'Mr Mungo? Yes he is,' Amelia agreed.

Harriet looked at her and smiled. 'Actually, Amelia, I meant your cousin, Mr Hawkins! Mr Mungo is very pleasant, but he is so very foreign that I find it difficult to judge his personality. But yes, he is a perfect gentleman.'

'But did you not find Cousin Ralph rather self-opinionated? Too sure of himself?'

'Not at all,' Harriet protested. 'His manner is easy and rather familiar, I agree, but I consider that is merely a result of living in a new country without the rigid rules of the old one. His up-bringing and environment would surely shape him, but that doesn't mean to say it is a fault in his character.'

She leaned forward. 'I couldn't help over-hearing that he was going to look for family connections whilst he was here in York. Did his family emigrate from York? Were they in a profession or trade? I ask because it would be so interesting if we should have heard of them.'

'Oh,' Amelia said. 'I beg your pardon. Of course you don't know. Cousin Ralph was adopted by my mother's brother and his wife.' She hesitated. 'They were not emigrants, Harriet,' she said quietly, 'nor were they from York. They were convicts, transported to Australia.'

Harriet looked stricken. 'Convicts! And they never came back?' she questioned in a whisper.

'Why no!' Amelia replied. 'Very few did. Most had no money and many were forbidden to come back. That was part of the punishment. It was total exile.'

'Yes, of course it was,' said Harriet and her eyes filled with tears. 'Poor souls,' she whispered. 'Poor, poor souls.' She swallowed hard. 'Amelia,' she said. 'Do you – ? That is – '

'Yes?' Amelia was disturbed to see her friend upset as she so obviously was. 'What is it, Harriet?'

'Oh – no, it's nothing! Nothing at all.'

She appeared to have been about to share a confidence, Amelia thought, but then had thought better of it. Yet she seemed to be still in a quandary as she clasped and unclasped her hands and pursed her lips. 'Amelia,' she said eventually. 'Would you – ? Do you think any the worse of your cousin because he is the son of convicts? Is he tainted because of his parents' background? Please,' she said earnestly. 'I would like an honest answer. It will not go any further than these four walls. It is so very important to me.'

'Harriet,' Amelia began. It was now time for total revelation. She had not told Elizabeth or Harriet of her mother's past, simply because she had thought they were too genteel and un-worldly to understand. 'There are two things I must tell you and then if you wish you may ask the question again. First of all: what I said – was, that Ralph Hawkins is the adopted son of my mother's brother and his wife, Meg, so he is not a proper cousin. However, his own mother was also a convict, but she died and Aunt Meg looked after him. The other thing I must tell you is that my own mother was also a convict when she was only a girl, but because of my father's campaigning on her behalf, he obtained a free pardon and brought her home.'

Harriet's eyes never left Amelia's face as she was speaking and her lips parted and then closed.

'So you ask, is Ralph tainted because of his parentage?' Amelia spoke quietly. 'Then you must look at me and my brothers and sisters, and ask the same question.'

'Oh, Amelia!' A look of pure joy lit Hariet's face. 'I am so pleased that you told me! May I tell Elizabeth when she returns? It will mean so much to her. To both of us.'

Amelia was bewildered. This wasn't the usual reaction when people found out about her background. 'You may of course, but why? Why does it mean so much?'

'I can't explain now. Not until I have told Elizabeth.' Harriet, usually so blithe, suddenly became overcome with emotion and started to weep and Amelia, startled, thought of Elizabeth, who had also had a weeping fit during her visit to Holderness and had become unwell. Whatever is wrong? she worried. Whatever can be the matter?

'So why have you really come to York?' Edward Scott's voice was brusque.

Ralph put on a surprised expression. 'As I said, sir. The confectionery – '

'And have you found any relatives?'

'No, not yet,' Ralph lied. 'Although I understand my mother probably came from York. It's very difficult to find records as a matter of fact. The authorities didn't always make an entry. I have yet to do some research.'

'I shouldn't bother if I were you,' Scott said gruffly. 'Best to let sleeping dogs lie.'

But he then went on to ask questions in a casual manner, about Ralph's age and where he was born, dropping them into the conversation as if they were of no real importance.

There came a knock on the door and a woman entered. 'Morning, Eddy. Oh, beg pardon. I didn't realize you had company.'

She was of middle years, with dyed straw-coloured hair and dressed unbecomingly in a gown more suited to a younger woman. She spoke in a vapid, commonplace voice.

'Come in Dolly.' Scott didn't rise to his feet as Ralph did, but stayed at his desk. 'This young fellow has come over from Australia.'

'How do you do, ma'am,' Ralph gave a short bow. 'Ralph Hawkins.'

She floated towards him and extended her hand. 'From Australia! On business?'

'He's going into the sweet industry,' Scott interrupted.

'Enquiring into the possibility, ma'am. Mr Scott was recommended to me.'

'And who is that waiting in the hall?' she asked. 'Such a handsome man, Eddy, and as dark as that bureau.'

'My manservant, Mrs Scott,' he acknowledged, thinking that she was being most familiar. 'He accompanied me from Sydney.'

'Oh, I'm not Mrs Scott,' she replied. 'I'm Mrs West. An old friend of Mr Scott's. We've known each other a long time, haven't we Eddy? Of course,' she added, rather hastily, Ralph thought, 'I was a friend of Mrs Scott's too. I was just passing this morning, and thought I'd drop in for coffee. We have coffee together most mornings, don't we Eddy?'

'You'd better ring for it, then,' Scott said sourly, 'the girl won't think of bringing it if you don't.'

'I did already,' she said sweetly. 'It'll be here in a minute.'

'Mr Hawkins is a convict's son,' Scott announced. 'He's looking for relations.'

'Really!' Her eyes grew wide. 'Do you normally tell people?'

'It's no shame in Australia to be the son or daughter of convicts,' Ralph answered coldly. 'There are so many of us. Besides we can't be answerable for our parents' crimes or misdemeanours.'

'Of course not. But in England you'll find it different. If I were you I should be careful who you tell,' she whined. 'In the better circles anyway.'

To which you don't belong, madam, he sneered silently.

'So what crime did your father commit, to be sent out to Australia? And I suppose your mother followed him out there?' she enquired. 'A lot of women did. Or so I'm told.'

'It was his mother, Dolly,' Scott interrupted. 'His mother was sent out. But she died on board ship.'

Ralph watched her intently as her mouth worked and her cheeks beneath the painted colour paled. 'How sad,' she said hoarsely. 'And – and, how old were you?'

'I was only a few days old when she died.'

'So you were born on the ship? She died of childbed fever, I expect?' Her head nodded as she spoke.

'I'm not sure.' He found it quite easy to lie to them. He had no desire to tell either of them what he knew. Not yet at any rate.

'So, you know nothing of her, then?' She looked at him intently. 'Nothing of how she came to be on the ship?'

'Not yet,' he said easily. 'But I intend to find out.'

'Are you a married man, Mr Hawkins?' Scott asked abruptly.

'No sir, I'm not.'

'But you have come of age.'

'Why yes, sir, why do you ask?'

'I wondered how you would set up this business. Will you get a bank loan? Or perhaps your relatives will help you? Captain Linton is a relative I think you said?'

'Relatives of my adoptive parents, not, strictly speaking, my own. But no, I won't be seeking any financial help. I have sufficient funds to start up a business on my own.'

Edward Scott nodded, then gave a thin smile. 'Then I think I can probably help you, Mr Hawkins. If you take the benefit of my advice there is money to be made.'

Odd, thought Ralph. He previously said that I wouldn't make a fortune.

'It needs to be set up properly. I recommend that you use my accountant. Henderson knows how to look after money. He'll keep yours safe until you're ready to start.'

'But – I only need information at this point,

sir.' Ralph was startled at the swift turn of events. 'I intend to start up in Australia, not here in England!'

'Yes, yes,' Scott blustered, 'but you need credentials to open accounts, you'll need to show you have sufficient money to start up in business.'

Ralph looked at the satisfied expression on Scott's face and began to feel uneasy. He's up to something. I'm sure of it.

Chapter Nineteen

'What do you think then, Eddy?' Dolly West chewed on her lip, watching from behind the curtain as Ralph rode down the drive. 'He can't be her lad, can he?'

Edward Scott scowled. 'There were hundreds of women sent out, there's no reason why he should be. Besides I wasn't told she'd had the child.' But he fiddled with papers on his desk. 'He didn't look like me, did he?'

She shook her head. 'No, not a bit and he didn't look like her either, too tall for one thing. But still,' she looked anxious. 'It seems funny though. He's the right age and everything.'

'What do you mean?' he said sharply. 'What's *everything* mean?'

'Well, you know – his mother dying on board ship. And her babby'd have been due before they got to Australia. Seems funny,' she repeated.

'It's not funny,' he growled. 'Not funny at all. I don't want some stranger claiming me as his father and expecting God knows what from me.

But on the other hand—' An idea which had come into his head earlier took deeper root. 'He's not poor by the look of it. He's brought a servant with him.'

Her eyes sparkled. 'You should have taken a peek at him, Eddy. He's ever so handsome, though I don't usually take to darkies, but his skin was a sort of treacly colour and he looked very muscular and strong.'

He gave her a withering glance. 'He's an Abo! A native. Not a proper person. They've been almost wiped out and quite right too, in my opinion. They're of no use. They serve no purpose except as servants, and there are plenty of white folks who can fill that role.'

She shrugged. 'Like Ada, you mean,' she said, speaking of the maid. 'Well, she won't stay long. She'll be on her way soon if you ask me.'

'Well I didn't ask you, so shut up,' he answered sharply. 'Now go and make yourself useful and then come back in half an hour and you can post a letter. I'm going to write to Henderson and arrange a meeting for Mr Hawkins. Then we'll find out who he is and if he has any money.' A sly grin came to his lips. 'And if he has, well, I might just discover my long-lost beloved son.'

Reluctantly she went towards the door. 'But you won't get up to anything, will you Eddy?' She turned towards him. 'We shouldn't push our luck too far.'

He dismissed her with a curt wave of his hand, then he sat staring at the door as it closed behind her. She had her usefulness, had Dolly, but sometimes she weakened and he couldn't be doing with that. She was expendable. He'd not be questioned or have his hand stayed from its purpose, not by anybody. His wives had discovered that to their cost.

'I'm curious, Jack. That's why I've agreed to meet this accountant fellow. But I shan't part with any money, you may be sure of that.' As they rode back into York, Ralph outlined what had happened.

'Is he your father? Did you find out?'

'He didn't respond too much when I said I was looking for relatives. But she did. Mrs West.'

'Mrs West? Was that the woman at the house? She came down the stairs and was going towards the door when she saw me,' Jack said. 'Then she turned round and went into the room where you and Scott were.'

'She said she was passing the house and decided to call,' Ralph grinned. 'I thought I hadn't heard the doorbell.'

'West!' Jack considered. 'Wasn't that the name of the witness at your mother's trial?'

'Of course it was! It hadn't ocurred to me. And he called her Dolly which is short for Dorothy. Mrs Dorothy West!'

'It's a strange house,' Jack said thoughtfully. 'It had bad feeling there. I could sense it. There has been a great deal of unhappiness within those walls.'

Ralph glanced at his friend. He knew better than to scoff. Jack was very sensitive to atmosphere. He nodded. 'It wasn't a welcoming house.'

'No,' Jack said softly. 'There was a smell of death there.'

Henderson was a small man, thin, and nervous as a cat as he ushered Ralph into his office and bade him be seated. He looked apprehensively at Jack who stood immobile and glassy-eyed inside the door where he had followed them.

'It's all right,' Ralph assured Henderson. 'He goes everywhere with me.'

'But – er, in private discussion?'

Ralph nodded. 'He won't understand what we're talking about.'

'Ah.' Henderson shuffled about on his desk to find the paper he wanted and then, with another quick nervous glance at Jack, said, 'I understand from Mr Scott's letter that you are thinking of starting up in the confectionery trade and might be needing financial advice.'

'No,' Ralph said calmly. 'I never said I needed financial advice. Mr Scott suggested that I came to see you, that you were the man who could advise me on the *possibility* of starting in business, but not here – in Australia.'

Henderson became more nervous and agitated and glanced down at the letter in his hand. 'But, erm, Mr Scott suggests that you should gain experience here, perhaps by buying a shop or small factory – there are several on the market at the moment, erm, he, Mr Scott that is, knows the owners personally and I could,' he pushed his glasses up his nose, 'I could arrange it for you.'

He glanced again at Jack and then at Ralph. 'He – er, we will of course need to have your financial credibility ascertained before we could proceed with any transaction.'

He's sweating, Ralph noticed. Why is he so nervous? 'Have you known Mr Scott for long?' he asked abruptly.

'Yes, yes,' Henderson stammered. 'Thirty years or more. We started up in business together when we were young men.'

'So you have shared his troubles?' Ralph said softly.

'His troubles?' Henderson looked up directly at Ralph, an alarmed expression on his face.

'His wife? I understand she died rather tragically.'

'Oh, yes, yes. He told you did he? Yes, poor lady. She fell into the Ouse; she was dead when they got her out.'

'Oh! Then there must have been another Mrs Scott?' Ralph, startled, glanced at Jack whose expression never changed.

Henderson put his hand to his chin and worried his fingers through his sparse beard. 'I thought you meant –. He told you of the other, did he? That poor lady died in her bed. She hadn't been well for a week or two, a stomach upset, I believe. She had some kind of violent fit, the doctor said. It was unfortunate that Mr Scott was out that evening or she might have been saved.' He gazed vaguely across the room. 'She might have been. There was only Mrs West in the house and she was downstairs and never heard anything untoward.'

Ralph swallowed. It's not him then. Scott is not my father. A feeling of relief swept over him. 'I think I might be having second thoughts about this confectionery business,' he said, 'and I don't quite know how long I will be staying in York. My primary aim, Mr Henderson, is to look for relatives.'

Henderson seemed to relax as he spoke, but then said with a catch in his voice, 'Mr Scott will be very disappointed, very disappointed, but still – if you have changed your mind, and of course it would take a deal of money to set up.'

'It's not the money,' Ralph said vaguely. 'But I really must concentrate on trying to locate my father.'

'Your father?' Henderson raised his eyebrows. 'How is it you have lost your father?'

'I have spent all of my life in Australia, Mr Henderson. My mother gave birth to me on a ship, a convict ship, and I have discovered recently that she came from York and that there is the strong possibility that my father still lives here.'

He broke off abruptly as he saw Henderson's face change colour and his hand clutch at his collar. He rose to his feet. 'Are you unwell, Mr Henderson? Shall I get you some water?'

Jack moved swiftly towards the desk and, standing behind Henderson, gently bent his head and shoulders towards the desk. 'Breathe deeply sir,' he said softly. 'Relax. Don't be alarmed.'

'Thank you, thank you.' Henderson lifted his head after a moment. 'I'm all right, really.' His colour was returning but he wore a frightened expression. 'Just a sudden turn. I have them from time to time.'

'Then I trust you have seen a doctor?' Ralph asked and as Henderson shook his head, advised, 'it would be a precaution, sir, if you don't mind my saying so.'

Henderson cleared his throat. 'Yes, yes, indeed. Mr Hawkins, may I ask you a personal question? Where is your mother now? Did she survive the journey?'

'No sir, she did not. She died on board ship. I was adopted.' I must write to Ma and Da, he thought. I have sent them only brief correspondence since arriving in England. Ma will want to know what is happening and if I have found news of my mother's family. I must write and tell her of this stalemate, and of the relief to know that the man I thought was my father, is not. That probably, somewhere in this city is another man with the same name, and as far as I am concerned he can stay anonymous.

'And was she tried at York County Court?'

'She was, sir.' I'm sick of this palaver, he thought. I want to get out of here and go back to Holderness. Suddenly he missed the open spaces, which, though considerably less in size than Australia, gave him the feeling of home.

'On what charge, may I ask?'

'On attempted murder, Mr Henderson.' Ralph stood up to go, to finish the discussion. He would leave the whole issue. He knew now who his real parents were, they were Meg and Joe Hawkins who had brought him up, had lavished love and care and discipline upon him as if he was their own. 'She had apparently attempted to kill her husband. Perhaps he deserved it, I don't know.'

Henderson stayed at his desk. He seemed to have lost his nervousness and had a calm resigned expression on his face. 'Please sit down, Mr Hawkins. I have something to tell you.' He looked into the distance, but it was as if he wasn't seeing his surroundings and was elsewhere. Then his gaze returned to Ralph.

'I may be starting all kinds of repercussions,' he said softly. 'But that can't be helped. I have lived with a troubled conscience for so many years and here may be my chance to gain peace of mind.'

Ralph stared at him. 'I don't understand, Mr Henderson.' He sat down again as he was bid. 'What do you mean?'

'I once had a client, a widow who came to me for advice. She had been left an inheritance by her late husband and wished to start up in a small business. I introduced her to someone I knew, Mr Thacker, a very sound gentleman, who was then in the confectionery business. On his advice she bought a shop and ran it very successfully. It just so happened that Thacker knew Edward Scott, and I don't know how or why, but Mr Scott and the widow were introduced. They subsequently married, Mr Hawkins, but things went wrong. There was violence within the marriage and Mrs Scott was accused of attempted murder. She was transported even though she was with child and had other children to consider.

'Mr Hawkins,' he said softly. 'I may be doing you a disservice by telling you this, but I do believe that Edward Scott is probably your father.'

Chapter Twenty

The days were cooler now in the hills above Sydney. Autumn had arrived and with it softer weather and rain which cooled the land.

Meg sat on the veranda with Ralph's latest letter which had been sent many weeks before. It was brief and written in haste and didn't tell her all she wished to know. Ralph had said that he was going to York again to look for details of Rose Elizabeth Scott. He was careful to call her by her full name and not refer to her as his mother, and for that Meg was grateful. He'll come to know he belongs to me, she thought, as she gazed down at the hundreds of ships in the harbour. There was a regatta taking place at the weekend and Sydney was swarming with visitors from the outlying districts.

I want to know about my own town, she mused. Has Hull changed, I wonder? Are there steamships on 'Humber where once there was sail? Does the market still bustle the way it did? Do they still have soup kitchens for poor folks beside 'King Billy statue? All her memories flooded back, but they were mostly painful ones. Have they pulled down the house of correction where Emily and I met? I don't suppose Emily goes into Hull much, it will be painful for her too.

She thought often of Joe's sister in her grand house in Holderness. Emily had written of it many times when she had first married Philip Linton and taken up residence there. She had sent lavish descriptions of the house and detailed the layout of the rooms and the colour of curtains and carpets and from this, Meg, who had had no knowledge of design or style, fashioned her own home at Creek Farm on the plan of Elmswell Manor. She had asked Emily's advice on the type of material to be used for drapes and hangings, knowing that heavy velvets and brocades would not be suitable for the climate of Australia as they were in the north of England. Emily had suggested muslin and chiffon for the summer and heavier cottons for the winter, and Chinese rugs scattered about the polished wood floors, and not to buy horsehair furniture on any account for it tickled so.

That the house and its furnishings were a success, she knew, for Lucinda Boyle had exclaimed in delight on her very first visit. 'How elegant,' she had said. 'So like an English country house, and yet with colonial touches which makes it just right for this continent. How very clever you are, Meg.'

And Meg had smiled and thanked her and not told her, until she knew her better, that it was Emily, her dearest friend, who had advised her.

She poured herself a glass of ale and sat sipping it, enjoying its cool aromatic flavour. As she rocked on her chair she wished that Daisy would come over to keep her company. Peggy had gone off to join some friends to watch the sailing, and Joe had gone down into Sydney to negotiate the sale of wool and visit the bank. Although she could have gone with him and whilst he attended to his business could have strolled in the scented arbours of the tropical Botanical Gardens and listened to the regimental band which played beneath the jacaranda trees, she had decided against it. Joe liked to call in at a tavern, smoke a pipe of tobacco and drink a tankard or two of ale and listen to the gossip of settlers and farmers, and she didn't want him to feel he had to rush to collect her.

Joe was happy in Australia. He had found his niche and was known as a successful man. Many in Sydney tipped their hats to him, though there were others amongst the Free Colonists who would ignore him and name him an Emancipist. This view, contrarily, gave Joe immense satisfaction; he knew that he had survived and succeeeded against all odds, whereas people such as Captain Boyle, who thought himself so superior and could join the best clubs in Sydney, could barely afford to keep his wife and daughter in ribbons.

I miss Mrs Boyle, Meg mused as she rocked. I miss her company. I wish, though, that she didn't have to hide our friendship from her husband. What a dreadful man he is; if she only knew him as others do, I swear she would never come back from England. Her own experience with Captain Boyle from when she was on the convict ship, coupled with the rumours which both her white and Aborigine servants told her, increased her dislike of the man constantly.

She narrowed her eyes; someone was riding up the drive towards the house. She drew in a sharp breath. The servants had all gone off for an afternoon sleep, there were only a couple of the very young Aborigine children there and they were playing on the grass at the back of the house. She wasn't a nervous woman though she kept a pistol hidden, which she knew how to use, and a whip was always propped up against the veranda wall for the occasional wild dingo which might approach the house.

But there was something abut this figure riding up the hill towards her which unsettled her and brought back memories of more than twenty years ago, when Ralph was just a baby and she was here with Emily. He sits with the same posture, she thought, and she leaned forward better to see; it's as if he isn't comfortable on horseback.

She gasped. He's wearing uniform. It's him! She put her hand to her throat. What does he want? Has he found out about Mrs Boyle? Does he know about Ralph admiring his daughter?

But there was something more about him which disturbed her because she was alone. In her past she had been an experienced woman in the ways and desires of men, and she knew without a shadow of doubt that Captain Boyle, and it was he who was now approaching the house, had lusted after her when she was a convict woman in chains, and did still, for she saw it in his eyes whenever they should chance to pass in the streets of Sydney, even though she was now a respectable farmer's wife.

Captain Boyle grunted as he dismounted, then straightened his jacket and took off his hat. 'G'afternoon, Mrs Hawkins.'

Meg inclined her head. 'We've not seen you up here in a lot of years, Captain Boyle. Is something amiss?'

He climbed the steps towards her and she wondered if she should offer him a drink. He was sweating from the exertion of the ride.

'Nothing amiss, Mrs Hawkins.' He gave a sly smile. 'Just a neighbourly call.'

'It's a long way up for that and I'm afraid Joe is out.'

'I know.' His smile grew wider. 'I saw him down in the market place. He was drinking with some cronies, ex-convicts by the look of them.'

She didn't answer. The men that Joe knew were settlers or farmers; some had come out as emigrants, one or two had been convicts but had established themselves with hard work and endeavour as Joe had done. None of them had travelled with them on the convict ship the *Flying Swan*.

'Or they might have been miners,' he drawled, 'they had the look of labour on them anyway.'

She watched him draw off his white gloves to reveal his soft hands. 'Not gentlemen, then, Captain Boyle, such as yourself?'

He glanced swiftly at her, then grinned. 'Hardly! And I imagine your husband would be offended should such a description be applied to him?'

'He would. Joe knows exactly who he is and is happy with his status.'

'Just as well,' he said ironically, 'for there is no likelihood of him changing it.'

'Why have you come, Captain Boyle?' Her tone was icy. 'Not to discuss the merits of my husband?'

'Still got a sharp tongue in your head, Meg,' he said softly. 'I like a woman with spirit. It was one of the things which attracted me to you all those years ago.'

'Aye,' she snapped. 'That and 'chains which were binding me. It excited you, didn't it, seeing all those women in fetters?'

'Come now,' he said placatingly. 'I haven't come to quarrel. That was all a long time ago. We have changed, all of us. We could be friends.'

She laughed. What a nerve the man had. 'Friends! How could we ever be friends wi' likes of you?'

He gave a small dismissive gesture. 'Don't think of yourself as inferior, Meg. You are the wife of a successful man, and if I might say so, you are still – no, even more so, a very handsome woman.'

She roared with laughter. 'You haven't changed, Captain Boyle, you are still as obnoxious as ever – and I *don't* think myself inferior!'

She leant towards him. She hadn't invited him to sit down and he hovered on the top step of the veranda. 'But 'reason we can't be friends wi' likes of you is plain to see when Joe takes his shirt off every night and I see 'scars which you put there. We'll not forget you. Not ever, nor others of your kind who sent us here.'

Bitter memories spilled over and she had to bite her lip to keep back angry tears. She didn't often cry, but sometimes the past was too painful to remember.

Captain Boyle gave her a wry look and moved towards her. He touched her arm. 'That's done with, Meg. I'm here to make amends. We're sensible people, we must try to forget what went before. Look,' he said. 'You're alone. Your husband is busy. I don't suppose he gets a great deal of time for socializing – my wife is away in England. We could perhaps have an evening together at the theatre, or maybe supper? All above board of course.' The pressure on her arm increased and he stroked her flesh with his thumb. 'I would like that, Meg. I really would.'

She lifted her head and stared at him coolly. 'And then,' she said softly, 'we could go back to your house for coffee, and the servants would be out so we would have to have a glass of wine instead, and as the weather was warm you would invite me to take off my jacket and make myself comfortable – '

His eyes narrowed. 'I wasn't suggesting – '

'Oh yes you were, Captain Boyle. I haven't forgotten what I learned at my trade,' she said bitterly. 'The men then might not have been your class but you run to type. If there was one thing I did learn, it was when a man was making a suggestion and pretending he wasn't.'

'Well, seeing as you mention it,' he said smoothly. 'Why not? An occasional rendezvous would bring a little excitement into our lives, would it not?'

'You're right of course, Captain Boyle,' she said quietly and moved towards him. 'We can all do with a little diversion now and then.' She ran her fingers slowly down her throat and neck and fingered the neckline of her gown, watching his eyes glisten as he followed their trail. Slowly she unfastened the top button of her gown and then the one below. She was wearing a low-cut lacy cotton chemise beneath it and she saw his eyes linger. He licked his lips and she fought back a shudder as she stretched out her hand to reach him.

'We allus get what we want if we try for long enough,' she murmured. 'And I've never told a soul that I've yearned for this for many a year.'

She heard the rear door of the house open – it had a decided click and she knew that someone, maybe one of the Aborigine children, was entering the kitchen.

'I knew it.' Captain Boyle's lips were wet as he mumbled, 'I knew your desires were the same as mine. I can always tell a lustful woman. What a time we can have, Meg. I can't wait! Come with me now. Where can we go?'

'You can go to hell and back,' she yelled as she gave him a great shove on his chest. 'And just see how you like it.'

He fell with a thump down the veranda steps and flat on his back on the ground and lay there groaning. 'My back! Oh, God. My back! You've broken it, you bitch. You whore!'

She reached for the lash and shouted, 'Tommy! Barai! Sal!' This last name to her housekeeper, a convict's daughter whose mother had died at the hands of a rough settler and had had to fend for herself since she was eight.

Sal came running through the house at her call. 'What's up, missus?'

'An intruder,' Meg gasped. 'He tried to assault me.' She stepped down the veranda steps and, flourishing the whip high above her head, she thrashed it so that it whistled and cracked as it cut through the air.

'Don't come near me, I'm warning you.' Captain Boyle tried to rise to his feet but fell backwards and grimaced in pain. 'You bitch,' he groaned. 'I'm in agony.'

She stepped forward, nearer to him, and once more the whip whistled through the air. 'Do you remember that sound, Captain Boyle? Do you remember when you lashed Joe after half-drowning him? And do you remember you were going to lash me?'

The thin leather strap whistled towards him and Boyle put his hands to his face. 'Don't! Don't,' he whined and she felt a pleasing sense of power.

'Why not?' she jeered, and with swift rapid movements spun the whip above her head and lashed out towards him. Boyle ducked as she knew he would and the whip hit his shoulder, cutting through the fabric of his wool coat. 'It feels good, doesn't it Captain? To be in control. In command!'

'Shall I fetch the men, missus?' Sal said eagerly. 'They'll know what to do with likes of him.'

'Yes,' Meg said, staring down into Boyle's face. 'And tell them to fetch a rope to tie him in case he becomes violent.'

Sal ran off and Boyle, groaning, eased himself onto his hands and knees. 'I never touched you,' he grunted. 'You're a damned liar.'

'Only you and I know that,' Meg sneered. 'But

this time, Captain, I shall be believed. I am now a respectable woman and you are a well-known rake.'

He stared at her, his mouth open. 'What – what do you mean?'

'I mean that your reputation has even come up here to Creek Farm. You have been seen entering the brothels of Sydney. It's well known that you frequent the houses of the Aborigine women whose only means of living is to satisfy the needs of white men like you. Even there, Captain, your reputation stinks!' She went on contempuously, 'and you have sunk very low indeed when you have to enter the Rocks for your pleasure.'

'Well, you should know all about that, Mrs Hawkins,' he spat. 'No doubt you have friends there.'

Her expression froze. 'I have few friends,' she said icily. 'But those I have I value dearly and one of them is your wife.' She saw the alarm on his face and instantly could have cut off her tongue. How would he react towards Mrs Boyle on her return from England after such a revelation? Would he make that gentle lady's life a misery?

'My wife?' He staggered to his feet. '*You* are a friend of my wife's?'

She lifted her head proudly. 'I am! She is a gracious lady and doesn't deserve to be tied to a reprobate like you. I could be very worried for her health!'

'You needn't be,' he snorted. 'Women like Mrs Boyle are purely decorative and an asset to a marriage. Unlike women like you, *Mrs Hawkins*.'

Meg wasn't hurt by his insults, she had heard worse but not in a long time. She glanced across the fields. Men and dogs were running towards them with Sal trying to keep up behind. The dogs were barking and children were shouting. Most of the men were Aborigines and carrying sticks.

'You'll get your come-uppance one day, *Captain* Boyle, that I'm sure of. Now go,' she urged. 'I can't guarantee your safety.'

He too glanced up and started to hobble towards his horse. 'I shan't forget this,' he panted. 'You've just about crippled me.'

'You'd better forget it,' she said. 'Or I shall tell Joe and then you'll be really sorry that you came.'

He threw a glance of pure venom as he eased himself into the saddle. 'And stay away from my wife when she returns,' he spat out as he slid his feet awkwardly into the stirrups. 'I shan't allow her to mix in your company.'

Meg smiled, though she felt not in the least humorous but only anxious now about Mrs Boyle. 'Is that so? And what about your daughter and my son?' she said. 'Did you know about that?'

Anger flushed his face but he glanced anxiously at the approaching crowd which had now reached the paddock. 'What?' he bellowed. 'What are you talking about?'

'That there might be a wedding,' she scoffed and fervently hoped that there wouldn't be. 'But get on your way or you might not live to see it.'

Chapter Twenty-One

Captain Boyle grimaced in anger and discomfort as he rode. The pain in his back increased with every movement from the horse beneath him. Blasted woman; but he should have expected as much. She'd got uppity now that she had money. If she'd been down on her luck she would have welcomed him. Then an unwished-for doubt crept in: or maybe her husband keeps her satisfied. A picture of Joe Hawkins, strong and defiant even though he had been in fetters, came into his mind. He hadn't been able to break his spirit all those years ago, not with the ducking overboard or the cat-o'-nine-tails.

And what does she mean, I'll get my come-uppance? Will she tell Hawkins? Or will she send somebody to frighten me off? No, she was bluffing. But I shan't go up there again, even though I'd like to bed her. His salacious appetite sharpened at the thought of Meg Hawkins's fine figure. She's been a whore, and once a whore, always a whore.

But what Meg Hawkins had said was true; the sight of so many women in chains had excited him, and it was for that same reason that he visited the brothels in town and on occasion the Rocks, the most notorious of districts in Sydney. The women there were so downtrodden they were willing to do anything to earn a copper.

He felt himself stirring as he remembered the last time he had visited the Rocks. He had seen a young girl, maybe fourteen or perhaps younger, attractive in spite of the dirt on her face and her torn clothes. He had beckoned her to come with him, and her mother, her face haggard and worn, and dirtier even than her daughter, had pushed her forward, even though the girl had been unwilling.

He'd held her tightly by her thin wrist so that she wouldn't run away, and taken her to a seedy downtown hotel and ordered a room with a bath and hot water. He'd watched her as she stripped off her dirty dress and stepped gingerly into the water, tears streaking her face.

He had lain on the bed chewing on a cigar and watched her as she soaped her thin body as he directed. He'd felt the excitement growing inside him at the sight of her small round breasts and buttocks, at the soft downy pubescent hair, until he could bear it no longer. He'd pulled her out of the bath and without permitting her to dry herself he pushed her onto the bed and held her down with one hand whilst he tore off his trousers.

She'd screamed and cried, but in that area of the town no-one had enquired about the noise and when he had finished with her he threw some money at her and told her to go. She gathered up her clothes against her naked body and staggered out of the room. He saw that she was shaking and crying but he simply turned over on the none too clean sheets and slept for an hour before going home.

He thought of the girl now. Perhaps I could find her again, or someone like her. His anger over Meg had increased his frustration and brought his licentious desires to the fore. I'll go home and bathe and change out of these clothes. He was hot and sweaty and his back ached. He hated blasted horses and wished he'd brought the trap, but that wouldn't have cut much of a dash. Women's transport! If only I could afford a curricle.

Perhaps if Edwin is at home, he mused, I could persuade him to come with me into town. Edwin had a position at Government House, but puzzlingly didn't go into the office regularly but often slept late in the morning and went to the office in the afternoon, working until very late in the evening, so that his family saw little of him.

Yes, if he's at home, that would be good, he thought. I'll persuade him to take the rest of the day off. We could get two girls. A pain shot down his back and into his legs, but he wasn't deterred. Maybe even bring them back for the whole night. I've never been able to do that before.

He had initiated Edwin into the charms of the brothel when the boy had reached seventeen. Edwin hadn't wanted to go, he'd made all kinds of excuses but his father had insisted and had waited for him in the reception area with a glass of wine in his hand, compliments of the management, feeling self-satisfaction that he had done right by the boy in helping him to achieve his manhood.

He and the madam had chosen the girl themselves, a pretty eighteen-year-old with plenty of experience and charm. He had been disappointed when Edwin refused to discuss the experience, saying that it was private; but the girl had had a merry gleam in her eyes as they came downstairs, and watched with a smile on her lips as he paid the madam. Yet he never knew if Edwin had been to the brothel again. He'd used the girl himself, quite often since then, but she wouldn't be drawn as to whether she had seen his son and it was almost as if Edwin had avoided conversation with his father ever since.

Smith, the Aborigine who had been employed to look after the two horses and tend the garden, had gone walkabout since Lucinda and Phoebe had left for England. He'd asked for his wages on the day they'd sailed and Boyle hadn't seen him since. He had employed a young half-black in his place but he never seemed to be there when he wanted him. He wasn't here now so he

230

tied the horse to a rail out of the heat and let himself into the house.

The blinds had been drawn against the sun and although the rooms were kept well polished and tidy by the maid, there was an emptiness which had settled since Lucinda had gone away. There were no flowers on the table and the fireplace was bare of decoration. There was no smell of cooking as he'd sacked the cook and told her he and Edwin would eat out, and on hearing this the young maid had declared that she would no longer live in, but would come in on a daily basis to do the washing and cleaning.

He walked back into the hall to ascend the stairs. He wouldn't take a bath after all, he decided, for there wouldn't be any hot water, and it was then that he noticed Edwin's hat on the hatstand. So the young devil is at home, but surely not still in bed, it was almost four in the afternoon.

He looked up the stairs. His own bedroom door was half open as he had left it, but Edwin's was firmly shut. He listened. Could he hear voices? He crept further upstairs. There was a low laugh. Edwin's laugh. He hadn't heard that in a long time. He was a most sombre young man as a rule. There it came again. He smiled. He's got a wench in there. Young reprobate. So he takes after his father after all.

He climbed stiffly to the top of the stairs. Wonder who she is? A street girl perhaps? A nerve though if she is, bringing her here! Not one of their crowd surely? The young people that Edwin and Phoebe mixed with were mostly decent, of good parents, though there were a few bad elements creeping in he'd noticed, like the Hawkins girl for one. He'd seen her one day on the arm of Edwin's friend, Marius Nugent, Lord Nugent's son, and had been wryly amused at the consternation that would ensue should Lord Nugent find out.

He remembered what Meg Hawkins had told him about her son and Phoebe, but he'd decided to disbelieve her. Phoebe would never choose someone like Ralph Hawkins, in spite of his money. Not with his background. He'd thrash her himself if she did.

He put his ear to the door and listened. They were having fun; he could hear the low laughter and soft murmuring. Young dog.

He turned the doorknob. It was locked so he hammered on the door. 'Edwin! What's going on in there?'

There was an immediate silence. 'Come on!' He grinned as he spoke. 'I can hear you. You've got a girl in there.'

He heard a muffled laugh, then, 'Just a minute, Father.'

He heard the creak of the bed and he waited expectantly. If it was a street girl then there would be no need to go out looking; that's if Edwin would agree to share.

The door opened a crack and Edwin looked out. His hair was tousled and he was clad in a silk dressing robe, not one that Boyle had seen before. 'What do you want, Father?'

'Want? I want to know who you've got in there.' He peered over the top of Edwin's head but could only see the bottom of the bed and the crumpled sheets.

'It's nothing to do with you who I've got in here.' Edwin's voice was low and tense, but under control.

'Nothing to do with me?' He was peeved. 'This is my house. Of course it's to do with me!' He put his hand on the door but Edwin held it fast. 'Come on, old fellow. Let's take a look. Is it that young wench from the brothel? Is it a street woman?'

'No. It is not. Do not insult me by such a suggestion.' There was anger in Edwin's voice. 'Now please go away whilst I get dressed.'

Boyle gave a snigger. 'I'm intrigued, Edwin. What a dark horse you are. You've been keeping some little filly hidden away for your sinful appetite, and I never guessed.' He gave a sudden push on the door and it flew out of Edwin's hand and banged against the wall.

His eyes were drawn to the bed; to the sheets which lay crumpled upon it and to the pile of clothing, shirt and trousers, which lay on the chair at the side of it, but his lascivious smile faded as he saw the fair-haired figure lying naked and unashamed on the bed.

His mouth dropped open; he felt his chest tighten and his breathing become rapid as all his own lecherous thoughts disappeared. 'Marius Nugent,' he breathed, 'but where's the girl?' He looked towards the small dressing room adjoining the bedroom, but the door was open and there was no-one in it.

'Where's the girl?' he repeated, turning to Edwin. 'Where's the girl?'

'There is no girl, Father.' Edwin's voice was low. His throat beneath the neck of his robe was flushed and he swallowed and licked his lips. 'There's only Marius.'

Boyle looked again to the bed. Marius sat up and drew a sheet over the lower half of his body. He raised a hand to Boyle as if in greeting.

'What!' Boyle's voice was hoarse in condemnation. He looked at his son and saw that beneath his robe he was as naked as Marius Nugent was.

Edwin's eyes held his and didn't flinch. 'It would be no good trying to explain to you, Father. I wouldn't expect you to understand.'

Boyle found his voice and raised it. 'You're quite right I wouldn't, you obscene, lecherous, debauched piece of dirt! You,' he pointed to Marius. 'Get out of my house and don't ever let me see you here again.' He felt sick. He'd been so proud of his son's connections with the upper-class members of Sydney society. 'What would your father say if he found out?'

Marius swung his legs onto the floor; his body was as fair as any girl's. 'I doubt if he would say anything,' he replied in a lazy drawl. 'He

234

wouldn't want his own reputation to be damaged.' He slipped on his white shirt, stepped into his trousers and buttoned them. 'And neither, I suppose, would you.'

His manner just missed being insolent. He didn't address Boyle as sir, as would have been fitting for a younger man in conversation with an elder, and yet he smiled quite graciously and appeared not at all put out at his and Edwin's unfortunate discovery.

Edwin stared at his father. 'I tried to tell you years ago that I wasn't interested in females, and all of those descriptions of me which you have so aptly recited could so easily apply to you, Father. You have been visiting brothels and hotels of ill repute for as long as I can remember, how then can you say such things to me? I have only ever had one lover and that is Marius.'

'Lover!' Boyle heard his own voice raised in reprehension. 'How can he be a lover? What you do is unclean. A crime. A sin!'

There was anger in Edwin's voice, yet he made no answer to his father's accusation and merely said, 'Please leave my room, Father. I want to get dressed, then I'm leaving. I'm taking rooms elsewhere.'

'What will your mother say when she finds out? She'll be heartbroken.' He saw the hesitation on Edwin's face and continued ranting. 'And Phoebe – think of the shame! How will she ever find a husband when she has a brother who takes part in such dissipated relationships?'

A ghost of a smile touched Edwin's mouth. 'Phoebe already knows about Marius and me, and whether she approves or not is immaterial to either of us; besides, Phoebe has other things more pressing on her mind. As for Mother – ' again he hesitated. 'When she eventually comes home *then* I'll try to explain. In the meantime she won't find out. Not unless *you* tell her.'

Edwin held open the door and Boyle backed out. He threw a look of loathing at Marius Nugent, who simply returned his gaze with his own steady stare and then turned his back.

Boyle staggered downstairs and headed for the brandy decanter. It was almost empty and he shook it to retrieve the last few drops. Dirty, filthy reprobates! How could they?

His first thought was to ride over to Lord Nugent's house to discuss the situation, but it was on the other side of Sydney and he wasn't sure what kind of welcome he would receive from a man he had never met. Would he believe his accusations about his son? Besides, he thought, both young men are adult and independent. What their fathers thought or said wouldn't make a difference. What was important was that it was kept quiet.

But where was Edwin going? If he was sharing rooms with Marius then there might be talk. He must put a stop to that. He went back into the hall and bellowed up the stairs, 'I want to talk to you, Edwin.'

The two young men appeared in the doorway and to Boyle's horror, Marius gave Edwin a brief kiss on his cheek before running lightly downstairs. 'It's no use trying to persuade him to stay, Captain Boyle,' he said as he passed him. 'It's all arranged. We've been planning for Edwin to move out for months.'

'He can't afford to keep himself, you know,' Boyle barked. 'He's only a jumped-up clerk after all. He's got no money of his own.'

Marius gave a slight smile. 'But I have, Captain Boyle, so you need have no worries on that score. I can afford to keep Edwin in more comfort than he has had here.'

'Get out!' Boyle shouted. 'Don't show your pretty face here again or I'll smash it so hard that even your mother wouldn't recognize you.'

Marius nodded. 'Good day, Captain. Try not to think too badly of us, it's the way we are made.'

Boyle shuddered. He remembered some of the convicts who were sent out on the ships he'd sailed in during his early career. The men were often packed in so close together that some with unnatural tendencies, as he was wont to describe them, were sometimes found indulging in indecent acts. They were brought up on deck and lashed until their flesh was cut and bleeding, and Boyle remembered the physical excitement he had felt as he watched their tortured writhings.

'I'm going, Father.' Edwin stood in the doorway. He had a leather travelling bag in his hand. 'I shall write to Mother and tell her I'm moving out, but I shan't say why. She can draw her own conclusions.'

'Go then,' his father bellowed, 'and don't expect that you can come crawling back, because you can't. I'm finished with you. You make me want to retch!'

'And you've sickened me for years,' Edwin retaliated. 'You've had no thought for my mother as you carried on in your dissolute ways. You might have brought God knows what home in the way of disease from the company you keep. I've been ashamed of you for as long as I can remember.'

Boyle felt his upper lip twitch as it sometimes did when he was angry. 'Get out!' he snarled.

Edwin opened the front door. The young Aborigine was sitting on the doorstep and he stepped around him and walked down the path to the road where there was a curricle waiting with Marius in the driving seat. As he climbed in, Boyle thought that no-one would ever guess; they looked just like two young men setting off to enjoy themselves at their club or going to meet young ladies in the park.

'You want me to dig the garden, Captain?' the boy asked. 'Or make you nice dinner?'

Boyle looked down at him. He was shirtless and his hands and knees were covered in mud.

'No.' He closed the door on him and turned back into his empty house.

Chapter Twenty-Two

'Harriet!' Amelia busied herself about the fire, putting on another log, brushing the ash from the hearth and keeping her flushed face away from her companion.

'Mmm?' Harriet was bent over a piece of linen, carefully hemming the edges to make a handkerchief.

'I wondered – what are your opinions on mixed marriages?'

'Religion, you mean? Well, I'm not sure if they work. One of the doctrines has to dominate and if the other partner has strong feelings then there is bound to be a clash.'

Amelia straightened up. 'No, I didn't mean that,' she said slowly. 'Although religion would have to be considered. No, I meant race – culture.'

Harriet put her head up and stared at Amelia. 'You mean Mr Mungo, don't you?' she breathed. 'Oh, Amelia! Have you become fond of him?'

Amelia sat down, the flush which had touched

her cheeks starting to pale. 'I – I think perhaps that I have,' she conceded. 'My feelings are certainly in confusion when he is near. And even when he is not,' she added. 'I have not felt this way about a man before.'

Harriet put down her sewing and folded her hands on her lap. 'I'm not sure what to say. My first thoughts are that it is madness, that it would be totally wrong.'

'Yes,' Amelia agreed. 'So are mine.' She swallowed nervously. 'Yet I feel so much emotion when he is near. Do you feel the same about your Mr Thacker?'

Harriet smiled. 'I went through such a stage when I wanted only to be with him, but I know, we both know, that our marriage is impossible until such time as our fortunes change, and so our relationship has changed. Our feelings are the same for one another, but restrained.'

'How sad for you both,' Amelia was genuinely sorry for her friend, 'that you must hold in your emotions.'

Harriet nodded. 'But it is only finance that is holding us back, there are no other barriers, Amelia. There are no prejudices such as you would encounter if you should marry Mr Mungo.'

Amelia was startled. 'There is no question – ' she began. 'I didn't mean – I only wanted your opinion on the subject, to be discussed impartially.'

'But the subject could not possibly be discussed impartially if the question should arise.'

'Why no! But let us only discuss it objectively, in a detached open-minded manner, without bias.' Amelia was becoming flustered. 'That is all I ask.'

'Very well.' Harriet sat back and, putting her hands together, gently tapped her fingers as she pondered. 'It would depend, I think, on the people involved. They would need to be exceptionally strong-minded in order to disregard the prejudices of others, for there is no doubt that there would be many who would find the idea abhorrent.

'There would also be a clash of cultures, depending of course on where the people involved chose to live. For instance, here in England the couple would find themselves ostracized and barred from society, whilst in Australia or – Africa, or wherever the person came from,' she added hastily, 'then the white person would probably not be accepted by the other's kin either.'

She continued, 'You and I, Amelia, have not been exposed to other cultures, to a different race or another totally different way of life. We have led such sheltered lives that we do not have any conception of how it would be in such a situation. I think that perhaps you should open up the discussion with Mrs Boyle or her daughter. They live in a country where there is another race. Ask their opinion, in a general sort of way, without being too specific.'

'I am being very foolish, am I not, Harriet?' Amelia gave a wan smile. 'Why should I ever think on such things? I thought I was such a sensible person.'

Harriet caught hold of her hand and gave it a squeeze. 'You are a sensible person,' she said gently. 'But even sensible people can fall in love.'

But I don't know if I am in love, Amelia pondered. My emotions play such tricks on me when he is near. Is it his manner? His looks? Or is it simply because he is different and therefore intriguing? I hope that no-one notices any difference in my behaviour towards him, I hope that *he* doesn't notice anything untoward. I would be *mortified* if my feelings were so transparent.

Harriet started as governess the next day and as her pupil lived in York, she was able to come home in the evening. 'I will be home in time to prepare supper, Amelia,' she said, picking up her bag. 'So don't put yourself out too much.'

'I won't.' Amelia opened the door to let her out. 'I trust everything will go well and that your pupil is amiable.'

She prepared the lesson which she was to teach to Elizabeth's pupil, who was due to arrive at nine o'clock, but by nine thirty she hadn't arrived. I do hope that she isn't going to stop coming, she worried. Elizabeth and Harriet will barely be able to manage their finances without any pupils. At ten o'clock there was a knock on the door and a message was given that the child was ill and wouldn't be coming for her lessons until the next day.

Well, she thought, Elizabeth will be home this evening, so she will be able to teach her herself tomorrow. I'm not needed after all. She busied herself around the small house, tidying books and papers, straightening pictures on the wall, and as she did so she stopped to read a framed tract, one which she had seen previously, but had not read. It was handwritten and faded, which was probably why it was in a dark corner to protect it from the light.

Someone, probably a child, had painted small blue flowers around the words, but the writing was unmistakably in an adult's hand.

'*To my dearest daughters,*' Amelia read, and reached to lift the frame from the wall, to see it better.

'*Oh, do not think, though far away,*
Thou are forgot by me;
Oh, no, believe there's not a day
But I'll remember thee.
From your ever-loving mother, Rose Elizabeth Fielding.'

How sad. Amelia felt her eyes prickle with tears. So who looked after Elizabeth and Harriet as children? Elizabeth had said she was only eight when her mother died. Relatives perhaps? Though I have not heard them mention any.

She prepared lunch for herself and was about

to put on her hat to go out for a walk when there was a knock on the door. It was Ralph and Jack Mungo, who both raised their hats in greeting.

'G'afternoon, Cousin Amelia,' said Ralph.

'G'day, Miss Amelia,' Jack smiled.

'So glad to find you in.' Ralph appeared rather anxious. 'Are you very busy? Is your pupil with you?'

'No, she is ill and couldn't come today.' She hesitated about inviting them in. Would it be proper? She saw one of Harriet's neighbours looking out of her window, directly towards them. 'I was about to go out for a walk. Would you care to join me?'

They agreed that they would and she slipped back into the house for her hat and jacket, and took a basket with her for she intended to buy something for supper.

Ralph smiled when he saw the basket. 'Are you playing at housekeeping, Amelia? Not your usual role?'

She took offence, she knew not why. 'I may not have had much experience,' she said sharply, 'but I am intelligent enough to know how, should the occasion arise, as it has today.'

She saw him wince and glance at Jack who lowered his eyes. I don't know why Cousin Ralph irritates me so, she thought vexedly. But he always seems to say the wrong thing. He is heedless and speaks as he finds, unlike Jack, who is so discriminating and mindful of the effect his observations might have.

'I wanted to talk to you, Amelia, but perhaps today wouldn't be a good day after all,' Ralph began.

'Why not?' She sounded waspish, she realized, and tried to temper her voice with warmth. 'It's a sunny day, just right for pleasantries.'

She heard him give a small sigh, and then Jack broke in. 'Might I suggest we walk by the river for a little while and then perhaps call in somewhere for coffee, there are several pleasant places to stop to eat or drink.'

'Yes,' she answered quickly, 'that would be very nice.' He is so thoughtful, so considerate, always ready to smooth out difficulties. She gave him an appreciative smile.

They chatted as they walked; generalities, of the differences in climate between Australia and England, of the food crops which grew in one country and not another and of the wildlife in Australia.

'Your brother Roger would like to see the flora of Australia,' Jack remarked. 'He is so interested in all growing things.'

'Did he say that he would?' Amelia expressed surprise, 'I have never heard him say that he would like to travel.'

'Perhaps he feels his life is mapped out for him here,' Ralph said. 'It is sometimes expected that a son should carry on in the tradition of his father.'

'But in that case, he would follow in our father's footsteps and have a seagoing career,'

Amelia replied. 'And he has never suggested that. It is our mother who runs the estate with Samuel. Papa takes an interest of course, but he is first and foremost a seaman.'

Ralph shrugged. 'Then as eldest son, Roger must think he has to eventually take over the estate from your mother and Samuel. Joseph is too young and,' he glanced at her and added, 'presumably you don't want to? You will no doubt marry well and move away from the district.'

She felt herself grow hot and she answered pertly. 'I shall only marry *well*, cousin, when, or if, I find someone to suit me. It is not an absolute requirement!'

They came back into the main thoroughfare and Jack once again suggested they stop for coffee. They were close by the Minster and the bells were pealing; there was a small café across the street so they crossed over and took a table by the window, ordering coffee and cakes.

Amelia and Jack chatted as they waited for their order, but Ralph was silent until Jack asked quietly, 'Are you going to discuss the issue of Scott with Miss Amelia, Ralph? Or will you wait until we are back in Holderness?'

'I don't know if the time is right,' Ralph said abruptly. 'Besides, it only affects me. No-one else.'

Amelia glanced at him. He was worried over something. Had she been rather sharp? Was his indiscreet attitude the result of the matter which was bothering him and not really directed at her?

'Perhaps a problem shared – ?' she suggested.

'I doubt if you could understand the situation, Amelia,' he replied, adding swiftly, 'and that does not mean to say that I consider you to be without understanding or compassion.'

He waited as the coffee was brought and poured and then continued. 'The circumstances are rather unusual. Less than twelve months ago, I was part of a normal family life. I was a son and a brother, and then I was thrown into turmoil. I was no longer who I appeared to be. My mother was not my mother, my father was not my father and my sister was not my sister. So who am I?

'I came to England to find out and now I think I have discoverd who I am, or at least who my father is. My mother is still an enigma.'

Amelia leaned forward eagerly. 'You have found your father? Is this the man you have been visiting? Scott, the man you and my father went to meet?'

Ralph nodded. 'The same.'

Amelia waited for more revelations but when none came, asked tentatively, 'So – what are your feelings? Have you told him? Does he know he has a son?'

'I haven't told him.' Ralph stirred his coffee and gazed down at the swirling liquid. 'And whether he knows of my existence I couldn't say. But as for my feelings towards him, on the brief meetings I have had with him, I can honestly say that I don't like him. I would, I think, be ashamed to call him Father. It seems to me that the man has no soul. I believe that he has sold it to the Devil.'

Chapter Twenty-Three

Captain Linton escorted Elizabeth back to York that evening, but there was scarcely time for more than a greeting for he was anxious to get back to Holderness immediately, as the next day he was travelling to London on Navy business.

'Thank you so much for your kindness in bringing me home, Captain Linton, and please thank Mrs Linton again most sincerely, for her compassion when I was unwell.'

'Are you feeling better, Elizabeth?' Amelia asked. 'You don't look as peaky.'

'So much better,' Elizabeth said gratefully. 'I feel more relaxed in spirit as well as in health.'

'Goodbye, then, Amelia,' Harriet said. 'You have been such a tonic. Do come again to visit us.'

With promises that she would, Amelia joined her father, Ralph and Jack at the carriage, and waved goodbye to the two sisters as they stood by their door.

'How is your new position, Harriet?' Elizabeth

took off her hat whilst her sister put the kettle on the fire.

'I think it will do very well. Amy is a pleasant child, not given to tantrums, though she is not the brightest pupil I have taught.' She turned to Elizabeth. 'You look very well, the nervous strain appears to have gone from you.'

'Yes.' Elizabeth sat down in the chair. 'The Linton family have a way of putting one at ease.' She ran her fingers over her lips meditatively. 'Such an extraordinary thing, Harriet, and I couldn't tell you before when we were at Elmswell Manor, because I felt so unwell. But it was something which was said by Mrs Linton and Mrs Boyle which made me ill.'

'I cannot think that they were unkind or disparaging!' Harriet said in astonishment.

'No! No!' Elizabeth was quick to deny it. 'It was what was said about Mrs Linton's past – we didn't know, because Amelia had never remarked on it –'

'That her mother had been a convict!' Harriet finished for her. 'I know. Amelia discussed it with me. Oh, Elizabeth.' Harriet knelt by her sister's chair. 'Could we tell her of Mama? It would be such a relief to speak of it, and especially now that we know of Mr Hawkins too.'

'Mr Hawkins?' Elizabeth frowned. 'What of him?'

'You didn't hear? Well, Mrs Linton's brother and his wife are not Mr Hawkins's real parents, and they too were transported.'

'That must be Meg, of whom Mrs Linton spoke most affectionately,' Elizabeth said thoughtfully.

'Indeed. Amelia refers to her as Aunt Meg,' Harriet explained. 'But Mr Hawkins has come to England to look for his natural parents, or at least for his father, for his mother died. Please, Elizabeth,' she begged. 'May we speak of our own past troubles, even if only to Amelia and her mother? They would, I'm sure, be so understanding.'

Elizabeth nodded. 'You are right, Harriet. It was such a relief when I discovered that it wasn't only wicked people who were transported. Mrs Linton wasn't wicked, I'm convinced of that, she is far too gentle even to have bad thoughts.' Her lips trembled and her voice was choked as she whispered, 'Mama wasn't wicked either, even though they said that she was, even though *he* kept on telling us that she was. *Telling. Telling. Telling*,' she said fiercely and tears started to fall.

Harriet stroked her hand. 'Don't upset yourself, Elizabeth. He is the one who is wicked. We both know that, and one day he will answer for it.'

'I wish I could say that the matter was resolved, sir,' Ralph replied in answer to Philip Linton's question on how his enquiries were progressing. 'It seems most likely that Edward Scott is my father and I am not overjoyed by the revelation. But from what Henderson has said, and he opened up considerably – the poor fellow seems to have been burdened by Scott's dealings for many years – it would appear that Scott's wife was with child when she was transported.

'Everything fits,' he said morosely, 'the year, the trial. But what I don't understand is why Scott didn't plead for leniency.'

'You need to give yourself some time to think this through,' Philip Linton said, 'and of course you do not have to go any further with this. You may save yourself a great deal of pain by just leaving things as they are – '

'I can't, sir,' Ralph interrupted. 'I may open a cask of worms, but I must continue.'

Philip nodded. 'Very well. Then you must go back to York and look at the deposition. I believe that murder cases come under a special section, but you should be able to find written evidence from the witnesses, therefore Scott's evidence should be there also. But take time off,' he urged. 'See the countryside, help on the estate if you wish. There is nothing like physical work to take your mind off problems.'

'Thank you, sir,' Ralph was grateful. 'I think that perhaps I will do that.'

He was out early the next morning with Roger and Samuel to look over the estate, leaving Jack to be entertained by Amelia and her mother. Mrs Boyle and Phoebe were still away.

'May we ride out somewhere, Mrs Linton?' Jack asked. 'Or at least if you and Miss Amelia should care to ride I would walk.'

'I must decline, I'm afraid,' Emily Linton said regretfully. 'I have a meeting planned for today with some of our tenants. They come to lunch once a month and discuss various issues or problems, if they have any. But Amelia, you would enjoy that, I think? And one of the grooms could go with you and take a spare mount for you, Jack, in case you tire of walking.'

She smiled as she spoke, remembering his father Benne and knowing that if Jack was like his father then he wouldn't tire. Walking or running was part of the Aborigine tradition, born of long ago when they had been huntsmen, tracking for days in search of prey.

'Perhaps we could ride to Hedon and then follow the Haven down to Paull,' suggested Amelia, for whom the thought of a morning alone with Jack, apart from the groom, was already being anticipated with such pleasure and apprehension that she felt quite giddy.

'Ask Cook for a little cold chicken and a drink to take with you, Amelia. It is quite a long way, but you will enjoy it.' Her mother turned to Jack. 'You will see the ships en route for Spurn and although Paull is not the port it was, it is still an interesting place, and you may see the shrimpers there,' she added. 'You could buy some, Amelia,' her face brightened, 'and bring them home. I used to love the shrimps from Paull when I was a girl.'

'Mother spent her childhood by the river,' Amelia explained as they got under way. 'She becomes very nostalgic when she talks about the Humber. Uncle Sam taught her how to fish and to row a boat.'

'Mrs Linton is a very unusual lady, Miss Amelia.' Jack walked with a long stride alongside her horse. 'She appears to adapt to any circumstance in life.'

'Yes,' Amelia agreed. 'She does. She has had an unusual life. But,' she hesitated. 'Surely, you too have had to adapt to a different situation from the one which your father and grandfather had?'

'Different from theirs, yes,' he said. 'But I have known no other. From the time I was born, my life has been spent on a sheep station. My father and Ralph's father had agreed their partnership long before I was born. I am not a typical Aborigine.'

He looked up at her and she felt herself grow pink. 'I have a settled existence, I have wealth and there are very few of my race who can say that. Most are poor, many are in ill health and even those with some education are not accepted by the white race, any more than I am,' he added, and as she looked down at his dark eyes, she wondered if there was some kind of caution or hint in his words, that she should beware.

'But that does not appear to worry you,' she said lightly. 'If you have all that you want or need, you do not require society's good opinion?'

'I still have to live in the world, Miss Amelia. I still have to brush shoulders with my fellow man. I have white blood within me. I need the companionship of others.'

They travelled in silence for a while and then spoke of popular topics, and Amelia pointed out various landmarks and farms which were scattered intermittently in the empty undulating landscape. Eventually they reached the market town of Hedon. Amelia looked straight ahead as she saw shoppers and pedestrians turn to watch their progress. She heard the shouts of small boys to come and look at the black man, and old women stopped in their tracks to gape and point.

'How do you abide it?' she burst out as they took the grassy track by the muddy waters of the Haven which trickled towards the Humber. 'People are so rude to stare.'

He put his hand up to hers as she held the reins and she gave an involuntary start. 'It is nothing,' he said softly. 'Do not disturb yourself on my account.'

'Miss Linton!' Briggs called from behind where he had been following them. 'Allow me to go in front. It gets very wet along here. It's very low-lying.'

She paused to let Briggs go by and then asked Jack if he wouldn't like to ride the spare mount. 'Very well,' he smiled. 'I will, and then we can travel on an equal level and you won't have to look down on me.'

255

'I would never do that,' she said softly, and waited as he mounted. 'You are more than my equal.'

He turned to look at her. His eyes were deep and impenetrable and she felt her heart hammering so loud in her breast that she was sure he would hear it.

She followed behind Briggs on the narrow path and Jack followed behind her, and she was disturbingly conscious all the way that his eyes were riveted upon her, infiltrating into her secret self.

When they arrived in the village of Paull the wind was blowing gustily and Amelia gathered her riding cloak closer about her. They dismounted and Briggs asked if he might light a pipe of tobacco if they found a sheltered spot. Amelia suggested that he take the horses to the tavern yard and that he should have a glass of ale. 'Mr Mungo and I will walk by the river and then join you there. It is too cold after all to sit for a picnic.'

Jack gave a shiver as they walked by the bank. 'This is your summer,' he complained, offering his arm. 'How cold is it in winter?'

'Much colder than this.' She put her hand lightly on his arm. I feel quite reckless, she mused. I would not expect or desire this familiarity from an Englishman on so short an acquaintance. Goodness, am I conventional after all? And yet I cannot be, she further meditated, for I like the sensation of his arm next to mine. I do believe I am in the midst of a forbidden romance, and I thought that romance of any kind would never come to me.

There were ships on the river heading towards the open sea, and tugs and coggy boats, and Amelia realized that Jack had been talking as she had been inwardly defining her emotions.

'The harbour at Sydney is full of ships from all over the world,' he was saying. 'So many that they are uncountable, and yet less than one hundred years ago the Cove had only soft white sand and streams running down to it, with the bush beyond, and the only inhabitants were the Aborigines.'

They continued on round a slight bend in the path and Jack turned to her, slowing her footsteps. 'Can you imagine how those inhabitants must have felt when they saw those great ships and the strange white people on their shore?'

'No, I cannot. Except that I think they must have been fearful as well as curious.' He was close to her and she was very aware of his presence, of his strength, his high cheekbones, heavy eyebrows and full generous mouth which now smiled gently at her. 'They cannot have known what to expect,' she murmured, conscious of her bated breath, the pulse hammering in her ears and the melting of her bones.

He bent towards her and placed his lips on hers. They were warm and soft and fitted her own parted lips as if they were meant to. He drew his hands down her cheeks – his touch was gentle and she didn't draw away as she knew that she should.

'Forgive me,' he said softly. 'But I could not help myself. You remind me of a flower in bud about to open.'

It is true, she reflected. I have been awakened as if from a deep sleep. I have not been aware of myself or of what is around me. Suddenly her physical senses seemed heightened. The sky was brighter, the waters of the river glistened and she could smell the salt of the sea. The shrieking of gulls as they flew low over the river piped in her ears and the breeze caught and tangled her hair. Everything told her of an intoxication, the arousing of passion, hitherto unknown to her.

He kissed her again and then drew away. 'I should not have done that, Miss Amelia.' He took hold of her hand and stroked her fingers. 'I forgot that in England such a gesture would be misconstrued.'

She gazed at him. 'You mean', she said huskily, 'that a woman would consider it as a commitment of intent? Is it not so in Australia?'

'Perhaps with the English community,' he said softly. 'With my race we are more affectionate, more able to show our feelings without a sense of obligation.'

He continued to look intensely at her and she swallowed hard. Was he saying that the kiss meant nothing? Just an impetuous kiss, not a deep-felt desire?

'But you have English blood. Are your English feelings subdued when it comes to the matter of affection?'

'I am a man of appetite, Miss Amelia.' He touched a wisp of her hair. 'I can be reckless when I am in the presence of an alluring comely woman. I do not practise caution and then live with the regret that I missed the pleasure of treading on enchanted ground.'

She gave a sudden laugh at his extravagant words. 'You are bold, Mr Mungo! You have taken advantage of me. I should be running screaming for Briggs at your audacity.'

'No,' he said solemnly. 'If I had thought that you didn't want the kiss as much as I did, then I shouldn't have given it. But I knew that your desire was as strong as mine.'

She could not deny it, but she was confused. Did he bestow his kisses on all females who were attractive to him? 'I fear that you would not make a faithful husband,' she murmured.

'With the right wife, I would be, but there will be many considerations to be resolved before I take a wife.'

'And those are?'

He took her arm and they started to walk slowly back the way they had come. In the distance she could see Briggs sitting on a bench outside the inn.

'I must decide in which direction my life will take me. Is it with my native brothers or in the half-life between black and white?' He looked directly at her. 'If it is the latter then I shall need a strong determined woman to share that life, and all of its difficulties, with me.'

Chapter Twenty-Four

Amelia had promised Jack during their journey home from Paull that she would take him to the town of Hull. He had expressed an interest in seeing the docks after she had described the ships which came from all over Europe. 'The port will not compete with the harbour at Sydney, I don't suppose,' she said, 'there is no fine beach or white sand, but Hull is a busy town and even though the whaling trade has come to an end, the seagoing trade is second to none.'

She was not familiar with all the streets of Hull, but made several visits a year for shopping or the theatre and the whole family always went to the annual fair which came in October. Ralph had agreed that he too would like to visit the town and her sister May said that she would come as she wanted to buy some new ribbons for a hat she was making.

However, on the day before they had arranged to go, Jack went down with a heavy cold and took to his bed. He sent a message down with

Ralph the next morning insisting that they went without him as the carriage was free that day, not being needed for anyone else. May was in two minds whether or not to go; her prime object in the outing was to be seen with the handsome, exotic Aborigine and boast to her friends of him.

'Oh, do come, May,' Amelia persuaded. 'There are several things which Mama needs, and you said you needed ribbons and I might not choose the right colour.'

'But Cousin Ralph is not so interesting as Mr Mungo,' May whispered. 'Mr Mungo pays such compliments and Ralph does not, I don't think he even notices what I'm wearing.'

Amelia raised her eyebrows. 'And what compliments has Mr Mungo paid you?' she asked.

May simpered. 'Only the other day, he came in from the garden with a rose in his hand and presented it to me,' she said, 'I was just coming down the stairs as he came through the door and he bowed so charmingly and said, "Miss May, a rose for a rose".'

'Really!' said Amelia. 'How delightful! And now I suppose you wish to stay behind to mop his brow?'

May opened her mouth to reply, but Amelia butted in briskly, 'Well Mama won't allow it, silly girl, so you had better come with us.'

She too was disappointed that Jack couldn't come and although she didn't always choose to be in the company of her artless sister, neither was she enamoured of the idea of being alone with Ralph, who had been rather morose and lacking in conversation of late.

He apologized though, as they drove, for his lack of attention. 'I have much on my mind, cousin,' he said. 'This business of Scott tends to distract me from other concerns.'

Amelia inclined her head. 'I do understand,' she murmured. 'It must be difficult.'

'I doubt that you do understand,' he replied and she looked at him sharply: he had said that once before. Did he think that she was unsympathetic?

'I doubt if anyone could unless they had been in similar circumstances themselves.' He seemed oblivious to the effect his words had upon her. 'Your father has been a great source of strength to me in his advice as to procedure, but even he admits that it is not a predicament in which he would care to find himself.'

Amelia was stung to the quick. 'It does not necessarily follow that because someone hasn't experienced such an ordeal, their sympathies cannot be extended or their understanding is of no value!'

Ralph sighed. 'I'm sorry. You misunderstand me. I merely meant that unless someone has been through this situation themselves, they cannot possibly advise on what is the best to be done.'

'Indeed not,' Amelia said coldly. 'I would not under any circumstance choose to advise you, cousin. I'm quite sure you are perfectly capable of making any decision on your own.'

He gave her a questioning glance. His eyes were very blue, fringed by dark lashes although he was fair-haired. 'Yes,' he said evenly. 'I started this undertaking and now I must finish it one way or another.'

Amelia's mood was rather deflated after their conversation and she was short with May, who dithered over her purchases and professed no interest in looking at the ships in the dock.

'May!' Amelia said abruptly. 'Suppose Cousin Ralph and I go and look at the ships and you wait for us in the coffee shop? Will you be all right on your own?'

'Oh, look over there,' May interrupted. 'There's Clarissa and her mother, I'll go and have a word. Yes,' she called as she hurried across the street, bent on catching her friend. 'I'll see you at Fieldings coffee shop at two o'clock.'

Amelia turned to Ralph. 'I'm so sorry,' she began.

He gave a sudden laugh. 'We seem to be spending the morning apologizing to each other, Amelia. Suppose we start afresh? I will do my best to rid myself of this shadow hanging over me, at least for today.'

'And I will try to be more sociable,' she agreed, 'and show you the sights of this merry town.'

And so they became a little more comfortable

with each other and Amelia led him down Nelson Street towards Victoria Pier where passengers gathered to catch the ferry across to Lincolnshire. They stepped over the long coils of rope which ran down the streets near the ropery, then walked back across the narrow town streets to the Queen's Dock, once the largest dock in England, which was crowded with steamers and ships laden with timber and other goods for trade.

She showed him the Market Place and the Holy Trinity church and the handsome triple-domed building which housed the Dock Company, and he stood by the statue of Hull's famous son William Wilberforce, and was delighted to see a man on a velocipede riding over the Junction Bridge towards the busy street of Whitefriargate.

'How Jack would like one of those,' he laughed. 'I'd like to buy him one.'

'You and Jack get on well together, don't you?' Amelia said as they took their seats in the coffee shop.

'We've known each other all our lives. We're almost family.' Ralph ordered coffee for Amelia and himself. They were early and Amelia commented that May was nearly always late.

'And do Jack's family accept you?' she asked, 'in the same way as yours accept him?'

Ralph hesitated over the question. 'His parents and brothers and sister, yes. Not all of his extended family, and there are many of them. They see all white men as the same, usurpers of their land; and as the Aboriginals don't have the same rights as white men, they are naturally suspicious of us. They have no say in how their country is run. They are shot by farmers if they go onto land which they consider free, but is no longer; and they cannot go into some areas of Sydney, such as the parks, because they are forbidden.'

'It is difficult then for them to integrate,' she murmured.

He nodded. 'Jack's grandmother legally married an Englishman, but I understand that she was never accepted by the whites. Daisy, Jack's mother, had a better life, or at least a better education, but she too was barred from social activities.'

'And today?' It is only curiosity that makes me ask the question, she told herself. 'What if a white woman should want to marry an Aborigine?'

He looked at her in some surprise. 'I have never known of it, although Jack jokes that he will marry a white woman and have children by an Aboriginal woman to keep his race alive.'

He saw the shocked look upon her face. 'I do apologize,' he stammered. 'I have offended you. I forgot for a moment to whom I was speaking. At home, amongst friends we are used to speaking freely.'

She put her fingers to her flushed face. 'No. No, it is nothing.'

'But it is,' he said earnestly, 'and I am embarrassed by my behaviour. You must think me crass and ill-mannered and I apologize most profusely. I must remember whilst I am in England to think before I speak.'

Indeed you must, Cousin Ralph, she thought. You are far too outspoken. But she enquired, curiosity again getting the better of her, 'But he was only speaking in jest?'

Ralph shrugged, unwilling now after such a blunder to continue with the conversation. 'I know of no white woman who would risk losing everything: her social standing, her family. It would be a very lonely life.'

May came through the door at that moment, her arms overflowing with parcels, so saving them both from searching for another topic of conversation. 'I have bought a dress, Amelia, ready-made, in such a lovely shade of blue,' she said breathlessly. 'Do you think that Papa will think me extravagant?'

'It depends on how much you paid for it,' Amelia said wryly, 'and whether you have overspent your allowance.'

'Oh, I have,' she said anxiously. 'By quite a large amount. It is Clarissa's fault, she persuaded me that it suited me so well.'

Ralph smiled and commented, 'It seems to me that you will have to find a rich husband, May. I hope you have started looking already.'

Her eyes took on a dreamy gaze. 'Yes, indeed, and I think I have found him.'

Amelia sighed and shook her head at her sister and wondered who the beau was. Ralph ordered more coffee, sandwiches and cakes, and Amelia glanced out of the window at the thoroughfare outside. There was some kind of disturbance going on and a crowd was gathering. Idly she watched. A rather large man was haranguing a young girl who was sitting in a doorway. The man was drunk and he was shaking his fist at her. 'Damned Irish.' His words were muted through the glass but Amelia heard them well enough. 'Get yourself back to your bogs and pigs, 'stead of taking work from decent people.'

The young girl kept her head down towards her knees. She had a bunch of drooping daisies in one hand and with the other held fast to her thin shawl. Another man came by and pushed the drunk to one side, urging him away and the crowd moved on, uninterested if there wasn't going to be a scene. The girl put her head up when they had gone and got to her feet. It was Moira.

'Oh, excuse me.' Amelia rose to her feet. 'I've just seen someone I must speak to.'

She hurried out of the cafe and across the road, leaving Ralph and May staring after her. She called, 'Moira, Moira,' but the girl didn't hear her and scurried on. Amelia followed but then lost sight of her as she turned down an alleyway. Amelia stopped as she approached the dark opening. It looked forbidding and was littered with rubbish.

'Amelia!' Ralph came rushing up behind her. 'Is something wrong? You seemed in such a hurry.'

'It's a young girl I used to teach in York. I have been meaning to come and look for her. I thought I saw her on my last visit to Hull. I think she might have been begging.'

'Begging? Is she very poor then?' He peered down the alley. 'She must be if she lives in a place like this.'

'You think she might live down here? Surely not! I thought she was just running away from that horrible man.'

'I see no reason why else she would come to somewhere like this,' he said. 'Shall I go and look?'

'I'm not sure,' she hesitated. 'Would it be safe?'

'I've seen worse places,' he said grimly. 'But it should be all right in daylight.' He and Jack had once wandered into a rough part of Sydney by mistake and it was only their combined muscular strength that had saved them from robbery and a beating by the residents of the area.

'I'll come with you,' she said. 'You don't know her.'

'No,' he insisted, 'I'll go and look to see what kind of place it is, then I'll come back for you if it is safe.'

Oh dear, perhaps I shouldn't have been so impulsive. Amelia hesitated at the end of the alleyway and was jostled by passers-by. What if

Ralph is attacked? It will be my fault. I'll go after him, she decided, and set off down the narrow alley. It was dark and tunnel-like and as she turned a corner she almost bumped into Ralph, who was standing with his hands in his pockets staring at the scene before him.

'I was wrong.' He turned towards her. 'This is worse than I have seen in Sydney. How can the authorities let this happen?'

Amelia put her hand to her nose. The stench was appalling. The alley opened out into a small courtyard with dwellings all around it and a high wall at the end. Many of the windows in the houses were broken and studded with paper and rags to keep out the weather and the doorways were blocked by shattered doors or pieces of wood, though some were wide open to admit any stray dog, cat or vagrant.

Amelia stared down at her feet. Pools of stagnant water gathered over the broken paving and mosquitoes hovered above them. There were piles of rubbish scattered about and in the far corner a standpipe dripped constantly into an overflowing barrel.

There was no-one about, though Amelia felt that she was being watched and she could hear a child crying.

'Your little friend doesn't appear to be here,' Ralph commented, 'unless she's hiding.'

'She didn't see me so she wouldn't need to do that. But how odd that everything is so still.'

'They're suspicious of us, that's why,' Ralph said, 'but there are people here all right.'

They heard footsteps behind them and a man appeared. He was shabbily dressed, his jacket was worn around the elbows and his trousers were greasy and stained.

'You looking for somebody?' he barked. 'They'll not be in if you're after money.' He had an accounting book under his arm and a leather bag tied around his wrist. 'They're never in during 'day when they know debt collectors or rent men will be calling.'

He went and banged on several doors and shouted up the stairs but on getting no response turned back towards the alley and the street. 'What a job,' he muttered. 'Who'd do it?'

'Excuse me,' Amelia said. 'Do you know if there's an Irish family here by the name of Mahoney?'

'Not one of mine,' he said. 'But they're mostly Irish down here and a few Eyeties.'

'Eyeties?' she frowned. 'Who are they?'

He looked her up and down. 'Italians, miss, though God knows what they're doing in a dump like this. I shouldn't hang around if I was you,' he added, looking at Ralph. 'Not unless it's very important. It's not a place for tourists.'

'What's her name?' Ralph asked as the man disappeared back down the alley. 'Your little friend?'

'Moira,' she said. 'Moira Mahoney.'

He looked around the court and then walked to one of the doorways. 'Moira,' he called. 'Are you there?' Then he jumped backwards as a boot was aimed down the stairs followed by a torrent of foreign language.

'Well,' he said. 'Those are the Italians, so let's try next door.'

He shouted Moira's name again in the next doorway and a voice yelled from an upstairs window, 'You'll find her next door unless you're collecting and then they'll be out.'

He grinned and went to the next door, then turned to Amelia. 'Would you like to call her? She might respond to your voice.'

Amelia nodded and stepped gingerly around the rubbish to reach the door. 'Moira! Moira. Are you there? It's Miss Linton here.'

She stepped back and waited. Why am I here? What can I do?

The stairs creaked and over the broken banister she saw a gingery head peering down at her. 'Moira? Is that you?' she called again. 'It's all right. You're not in trouble. It's just that I saw you out in the street and wanted to speak to you.'

The girl came slowly down the stairs, stepping over the broken treads. 'Hello, miss. I didn't know you lived in Hull.'

'I don't,' she said. 'I'm only here on a visit.'

Moira stood before her. She looked thinner than Amelia remembered, her feet were bare as they had been in York and were caked with dirt.

Her skirt was in rags and over it she wore a large shirt, big enough for a man.

'You shouldn't be here, Miss Linton,' she muttered. 'Sure it's not a fit place for a lady like you.'

A voice called down the stairs. 'See if they'll lend you a shilling or two, Moira.' The voice was female and slurred.

'That's me mammy,' Moira said. 'Take no notice, she's had a drop or two.'

Amelia put her hand to her purse but Moira shook her head. 'No, it's all right, miss. We can manage fine.'

'Did your father find work, Moira?' Amelia remembered that that was the reason why the Mahoney family came to Hull.

The girl pinched her lips together before saying, 'Aye, miss, he did too. Down at the docks. And the first week he was there somebody started a fight wi' him 'cos of him being Irish. There were two of them, Miss Linton, and he ended up in the dock under one of the barges. By the time they fished him out it was too late.' She crossed herself. 'And that's why me mammy has taken to the drink. She says she'll never get back to Ireland now.'

Amelia thought of the big proud Irishman who had chastised her because he had thought she was teaching his children to forget their Irish roots, and she was sad at his loss. She hadn't met Moira's mother but she recalled Mr Mahoney saying that it was her idea that the

273

children should go to school. 'And what of Kieran and Eamon?' she asked. 'Where are they?'

'Kieran goes to look for work every day, Miss Linton, but Eamon is sick and has gone to the workhouse infirmary. I go to see him once a week but it's a long walk so it's too far for me mammy to go.'

'And does your brother find work?' Ralph spoke up. 'How old is he?'

'Eleven, sir. He earns a copper by running errands but not enough to pay the rent. I'm the breadwinner now.' She put her chin up proudly.

Amelia smiled at her. 'So did your reading and writing help you to find a job, Moira?'

Moira looked downcast. 'Well, not exactly miss, but I can speak good English, and not everybody knows that I'm Irish. They won't give to me if they know, you see.'

'Give to you?' said Amelia.

'No, miss. I'm a beggar girl, you see.'

Chapter Twenty-Five

Whatever am I to do? Amelia pondered as they drove home. I gave her all the change I had and I saw Cousin Ralph give her something, but that will surely only last a few days.

'You're worried about the girl, Amelia?' Ralph asked.

'I am,' she said softly. 'I hate to think of the family being destitute.'

'Can she not get work?' May asked. 'Selling flowers or something?'

'She's only a child!' Amelia declared. 'Lily's age. And there are so many people looking for work. Besides, who would employ her when she looks so – so – '

'Wretched! Dirty!' Ralph interrupted. 'She needs a bath and clean clothes.'

'I can get her some clothes easily enough, but how can these poor people keep clean? Their living conditions are indescribable, and the flies,' she shuddered. 'There is no wonder they become ill.'

Ralph nodded. 'And no wonder they turn to drink or opium. There cannot be much pleasure in their lives. I'm reminded of the Aborigines who have lost all hope and only wait to die.'

Amelia and May both stared at him. 'I'm sorry if I shock you,' he said. 'But it is so.'

If Moira could finish her education, Amelia considered as they rattled their way along the Holderness roads. Or at least be able to read and write passably, then perhaps, with help, she could find work when she is older and get out of that dreadful place. Perhaps – an idea took hold. Perhaps if I paid Elizabeth Fielding to teach her, and if – Amelia grew quite animated as it became clearer. If Moira could live in the little room under the Fieldings' roof, then she could help Elizabeth with the housework. I noticed that their daily maid no longer came in.

She beamed at Ralph and May. 'If I can persuade Moira to return to York, I think I may have a solution.'

'But what of her mother?' asked May. 'She wouldn't want to leave her mother by herself, would she?'

Oh, no! Of course she wouldn't. Amelia's hopes were dashed. And I'm forgetting, Moira is so young, her mother wouldn't let her go to live with strangers.

Mrs Boyle and Phoebe were due back the next day, their friends in Harrogate having arranged to return them in their carriage. 'We have enjoyed ourselves so much, Mrs Linton,' Mrs

Boyle said on arrival. 'Harrogate is a charming town and we took the waters, or at least I did and found them very beneficial, but Phoebe declined.'

'I couldn't bear the smell.' Phoebe wrinkled her nose. 'It was appalling.'

'But we were so pleased to come back here, Mrs Linton. The air is so good and we both agreed, Phoebe and I, that we feel very much at home at Elmswell Manor. But,' Mrs Boyle turned to her hostess with regret, 'we do not wish to outstay our welcome. You have been very kind and hospitable, but we must soon be on our way again.'

'Please don't think that you cannot stay longer,' Emily Linton assured her. 'You are very welcome indeed, and especially whilst Ralph and Mr Mungo are here. We are such a happy party.'

Mrs Boyle glanced at Phoebe, who gave her an imploring look and said, 'Please don't make me go back to Hampshire, Mama. I shall die of boredom.'

When the young people had gone for one last stroll in the gardens before dark, Mrs Boyle, in a sudden burst of confidence, said, 'Phoebe doesn't wish to go to my brother's house because his wife is planning balls and outings in order to find her a husband. In a moment of weakness I told my sister-in-law that that was what my husband said I must do.'

'Oh, but I thought that there was an understanding between your daughter and Ralph!'

Emily Linton expressed surprise. 'Am I mistaken?'

'I am afraid so.' Mrs Boyle shook her head in mild exasperation. 'It is Phoebe's fault. She led me to understand, some weeks before we left Australia, that they were fond of one another.' She sighed. 'But I rather feel that she may have misled me. But in any case,' she gave an even deeper sigh, 'her father would not allow it.'

'Because he is a convict's son?' Emily said quietly.

'Yes.' Mrs Boyle straightened her shoulders. 'Though I find it disagreeable to say so, I'm very much afraid that Captain Boyle has ideas even above his own station. Money and title is what he is looking for for our daughter, and a lady of distinction for our son. He will be disappointed, I fear.' She looked frankly at her hostess. 'I have said this to no-one else, Mrs Linton, but my husband is an upstart and anyone of rank or quality will recognize that.'

Emily Linton took in a quick astonished breath but Mrs Boyle continued. 'Of course, I too want the best for my children. Should Phoebe marry Ralph Hawkins she would want for nothing material, for the Hawkins are very wealthy. But she would have no status.'

'She would have love and kindness,' Emily murmured.

'I have no doubt that she would.' Mrs Boyle gave a sad smile. 'But that would not be considered important in my husband's eyes, he

278

knows nothing of such things.' She lowered her eyes. 'And as for Edwin; he is of age, he must make the best of his life.'

Jack was still confined to his bed and as Amelia walked in the garden with Phoebe and Ralph, she decided that she would write to the Fielding sisters after all and ask their opinion on the dilemma of Moira. She also decided to discuss the situation with Phoebe and Ralph.

'I shall visit Hull again in a day or two to try to resolve this business of Moira. I shall take her some clean clothes and some soap and one or two things from the kitchen, and try to talk to her mother.'

'You can't go alone Amelia,' Ralph asserted. 'That's out of the question.'

'But of course I can!' she said sharply. 'Now that I have seen the place, although it is very dirty it did not seem threatening. I shall be perfectly all right. I won't stay long,' she assured him.

'I'll come with you, if you like, Amelia,' Phoebe said lazily.

'No,' Ralph insisted. 'Neither of you must go, not unless someone is with you. Wait a day or two until Jack is well and we will both come.'

'No!' Amelia answered. 'It is very kind of you both to offer, but we will be a crowd and neither Moira nor her mother would be willing to speak to me in such circumstances. I shall go alone.'

'What an exasperating person you are, cousin,

when you won't listen to reason.' Ralph scowled. 'You will be taking your life in your hands!'

'What nonsense,' she said crossly. 'Of course I won't!'

'Excuse me!' Ralph, tight-lipped, gave a small bow. 'I must have a word with Jack before he goes to sleep.'

'Oh dear!' Phoebe gave a wry smile as Ralph left them and hurried back to the house. 'I'm afraid you have upset him.'

Amelia stared after him. 'Well, I can't help that. He must take me as he finds me.' Then she remembered her manners. 'Do forgive me, Phoebe. I had no wish to embroil you in this matter, but I do feel very strongly about it, I thought Ralph would understand that.'

Phoebe looked quizzically at her, then took her arm and turned her around so that they were walking back to the house. 'I'm quite sure that he does. He is concerned for your safety, that is all.'

'He is infuriating! Do you not find him so?'

Phoebe didn't answer, but gave a little chuckle.

'Oh,' Amelia remembered and was suddenly stricken with guilt, 'I'm sorry. Of course you do not! You are to be affianced, are you not? I do beg your pardon.'

'No, Amelia, we are not. We do not have an understanding, although Mama thinks that we do and perhaps Ralph thought so too.'

'How is that so?'

'Because I said so,' Phoebe said cheerfully and then shrugged. 'But I didn't mean it, it was merely a whim.'

'But if Ralph thinks – he will be upset when he discovers that you don't care for him.'

'But I do care for him,' Phoebe assured her. 'He is a splendid fellow. But I'm not going to marry him. I would make his life a misery. He is so well meaning that he would give me everything I wanted and I would become more and more selfish and he would end up hating me.'

Amelia frowned. Ralph a splendid fellow? Phoebe's opinion did not correspond with her own judgement. She has known him for so long that she does not see him as he really is, outspoken and arrogant!

'Amelia is the most infuriating woman I have ever come across.' Ralph stared down from Jack's window as Amelia and Phoebe walked back across the lawn. 'She will not take advice.'

Jack blew his nose vigorously. 'Really? And how could you be the considered judge of that when you never take it either?'

Ralph turned towards the bed where Jack lay propped up on pillows. 'I? I always listen to reason! When do I not?'

Jack didn't answer and Ralph continued. 'She is nothing like Phoebe who always listens and doesn't argue.'

Jack laughed and gave a husky cough. 'Phoebe *never* listens, although she pretends to, and she doesn't argue because she has already made up her mind or opinion.'

'How do you know that?' Ralph was puzzled as to how Jack could come to that conclusion.

'I just know, that's all.' Jack slithered further between the sheets. 'Phoebe knows what she wants.' He smiled. His eyes were shiny and Ralph thought that he looked feverish. 'And she will get it.'

Ralph turned to the window again and watched the two figures below. Amelia kept her head lowered but Phoebe looked up and gave him a wave. 'I don't think she wants me,' he murmured dismally. 'I thought she did, but I am having doubts. I think she will succumb to family pressure and marry title. Someone poor but noble, not a rich barbarian like me.'

'I keep telling you. She is not for you, my friend.' Jack's voice was low. 'Phoebe will settle for a lesser man than you.'

'There is no-one less than me, Jack.' Ralph's voice was barely audible. 'I have the stain of scandal and disgrace hanging over me. I have never before thought of myself as base-born but that is what I am. My mother had murderous inclinations and I believe my father – if father he is – to be a liar and a cheat. I have no proof of that but that is what I believe.'

Jack sat up in bed. 'Get up off your knees! I don't like what I hear,' he croaked. 'You are the same man you always were. The one I have always known.' He searched for his handkerchief beneath his pillow, and blew his nose again. 'When I am out of bed we will go to York once more and confront this man Scott. We will settle this matter once and for all.'

'Excuse me, Mrs Linton.' Ginny gazed round at the assembled company in the breakfast room. Mrs Linton, Mrs Boyle, Miss Boyle, Mr Hawkins, Miss May, Lily. Jack was having breakfast in bed and Roger was already out on the estate with Sam. 'May I ask who is accompanying Miss Linton?'

'Accompanying her where, Ginny?' Mrs Linton looked up with a smile. 'I assumed she had slept late.'

'No, ma'am. She apparently took the trap very early and told the stable lad she was driving into Hull. He was supposed to give me a message to give to you, to say she would be back later in the day. Only he forgot.' She folded her arms in front of her chest. 'He has been chastised, ma'am, you may be sure of that.'

'But why would she go into Hull on her own?' Emily Linton put a nervous hand to her throat. 'It's such a long lonely road.'

'Don't fret, Mrs Linton,' Ginny placated her though she herself looked anxious. 'She won't come to any harm on 'road. There'll be plenty of farmers and travellers driving in to 'market. But I don't understand why she's gone on her own when one of 'maids could have gone in with her.'

'I think I can explain, Aunt Emily.' Ralph

glanced at Phoebe who nodded in agreement. 'Amelia wanted to visit the young Irish girl, to take her some food and clothing. Phoebe – Miss Boyle and I offered to go with her, but she said she preferred to go alone.'

'But that is unthinkable! How very annoying of Amelia.' Mrs Linton rose from the table. 'Excuse me, Mrs Boyle. I must find Roger or one of the men to go after her.'

'I'll go, Aunt Emily. If I can borrow a mount I can be off in ten minutes. I know where she has gone,' Ralph added, 'and Roger doesn't.'

'Would you?' The strain eased on her face. 'I would be grateful. It is foolish of me, I know, but sometimes bad memories come back to haunt me.' She clasped her hands together. 'I wish Philip was here.'

Ralph took her hands in his and bent to kiss her cheek. 'Don't worry, Aunt Emily. Amelia will come to no harm. She is well able to take care of herself.'

It was a fine morning and except for his annoyance at Amelia for causing her mother distress, he enjoyed the ride into Hull. The hawthorn blossom was almost gone but the creamy, fuzzy heads of the elder scented the air and in the hedgerows, bees buzzed amongst the pale pink dog rose.

I could live here, he mused, gazing across the waving pale heads of corn. It is softer, more gentle than home, not so extreme, yet it has a sweeping remote landscape which soothes and pacifies, and indeed as he cantered along the road he felt more at peace with himself than he had for some time.

He left his mount with a stable lad at the Cross Keys inn. He had remembered the golden statue of King William just across from it, and so took his bearings from there to look for Amelia. It was then that he also remembered his mother, Meg, speaking of the Hull Market Place and he paused briefly to look as if through her eyes, so that he could tell her of it on his return.

She spoke of King Billy with such affection, he recalled, and had told him that she had often sat beneath his feet. He looked up at the gleaming edifice and a lump came to his throat. *What a hard life she must have led, and Da too,* he saw the Holderness countryside when he was a mere boy, *just as I did today as a man. I must tell them of what it means to me.*

He walked towards the Holy Trinity church and cut through the crush of market stalls which were gathered around it. He went across Trinity House Lane where the Marine School which had educated Captain Linton was situated, and towards the street of Whitefriargate where he stopped to ascertain his whereabouts.

Somewhere around here, he mused. *Do I turn left or right? Right,* he decided, and set off once more. He found the alleyway without any difficulty and was halfway down it when he heard the sound. At first he thought it was cats, but then realized that there was a child crying, several voices shouting and above it all a woman wailing.

He started to hurry and turned into the courtyard, his heart hammering for fear of what he might find. A group of women stood there, all poorly clad. All had shawls over their heads and most had small grey-faced children clinging to their skirts. One had a very young baby in her arms who was crying fretfully. They turned as one as he entered the courtyard and he felt their hostility.

'Be off with ye,' said one. 'We're in mourning here. The likes of ye are not welcome.' She had a strong Irish accent and she stared him defiantly in the face. He glanced at them in turn. Some, he thought, looked defeated, but others clenched their fists in a menacing manner.

'I'm not collecting or wanting money,' he said placatingly. 'I'm looking for someone who might be in trouble. A lady,' he said.

One of them guffawed. 'A lady! We're all ladies and we're all in trouble. In God's name have we ever known anything else?'

'She was looking for a girl called Moira,' he persisted and searched his memory for the girl's surname, but couldn't remember it. 'She's Irish, lives with her mother, up there.' He pointed to the upper floor of one of the dwellings.

'We all live up there, mister,' said the woman who had first spoken to him. 'Three families to a room, men, women and children all sharing. Sure, such luxury as ye'd never dream of.'

'There is a lady up there.' A woman, younger than the others, spoke quietly to him. 'She's talking to Moira's ma. She's just lost one of her bairns.' She looked up. 'That's her ye can hear keening. We've come out so's to give her some air.'

'Can I go up?'

'I supppose so.' She shrugged and looked at the other women, but they turned their backs on him.

He trod carefully up the stairs and wondered how many had fallen and broken their limbs, especially the women who carried children. He called as he reached the first landing but then heard the keening from the floor above. There was no air and a stink of stale food, urine, and unwashed bodies emanated from each doorway that he passed.

'Amelia!' He called again. 'Amelia!'

He heard chair legs scraping on a wooden floor and then the swish of skirts. Amelia appeared in a doorway. She took a deep breath when she saw him and put her hand to her forehead. Her face was pale and she looked quite distraught.

'Ralph!' she said thankfully. 'Oh, I am so pleased to see you! I don't know what is to be done for this poor woman. Her son is dead and she will not be pacified.'

He took her by the arm and they entered the room together. A woman was sitting on a chair in the middle of the room, rocking to and fro and making a high-pitched wailing sound. On the floor by her side sat the girl, Moira, and standing over near the broken window was a young boy.

'It's a keening for the dead,' Ralph whispered. 'I've heard it before with the Irish in Sydney. Only usually they do it over the body.'

Amelia looked up at him. 'She had word only this morning that her youngest son has just died in the workhouse infirmary,' she whispered back. 'Moira says she's crying because she can't go to see him. She can't walk far, she is very lame.'

Ralph glanced towards the woman and saw a stout stick lying beneath her chair. 'Where is the boy?' he asked. 'Can we take her to him?'

Amelia beckoned to Moira to ask her. 'He's still at the workhouse, miss,' she answered. 'Then they'll take him to the paupers' graveyard. That's bothering Mammy too, she wants him to have a proper burial with a priest there.'

'All right.' Ralph made up his mind. 'Tell your mother we'll hire a cab to take you all to see your brother. Then we'll see what is to be done about the burial.' He turned towards the door. 'I won't be long.'

He came back within ten minutes to say a hackney cab and driver was waiting out in the street and, in the meantime, Amelia had persuaded Mrs Mahoney to cease her crying. Moira then wiped her mother's face with a damp cloth and plaited her long sandy-coloured hair.

'Thank you, miss,' Mrs Mahoney whispered. 'Moira has always said how good you were to her and Kieran. Ah! And to Eamon too, God bless him.' She seemed more composed now that she was actually going to see her boy for the last time.

The workhouse was a new building far out of town on the road to Anlaby, and Amelia and Ralph followed in a separate hansom cab behind the one holding the Mahoneys. 'Thank you so much, Ralph,' Amelia said gratefully. 'I was beginning to despair of what to do. She wouldn't be comforted and I didn't like to leave them without doing anything.'

'It is only when you see things at first hand like this, that you realize what miserable lives some people have.' He sat silently for a moment, then said, 'I keep thinking of Ma. I always knew that she had had a hard life before she was transported, but I had no idea just how bad it must have been. She must have lived much as these people are living.'

Without thinking, Amelia placed her hand on his. 'Yes,' she said softly. 'But how strange that the worst thing to have happened to her, transportation, should be the way to her change in fortune.'

He nodded and closed his other hand over hers. 'Yes, meeting your mother and Da – well, fate must have taken a hand.'

She wanted to say she was sorry. Sorry for being so awkward on so many occasions and to thank him for coming, yet she couldn't bring herself to utter the words.

They followed the Mahoney family into the workhouse and Ralph made the necessary arrangements for the funeral service, paying the matron for the expenses and arranging for a priest to say a mass.

'We are finished here, Amelia,' he said. 'There is nothing more that we can do.'

'But should we not wait and escort them back?' she asked, 'and I should talk about Moira's future. That is why I came.'

'No.' He bowed to the matron, who bent her knee respectfully, and escorted Amelia out of the door. 'The cabby will wait to take them back. Now they must be allowed to grieve. They'll not wish to think of anything more at the moment. We'll go home, your mother is anxious about you.'

There! Amelia deliberated. He is always right! That is what is so annoying about him!

Chapter Twenty-Six

Jack had had dreams again during his fevered sleep. He had tossed, hot and sweaty beneath his bedclothes, and only gained ease when he dived into the cool deep freshwater lake. Down into the depths were large fish which swam past him, undisturbed by his presence. He tumbled and rolled beneath their glistening bodies, then in a swift spiralling surge he swept to the surface, breaking the water's sun-cloaked mantle like a waterspout.

High beyond the lake edge were long white hills fringed by brown plains, whilst in the sheltered sand dunes, camps had been set up for the summer; fires were burning along the eastern edge and the women, his own amongst them, were preparing and cooking the golden perch or cod which they had caught in the lake. He could see them constructing the ovens in the sand, digging out shallow holes and lining them with stones, heating them with their fire-sticks ready to place the fish in them and then covering with grass and hot stones, to cook.

He stood up on the water's edge, avoiding the nets which were laid to dry, and raised his hand to his woman. She stood up in acknowledgement of him and he smiled at her. She was small and gracile, a different race from his own whose bodies were robust and sturdy. She sat down again by the fire amidst a heap of mussels which she had collected and would bury in the sand for consuming on another day. She is a good woman, he thought, as he strode towards the hills, a skilled gatherer of food, a wise teacher to our children.

He looked down from his vantage point on the escarpment. The lake was drying. Soon there would be no more fish or shellfish. Soon they would have to escape to the far hills to hunt kangaroo and wombat. His woman would crush and grind grass seed for bread. A great wind was blowing, dispersing the sand from shore and filling the lake, making it into desert and dune. He clasped the firestick which was now in his hand and felt its heat. It was time once again to move on.

'I'll help out with haymaking before I go back to York,' Ralph said to Jack, 'and by then you should be feeling better.'

'I feel better already,' Jack insisted, though as he put his feet to the floor there was a distinct rocking movement which hadn't been there before.

'You were delirious when I looked in last time,' Ralph said. 'Mumbling on about fire and ice.'

Strange images swam into Jack's mind. 'It was the fever I expect,' he said huskily 'and I was thirsty, I'd knocked my water over. But I'll be ready to get up tomorrow.'

'Good.' Ralph rose from where he had been sitting on the edge of the bed. 'All the ladies will be glad to see you downstairs again.'

'Will they?'

'Every one of them. Mrs Boyle, Phoebe, Amelia, even young May. They've all been asking about you.'

Jack gave a weak grin. 'It's my charm, I expect.'

'I expect it is,' Ralph agreed. 'Regrettably I don't have it as you do. I don't notice what the ladies are wearing or if they have a new hair fashion. And Amelia is set against me for something or other. I don't think she was too pleased about me following her into Hull.' He shrugged. 'My intentions were good. I knew her mother was worried, but it seems I can't do right for doing wrong.'

The whole family turned out for haymaking, though Ralph's main reason for being there was to put off the time when he should go back to York and confront Scott. Amelia, her mother and Ginny packed hampers of food from the kitchen – meat pies, baked potatoes, apple pie and numerous jugs of ale and lemonade – and drove down to the fields in the traps to feed the hungry workers.

'I've never done this before.' Phoebe, on top of a haywain, wearing an old cotton dress of Amelia's and an even older sunbonnet, looked down at her blistered hands as she wielded a hay rake. 'Such fun!'

Roger rode across on his bay mare and heard her comment. 'Such fun!' he said. 'It is, Miss Boyle, when you can stop if you're tired. But come ten o'clock tonight when the men are still working and they know they have to be up at five to start again, then it isn't fun, just hard work.'

Amelia looked around. She loved this time of year: the rich smell of new-mown hay, the swish of the scythes, the darting of goldfinches, the rabbits scurrying for cover and the children romping and calling to each other as they tumbled in the newly cut hay. She saw Ralph with his trousers turned up and his shirtsleeves rolled back and a battered felt hat on the back of his head, his face turning brown with the sun and heat, and she smiled. He looked right in that setting, she thought. He looks a true country-man, whereas he is usually so dapper in his fashionable clothes.

He came across to her and she poured him a tankard of ale. He mopped his brow and took a deep quenching drink. His forehead was red where the sun had caught it. 'It's a pity Jack isn't here,' he said, 'he would enjoy this.'

'He'll come tomorrow. We decided that the

dust would go on his chest and start him wheezing again,' said Amelia. 'He wanted to come.'

'Jack's coming!' Phoebe called from her vantage point on the cart. 'He's riding up now.'

They turned and saw Jack sitting easily on a mount and riding towards them. 'I didn't want to miss seeing Miss Boyle pretending to be a country girl,' he joked. 'What would your friends say if they heard, Miss Boyle?'

She looked down at him. 'They would be astounded, Mr Mungo,' she said. 'But I would enjoy giving them something to gossip about.'

Amelia, glancing across at them both, caught a look of understanding between them and she looked again more pertinently. Has he, I wonder, been charming Phoebe in the way he charmed me? Has he stolen a kiss from her? And did she object if he has? A pang ran through her, not exactly of jealousy, but of pique, that she wasn't the only woman who had been admired by him.

'Oh, Mr Mungo, I'm so pleased that you are well again.' May ran across the field to greet him.

He bowed his head in greeting. 'I have missed your company, Miss May,' he said gallantly. 'My days have been dull without it.'

May blushed prettily and sighed and Amelia laughed. What a philanderer he was, yet she was sure there was no harm intended. She glanced at Phoebe again and she had a wry amused look upon her face.

'Don't listen to him, Cousin May,' Ralph called across to her. 'He'll break your heart into little pieces and then leave you.'

May blushed even deeper and hung her head and Jack dismounted. 'I will not break your heart, Miss May,' he murmured to her. 'I am merely making it tender, ready for some young gentleman to desire.'

Amelia, catching his whispered words, felt a sudden understanding and a warm indulgence towards him.

Jack rode back to the house and Phoebe, tired now with the heat and her blistered hands sore, drove back with Mrs Linton and Ginny, and Amelia moved from group to group of workers with a basket over her arm offering food and refreshment. Her uncle Sam, and Roger had both discarded their cotton shirts and were scything at the bottom of the meadow. She walked down to them and after offering them drinks, she turned back and saw that Ralph too was pulling his wet shirt over his head. He was broader-chested than she would have imagined and his skin was brown in spite of him being so fair-haired.

'It's very hot, isn't it?' she said, avoiding looking at him directly. 'Although perhaps you don't find it so?'

'This is nothing compared with the heat at home. There I couldn't take off my shirt until the evening or I would scorch, and then Jack and I would swim in the creek.'

'It will be warmer still at harvest time,' she said. 'Will you still be here?'

He looked frankly and intently at her. 'Would you like me to be?'

The question caught her off guard and she was momentarily confused. 'I – I only meant, that is, I'm sure that Uncle Sam and Roger would be pleased if you were. They are always glad of extra help,' she added lamely.

'That isn't what I asked.' He continued to gaze at her. 'I said, would you like me to be?'

She felt a prickle of vexation. Why was he always so direct? But she bowed her head pleasantly enough and said yes of course, they would all, including herself, be glad if he would stay.

Jack was over his cold in just a few days and Ralph decided to go back to York. 'I want to come face to face with Edward Scott,' Ralph explained to Amelia and her parents, 'and ask him point-blank if he was my mother's husband and is he indeed my father.' He wanted to add, and to ask him, or was I the bastard child of another man? for that thought had crossed his mind. But he didn't want to upset the sensibilities of his aunt or Amelia by uttering such a statement, and he pondered whether that could have been the reason why Scott wouldn't speak for his wife at the trial.

'Perhaps if you have the time, you would call on the Misses Fielding and give them our regards?' Amelia asked, 'and do say that we trust that they are both in good health.'

What *she* didn't say was that she had written to Elizabeth Fielding and told her of the plight of the Mahoney family and of the death of the boy Eamon, and put forward her suggestion that Moira should go to stay with her.

Ralph and Jack booked in at an inn in York and Ralph hired a horse for the next day. 'I'll go alone to meet Scott,' he said, 'and give you the news on my return in the evening.'

Jack nodded. 'And I will acquaint myself with the antiquities of this city and learn of your ancestry, though the period is short compared with mine, a mere two thousand or so years.'

Ralph gave him a friendly shove on the shoulder. He knew that Jack was humouring him, trying to put him in a lighter frame of mind before he faced the ultimate change in his life.

He rode once more up the short drive of Scott's house, tied up the reins again and rang the bell on the front door. The maid, a different one from before, bade him wait whilst she asked if Mr Scott was at home. 'Tell him – advise Mr Scott I have something important to discuss with him,' he murmured. 'Most important.'

She came back to say that Mr Scott would see him if he would kindly come through. Scott was sitting at his desk as he had been the last time and he raised his head as Ralph entered, although he didn't get up from his chair.

'So, Hawkins, you return. Have you thought more on the confectionery business?'

'No. Not a great deal,' Ralph answered firmly. 'But I have other business to discuss with you if you will permit me. Business which concerns us both.'

Scott rose slowly from his chair. He had an unlit cigar in his hand and he rolled it gently between his fingertips. 'Really?' he said 'What kind of business?'

Ralph took a deep breath. His mouth was dry and he wished with all his heart that it hadn't come to this. 'I have reason to believe, sir, that you are my father.'

Chapter Twenty-Seven

Scott lowered himself gradually into his chair, then tapped the cigar several times on the desk. He laid it down and said, 'Sit down, Hawkins, and tell me why you should think such a thing.'

Ralph pulled up a chair and sat down. He cleared his throat. 'I have researched into my mother's past. Her name was Rose Elizabeth Scott, and I know that she was sent for trial at York County Court on a charge of attempted murder of her husband, Edward Scott.' He paused. 'The same name as yours, sir. It is not an unusual name, I know, but my enquiries have led me to discover that my mother was in the confectionery trade before her marriage and so, of course, were you.'

Scott stared at Ralph and slowly nodded his head. 'It is true,' he said, 'that my wife did attempt to murder me and was transported for the offence. It is an episode that I prefer to forget.'

He looked down at his desk and pursed his

lips and Ralph had an intuitive feeling that he was working out his next move, as if he was playing a game of chess. 'What is rather strange, however,' Scott continued, 'is that I didn't know that she was expecting a child. Rather odd that she wouldn't have told her husband, don't you think?'

'Ah!' So perhaps I was another man's child, Ralph considered. I think I would prefer it if it was so. Yet he remembered that Henderson, the accountant, had said that Mrs Scott was with child when she was transported. If he knew, then Scott must have known too.

'But I am not saying it is not possible,' Scott went on. 'Have you not managed to track down any other living relatives?'

'No, sir, there is no-one else.' As he said it, some information, vague and shadowy, slipped into his mind. But so indeterminate he couldn't recall its substance.

'I see! Well, shall we work out some dates, the trial, the voyage, your birth?' Suddenly Scott was extremely affable and giving Ralph a broad smile, got up, and leaning across the desk, put out his hand. 'I would be delighted to think that I had a son after all these years.'

He's lying, Ralph thought. He must have known. But if I am not another man's child, what was the reason for the offence? 'Why did your wife attempt to kill you?'

Scott looked sorrowful. 'I'm not sure if you will want to know this, if in fact your mother and my wife are the same person, and it is looking extremely likely. But,' he shook his head despairingly, 'I had a terrible life with her. She was, I'm sorry to say, a very wicked woman.'

Ralph stood up and started to pace. 'But she surely must have had some cause to commit such an act? A quarrel perhaps?'

'Of course you wouldn't wish to believe that your mother was wicked! But, a quarrel, yes. She was an extremely quarrelsome woman. Wanted everything her own way. Wouldn't take no for an answer.'

Henderson had said that there was violence within the marriage, Ralph remembered. 'And – and did you ever strike her?' he asked.

Scott looked shocked. 'Strike a woman? Never!'

'But there must have been a reason – '

'Why she picked up a knife?'

'A knife? I didn't know the weapon, sir.'

'A paperknife. It was lying here on the desk. Look,' Scott brought from beneath a sheaf of papers a slender silver knife. 'This very one.'

He kept it! Ralph thought. I would have wanted rid of it. He stared down at the implement. The handle was shiny but the blade was dull and rounded. 'Were you badly injured?'

'It was not the injury,' Scott said in an aggrieved voice, 'but the intent. But yes, I have a scar on my neck to this day.'

'Were you not told that she had died on the voyage?'

'Yes, I was notified,' he said briefly. 'I suppose she caught some disease? Those convict ships must have been breeding grounds for every kind of illness.'

Ralph fixed him with a look. 'She jumped overboard. She didn't die of illness, she killed herself!' He felt a sudden deep pain of sorrow for his mother, that she had been married to this heartless man. 'Her life must have proved unbearable at the end.'

Scott was silent for a moment, then he muttered, 'Yes. It must have been.' He returned Ralph's stare. 'Let's trust she repented of her sins.'

'Good afternoon, Mr Mungo. How very nice to see you!'

Jack turned at the sound of the voice. 'Miss Fielding!' He touched his hat and bowed. 'This is an unexpected pleasure.'

Elizabeth Fielding flushed shyly. 'Are you alone in York? Is Mr Hawkins not with you? Or Miss Linton?'

'Regrettably Miss Linton is not in York, and Mr Hawkins is on business elsewhere, but he will be joining me later in the day. I have been enjoying the delights of this most unusual city.'

'Would you – ' Elizabeth hesitated and then decided to be bold. 'Would you and Mr Hawkins care to have supper with us this evening? A gentleman friend of Harriet's and his father will be joining us.' She indicated her basket. 'I have just been buying provisions – only a simple supper,' she added. 'Nothing elaborate, I'm afraid.'

'So very kind,' he murmured. 'I would be delighted and I am quite sure that Mr Hawkins will be too. You must allow me to buy wine for the occasion.'

'Oh,' she demurred. 'There is really no need. Harriet and I rarely take wine and Mr Thacker and his son only occasionally.'

'I have given up grape and grain completely, Miss Fielding, but perhaps on this occasion you could be persuaded?' He smiled as he spoke and she agreed that perhaps just this once she could be coaxed into having just one glass of wine.

After a few more pleasantries, they said fare-well and Jack went off to make some small purchases. Thacker, he deliberated as he bought flowers, I have heard that name recently.

He bought chocolates too and cigars for the gentlemen, though he himself did not smoke, and then went back to the inn to await Ralph's return. He heard the sound of his footsteps on the stairs and opened the door of his room to greet him.

Ralph came in and threw his hat onto Jack's bed and, sitting down on a chair by the fire, put his head in his hands. Jack took the other chair. 'So! He is your father?' he said quietly.

Ralph gave a huge sigh. 'Yes. There is no doubt about it. Everything fits, although he says that he didn't know that his wife was expecting a child.'

'He's lying,' Jack murmured. 'Henderson said that she was.'

'He did, didn't he?' Ralph looked up; his face was pale and drawn. 'I thought that was what he'd said. But why would Scott lie?'

'It wouldn't look very good, would it, admitting that your wife was carrying your child when she was about to undertake a life sentence?'

'I wish that I had never started this,' Ralph muttered. 'No good will come of it.'

'You don't know that,' Jack replied. 'You can't see into the future, you can only see what has gone before. There may be great advantages before you. Be patient.'

'You're such an old sage, Jack,' Ralph grumbled. 'But you are usually right.' He got up and stretched. 'I'm going to my room to get changed and shake off the aura of Scott from me, then we'll go out and have a slap-up meal, shall we? To celebrate my good fortune in finding my father,' he added cynically. 'He wanted me to stay for supper, but I made the excuse I had arranged to meet friends.'

'Which is what we are to do,' Jack interrupted. 'We have been invited to sup with the Miss Fieldings and their guests.'

'Oh! Have we?' Ralph was slightly chastened. 'I'm not sure I shall be very good company for those delightful ladies.'

'Well, I will charm them with my wit and you

can make polite conversation with their friends, the Thackers.'

'The Thackers? Man and wife?'

'Father and son.'

'We had better buy wine and flowers then, oh and cigars. I do believe the ladies are in straitened circumstances.'

'No sooner thought than done, brother,' Jack laughed. 'We are of the same mind.'

'Elizabeth! Are you sure the food will stretch to six?' Harriet was in a tizzy when Elizabeth told her of their two extra guests.

'I hope so. I felt it only polite that I invite them. After all, the Lintons were so very kind to us in inviting us to their home, and Mr Hawkins and Mr Mungo were very pleasant towards us even though we did not have a great deal of conversation with them.'

'Of course. You are quite right and it will not be at all improper if Mr Thacker and Thomas are here to dine also.'

'Quite so,' Elizabeth answered. 'Although I am such an old maid now that I fear my days of being improper are almost over.'

Harriet sighed. 'And mine too, dear Elizabeth. I think that Thomas and I are doomed to grow old in single companionship only.'

Elizabeth chopped the rabbit she had purchased and divided it up into portions. She poured over it the last of the sherry which Mr Thacker had brought at Christmas, and then chopped several onions, a bunch of parsley and a potato and put it all in a pie dish and into the oven whilst she prepared the pastry to go over the top.

Harriet scrubbed potatoes and whilst they were boiling, she shelled new peas and set the table in the parlour. It was not dark but she lit a candle on the table and the lamp on the dresser, then put another log on the fire. 'There,' she said. 'See how cosy it looks. No-one would guess how very poor we are, Elizabeth.'

'How very cosy,' Ralph said as he was shown into the parlour. 'And can I smell rabbit pie?'

'You can, Mr Hawkins,' Elizabeth said. 'It is a favourite of ours.'

'And mine too,' he said. 'My mother makes it very often. Now you have made me feel quite homesick, Miss Fielding!'

'Oh, I am so sorry,' she began, but then on realizing he was teasing, said, 'but you must be enjoying your stay with the Lintons? I have recently written to Miss Linton. They are such a delightful family, so very hospitable.'

They were interrupted by the doorbell and introductions were made as Thomas Thacker and his father James came into the parlour. They were seated immediately as the room was too small for them to stand around, and Ralph asked if he might be allowed to pour a glass of wine for everyone.

'And are you in a profession, Mr Thacker?'

Ralph addressed the younger man as he gave him a glass of wine.

'Trade, Mr Hawkins. I am a clerk in a confectionery company. A lowly position, I'm afraid.'

'Were you in a similar occupation, sir?' Ralph now addressed Mr James Thacker. 'The confectionery business in York appears to flourish.'

'Indeed I was, I had a prominent position with one of the larger manufacturers, but alas, ill health forced me to retire early.'

Ralph heard Jack draw in a short sharp breath and turned his head slightly. Jack's eyes flickered from Mr Thacker to himself and back again, but he didn't understand the meaning of the intense glance.

Elizabeth brought in the pie and Harriet the vegetables, and they all exclaimed appreciatively at the aroma and the golden crust of the pie, and when their hostesses were seated, began to eat.

'Do you find York interesting, Mr Mungo?' James Thacker asked. 'It will be quite different from your native land, although I do believe that your culture must go back much further than ours?'

'I am surprised and pleased to hear you acknowledge that, sir,' Jack replied. 'So many people do not consider that the Aborigines have any culture at all, whereas in fact it is very ancient.'

'Ah, well, since my retirement I have much time on my hands, and I make it my business to read as much literature as possible in order to keep my mind from stagnating.' He put down his knife and fork. 'I have read of the advancements of the New World, but it seems to me that as the native Australian was already on that continent when the white man arrived, he must have been there for some considerable time. But how he got there I couldn't begin to imagine. One day, I am sure, there will be studies done.'

'What brought on your interest in Australia, sir?' Ralph asked. 'Politically it has always been controversial.'

'Indeed it has.' James Thacker glanced across at Elizabeth. 'But a very dear friend of mine journeyed there many years ago and I was curious to know what kind of country it was.'

'And in what part of the country did he settle?' Ralph asked. 'Sydney? Melbourne?'

'Regretfully I do not know. We lost touch unfortunately.' He picked up his knife and fork again and, turning the conversation, asked Ralph, 'And is your interest in York in a tourist capacity, Mr Hawkins? Or are you on business here?'

'Neither of those things, sir.' Ralph felt a deep depression coming over him as he realized that he now had a commitment to Scott. 'I came here to look for family connections.'

'Oh, how very interesting.' James Thacker popped a piece of rabbit into his mouth and chewed thoughtfully. 'I take it then that your family were immigrants. Were they from York?'

There was a sudden hush around the table. Both Harriet and Elizabeth stopped eating and looked at Ralph expectantly, and Jack waited, his breath tight in his throat, for Ralph to impart the tidings of his past to James Thacker. What Ralph had to say would, Jack was convinced, prove without doubt that Scott was Ralph's father.

'Excellent pie, my dear Elizabeth,' Thomas interrupted enthusiastically. 'The best I have ever tasted.'

'Thank you, Thomas.' Elizabeth smiled at him, then turned her attention back to Ralph. 'I understand, Mr Hawkins,' she said, 'that you think your father was a York man?'

Ralph nodded. His appetite seemed to have vanished and he pushed a piece of piecrust around his plate. 'That's right, and now I have found him and today I have advised him of my existence.'

Thomas looked up. 'You mean he didn't know? How is that?'

'He claims that he didn't know that his wife, my mother, was expecting a child.'

'How very odd,' Thomas exclaimed.

'Indeed, very odd, though there could be some truth in it. You see, my mother was transported to Australia as a convict. Perhaps she didn't tell him, though it seems unlikely.'

There was a sudden clatter as Mr Thacker's knife slipped from his hand.

'I say Pa, are you all right?' There was concern

in Thomas's voice as he saw his father's ashen face.

James Thacker clutched his chest. 'May I have some water?' he croaked.

'A little red wine, sir.' Jack was on his feet in an instant, proffering the glass to the old gentleman's lips.

'Thank you, thank you. I am all right,' but he trembled and Elizabeth insisted that he should sit in a more comfortable chair. A footstool was brought for his feet and he was adamant that everyone should continue with their supper, whilst he sat silent and meditative in the chair.

After they had finished, Harriet made coffee and Jack brought out the chocolates, then they pushed back the table and sat around the fire.

James Thacker heaved a deep sigh and clasped his hands together. 'Mr Hawkins. You may think me very impertinent, but may I question you? Not out of idle curiosity, but out of real concern.'

Ralph inclined his head to imply that he continue. 'Please do, sir,' he said. 'I cannot think that a gentleman of respectability such as yourself could ever be impertinent.'

'Be assured,' replied Mr Thacker, 'that on only our short acquaintanceship, I have your best interests at heart.'

He heaved another sigh and rubbed his chest. 'I am afraid that tonight such grievous memories have returned to me. Memories that have remained hidden for so many years. Your mother, Mr Hawkins. Is she in good health?'

Ralph started to smile. His mother, Meg, was always in good health. Then he hesitated, something disturbing his thoughts. 'My adoptive mother is in very good health, Mr Thacker. She and my da, they have a sheep farm above the hills of Sydney.'

He saw Jack shake his head. *Thacker! That's the name that Henderson mentioned!* 'But – my natural mother is dead. Sir,' he said quietly, 'did you know her?'

James Thacker put a trembling hand to his mouth. 'I believe that perhaps I did. And your father's name? The man you have just discovered?'

'Scott, sir. Edward Scott.'

Chapter Twenty-Eight

Elizabeth Fielding gave an anguished cry, half rising from her chair and then sinking back again, whilst Harriet rushed to her sister's side, to sit on the chair arm and clutch her by the shoulder. 'What does it mean?' Elizabeth's voice was full of fear. 'What does it mean?'

Ralph looked from the sisters to James Thacker and then to Jack, who appeared as puzzled as he himself felt.

James Thacker eased himself from his chair and stood up. He looked down at the sisters and said gently, 'It means, my dear Elizabeth, my dear Harriet, that you have a brother returned to you.'

He turned to Ralph who now was also standing, and offered his hand. 'Young man,' he said. 'This is probably as astounding to you as it is to these young ladies, but I for one am delighted to meet you at long last. It has been my heart's wish that you survived.' His voice was choked as he went on, 'I am only so sorry, so very sorry that your mother – and the mother of these dear ladies is no longer with us.'

'I don't understand—' Ralph began, but stopped as Elizabeth began to mourn and weep, rocking into herself.

'Mama,' she cried. 'Mama! Don't say that you have left me after all.'

Ralph turned to Jack. 'Henderson!' he said, and Jack nodded. Henderson had said that there had been other children to consider. Why had he not thought to question him?

Harriet tried to comfort her sister but she too wept and her lips trembled as she glanced across at Ralph. 'Please forgive us, Mr Hawkins,' she said. 'This is too much of a shock and I don't completely understand what has happened. I – we didn't know that our mother was expecting a child when she went away from us.'

Ralph went across to them and bent over Elizabeth. 'Elizabeth,' he said softly. 'I didn't know that I had any sisters. I came to England to search out relatives and thought that I had found only my father. He didn't tell me that he had daughters.'

'No!' Elizabeth cried out. 'Edward Scott is not our father! Our father, John Fielding, was a good kind man. Edward Scott is wicked. He was cruel to our mother and unkind to us. He told us that our mother had brought disgrace on us and was being sent away as a punishment, and that we as her daughters would never hold up our heads again. He said that he would divorce her and that she would live out her life in chains in a foreign land.'

She started to sob. 'All of my life I have waited for just one word from her to say that she was alive and well.'

'Did Scott not tell you that she had died on the voyage?' Ralph could not believe that Scott could keep this information from them.

Elizabeth lifted bloodshot eyes towards him. 'On the voyage?' she whispered, and he heard an exclamation from Mr Thacker behind him.

He looked at her tearstained face and decided that a small lie would suffice in this instance. Only Philip and Emily Linton in this country knew what had really happened, and they would not tell, he was sure of it. Then he remembered that he had told Scott the truth about his mother's death. He took a deep breath. He would deal with Edward Scott.

'Our mother,' he said, taking her hand and then also Harriet's. 'Our mother was not in chains when she died. She died a few days after giving birth to me. I know the surgeon who was with her,' he nodded. 'I am named after him. I know that she was well looked after at the end.'

In time, he thought, I can tell them more. But not yet. Not yet. He smiled. 'This is such a lucky day for me, to discover that I have two more sisters.'

'Two more, Mr Hawkins?' said Harriet, wiping away a tear.

'I have a sister, Peggy, in Australia,' he said. 'Born to my adoptive mother. She will be so pleased to know about you. And I think, Harriet, that perhaps you should call me Ralph.'

The hour was getting late and it was apparent that they should make their departures. Elizabeth was very fatigued and could hardly rise from her chair. 'Will she be all right?' Ralph asked Harriet in a low voice. 'This news has been too much for her.'

Harriet appeared anxious too, so he assured her that he would call round the following morning. He bowed to Elizabeth and then kissed her hand. 'Goodnight, Elizabeth,' he said. 'Have no fear of me. I will not impose myself upon you if you do not desire it.'

She gave him a slight curtsey but made no reply. She was very pale and held tightly to Harriet's arm.

'Goodnight, Harriet.' He kissed her hand too and was rewarded with a smile.

'Goodnight, Ralph, I look forward to talking to you tomorrow.'

The four men walked towards Sampson's Square and Ralph asked James Thacker if he and his son could be prevailed upon to go with himself and Jack to the inn where they were staying, so that they might further discuss the issue.

'I am very tired,' the older man replied,

'but it is perhaps necessary that we fit the missing pieces of jigsaw together to make the whole.'

Ralph assured him that he would order a cab to take them home when their discussion was over and so it was agreed.

'Mrs Fielding, as I knew her,' Mr Thacker cradled a brandy in his hands as they sat in a small private room at the inn, 'was a caring woman who nursed her husband when he was dying and was always a loving mother to her young daughters. Scott, of course, married her for the successful business which she bought with the annuity her late husband left her.'

He shook his head. 'I saw her only infrequently after she married Scott, he didn't encourage her to have friendships and certainly not with another man. But I knew, whenever I did see her, that she was desperately unhappy. I called one day at the shop which she had owned, and found her serving behind the counter, like an ordinary shop girl, which she certainly wasn't! She told me that Scott would no longer let her make decisions about the business and that he had taken it entirely out of her hands.'

'Was he unkind to her as Elizabeth said?' Ralph asked.

'I think he was,' he said regretfully. 'But there was nothing I could do. She was a married woman under her husband's domination.' He sighed. 'If only – you see, Hawkins – ' He looked up at Ralph. 'Should I call you Scott?'

'Certainly not,' Ralph answered firmly. 'I have no intention of changing my name.'

'Quite right,' said James Thacker. His son Thomas sat silently in his chair, listening to their conversation. 'You see, Hawkins, if only I had been braver, and richer, none of this would have happened. I cared for Rose Fielding, but I was a widower with a young son to bring up and I could only offer my esteem, which seemed very little at the time. I realized later that she did have me in high regard, for she wrote to me when she was in prison, saying that there was no-one else she could trust. She was fearful for the child she was carrying, which Scott did know of, no matter that he denies it, and she asked me if I would watch over her daughters and make sure that they came to no harm.

'Regretfully, by the time the trial was over, Scott had whisked them away to boarding school and wouldn't tell me where they had gone. He married again,' his voice dropped, 'which is why I always suspected that Rose was dead – he wouldn't have gone through the messy business of divorce. His second wife was also a widow with property and when she died he was even richer than before.'

'And his third wife?' Ralph asked. 'I understand that she died also.'

James Thacker nodded, 'I know nothing of that marriage, I can only draw conclusions.'

After the Thackers had gone, Ralph and Jack

sat talking far into the night. 'I must look after Elizabeth and Harriet, Jack,' Ralph said. 'They deserve some comfort after all they have been through.'

'They need more than money,' Jack said swiftly. 'They need you as family.'

'I didn't mean just to give them money. I will be a brother to them if that is what they want. But at the moment I am a stranger to them, I can't push myself into their lives. We must learn to know each other first. Harriet, I think, will be easy to care for, she has a friendly outgoing nature. But Elizabeth.' He stopped and pondered. 'She has been badly hurt by what has happened, and I don't think that having a brother arrive on her doorstep is going to salve that hurt.'

Jack stood up. 'I'm going to bed,' he said. 'You should do the same. Tomorrow there will be decisions to be made.'

Ralph nodded absent-mindedly. 'Yes. Good-night. I'll see you in the morning.'

Decisions, he thought. And ways to deal with Scott! But the more pressing need was Elizabeth. He was worried for her. She had been very distressed. It is not proper for me to make suggestions, she is a woman and she barely knows me. Amelia, he thought, and Aunt Emily. They will know what to do.

He rose from his chair and went upstairs and tapped softly on Jack's door. 'Jack,' he said, when the door was opened. 'Will you ride to Holderness and fetch Amelia or Aunt Emily?'

'Now?' Jack was astonished. 'It's half past two in the morning!'

'Oh!' Ralph consulted his pocket watch. 'So it is! Well, first thing in the morning then?'

Chapter Twenty-Nine

'Mama! May I go to Hull?' Amelia had Elizabeth Fielding's letter in her hand. 'I have received a letter from Miss Fielding and she is willing to take Moira Mahoney to live with them. I'll ask Ginny or one of the maids to go with me if you agree.' She knew better than to attempt to go alone again.

'Very well,' her mother smiled. 'Ask Ginny, she might enjoy a day out looking at the shops.'

Ginny grumbled at her as Amelia expected she would, but agreed to go the following morning. It was a fine day and Ginny brightened up considerably as the carriage neared Hull. 'I was born in Hull, you know,' she chatted, 'and worked in service here. That's how I came to know your mother. She was so beautiful, and so gentle. Still is,' she added.

'I know,' Amelia nodded. 'Did you know Ralph's mother? Aunt Meg, I mean, who adopted him; she was from Hull.'

'I didn't know her though I saw her once.'

Ginny gave a slight smile. 'We moved in different circles. I was very much mistaken about her. It just goes to show', she said, 'that you should never make rash judgements about people or their circumstances.'

They decided that they would visit the Mahoneys before shopping and Amelia led the way down the alley towards the court. 'God in heaven!' Ginny muttered. 'Do people still live down here? I thought it had been condemned years ago.'

'Irish and Italian people live here,' Amelia commented. 'It seems that no-one cares about their well-being.'

She knocked on the broken door of the house where she had previously been, and called up the stairs. A faint voice answered her but she could not make out the reply. 'We'll have to go up, Ginny,' she said. 'It's not very pleasant, I'm afraid.'

They clambered up the worn treads and through the open doorway of the Mahoneys' room. There was a bed in the corner and under a dirty blanket lay Mrs Mahoney. 'I thought it was Moira come back,' she breathed in a rasping voice. 'She's been gone all morning and I feel as if me throat's cut, I'm that desperate for a drink.'

Amelia looked around the room and saw an uncovered half-full jug of water on the table. She picked up the jug and looking into it, she grimaced. 'I'll get some fresh water if you'll tell me where to go.'

'In the yard, miss. That's as fresh as it comes.'

'I'll get it.' Ginny took the jug from Amelia. 'You find out where Moira is and then we'll be off.'

'Aye, you wouldn't want to be hanging around here, missus.' Mrs Mahoney peered up at Amelia. 'It's Miss Linton, isn't it?'

'Yes. I came to ask if you would allow Moira to go and live with the Misses Fielding, Mrs Mahoney? They would give her lessons, and feed her in exchange for a few duties. Nothing arduous,' she added swiftly. 'Just a little dusting and shopping.'

'Glory be to God!' Mrs Mahoney closed her eyes. 'The angels have come!'

She opened her eyes again. 'I knew when I first saw you, Miss Linton, that you'd be our saviour and you're only just in time.' She started to cough. 'I'm not long for this world, a few weeks only, and my dearest wish is to be with my Daniel and young Eamon.' She pulled herself up to a sitting position and the effort appeared to be painful. 'But I knew I couldn't go until Moira and Kieran were taken care of.'

'Don't worry about Moira,' Amelia said and turned her head as Ginny came back into the room and poured water into a cup.

Ginny knelt by the bed and helped the woman to sip the water. 'You need something stronger than that,' Ginny muttered. 'What is it you've got? Consumption?'

'Aye, and it's galloping away faster than a man

on horseback.' She turned to Amelia. 'Will you take my boy as well as Moira? I'd die happy if you would.' She must have seen the uncertainty on Amelia's face, for she added, 'He's a good worker, takes after his dada. Turn his hand to anything.'

They heard footsteps on the stairs and she grasped Amelia's arm. 'Not a word about me,' she urged. 'I don't want the bairns to know. They think I drink and that's why I take to my bed, but where in the world would I get money to buy drink when we can barely afford food?'

Moira came up the stairs followed by Kieran. The girl was very pale and thin and the boy was sallow-complexioned.

'Why, miss, what you doing here again?' Moira gave her a smile but glanced anxiously at the bed where her mother lay. 'Mammy,' she said. 'You should be out of bed at this time of day. Come on,' she urged. 'You'll have to help me with the begging. I've only earned sixpence this morning.' Her eyes filled with tears. 'There's not enough money to buy our dinner and pay the rent.'

'What about you, Kieran,' their mother said wearily. 'Did you manage to get a job?'

He shook his head. 'No Ma, I didn't. But I've to go back to the docks in the morning and I might get taken on as apprentice on a fishing boat.'

Mrs Mahoney gave a low cry. 'Never,' she said. 'You're a farmer's boy, not a seaman. You'll not last a day on a boat.' She gave an imploring glance towards Amelia. 'Please, miss. I beg you.'

'Moira.' Amelia turned to the girl. 'Miss Fielding in York is willing to take you back and teach you if you will help her in the house. You can live in a cosy little room at the top of the house where I used to stay when I was teaching. Your mother says that she is willing for you to go.'

Moira frowned. 'But who'll earn money if I'm not here? And besides there's bad things happen in York. I've seen them with my own eyes.'

Amelia was startled, but Mrs Mahoney said, 'Away with you, child. Forget about that. Bad things happen everywhere, not just in York. Sure it's a fine city and Miss Fielding will take good care of you. Besides,' her voice was breathless. 'I've the promise of a job in a big house, but I have to live in and I can't take you and Kieran with me.'

'A job—' began Moira but was interrupted by Kieran who complained, 'But Mammy, what about me? Where will I go?'

'You'll come with us,' Ginny broke in. 'I'm looking for a willing lad to fetch and carry, and help with the coals. Can you do that?'

He nodded. 'Will I be able to see Mammy or Moira?' he asked.

'Probably not often,' Ginny answered truthfully, 'because we live in the country. But you know as well as me that once you start work you generally only see your family once a year.'

'What shall I do, Mammy?' he muttered. 'I'd like the job.'

Mrs Mahoney put her hand over her mouth and swallowed hard. 'Take it, my brave lad, and make your mammy and dada proud of ye.'

Amelia and Ginny went off then to do their shopping with the promise that they would be back at three o'clock to collect the two children. 'But first,' said Ginny, propelling Amelia towards an inn, 'we wash our hands thoroughly and I hope in God's name that those two children haven't caught what their mother has. It can go through a family like wildfire and I wouldn't like to think they were bringing anything home to our family.'

'Oh, Ginny.' Amelia was horrified. 'I didn't think! They were both very pale and sickly-looking. We must let the doctor see them before they meet Lily or the twins!'

'You'd be pale, Miss Amelia, if you lived the way that they do. I'd forgotten,' she muttered. 'I used to see it all the time when I lived in Hull. I didn't realize that it was still here.'

The doctor checked Moira and Kieran over the following day and pronounced them free of disease but suffering from lack of proper food. 'They've probably been living on bread and water,' he remarked as he looked them over. 'Give them some good food and they'll be as right as can be. They seem to have good constitutions.'

Ginny went back into Hull armed with a

basket of provisions and returned to tell Amelia that she had arranged for Mrs Mahoney to go into the workhouse hospital, the same one where her son Eamon had died. 'She said she would be happy there where he had been,' she told Amelia. 'So you are not to worry about her. I've arranged for a priest to visit her and we'll tell the bairns all in good time.'

'Thank you, Ginny.' Amelia was grateful. 'How good you are.'

'Ah, well,' said Ginny. 'There but for the grace of God go I.'

Early the next day, Ginny knocked on the bedroom door and called softly, 'Mrs Linton!' and entered the room.

'What is it, Ginny?' Emily was standing by the window in her night robe. 'Has someone arrived?'

'Yes. Mr Mungo. He's ridden urgently from York and asks to see you and Miss Amelia. There's a message from Mr Hawkins.'

'I'll get dressed. Has Philip gone out?'

'Captain Linton left with Master Roger an hour since.' Though Ginny called her mistress by her first name when they were alone, she always observed propriety with Captain Linton. 'Shall I call Miss Amelia?'

'Please. It must be urgent for him to have come so far so early. I do hope nothing is wrong.'

Nothing was wrong, Jack assured them. On the contrary, there was good news, but their presence was needed as Miss Fielding appeared to be unwell.

Jack joined Amelia and her mother at breakfast and told them of the events in York. 'So, you are saying that Ralph is the brother – or at least the half-brother of the Misses Fielding?' Amelia said in astonishment.

'It seems so incredible,' said her mother, then paused in thought. 'That time when Miss Fielding was ill. It was after Mrs Boyle and I were discussing convict transportation. Why did she not tell us then of her mother?'

'Too ashamed, Mama,' Amelia confided. 'Harriet asked me questions about Ralph and then I told her about your past and she too became very agitated. They have kept their secret hidden for so many years.'

'They were told to,' Jack interposed. 'By Edward Scott. Mr Thacker told us that Scott had threatened them when they were children that they must never tell anyone.'

'Poor things,' Emily Linton murmured. 'He doesn't sound like a very nice man. Come along, Amelia. We must do what we can. Thank you so much,' she said to Jack. 'You have been so kind.'

'Shall I return to York with you, ma'am?' he asked.

'There is no need to trouble yourself. Perhaps – would you be kind enough to look after Mrs Boyle and her daughter whilst we are gone? And give them my apologies for deserting them?

I'm sure they will understand. My husband and Roger will be back this evening for supper.'

They took Moira with them; she was scrubbed and clean and wore a neat grey dress, with a cotton bonnet on her head. She preened as she sat in the carriage next to Amelia and wriggled on the cushions, and Amelia asked her, 'What bad things happened in York, Moira, that made you think you didn't want to go back?'

She hung her head. 'My mammy said I shouldn't talk about it, miss, that I'd make trouble for myself.'

'If that's what your mother said, then perhaps you shouldn't,' Mrs Linton advised. 'But if it worries you then you may tell us in confidence, or Miss Fielding, and perhaps we can put your mind at rest. You are only young, perhaps it was an incident that you didn't understand.'

'Oh, I understood it all right, ma'am.' Her eyes were bright and frank and seemed older than her years. 'Sure I understood it right enough.'

When they arrived in York they found Elizabeth Fielding in a very nervous state, mainly it seemed over the confirmation of her mother's death. Harriet, however, was in a condition of feverish excitement over the discovery of a brother she didn't know she had. Her mood broke out from time to time in a flurry of exclamations and utterances.

'I can hardly believe it, Amelia,' she gasped, for what seemed like the hundredth time. 'And

329

he is so kind and considerate towards Elizabeth. I'm sure she will take to him eventually. Not that she dislikes him, you understand,' she added quickly. 'No, nothing like that, she is just so upset over our mother's death. Oh, goodness!' she exclaimed yet again. 'I cannot believe it! Do you think he will protect us from Scott, Amelia? I do hope that he will. Yet still – perhaps not, he is Scott's son after all.'

'Protect you? In what way, Harriet?' Amelia was puzzled. 'Was Mr Scott not your guardian when you were young?'

Elizabeth came into the parlour as she spoke. She wore a loose gown and her hair was not dressed but hung down her back, making her look young and vulnerable. 'He became our guardian when Mama went away,' she said. 'He said there would be no-one else willing to look after a convict's children, and if it wasn't for him we would be in the workhouse. But I discovered later that he took on our guardianship so that he would have control of the annuity which our own father had left us. There was very little left when we came of age.'

'And now?' Amelia asked. 'Does he not enquire about you?'

'Oh yes.' Elizabeth gave a cynical smile. 'He comes to remind us of our faults and of our mother's sins. He comes regularly to torment us.'

Amelia related this to Ralph later when he called. 'I do believe that Elizabeth is frightened of Mr Scott,' she said. 'She cannot bring herself to tell him not to come to the house.'

'There are some people who find pleasure in hurting others, they like to manipulate and take control,' Ralph said slowly and thoughtfully. 'They are inadequate in themselves, yet want to feel power – like small boys who pull the wings off flies to see them squirm and suffer. I believe that Scott is like that.' He gazed at Amelia and she saw sadness in his eyes. 'I am ashamed to call him my father.'

'It is not your fault,' she said urgently. 'You cannot take the blame for him.'

'No,' he answered. 'But I must try to make amends for the hurt he has done, to my mother and to my sisters.'

Have I been mistaken about him? she thought. He appears to be most considerate and thoughtful. But she was startled and disconcerted when he spoke again in a harsher tone.

'Perhaps I shouldn't say this to you, Amelia. You are a woman and not given to violence and wouldn't understand.' He curled his fingers into a tight fist. 'But I could meet that man who brought me into being, and thrash him until he begged for mercy.'

Chapter Thirty

Lucinda Boyle looked out of her bedroom window. She had retired to her room for a rest after luncheon, but had caught sight of her daughter and Jack Mungo walking together in the garden below, and she now sat in an easy chair gazing thoughtfully at the pair.

He was talking, moving his hands expressively as if explaining a point and Phoebe was shaking her head. He must be telling her of the extra-ordinary happenings at the Fieldings' house, she pondered. How considerate it was of Miss Fielding to invite him to their supper party. That wouldn't happen in Australia, she mused. I can't think of one of our acquaintances who would invite an Aborigine into their home, unless it was to perform some menial task.

Her thoughts went then to her husband. He would be appalled at the very idea of social intercourse. Aborigines, convicts and dingoes were in the same class as far as he was concerned and he would shoot them all.

I don't want to go back. The small nagging thought, which had been with her from the moment she had stepped onto the ship in Sydney Harbour, came back with full force. *Yet how can I stay here without support? My brother would have to take me in, but I would be ostracized from society if it was known that I had left my husband.*

And what would happen to Phoebe then? No man would marry her if her parents were separated. There would be such shame on her head! She gave a deep depressed sigh and peered down into the garden. Phoebe and Mr Mungo had moved out of sight, though now and again she caught a flash of white from Phoebe's dress as they moved amongst the bushes and the herbaceous borders. *Phoebe won't want to go back to my brother's house, not after such freedom here at the Lintons'. She will consider it far too staid and stuffy. But how else will I ever find her a husband?*

The couple below appeared again from beyond the trees. This time Phoebe appeared to be doing all the talking. She had her hands clasped near her face and she was smiling. Jack Mungo was looking at her, though Mrs Boyle couldn't see his expression as he had his head turned away from her. A sudden worry seized her. *I ought to fetch Phoebe in.* The sensibilities and prejudices of her own up-bringing came to the fore. It was not seemly to spend so much time alone with a man who was not your husband or your intended, even though Phoebe and Mr Mungo were in full sight of anyone who cared to be interested.

She stood up against the window intending to tap and call, but Phoebe looked up at that instance and smiled and waved and Jack too looked up towards her. She saw him say something and Phoebe nodded and they turned towards the house.

'I must speak to Ralph,' Jack was saying. 'He is my friend and he wants to marry you.'

'No, he doesn't. Not really.' Phoebe clasped her hands beneath her chin and smiled. 'Besides, if *you* won't marry me, then I won't marry anyone.'

He wanted to reach out and hold her, but was aware, as they both were, that they were visible to any watchers at the house. 'It would be so hard for you, Phoebe. You know of the difficulties you would encounter. How can I ask you to share such a life?'

'Because I love you,' she said simply, 'as I always have, and because I am strong.'

'What shall I tell Ralph? He will feel betrayed.'

'Tell him he should marry Amelia. She would suit him much better than I.'

He laughed. 'They don't suit at all. They are always at odds with one another.'

'All the more reason why they should marry, they will settle their differences then.' She gazed tenderly at him. 'I'm a woman, I know about these things.'

'I know that you are a woman,' he said softly. 'I have never had any doubt about that.'

She glanced up at the house. 'Mama is looking at us.'

He turned and looked up. 'We'd better go in, she will start to worry.'

'You are so considerate, Jack.' Phoebe gazed at him. 'You deserve someone so much better than me.'

Can his father be so very bad? Amelia deliberated as Ralph issued the statement so harshly. Is it possible to hate or love a blood relation on such a short acquaintanceship?

Her mother came into the Fieldings' parlour. 'Amelia dear, I think I will take Miss Fielding home with us until she is feeling better. Harriet too if she wishes.'

'Harriet has to work Mama,' Amelia reminded her. 'But I could stay here with her as I did before, if Elizabeth goes home with you.'

'What are your intentions, Ralph?' her mother asked. 'Will you stay to renew your relationship with your father?'

Ralph's mouth tightened. 'I will stay a little longer, Aunt Emily. I need to find out the truth.'

His aunt nodded. 'Then I will return home with Miss Fielding.' She added, 'I think that I have almost convinced her that as we are practically related, she need not feel obliged towards us in any way. She is so bowed down with guilt.'

'Yes,' Ralph agreed grimly. 'And it is because of Scott!'

When her mother had gone from the room, Amelia rationalized, 'There is nothing you can do about what has gone before, Ralph. All those circumstances are in the past. You may feel hatred towards your father because of what he did, but you can't undo it.'

'You don't understand,' he burst out passionately. 'I need to pay him back!'

'Please! Don't keep saying that I don't understand!' Amelia jumped to her feet. 'Of course I understand! Scott hurt your mother and your sisters and by doing so, you too have been hurt. But you are a different man from the one you would have been! You too might have been downtrodden and under Scott's influence if your mother hadn't taken that knife in her hand.'

Her voice had risen in anger and she didn't hear the door open or see Elizabeth Fielding standing there. 'You wouldn't have been as self-opinionated and arrogant as you are.'

Amelia swept towards the door and gasped as she saw Elizabeth standing there. 'Excuse me,' she muttered. 'I do beg your pardon,' and hurried out of the room.

'I'm so sorry,' Ralph began, but Elizabeth put up her hand as if she was listening or thinking of something.

'That's what it was,' she breathed, her eyes vacant. 'It was a knife! It was lying on his desk.'

'Yes, I've seen it. He still has it.' He was

bewildered and annoyed. What did Amelia mean? How was he arrogant?

Elizabeth looked at him; it was as if she was awakening from a deep sleep. 'It was because of me that Mama picked up the knife! That is why I have felt so guilty all these years.'

Ralph remained silent. Something momentous was about to be said.

'He was going to strap me,' she whispered. 'Because of something I had forgotten to do. I can't remember now what it was, something trivial – children do forget to do what adults tell them. He kept the strap beneath his desk. I had had a taste of it before, only Mama didn't know. But this time he told me that when he had strapped me, he would strap Harriet as well, and that would make me always remember to do what he told me.

'Mama came into the room as I stood with my hands out and she started to scream at him; she said she wouldn't allow him to start on us children no matter how he treated her.'

Ralph gently eased her down into a chair. 'He lashed out at her then,' Elizabeth continued in a low voice. 'I remember that his face was scarlet with fury because she had defied him, and he was hitting out wildly with the strap, knocking over ornaments and the papers off his desk and chasing her around the room, and I ran behind a chair. It was then that Mama picked up the paperknife from the desk and struck out at him.'

She shook her head. 'It was only a glancing

337

blow, a mere scratch and there wasn't any blood, but he made a terrible fuss about it. Mama and I went upstairs to our room, and later in the evening he called a doctor and a constable and showed them the wound. It was just below the collar bone and much deeper and bloodier than it had been before.'

She gazed at Ralph and her eyes were large and luminous. 'I don't know what happened next as Mama was taken away and we never saw her again. We were not allowed. We were sent to stay with Dolly. She was a friend of Scott's,' she said in a low voice. 'But not of Mama's.'

'I have met her,' Ralph responded. 'She was visiting Scott.'

'She's always there,' she muttered. 'Even after he married again. Dolly was always there.'

'It's finished, Elizabeth,' he insisted. 'You need fear him no longer. Go to Holderness with Aunt Emily and rest. I'll make sure that Scott doesn't ever bother you again.'

She looked up at him and said in a hesitant voice, 'You will make it up with Miss Linton – Amelia, won't you? I should hate to think it was because of us that you quarrelled.'

'Because of you? Why should you think that?' She seemed to take the troubles of the whole world on her shoulders.

'I couldn't help overhearing,' she confessed. 'Amelia said—'

He took her hand in his. 'Our difference of opinion is not because of you or Harriet, but because of me. I believe that Amelia thinks that I shall seek vengeance with Scott over this. But she is quite wrong,' he lied. 'So you are not to worry about it.' But Amelia is quite right, he deliberated as Elizabeth left the room, for that is exactly what I intend to do.

He left shortly afterwards, bidding Aunt Emily and Elizabeth a cordial goodbye, but giving Amelia only a polite bow, saying that he would call on her and Harriet the following day.

After Amelia closed the door behind her mother and Elizabeth, she burst into floods of tears. Her emotions, kept pent up inside her since her argument with Ralph, erupted.

Whatever was I thinking of? she wept. I was so rude! How could I say such things? He will never forgive me and rightly so. His father *has* been wicked in keeping secret the news of their mother's death from Elizabeth and Harriet. Elizabeth, especially, has lived in hope since childhood that her mother would come back. It is natural that Ralph would feel anger against him.

She wiped her eyes. I will apologize tomorrow when he calls. He is not arrogant. Certainly not. How could I think it when he has behaved so well towards his newly discovered sisters?

Moira knocked and came into the room. 'Would I go and do some shopping, Miss Linton?' she started to say, then stopped when she saw Amelia's tear-stained face. 'Or maybe I'll make you a nice cup of tea?'

'Please,' Amelia said, and blew her nose. 'And then we'll think about what to get for supper.'

'I hope everything's all right, Miss Linton?' Moira hesitated, not yet knowing how she should behave in her new position.

'I'm sure it will be, Moira,' Amelia gave her a weak smile. 'It has been quite an eventful day, but things can only improve.'

That evening Ralph ate supper at the inn, though his appetite was listless as his thoughts returned time and again to Amelia's opinion of him. Why does she think such things? I speak my mind and do not pander to convention, it is true, but does that make me opinionated or arrogant? I'm honest in my beliefs and surely that is worth more than spouting trivial platitudes? Or is that what young women expect?

After a disturbed night's sleep in which he had heated imaginary conversations with Amelia, he awoke, irritated and restless, and decided that he would call again on Scott that morning and confront him about misleading him over his half-sisters.

Dolly opened the door to him and haltingly excused the lack of a maid. 'So difficult to keep them, you know,' she whined. 'They want so much these days.'

'I am sure you are managing perfectly, Mrs West,' he said with a cynicism he didn't bother to hide, and followed her into Scott's study.

'Please stay,' he said, as Scott indicated that

Dolly should leave the room. 'Perhaps you can help me with my dilemma. Your friendship with my father must have been a great comfort to him throughout his unfortunate misadventures in life. You have been unstinting in your endeavours to help him through the sorrowful times he has encountered over the years.'

She looked at him in confusion and then glanced at Scott, who growled at Ralph, 'What do you mean – misadventures?'

'Why surely, sir, there cannot be many men who have been unfortunate enough to lose three wives! The first – my mother. I accept that you said that she was a bad woman and therefore probably deserved to be punished and sent away, but your second wife, so sad, she died after a short illness I believe? And the third Mrs Scott – so dreadful for her to feel the waters of the river closing over her head and no-one able to help her!'

It was with some satisfaction that he noticed Dolly West's face losing colour as he spoke, and that she was biting hard on her forefinger. He addressed her. 'It would be tempting fate to become the fourth Mrs Scott, would it not, Mrs West?'

He uttered this in a part serious, part jovial manner and Scott with narrowed eyes said harshly, 'It is not a joking matter. Is this how you discuss death in Australia?'

'Yes, indeed it is. Our forebears have all faced death in one form or another, by treadmill or the rope, by flogging or hard labour and the only way they could confront or cheat it was to take it firmly by the throat and laugh in its face.'

Scott stared at him. 'I was going to send for you to come,' he said coldly. 'I want you to sign some papers.'

'What sort of papers?' Ralph was immediately on guard.

'I've seen my lawyer. He needs you to sign a statement confirming that you are my son.' Then he added in a lighter tone, 'And I need to change my will. I was going to leave what I had to various charities, but now – '

'I don't understand the legalities,' Ralph said in a light-hearted manner. 'I suppose it's a kind of affidavit? Will the estate not come to me automatically?'

'No! We both have to sign papers.'

'I suppose I shall have to change my will too as I have no other living relative?'

He thought he detected a glimmer of a smile in Scott's eyes, but he was distracted as Mrs West got up from her chair and started to pace the room.

'Sit down, Dolly,' Scott barked, 'or else go and make some coffee.'

She started towards the door. 'Before you go,' Ralph detained her. 'As I was saying, I have a dilemma. I had almost forgotten, but some months ago when I was searching through reports to look for relatives, I came across my mother's name in an Admiralty medical journal which the surgeon superintendents are required to keep on board ship. A sort of log book,' he explained. 'In it, it was stated that I was not my mother's first child, that she had borne other children.'

He waited for this to sink in. Dolly West stood motionless by the door and Scott continued to stare at him. 'I just wondered if you could throw light on the matter,' he continued. 'Had she lost children at birth? So many women do. Or, as you say that she was a bad woman, and although I find this totally abhorrent and I hate to offend you by what I am about to say, did she, sir, give birth to children before you married her?'

Scott was silent for a moment, then said, 'Let's get these papers signed and out of the way, and then I'll tell you what happened.'

Ralph shook his head. 'I'm sorry, I can't possibly do that. There might be other children to consider, brothers or sisters. They would have a claim on my estate, which I must tell you is quite substantial. I must consider them. They may be in dire circumstances and glad of a helping hand.'

Scott's face grew red. 'There are no other children! She had had two stillbirths before I met her. Now can we get on with this paper-work!'

'Of course,' Ralph nodded. 'I'll arrange for a lawyer to act for me and for Mr Mungo to act as witness. Will Thursday be convenient? I can't get hold of Jack before then.'

343

'You'd have an Abo as a witness?' Scott queried harshly. 'Can he sign his name?'

'Well enough,' Ralph said smoothly, though he was seething with anger. 'And Mrs West will sign for you, I expect?' He gave a deep sigh. 'Such a pity. I had hoped that I might have had siblings. It would have been such a pleasure, would it not, to meet a brother or sister face to face? Still,' he said, with regret in his voice. 'If it is not to be.'

'No,' said Scott. 'It is not to be.'

Chapter Thirty-One

'He could find out!' Dolly West's voice was even shriller than normal and Scott cringed. 'He could find out,' she repeated querulously. 'If he starts poking about in the record books he might find out about them two.'

'Shut up, will you! He can't possibly find out. There's no reason why he should start searching the records again. They've got a different name, haven't they? He doesn't know his mother was widowed before I married her.'

A thought struck him. Except that I sent him to see Henderson. Would he have told him? No, he decided. That fawning spaniel is frightened of his own shadow, let alone of risking my anger.

But as the day wore on into evening, his thoughts continued to draw back to his stepdaughters. If Hawkins should discover them, then he wouldn't sign the papers. He thought of Ralph Hawkins quite dispassionately. There was no warm or tender emotion at the discovery of a long-lost child, born of his own flesh and blood.

But he did feel a profound, inspired intoxication when he thought of Ralph's estate. There's money in sheep, he debated. And I wouldn't be surprised if there wasn't gold. He hedged when I asked him about that, didn't give a proper answer.

'Dolly!' he yelled out of the study door. 'Get ready. We're going to visit those Fielding ladies.'

Ralph raised his hand to knock on the door, then lowered it again. It was early, only just after four o'clock, and Harriet wouldn't be home yet. Can I face Amelia alone? he deliberated. If Harriet is late for any reason, Amelia and I will be forced into an embarrassing situation. What will we talk about? The English, I believe, discuss the weather, but I am not stamped in that mould.

But there! That, I suppose, is what Amelia means, he thought as he hesitated on the doorstep. My manners are lacking in refinement. I must apologize for my boorishness. She, of course, will be used to formality in the men she has met. Probably well bred with charm and finesse. He raised his hand again and gave the knocker a sharp rap. Polished and polite they will be in the art of conversation; and infinitely boring!

Moira answered the door. She gave him a neat curtsey.

'Is Miss Harriet at home?' he asked. 'Or Miss Linton?'

'Miss Harriet isn't back yet, but Miss Linton is in. Should I tell her you're here, sir?'

'Ask her if she will receive me,' he said formally. Drat, he thought, I should have brought flowers as a peace offering. If Jack had been here he would have reminded me. I can't seem to do things right.

'Cousin Ralph!' Amelia invited him into the parlour. 'I, er – we didn't expect you until later.'

'I came along the city walls. It took less time than I expected. Such lovely weather we are enjoying at present!' he added.

She gave him a surprised glance. 'Indeed we are.' She gave a slight smile. 'But it is to be expected in the summer!'

'Quite so,' he agreed. 'Amelia—'

'Ralph!' she interrupted. 'I was so very rude to you yesterday. I said such dreadful things and I do apologize.' Her eyes glistened but she looked directly at him. 'I don't know what came over me, for what I said was quite untrue.'

'No,' he said. 'You are right. I am self-opinionated. Jack says I am.' He considered. 'I don't know if I am arrogant, I don't consider myself to be better than others, quite the opposite in fact, especially if I compare myself with Englishmen.'

'Oh, please,' she said in some distress. 'Please don't compare yourself with anyone. I was quite wrong.' She put her fingers to her eyes to move a tear and then gave a shaky smile. 'You cannot

347

compare youself with anyone else, for you are quite unique.'

'Unique! That is one description I have never heard applied to my character.'

They both laughed. How very attractive she is, he thought. Not pretty as Phoebe is, but fine bone structure and a lovely mouth when she smiles as she is doing now. He put out his hand. 'Can we be friends then?' he said softly. 'Do we accept each other as we are?'

She blushed and put her head down as she gave him her hand, and nodded. 'But I am still so sorry for what I said.'

'I probably deserved it,' he murmured and impulsively kissed her on her cheek.

Her eyes opened wide and she gave a small gasp. 'Is this an Australian custom?'

'No,' he smiled. 'Why? Have you had such another? Don't tell me,' he bantered. 'Has that Jack-a-dandy stolen a kiss?'

He felt a fleeting moment of apprehension. Had Jack stolen her heart? He was such a buffoon sometimes. Did he not realize that women, especially sensitive Englishwomen, might take him seriously? The implications were too appalling to think about. He and Jack and others such as Phoebe, and Peggy his own sister, knew of the pitfalls, the ostracism, the exclusion and isolation that friendship between black and white could bring.

But Amelia knew nothing of these, and as he teased, he vowed that he must warn Jack not to give out his affection too freely lest it be taken wrongly. The time has come, my friend, when you must choose, he pondered. Take a wife. Choose a good woman from your own race, one who will bear you children. Or marry a white woman like Phoebe, strong in stamina, character and determination, who would not be bowed down by prejudice or disapproval.

'Ralph? Are you listening?' He started as Amelia spoke.

'Sorry,' he said. 'I was thinking about Jack and Phoebe.'

'Jack *and* Phoebe?' She looked puzzled.

'Yes,' he said thoughtfully. 'She understands him. I hadn't realized it before.' A picture came into his mind of Phoebe on the hay cart gazing down at Jack as he dallied with the affections of Amelia's young sister May. Phoebe was amused by his behaviour and not in the least put out by it. And he remembered too how Jack had walked Phoebe back to her cabin on board ship.

Jack doesn't pay compliments to Phoebe and it has nothing to do with her so-called white superiority or the knowledge of her father's hatred of Aborigines. He doesn't need to. The reality struck him. He doesn't need to, because he is assured of her affection as she is of his.

'I've just realized. Phoebe loves Jack!' He blinked and gazed at Amelia. 'I am convinced of it!'

'Surely not!' she began, 'I thought that you and Phoebe were – ?'

349

'No,' he said vaguely. 'I don't think so. In fact, I have been so wrapped up in this business with Scott that I haven't really thought about Phoebe at all.' He gave an apologetic laugh. 'Which is not the way to conduct a courtship.'

'She is not the one for you, Ralph, though I think you are mistaken about her and Jack. He will surely take a wife from his own race?' She wrinkled her forehead, considering. 'Though if what you say *is* true, then if they stayed in England, it would perhaps be less difficult than in Australia?'

Stay in England! I hadn't thought of that, he pondered. And what do I do now that I have discovered two sisters? Do I take them back with me or do I stay? Or do I leave them an annuity and then go, never to see them again? He looked at Amelia as she gazed at him and felt a strange stirring within him. And there are others to be considered. Had his confrontations with Amelia been covering other emotions? 'Yes.' He answered both Amelia and himself out loud. 'Perhaps so.'

Harriet arrived shortly afterwards and Ralph told her of his meeting with Scott. 'Are you saying that Edward Scott has denied our existence?' she asked incredulously. 'I cannot believe that even he could stoop so low. I don't remember our own father,' she said. 'And Scott never allowed us to call him father. Not that Elizabeth ever wanted to but I always wanted a father figure. It wasn't until Mr Thacker came back again into our lives, after we had returned from school, that I realized that he could fill that role.

'He was very kind to us, but it was difficult for him,' she added. 'For we were then living with Scott and his wife Bella, and Mr Thacker wasn't allowed into the house.'

She looked around the small parlour. 'We moved into lodgings as soon as we were old enough, and then Mr Thacker arranged the lease on this house when Elizabeth started teaching.'

'I think that Scott will come here,' Ralph said quietly. 'He will come to threaten you not to say anything should I come enquiring.'

Harriet shuddered. 'I'm so glad that Elizabeth isn't here. She is very frightened of him,' she whispered.

Amelia put her arm around her. 'There is no need for either of you to be frightened again,' she said. 'You have friends and family now to protect you.'

'May I stay?' Ralph asked. 'I want to be here when he comes.'

Harriet hesitated for only a moment, then said, 'I wish that you would. I feel safe now that you are here.'

They ate a simple supper, then Moira cleared away and they waited, for Ralph was convinced that Scott would come that night.

Just before eight o'clock, as Harriet was deciding that it was too late for him to come, there was a hammering on the door. Amelia and Harriet both jumped, the noise was so loud and insistent.

'It's him,' Harriet whispered. 'No-one else would come so late or knock so loudly.'

'Send Moira to ask who it is,' Ralph whispered back. 'Tell her not to open the door.'

Harriet did so and Moira asked through the letter box who was visiting at such a late hour. 'I don't know who you are,' a voice bellowed back, 'but tell Miss Fielding it's Scott and I need to speak to her immediately.'

Moira came back and repeated the message and was told what to do, whilst Amelia and Ralph escaped into the kitchen where they squashed up against the door, listening.

Moira opened the front door then let it crash against the wall as Scott and Mrs West came in.

'So who are you?' Scott demanded.

Moira flattened herself against the wall. 'New maid, sir,' she whispered.

Scott grunted. 'Humph. Fortunes must be improving if they can afford a maid! Well, look sharp, show us in. Tell Miss Fielding we're here.'

Moira had been told to say that Miss Fielding was out and that only Miss Harriet was at home, but she seemed to be struck dumb, and, grey-faced and trembling, opened the parlour door to where Harriet was seated by the fire. As she closed the door behind them she folded up into a heap and moaned softly to herself. 'Oh, God in heaven,' she cried. 'I knew something bad would happen if I came back.'

Amelia quietly opened the kitchen door and pulled her inside. She put her finger to her lips and whispered, 'Whatever is the matter, Moira?'

'Oh, miss,' she croaked hoarsely. 'It's him! It's him that I saw do something bad. If he finds out I saw him, he'll kill me for sure.'

Scott, as he entered the parlour, glanced around. 'You've come into some money then if you can afford a maid?'

'No,' Harriet said, more calmly than she felt. 'I have obtained a position as governess and the girl is here in exchange for lessons. Our finances are the same as always. Depleted. Thanks to you,' she added boldly.

He scowled. 'I only took what was due to me for looking after the pair of you. Where's Lizzie?' he demanded. 'It's her I want to talk to.'

'She's not here.'

'Then where is she?' He sat down in a chair. 'I'll wait.'

'You will have a long wait.' Harriet folded her hands in front of her and stared at Scott. She had so far refrained from looking at or speaking to Dolly. 'She is away. Not in York.'

'Not in York? Who does she know who doesn't live in York?' His manner was rough and his tone harsh.

'That really is nothing to do with you,' Harriet replied. 'And if you are going to be so disagreeable I shall have to ask you to leave.'

He stared at her as if she had taken leave of her senses and Dolly gasped. 'How dare you speak like that?' she trilled. 'When you have had so much done for you.'

Scott put his hand up to silence Dolly. 'Now look here, Harriet. I've something to say to you and you must tell Elizabeth as soon as she gets back. There's somebody sniffing around, pretending to be somebody he's not, and you must tell Elizabeth that if he comes here, she's not to let him in or listen to what he says.'

'Why would anyone come here to us?' Harriet asked innocently. 'We don't know anybody.'

He shook his finger at her. 'You don't know anybody because you have kept quiet lives, and you have kept quiet lives because of what your mother did. That shame will lie with you for ever and will never leave you. Remember that as Elizabeth remembers it. Elizabeth feels the shame and *you* are getting far too uppity, young lady! Now, I'll tell you,' he glared at her. 'If I want to, I can find out who your employers are, and if they should hear of your mother's past, well – how long do you think your employment would last then? Eh?'

Harriet was silent. She was afraid of him, just as Elizabeth was.

'Eh?' he asked again. 'Not long, I can tell you!' He glanced across at Dolly who nodded in agreement and looked down her powdered nose at Harriet.

'Not long at all,' Dolly said in a satisfied tone.

'They wouldn't want a convict's daughter working for them. Who would in their right mind?'

The door slowly opened and Ralph came in, followed by Amelia. He closed the door and stood against it with his arms folded. 'And who then, in their right mind, would claim a convict's son as their own?'

Chapter Thirty-Two

Scott's face showed shocked surprise, whilst Dolly's expression was one of incredulity tinged with fear. But Scott soon recovered and he gave a sly grin. 'So, you got here first! I wondered if you would. You're smart, I'll say that for you. I had a wager with Dolly here as to whether you would find out, didn't I, Dolly?'

Dolly nodded, keeping a mesmerized eye on Ralph.

'Yes. You've come up to expectations!' Scott expanded his chest and looked smug. 'It's a wise father who knows his own child,' he quoted.

'You hypocrite,' Ralph spat out. 'You had no intention of telling me of my sisters. You deliberately lied when I asked you if there were any other children.'

Scott shrugged. 'I wanted to see what you were made of, if you would just accept the facts that you were given.' His gaze locked into Ralph's. There was no shame, no contrition. 'How did you find out? Who told you?'

'No-one told me.' Ralph found that lying to Scott was quite easy and he had no intention of disclosing Henderson's name. 'I searched the records for my mother's maiden name and found Fielding instead. The rest followed. I had hoped,' he looked Scott up and down, 'I had hoped that my father was a man of honour. I did not expect to be told lies.'

'Now look here,' Scott began persuasively. 'Let's begin again. We're both men of the world.'

'If being men of the world means ill-treating the children of your wife and having that same wife sent away so that you could marry again,' Ralph's fists clenched and unclenched in his anger, 'then I am not one of them. And if that other wife should *unfortunately* die whilst in the care of my mistress, then that is definitely not my style. What was it you gave her?' he accused them. 'Arsenic?'

Harriet gave a gasp. 'Not Bella?' she trembled. 'Oh, no!'

'No,' Dolly whispered, her face ashen. 'It wasn't me, I never—!'

'Shut up,' Scott bellowed. 'He's making it up. There's no truth in it.'

'There's more,' Ralph said quietly. 'It has just come to my attention that the third Mrs Scott did not accidentally drown after all.'

'What do you mean?' Scott's voice was low and menacing. 'What do you know about it?'

'You were seen!' Ralph said. 'By a witness. Someone who is willing to swear in a court of law that you, and your friend here,' he nodded over to Dolly West, 'walked one on either side of that poor woman, holding her up. The witness assumed at first that she was the worse for drink, but now thinks she was probably drugged. Mrs West then walked away, leaving you and your wife by the river's edge.

'Do you wish me to go on?' he asked a silenced Scott. 'Shall I tell how the witness saw you stand your wife at the edge of the river and then turn away to fasten your bootlace? As you turned away, you pushed her into the water.'

Dolly gave a sharp scream. 'I knew you'd be found out! I said that somebody would see. It wasn't me,' she urged Ralph. 'It was his idea.'

'Be quiet,' Scott shouted again and raised his hand to her. 'Stupid woman!' he sneered and asked, 'So why didn't this witness come forward before?'

'Too frightened!' Ralph said. 'But a priest was informed, and—' He held up his hand as he saw the derision on Scott's face. 'Yes, I know that a priest cannot divulge details from a confessional, but the police will take note of it.' He gave a wintry smile. 'They will only have to look at your bank accounts to know that you only ever marry ladies with property. I expect you have some other lady waiting in the wings?'

Dolly looked at him sharply as he made this remark and then lunged towards Scott. 'You said,' she shrieked, 'you said there would be no more! I've waited all these years for you.'

'I do but jest, Mrs West,' Ralph assured her with considerable irony. 'He thought he had found a long-lost son to support him instead.'

Dolly stood with her mouth open as she realized her blunder and then staggered as Scott hit her across the face.

Ralph rushed to seize him but as he grabbed his arm there came a sharp rap on the front door. They all started, Harriet and Amelia both clutched their throats and Scott loosened his grip on Dolly.

'Probably the constables.' Ralph cast a concerned glance towards Amelia. 'Pehaps I'd better go.'

'I'll go,' Amelia whispered. 'Scott is not to be trusted.'

Which he wasn't, for as soon as the door was heard to be unbolted, Scott tore out of Ralph's grasp and out of the room and through the front door, knocking Amelia to the ground and almost unhorsing the rider who waited outside. Dolly ran screaming after him, shouting that she wasn't going to be blamed, and in the houses across the narrow street curtains were drawn back and faces peered from windows in an attempt to see what was happening outside.

'Amelia?' Ralph knelt beside her. 'Are you hurt?' He raised her to a sitting position.

'Ooh,' she groaned. 'I banged my head on the wall. Did he get away? Who is it at the door?'

'Your servant, Miss Amelia!' Jack leant down from his mount and looked in through the open door. 'What's happening, Ralph? I can't leave you for a minute but you're in trouble. Who was that? Not a thief?' He gathered up the reins. 'I'll go after him!'

'No. Don't! It was Scott. He thought it was the constables come for him. Come inside and I'll explain.'

Jack looped the reins to a ring in the wall and followed Ralph who assisted a shaky Amelia back into the parlour. Harriet put her hands to her face and started to weep. 'Such a dreadful man,' she cried. 'Did he really do those terrible things? Will he come to trial? Is the witness reliable? How did you find out?'

Ralph and Amelia exchanged a glance. 'I doubt if it would come to a trial, Harriet,' Ralph said. 'Amelia, could you – are you feeling all right?'

'Yes.' Amelia turned to go out of the parlour. 'I'll fetch the witness, if she's still here and hasn't run off in fright.'

She found Moira still cowering behind the kitchen door and after being persuaded that the villain had indeed gone out into the night, she clutched Amelia's skirt and followed her back into the parlour.

'Here she is,' Amelia gently pushed the trembling girl forward. 'Here's your witness.'

Moira looked up at them all with wide blue eyes. 'I swear to God on my mother's name,' she whispered, 'that what I said was true. I saw that man push the poor lady into the water.'

'But she's only a child,' Harriet breathed. 'She couldn't give evidence.'

'She could give it,' Ralph said. 'She could be called to the stand. But it wouldn't be enough.'

'Tell Miss Harriet what you saw, Moira,' Amelia said gently. 'Just as you told Mr Hawkins and me. You needn't be afraid.'

'I'd been to the market, miss,' she said nervously. 'They sell stuff off cheap at the end of the day, and I took a short cut home by the river, and then,' she glanced across at Jack and Ralph and hung her head. 'And then,' she said so softly that they had to strain to hear her, 'I had a call of nature, miss. I just couldn't wait so I went into the bushes. I was just – I was just straightening meself up, when I happened to see the three of them walking by the water, and it was the way they were holding up the lady in the middle that made me look again.

'I thought, glory be to God, it's a bit early in the evening to be on the bottle, especially for a lady, though I knows as there's some who couldn't be called proper ladies, have a drop quite early.'

She took a breath. 'But I could see by the look of their clothes that they were proper ladies, and he a gentleman all right. And then I saw it as I told Miss Amelia and Mr Hawkins, and I never want to see such a thing again for I didn't know what to do! And then after a few minutes, he, that man, started running up and down and shouting for help, and he ran up the grass towards the bushes and I was so scared he would see me and kill me, so I crouched down again, and then some people came and I saw another man jump in the river to fish her out.'

She started to tremble and Amelia drew her to a chair and sat her down. 'There's no need to worry about it any more,' she assured her. 'They've gone now.'

'Will I have to go to the police, sir?' Moira implored Ralph. 'I'd rather not. They'll not believe a poor little Irish girl.'

Jack looked at her with some sympathy and shook his head, and Ralph, interpreting his thoughts, knew that he and Moira were right. 'No, I think not,' he said softly. 'But I rather feel that we have seen the last of Scott and his friend Mrs West.'

'But the constables?' Harriet asked. 'You'd sent for them. You thought they were at the door!'

Ralph looked sombre. 'I regret that I have told a few lies, Harriet. In this respect I am like Scott. I did not send for the constables. There was no time and what could we have told them?'

'But Scott believed you, Ralph, therefore the lie justified the outcome.' Amelia had a catch in her voice as she spoke. 'And you are not at all like him! How could you be? He has had no influence on your life.'

They all remained silent as they mulled over the evening's events, then Ralph looked up. 'Jack,' he said suddenly. 'What are you doing here? I wasn't expecting you, though your arrival was timely!'

Jack avoided Ralph's eye and looked down at his boots. 'I needed to talk to you,' he murmured. 'Something important to discuss. I borrowed a horse from Captain Linton's stable.'

'Something important?' Ralph raised his eyebrows.

'It seemed so at the time. I went to the inn, but you weren't there, so I came to Miss Harriet's.'

'There's nothing wrong with my sister?' Harriet asked anxiously.

'I saw Miss Fielding only briefly,' he said. 'But she seemed in good health. This is a matter which concerns only my friend Ralph and me.' He smiled reassuringly. 'Do not worry yourself, Miss Harriet.'

Ralph, puzzled, gazed hard at Jack, but there was no hint on his placid face of any anxiety which he could interpret. 'Then we had better be going.' He rose to his feet. 'Sleep well, Harriet.' He bent and kissed her cheek. 'You too, Amelia.' He bowed and kissed her hand and she blushed.

He turned to Moira. 'Thank you, Moira. We shall be forever in your debt.' He patted her cheek. 'You're a good brave girl.'

As they bolted the door behind the two men, Moira turned to Amelia and Harriet and breathed, 'Sure, isn't he the kindest, handsomest gentleman you could ever wish to meet?'

Harriet smiled and raised her eyebrows

questioningly at Amelia who turned her gaze away, then smiling answered in a pseudo-Irish voice, 'Sure, and I think the child is right!'

Ralph, with Jack leading the horse, walked across the deserted St Sampson's Square. In the distance they heard a church clock strike eleven. 'So what was so important that you had to ride immediately to York?' Ralph asked. 'Has something happened?'

'There have been no changes since you left the Lintons' house,' Jack replied quietly. 'But I have come to a decision and I would like to discuss it with you.'

'If you have already made the decision,' Ralph bantered, 'why does it need discussion?'

'Because I need to know your feelings on the matter and I want to know if I will still have your friendship.'

Ralph stopped in his tracks. 'We have been friends all of our lives. Why should our friendship not continue?'

Jack put his free hand on Ralph's shoulder. 'Because you want to marry Miss Boyle – and so do I.'

Chapter Thirty-Three

'Mama! May I speak to you?' Phoebe found her mother alone in Emily Linton's sitting room. 'Are you expecting Mrs Linton to join you?'

Mrs Boyle looked up from the piece of embroidery on her lap. 'No. Mrs Linton is with Captain Linton and Roger. Seemingly their son is anxious about something which he wishes to discuss with them. Come and sit down, dear. I have hardly seen you over the last few days.'

Phoebe sat down on a nearby chair and tried to compose in her head what it was she wanted to say without giving heartache to her mother, who she knew had her own private problems.

'I understand that Mr Mungo has gone to York.' Mrs Boyle picked up her sewing again.

'Yes. He has something to discuss with Ralph. Mama!' she burst out nervously. 'Why are you now calling him Mr Mungo, when previously you used his first name?'

Mrs Boyle chose a thread of silk before

replying. 'When we were on board ship,' she said softly, 'when we had cast off from the shore, it was as if we had cast off outdated values and didn't have to conform to the rules of society in the same way. Oh, I know that essentially we did – for instance, Mr Mungo wasn't able to dine with us, but it was easier somehow. At least,' she added, 'that is the way I felt then, but now – ' she sighed. 'I suppose we must conform.'

'Jack dines with us here,' Phoebe said quietly.

'Yes, I know,' her mother replied, 'but the Lintons are different from any other family I know. Almost Bohemian, I suppose. And yet they are not.'

'I have something to say to you, Mama.' Phoebe rose from her chair and started to pace the room. 'I need to prepare you before Jack and Ralph come back from York.'

'Prepare me?' Mrs Boyle said in alarm. 'For what? What has happened?'

Phoebe came and sat beside her mother. 'You know, Mama, that I suggested to you that Ralph was fond of me?'

'Yes.' Her mother frowned. 'But I have been inclined lately to think that you had misled me.'

'I had my reasons for wanting you to believe it,' Phoebe admitted. 'Though in part it was true. Ralph, I do believe, thought that he cared for me.'

'Thought that he did? You mean that perhaps now he does not?'

Phoebe nodded. 'That is why Jack has gone to see him. To ascertain his feelings towards me.'

'I fail to comprehend – ' began her mother. 'Why should Mr Mungo – ?'

'Because,' Phoebe took a deep breath. 'Because Jack cares for me as I do for him.' She hesitated a moment to let her mother absorb what she had heard, and then said, 'Jack will ask to speak to you, Mama. We wish to marry.'

Mrs Boyle put both her hands to her face; her needlework slithered from her lap and lay undisturbed on the floor by her feet. 'Oh, Phoebe!' she said in a shocked voice. 'You don't know what you are saying. How can you think of such a thing? Mr Mungo – he seems such a considerate, thoughtful person, how can he contemplate asking to marry you?'

'He is a considerate person, and he loves me,' Phoebe said patiently. 'And I love him. I always said that I would choose the man I wanted to marry, and I have. There is no-one else.'

Mrs Boyle started to weep. 'This is my fault,' she cried. 'I have been far too lenient with you. I have not guided you as I should.' She drew in a quick sobbing breath. 'What will your father say? He will not allow it, of course. You know how he feels about – about – '

'About the Aborigines? Yes, we all know Father's views on the Aborigines, the convicts and anyone else who is downtrodden and tries to raise themselves up.' Phoebe couldn't help but let scorn creep into her voice. 'But I don't really care what Father thinks and I intend to marry Jack anyway, if not now, then when I come of age.'

'But you hardly know him, Phoebe. You have had only a short acquaintanceship – the ship, here at the Lintons.' Her mother strove for every possible excuse.

'I have known him for years, Mama,' Phoebe said quietly. 'He used to come with Mrs Hawkins sometimes to collect Ralph from dame school.'

She gave a smile of remembrance. 'We used to give a secret wave to each other when no-one was looking. I think I knew even then that he was the one for me. That was', she confessed, 'the real reason I wanted to come to England. When I heard that Ralph was coming and that Jack was travelling with him, I knew that it was the only way that we could meet and get to know each other.'

'But think of the consequences, Phoebe.' Tears rushed down Mrs Boyle's face. 'No-one will speak to you, you will be cut entirely from society, even Mr Mungo's family won't accept you.'

'I know there will be difficulties. We are both aware of that, and if people cut me then so be it, Jack is more important to me than anyone else. But you forget, Mama, that Jack's mother has white blood, her father was an Englishman. She, at least, will accept me.'

'I would never be able to see you! Your father would forbid it.'

Phoebe was silenced. It was true. Her father would forbid her mother to visit her. Their meetings would have to be secret, as her mother's meetings with Meg Hawkins were secret. 'Ralph's mother!' she exclaimed.

Her mother looked at her sharply. 'What about her?'

'We could meet there. Mrs Hawkins would be happy for us to do that.'

Mrs Boyle gazed at her daughter. 'You know that Meg is my friend?'

'Yes,' Phoebe said softly. 'I have known for a long time and Ralph knows too, but no-one else,' she assured her.

'I must go and lie down.' Her mother's eyes were bloodshot and she compressed her lips into a narrow line as she fought to check her emotion. 'I have a headache and I must be alone to think what is to be done.'

'There is nothing to be done, Mama,' Phoebe said steadily. 'I have decided. And if you will not give your consent so that we can be married in England, then when we return home I will live with Jack as his wife until I am of age to marry him.'

Her mother staggered as she stood up and put her hand to her head. 'I cannot believe I am hearing such things from your lips, Phoebe.' She gazed at Phoebe pleadingly. 'Tell me that nothing has happened between you and Mr Mungo? That there is no shame to impart?'

Phoebe shook her head. 'There is no shame.

Jack Mungo is and always has been a man of honour. He has always respected me. But if I cannot legally marry him, then I will go with him as I have said.' She put her hand out to her mother, who turned away from her. 'I'm sorry, Mama, to upset you.'

After her mother had left to go to her room, Phoebe crossed the hall, intending to walk in the garden. As she descended the outside steps she saw Mrs Linton sitting on a seat near the rose walk. She did not feel much like conversation but Mrs Linton had lifted her head and seen her, so she was obliged to walk towards her.

'Are you well, Mrs Linton?' Phoebe thought her hostess looked rather peaky.

'Well enough, my dear,' she said, 'but in rather a meditative mood. Life is full of surprises and it would seem that ours is about to change.'

'You must have seen many changes, Mrs Linton,' Phoebe said. 'More than most.'

'Yes, certainly in my early life. Circumstances over which I had no control. People, one person in particular, who did not care what happened to me, changed my life beyond all recognition.' Then her face lit up with a smile. 'But I had the strength of love to sustain me. Without that I could not have survived.'

'So', Phoebe said slowly, 'love is important above all else, would you say, ma'am?'

'Oh, undoubtedly. If you have never loved then you have never lived.'

Phoebe reached out to touch her hand. 'Thank you, Mrs Linton. Thank you so much.'

Emily Linton looked puzzled. 'For what, my dear?'

'For confirming what I already believed. Mrs Linton, would you be kind enough, a little later, to seek out Mama? I have given her news which has upset her and she needs a friend to talk to.'

'Of course. I too need to talk. My husband and I have had a long discussion with Roger. When you and your mother, Ralph and Mr Mungo – Jack,' she smiled, 'return home – ' She gave a great sigh. 'Our son Roger wishes to go with you. I will miss him so much,' she said in a low voice. 'But we must let him go, so that he will come back.'

'So you will lose your son and that saddens you and I have just told Mama that she is to gain one, and that saddens her.' Phoebe felt a sudden rush of emotion towards her mother and Emily Linton. What great strength was needed to be a parent and how selfish children were.

Emily Linton gazed quizzically at her. 'Do you wish to tell me about it? Are you to be married?'

Phoebe nodded.

'To Ralph?'

'To Jack Mungo.'

'Ah!' Mrs Linton exclaimed softly. 'Your mother will be concerned for you! For the difficulties and prejudices that you will surely encounter.' Then she turned to Phoebe and put her arm around her. 'How very brave you are. You must love him very much.'

Phoebe burst into tears as she received the comfort she was seeking. 'I know how difficult it will be,' she sobbed. 'I shall have to leave Sydney and all my friends. My father won't speak to me, but I shan't care about that; he has never shown either my brother or me any affection; but my mother will have to meet me in secret for my father will forbid our meeting. And, the worst thing of all – ' She hesitated: she had not confessed this fear to anyone else. 'Is that – in spite of the fact that I know Jack loves me, he might take another "wife" – an Aborigine woman to give him children so that their race will not die out.'

Mrs Linton gave her a handkerchief to wipe her eyes and said gently, 'And in spite of all that, you still wish to marry him.'

'Yes,' she said. 'I do.'

'You want to marry Phoebe?' Ralph confronted Jack. 'But you know how I have felt towards her! How can you possibly do this to me?'

He saw contrition written on Jack's face and decided that he wouldn't let him off easily, even though he felt a release inside himself. Phoebe wasn't for him, he now knew. She and Jack were right for each other, in spite of their obvious cultural and racial differences.

'I'm sorry, Ralph,' Jack began. 'I have tried to

tell you so many times that she was not the woman for you.'

'And so you sneaked up behind my back and charmed her with your sweet talking, just the way you do with other ladies!'

'No!' Jack protested. 'It has never been like that. You know that I only ever jested with others. No-one ever took me seriously!'

'What about Miss Linton?' Ralph barked at him. 'Did she not take you seriously?'

'Miss Linton! Ah,' he breathed. 'She is an admirable lady. I have a great fondness for her. But she is not the one for me. She requires a special kind of man for a husband.'

Ralph put his hands to his head in mock despair and Jack frowned. 'I didn't think that you would take it so badly! I didn't realize that your feelings ran so deeply. Phoebe isn't aware of them.'

'You have spoken to her then?' Ralph glared at him.

'We have spoken of our feelings for one another many times.'

'Traitor!' Ralph bellowed. 'And you were supposed to be my friend.'

Jack looked distressed and bewildered, and Ralph thought that perhaps he had gone far enough. 'There's only one thing for it,' he insisted. 'I challenge you! We must fight for her.'

Jack's mouth dropped open. 'Fight!' he said. 'But – '

'Isn't that what your people do when two men want the same woman?'

There was a lightning flash of anger on Jack's normally peaceful face. 'Yes, and I have also seen white men fight over a woman.' He unbuttoned his jacket and threw it over the saddle of the horse. His white shirt gleamed in the darkness and the whites of his eyes glistened in his dark face. 'If that's what you want, then I will wrestle you. But take heed. It is at your own peril. I will win as I always do.'

'We'll see!' Ralph too unbuttoned his jacket and threw it down. He rolled up his shirtsleeves. 'We'll see.' A man and a woman walking through the square stopped for a moment and then crossed over and hurried away, but a tramp sitting in a doorway got up and came nearer, settling on the ground near them for a better view.

Ralph stretched his arms and hands in a downwards position as he was the challenger, and Jack put up his arms in a passive position and they walked towards each other. Someone in a room over a shop opened a window and leaned out to watch, calling encouragement to Ralph. 'Don't let the foreigner win, mate,' he shouted.

'We're both foreigners,' Ralph shouted back, and launched himself at Jack.

It was an uneven match. Jack was angry and his weight weighed heavily into his torso, legs and feet, and Ralph couldn't shift him, no matter how he heaved. Then Jack suddenly lightened himself and allowed Ralph to toss him and he landed lightly on his feet.

A small crowd gathered. Late-night revellers, drifting home from club or theatre, stopped to watch the unusual fight where no violence was used, no fist or feet, no knife or glass.

Two more rounds and Jack was the challenger and Ralph prepared himself to be thrown. He landed awkwardly on his feet and fell, rolling over onto his side where he lay still.

'Get up!' Jack nudged him with his foot. 'We're not finished yet.'

Ralph didn't answer but his shoulders started to heave. Jack leaned over him. 'Get up,' he shouted at him. 'What's the matter with you?'

He pushed him again with his foot and Ralph rolled over onto his back, shaking with laughter. 'Hah,' he roared. 'If you could have seen your face!'

'What!' Jack glared at him as Ralph continued to roar with laughter. 'Are you – ?' Realization hit him as Ralph sat up, still laughing. 'You! You White Devil! You're fooling!'

''Course I'm fooling.' Ralph put his hand up for Jack to pull him up. 'Would I let even a lovely woman come between us?'

'Yes,' Jack answered softly. 'You would if you really cared for her.' He put out his hand, then grabbed Ralph around the waist and threw him and Ralph, totally unprepared, landed with a crash on the ground. A cheer went up from the crowd. They drifted away and Ralph lay groaning.

'That wasn't fair,' he grumbled. 'I wasn't ready.'

Jack pulled him up. 'Always be prepared,' he grinned. 'Even your best friend can turn on you.'

Ralph slapped him on the back. 'Good luck, old fellow,' he said with feeling. 'You have my good wishes, both of you.'

Chapter Thirty-Four

They were all gathered together in the drawing room of Elmswell Manor. Supper was over and empty coffee cups and brandy glasses were being cleared away. Although the evening was still warm, a cheerful fire burned in the grate, enhancing the perfume of lilies which were placed in vases around the room. In front of the hearth on a Chinese rug, a young dog lay snoring gently and a black and white kitten slept between its paws.

Harriet had not returned to Holderness with them but Elizabeth was still there. Her countenance had lost its pinched, tense look and she seemed more at ease than they had ever known her. 'My one desire', she was saying to Mrs Boyle, 'is that Harriet should marry Thomas. He has been so faithful all these years. For myself I want nothing more than to continue teaching. I am content now that I know my mother is at peace.'

Ralph heard her quiet words and reluctantly

turned his eyes away from the piano where Amelia was playing softly whilst Roger turned over the pages of music. Ralph had not heard her play before. They had been so busy chatting and discussing, to-ing and fro-ing between Holderness and York since they arrived on their visit, that they had not all gathered together in one group since their first evening, and he had not heard Amelia play or sing as she was doing now or even known that she could.

Elizabeth shall have her wish, he thought. I have money enough. I will give Harriet a dowry so that she might marry her Mr Thacker, and Elizabeth shall be comfortable in her little house. He turned his eyes back to Amelia and gazed at her profile. She had a faint smile on her face as she played a gentle melody, yet there seemed to be a sadness there. She glanced towards the windows which were open, letting in the soft smell of rain which had come earlier. He followed her gaze and saw the huge orange harvest moon filling the aperture of two panes of glass. Tomorrow the gathering of the harvest was to begin and after that the visitors would start their preparation for the journey home.

He closed his eyes as a pulsating agitation seized him. I don't want to go! Not yet. He swallowed hard as the knowledge threatened to engulf him. Why don't I? I want to see Ma and Da and Peggy. I have missed them, more than I thought I would. He had written to them and told them of all that had happened and that he had discovered that his natural mother, Rose Elizabeth Fielding, had been a good person and Edward Scott, of whom he could never think as his father, was a bad one.

He opened his eyes as he heard the words, 'I don't want to go back,' and thought that he had spoken out loud. Amelia was looking towards him but as he caught her gaze, she turned away.

It was Mrs Boyle who had uttered the words. 'I can't,' she said with despair in her voice, and although she was speaking to Mrs Linton they had all caught the words and had fallen silent, all but Amelia who continued to play softly in the background.

Mrs Boyle, after much heart-searching, had agreed that an accommodating priest could be sought who would marry Phoebe and Jack with the consent of one parent. There was, she had decided, no other alternative.

'I cannot return and face the anger and hostility of Captain Boyle,' she continued. In her anxious and agitated state, she no longer cared who knew or heard her opinion of her husband. 'I shall live with my mother and brother and his wife, and although I shall always be the poor relation, it will be preferable to returning to a man who has no compassion and is blind and deaf to my concerns or emotions.'

There was an awkward silence, then Phoebe said in a low voice, 'But you will not see me or Edwin again, Mama. Does that not upset you?'

'Of course it upsets me!' Her mother took out a handkerchief and pressed it to her eyes. 'But as I said before, your father would not allow me to visit you. And as for Edwin, I see so little of him anyway. He prefers to spend time with his friends than to be at home.'

Phoebe gave a sudden blink of her blue eyes and clenched her lips, but said no more, only exchanging a glance with Jack who was sitting close by her and reached out his hand to enclose hers.

'I understand your feelings, my dear.' Emily Linton spoke quietly and compassionately to Mrs Boyle. 'To look ahead and only see emptiness in front of you. I have been through that and am aware of the turmoil that is besetting you.' She looked towards Ralph and raised her eyebrows questioningly and he nodded. 'I think also of someone else in my time of trouble who was going through that same turmoil, and who took a way out which was consequential, and is why we are sitting here today.'

She turned to Elizabeth Fielding. 'I have spoken to Ralph of your mother, and we decided that you are now well enough to know the truth of your mother's death.'

She hesitated; the past was still very painful to her. 'It was dark below decks on the convict ship and we were all sick. I remember your mother handing her baby to Meg as she couldn't pacify him or stop him crying. Meg had no experience of babies and yet a bond was made immediately.

I believe that your mother saw that and was comforted by it.'

As Emily Linton looked back into the past, the image flashed before her of the woman poised on the ship's bulwarks before she took the final step, and she shook her head to dispel it and return to the present. 'I believe that your mother, who had given all her love and strength to her two young daughters and yet had lost them, thought that she would lose this child too when she reached Australia.'

She caught her husband's eye and saw the agreement in his face. 'She undoubtedly would have done, he would have gone to an orphanage and she to the womens' prison. When she saw Meg, who was brave and fearless, with her child, she knew that with her he would stand a chance of survival. Which he did,' she smiled at Ralph, 'For Meg fought like a tigress to keep him, vowing that he was hers and that my brother Joe was his father.'

'So, what you are saying, Mrs Linton,' Elizabeth said slowly, understanding at last, 'is that our mother gave up her own life so that her child, Ralph, our brother, would survive?'

'Yes,' said Emily Linton quietly. 'That is what I am saying, and I am also saying that you should be very proud to have had such a mother.'

Shortly afterwards Roger left them. He, and his Uncle Sam, who had had supper with them, were to have an early start the next morning to see the harvesters begin their work of bringing in the corn. Ralph and Jack had pledged their support but were not expected quite as soon as the labourers.

'Would you care for a walk, Amelia?' Ralph asked. 'A turn around the garden perhaps?'

As she agreed and gathered up her shawl, Jack rose to his feet. 'That's a good idea. Phoebe?'

'Yes,' she smiled. She had been subdued since her mother's outburst. 'That would be pleasant. Miss Fielding?'

'Thank you, no.' Elizabeth declined. 'I have walked several times today. I think I will retire early and I must think now of returning home, Mrs Linton.'

'You must come again soon,' Emily Linton declared. 'And bring Harriet with you. The house will be so quiet when all of these young people have gone, and especially,' she added huskily, 'if Roger goes with them.'

'Don't fret, Mama.' Amelia came across to her and laid her hand on her shoulder. 'There are still a few of your chicks left.'

'But for how much longer?' she replied softly as the four young people went out of the door.

The air was quite still and the moon lit up the garden as if it was daylight, highlighting the ash and oak trees and suffusing the grass with a glistening lustre. 'We're walking on diamonds,' Amelia said softly. 'See how the grass sparkles.'

'Yes,' Ralph murmured. He had not noticed the grass, only how the moonlight lit up the dark sheen of Amelia's hair so that he wanted to stroke it.

Phoebe and Jack walked in front of them, their heads, one so fair, the other dark, close together. Presently Jack's arm stole around Phoebe's waist. Ralph glanced at Amelia for her reaction and asked, 'Do you think Jack is being too forward?'

She shook her head. 'No. They are committed to each other. They want to show their love, that is understandable.' She paused before adding, 'They must continue to show it. They will have such hardships when they return home.'

'More than you can possibly imagine,' he answered and turning towards her, said abruptly, 'I shall miss you, Amelia,' and as she drew in her breath in bewilderment, added, 'I shall miss your company, our disagreements.' He smiled as she started to demur. 'Oh yes, come! We have had a few. We have had some lively conversations. That is what I shall also miss when Jack is married to Phoebe,' he told her. 'We have spent so much time together since our childhood.'

'Surely your friendship will continue?' Amelia said. 'He, they – will need it more than ever, I would have thought?'

'And they will always have it, but they will have each other, they will not need a third party.'

As he spoke, Phoebe and Jack turned around. 'I have just been hearing about your fight with Jack, Ralph,' Phoebe called to him. 'Jack said how upset you were when you heard the news!'

'You fought with Jack?' Amelia asked in astonishment. 'Why ever did you do that?'

'It was in the middle of York,' Phoebe called to her. 'They took off their jackets and fought like common louts!'

'But I won.' Jack laughed and kissed Phoebe's cheek. 'He is no match for me.'

'It was a jest,' Ralph muttered awkwardly. 'I was fooling, that's all.'

Phoebe didn't hear or pretended not to hear his remark, and went on, 'It is the very first time that anyone has ever fought over me.' She seemed to have recovered her spirits and laughed as she spoke.

Amelia, on the other hand, seemed to freeze. Ralph felt her iciness as she whispered, 'You fought with Jack over Phoebe? But I thought that you said, you said – they were right for each other?'

'I did,' he stammered. 'They are.'

'But you were still hurt? You do still care for her? That is the reason you fought?' He saw her face become rigid and her speech was restrained.

'No,' he insisted. 'It was a jape,' and he turned towards Jack for him to confirm it. But Jack and Phoebe had disappeared. Somewhere in the garden they had found their own secret place and Ralph and Amelia were excluded from it.

'Excuse me,' Amelia said. 'I am feeling chilly. I shall go inside.'

384

'I'll walk you back,' he said, his thoughts confused.

'No, really. I can manage. Thank you,' and she hurried off at such a pace that he was left standing alone.

'Damn!' he muttered as he saw her gather up her skirts and run up the steps. 'Damn! Damn! Damn!'

Chapter Thirty-Five

The following morning Ralph was up early. He dragged himself out of bed as dawn broke and sat in a chair by the window, staring out as the sky lightened and the sun came up in the direction of the sea.

At first sight the streaks of dawn were silver, shot with gold and rose, soft subtle shades, not a flood of incandescent brilliance such as he would see at home in Australia. Then, as if someone with a paintbrush had dipped deeper into a paint pot to bring out stronger tones, the sky changed to deeper colours, to splashes of apricot, aquamarine, ruby and bishop's purple.

The chorus of songbirds began, breaking the silence, with the thrush taking the lead, its clear voice urging the other birds to join in welcoming the new day. Swallows flew around the house in swift disarray, then gathered together on treetops and barn roofs, preparing for departure.

'Just like me,' he murmured. 'I feel as if I am in disarray. Like Mrs Boyle, I don't want to go, but for quite different reasons.'

He washed and dressed and then stole along the corridor to Jack's room and tapped on the door. He could hear the muted sounds of servants in the kitchen downstairs, the rattle of pans and of smothered conversation and laughter. There was also a faint aroma of baking drifting up the stairs, of pastry and bacon and ham.

Aunt Emily came along the corridor as he waited at Jack's door and he exclaimed a surprised, 'Good morning. I didn't expect you to be up so early, Aunt Emily!'

She looked crisp and fresh and had a large white apron over her blue cotton gown. 'It's all hands to the pumps today, Ralph,' she smiled. 'The kitchen staff have been up for several hours making bread and pies to feed the workers. The itinerant labourers come to help with the harvest and the hind's wife will be preparing food for them.'

'The hind's wife?' he questioned.

'The steward's wife,' she explained. 'Normally she does most of the cooking, but she's broken her arm and so Cook agreed to help her out.'

Jack opened his bedroom door. He was dressed and ready for breakfast and the three of them went down to the dining room to find the whole family there already, Amelia, May, Lily and the twins, who could barely keep still in

387

their excitement to help with the harvest and see the new sail reaper which had recently been purchased. Phoebe wasn't there, but Amelia murmured that she had knocked on her door as she'd passed, for she had said that she too wanted to come to see the harvest gathered in.

Amelia seemed subdued and she had faint shadows beneath her eyes. She answered Ralph's greeting but avoided his gaze and got up from the table to help her mother dish up the bacon, eggs and ham, which lay hot and sizzling in dishes on the dresser. She poured coffee and handed a cup each to Jack and to Ralph.

'Thank you, Amelia,' Ralph murmured and wondered how he could possibly gain a warm smile from her, such as Jack had received as she'd given him his coffee. She has an affection for him I do believe, he thought with a touch of resentment. Even though she knows that he is affianced to Phoebe. Perhaps that is why she is so spiritless this morning.

They moved off to the fields at eight o'clock, piling into a trap with the twins and Lily running on ahead. Lily had had a secret, knowing smile on her face since it was announced that Mr Mungo and Miss Boyle were to be married, whilst May had adopted a dreaming faraway expression each time she met up with either of them.

One of the fields was being cut by hand and Sam and six other scythe men were working their way across the corn. The scythes made a gentle swish, swishing sound and as the corn fell, women and older children gathered it into sheaves ready for the bindsters to tie and stook.

In a further field, Roger was watching with his arms folded across his chest as the new sail reaper, pulled by two horses and driven by one man, was cutting the corn with its swirling blades, whilst behind him a bevy of gatherers were bent low over the swathes, for manual labour was still essential even with the new machinery.

'Mama and Roger would like to bring in more machinery,' Amelia said, shielding her eyes from the sun as she too watched. 'But Uncle Sam is worried about the workers. He says there will be no work for them eventually. Perhaps,' she said thoughtfully, 'that is one of the reasons why Roger wants to go to Australia. He must feel very frustrated. He doesn't like to go against Uncle Sam, yet he wants to see progress. He says we won't survive if we don't bring in modern methods.'

Phoebe was pensive as she stood alongside Amelia with a jug of lemonade in her hand, and it was as if she was barely listening. 'I shall remember this time for ever,' she said softly. 'Jack and I would never have been allowed to be in each other's company at home in the way we have been here. It would have been forbidden. We could only have ever met in secret. This will be, I'm sure, one of the happiest years of my life.'

'There will be many more,' Amelia encouraged. 'Once you are married and don't have to hide your feelings for Jack.'

'There will be hurdles to climb and objections, that I accept, and I know that I shall be abandoned by society and my friends. And I do worry,' she admitted. 'Jack and I must be strong to withstand the difficulties that our marriage will bring. But I so desperately want to help him. To bring about his dream of freeing his people from the servitude of the whites.

'They are not ignorant, you know,' she turned towards Amelia and there was an appeal in her eyes, 'the Aborigines. They have their own languages, their own culture and history. Their only ignorance is that they do not realize that they are slowly being removed from the country which belongs to them.'

'Removed?' Amelia murmured. She was looking over towards where Ralph and Jack were raking the loose stubble, clearing the ground, so that the sheaves could be set up in stooks to dry.

'Yes,' Phoebe answered. 'By disease, bullet and despair.'

'You have learned all this from Jack?' Amelia asked.

'Not only from Jack,' Phoebe replied. 'But from observation too. I remember when I was very young how my father, and other men like him, treated the Aborigines. With either callousness and hatred or as if they didn't exist, and it disturbed me even then.'

'You are so brave.' Amelia poured lemonade for a young Irish worker. She was as dark as a gypsy and had a baby strapped to her back. 'Ralph was right when he said that you and Jack were made for each other.'

'Ralph said that?' Phoebe took off her large straw hat and fanned herself. She smiled. 'I do tease him so.'

'He still cares for you. He hides his feelings very well.' Amelia watched her friend's face for her reaction. 'It will be hard for him to accept your marriage.'

Phoebe laughed. 'Nonsense! Yes, he cares for me, as I care for him.' She looked Amelia in the eyes and said earnestly, 'But he does not love me.'

'Then why – ?' Amelia faltered. 'Why did he fight with Jack over you?'

'I was teasing, Amelia! They did not fight! Ralph pretended that he was devastated over my choosing Jack instead of him and challenged him to wrestle. They are like brothers, those two,' she added softly. 'I could not come between them.'

Amelia thought of the previous evening when she had rushed away from Ralph. Her feelings had been hurt and she had spent a restless night. Yet I don't know why, she pondered. He has given no intimation that his feelings might lie in my direction. And I, I have given him no reason to suppose that I might care for him. Quite the opposite in fact. I have been impatient and short-tempered with him. And yet, she mused, he started to say that he would miss me.

Her emotions were churning. He is not the man I would choose, she argued. He is outspoken and sometimes flippant, though I confess he is also spirited and enthusiastic. And bold when he is roused, she deliberated, as he was when he confronted Edward Scott.

As that fateful evening in York came into mind, she thought of how she and Ralph had hidden in the Fieldings' tiny kitchen. They were squashed together behind the door with Ralph trying to hear what was being said out in the hall. She had opened her mouth to whisper something but he had gently laid his finger on her lips to silence her, and gazed down at her with eyes which now seemed such an alluring blue. His hand dropped softly onto her shoulder and remained there until they heard Moira's cry.

She found that Phoebe was smiling at her, her eyebrows raised questioningly, and she gave a start.

'You were miles away, Amelia, not with me at all!'

'I beg your pardon,' she stammered. 'It is the heat, I think. It is making me feel quite dizzy.'

At noon the workers took a break; some retired to the shelter of the hedges and others leaned against the wagons whilst they ate their midday dinner. Ginny and Mrs Linton and some of the maids had brought meat pies, cheese pasties and bread rolls, whilst the hind's wife and her helpers brought apple pie, cold tea and jugs of freshly pumped cold water.

Ralph and Jack were lying in a corner of the half-garnered field. Ralph was turning a deeper shade of brown and he compared the colour of his arm with Jack's. 'You'll never get so dark.' Jack chewed on a length of straw. 'Your skin's too fair.' He suddenly sat up as in the distance he saw Amelia and Phoebe moving between the groups of workers with their jugs and baskets of food.

'Am I doing right, Ralph?' His voice was urgent. 'Am I being selfish to expect Phoebe to face the pain and opposition which will undoubtedly come if we should marry?'

Ralph too sat up and looked over in the direction of the two young women. 'She's strong and determined,' he said positively. 'There is no-one else I know who could take on such a challenge.'

'I don't mind the insults for myself,' Jack insisted. 'Nor the stone-throwing or being spat at. I am used to it. But I couldn't bear it if that happens to Phoebe. I would have to fight back.'

'And you know that if you do, you'll be thrown into jail. You will have to learn even more forbearance, my friend. To turn the other cheek.'

Jack nodded. 'She wants to set up a school,'

he continued. 'For the children and for their parents, if they will come. Not a school such as the missionaries have where they are taught English history and religion. Phoebe wants to teach them to read and write and for me to teach them about their own culture. Before it is lost,' he added. 'She thought of it after Amelia told her about the Irish children at the school in York.'

'It is an admirable idea.' Ralph was watching Amelia. She was coming closer, working her way towards them. She was smiling now, and had lost her morning languor and looked quite happy. 'Though it will be hard,' he admitted, almost absent-mindedly, as other thoughts came into his head. 'The authorities will be against it. They'll do everything in their power to stop you.'

'Jack!' He spoke in a low urgent voice and had half risen to his knees as Amelia approached. 'What would you think if I said that I wasn't going home?'

Jack gave a thin whistle, but didn't have time to make a reply before Amelia joined them. He accepted the cup of water which she offered, gulping it down before giving a quick glance at Ralph and then excusing himself to Amelia, saying he wanted to speak to Phoebe.

'No, nothing to eat, thank you.' Ralph waved away Amelia's offer of bread and cheese or meat pie. 'I'm not hungry. Only thirsty.' He too took a long draught of water, then said, 'Why don't you sit down for a few minutes, Amelia? Here.' He raked up a pile of straw into a cushion. 'Come and sit here.'

She hesitated and looked around and he gave a half-grin. 'Oh! Have I breached some etiquette? I can't seem to get things right!'

She laughed and put down her basket and sat down. 'No,' she said. 'Not really, though the farm workers will start to gossip about Miss Linton and the young man from abroad.'

'Will they?' He sat down beside her. 'And what do you think they will say?'

She blushed slightly and looked embarrassed. 'I don't know.'

'Do you mind what they say?' He gazed earnestly at her but she didn't meet his eyes.

'I – yes! I suppose I do. I would not like my behaviour to be the subject of idle tittle-tattle.'

'You could not then – ' he hesitated, then dared. 'You could not do as Phoebe is about to – enter into a controversial marriage and be the subject of abuse and hatred? Have silence fall in a room as you entered?'

She lifted her eyes then and answered slowly. 'I would have to be very sure that my love was constant and sincere.' She blushed again as she spoke so frankly, 'And not merely physical attraction. Phoebe and Jack are very brave to go into such a marriage. They obviously have no doubts.'

He gazed silently at her and although he

could see beyond her shoulder that the workers had gone again to their tasks, he did not attempt to move. 'I told you yesterday, Amelia, that I would miss you when I went home. Then you ran away from me,' he added softly. 'Before I could ask if you would miss me!'

She opened her mouth to speak, but then thought better of it and swallowed hard. She seemed tense and he put his hand over hers and held it there. 'Can you not say?' he asked quietly. 'Am I being too bold?'

Oh God. I'm doing this all wrong! He felt an overwhelming panic. This is not what young Englishwomen expect! They like to be wooed, to be showered with gifts and flowers and compliments, and I have done none of these things!

'It is not that you are too bold.' She raised her eyes to his but then looked away. 'Honesty and sincerity are things which I have always admired in others. It is just that I did not expect – that is to say – I had not considered that my opinion was so important to you.'

He felt a tightness in his chest as if emotion was swelling it to bursting point. She said once before that I was arrogant! A cold sweat came over him. Does she mean that I only consider my own opinion to be important? Is this what she means?

She gave a shy smile. 'But to answer your question directly as I know you would prefer it. Yes. I will miss you.'

He let out a great whoosh of air, not realizing that he had been holding his breath. 'As much as you will miss Jack?'

She put her head on one side. 'Jack?' she quizzed.

He said huskily, 'You have become fond of him, I think?'

'I have become fond of him,' she said mischievously and her eyes sparkled. 'As you are fond of Phoebe! Fond enough to fight over her!'

'Oh. That was a jest!' He spoke quickly as if embarrassed. 'Phoebe told of that incident deliberately, I'm sure of it.'

'Did she?' Amelia was astonished. 'Why would she do that?'

He smiled and shook his head. 'I can't imagine. Women are a mystery to me. They are wily and artful and full of tricks and games to get their own way.'

'I'm not,' she said swiftly. 'I'm not at all like that.'

'No.' He gazed at her. 'I don't believe you are,' he agreed. 'So if you were asked a question you would give a straight and honest answer?'

She considered. 'Yes. Unless I thought a truthful answer would cause unnecessary pain.'

'It would cause me a great deal of pain, if your answer to my next question was no.' He took hold of both her hands and lifted them to his lips, so that she would have no doubt of what the question would be.

'That is unfair,' she breathed. 'That leaves me with only one other answer.'

He leaned forward and as she didn't turn away, he gently kissed her cheek. 'It is the only one I want, Amelia. I love you. Will you give me permission to speak to your father?'

Chapter Thirty-Six

Amelia's father was at present away from home and the marriage of Phoebe and Jack had been arranged for the following week, so Ralph impatiently waited until after the wedding in order to speak to Captain Linton.

The ceremony was a quiet affair, conducted early one morning with Ralph and Amelia acting as witnesses and Captain Linton escorting the bride to meet her groom. Afterwards the whole family celebrated with a sumptuous breakfast, though Mrs Boyle ate little, spoke little and had dark shadows beneath her eyes. Mrs Edwards, Deborah and Sam came to stay at Elmswell Manor and gave up their gatehouse to the newly-weds so that they might have some quiet time alone.

'How very considerate everyone has been,' Phoebe said as she and Jack walked one evening in the garden. 'I shall never ever forget their kindness. It will sustain me whenever we have difficulties with others.'

'Don't think of the difficulties now.' He put his arm around her. 'We must live only for the moment and not wait in anticipation of what might or might not come.'

She sighed and put her head against him. 'I am prepared,' she murmured. 'And with your love I will overcome whatever is in front of us.' Then she drew away and took a deep breath. 'But there is just one thing I am not yet prepared for, and I must ask you to tell me so that I can strengthen myself in anticipation.'

He gave a puzzled frown. 'You must not worry about anything, not my family or the other Aborigines. I will protect you with my life.'

Tears flooded her eyes and she spoke in a choked voice. 'That I believe. I know in my heart that you truly love me.'

'So what then?' He stopped and turned her towards him. 'What is it that makes you cry?'

She lowered her head but he put his hand under her chin, lifting it. 'Look at me, wife. We must never be afraid to ask anything of each other.'

Her tears flowed down her cheeks and he gently kissed them away. 'Tell me,' he whispered.

'I need to know, so that I am prepared. When someone points a scornful finger or whispers behind their hands.' She gave a small sob. 'I should wish to be the first to know.'

'What? Tell me!'

'When, or if, will you take another wife? An Aborigine woman to give you children of your own race?'

He stared at her for a moment, then muttered something in a language she didn't understand. He shook his head, then took her face between his hands and kissed her on the mouth.

'Did you marry me and make vows in your church, thinking that I would take another wife to beget children?'

'Yes,' she whispered. 'I did. I wanted you, even knowing that.'

'Then I know that you truly love me as I love you. How could I take another woman, white or black?' His dark eyes glistened and his full mouth was soft as he spoke. 'When I have lain with my body next to yours? With your flesh close to mine so that we are as one? How could you think such a thing?'

'It is said that is what happens,' she began tearfully.

'Not with me.' He stroked her face. 'You will be a wife like no other. I will show you such memorable sights and take you to places that no other white woman has ever seen. We shall sleep beneath a canopy of stars and call the earth our home, and we shall raise our children to be proud.'

'Sir.' Ralph declined the offer of a seat as Captain Linton invited him into the library. 'I wish to ask for the hand of Amelia in marriage.'

He had rehearsed for days and his speech came out stiff, bald and unemotional.

Captain Linton gave a small smile. 'I have been expecting something of the sort.'

'You have, sir?' Ralph was astonished. However could he have guessed?

'Sit down, do.' Amelia's father again waved him to a chair. 'I have been young too, remember. I know all the symptoms.'

Ralph sat down in relief. Well, now it was out. He liked Amelia's father. Why had he been so nervous?

'Do you love Amelia?'

'Oh yes, sir. I do.'

'And does she love you?'

Ralph hesitated. 'I think she has a fondness for me, sir, she wouldn't have agreed to my coming to see you otherwise.'

Philip Linton smiled. 'Indeed she wouldn't. Of that you can be certain.'

'But,' Ralph felt he had to be honest, 'I do believe that she regards me as unconventional and outspoken and lacking in refinement.'

Captain Linton demurred. 'Surely not. Amelia is outspoken herself. She would not regard it as a fault in others.'

'Nevertheless sir, that is the impression that I receive. So what I would like to do, sir, with your permission, is to pay court to your daughter as an Englishman would. To call on her and show her that I can be well mannered and cultured – that I am not a Philistine. I do attend concerts and listen to chamber music in Sydney,' he added disarmingly, and Philip Linton put his hand across his mouth to hide a smile. 'And I'll bring her flowers and take her out driving, if that is permissible, for that is what young ladies expect!'

'Well,' his host replied. 'If that is what you feel Amelia would like, then certainly you have my permission to call upon her. But I assure you that not all Englishmen are gentlemen. Some may call themselves such and I can think of several who do, but it would be palpably untrue.'

'Yes, sir.' Ralph thought of Edward Scott who had the veneer of a gentleman, but who plainly was not. He felt a sudden sinking of despondency. I would hate to be like him.

He threw himself wholeheartedly into the art of wooing, even to the extent of moving out of the Lintons' house and taking a room at the Sun Inn in the market town of Hedon, just a few miles distant. He bought a sturdy mare and a small trap and arrived on the doorstep of Elmswell Manor each afternoon with flowers, chocolates or gifts of lace or sweet-smelling sachets for Amelia's pillow.

'There is no need,' she demurred one day when he brought her a posy to pin on her dress, and he responded with a polite bow and the words, 'Oh, but there is.' And with a gentle smile she accepted it.

He would first of all enquire about her health and then that of her mother, father, sisters and brothers, then as she convinced him that they were all in excellent spirits, he would comment on the weather, if it was fine and likely to stay that way or whether rain was imminent.

As they set off on their drive, usually with May as chaperone who would do her best to pretend she was not eavesdropping on their conversation, he would comment on Amelia's gown and how the colour suited her, and she would give a whimsical smile.

They drove through the lanes of Holderness and saw the leaves on the trees changing colour as autumn caught hold. The stooks glowed a pale gold and the earth where it had been turned was a deep rich brown. Amelia pointed out which land and farms belonged to the estate, which farms grew root crops for the local markets, which meadows were best for sheep and which field grew the best oats, or commented on which farm had the best hedge-layer and who was the champion ploughman.

'You are a true farmer's daughter, Amelia,' he complimented.

'I have known it all of my life,' she said. 'If I had been born a boy I would have been a farmer.'

'Could you face leaving this place if you had to?' he asked quietly. 'As Roger is going to.'

She hesitated. 'I'm not sure.' It was a question she had asked herself time and again since Ralph had said he loved her. Would he expect her to go with him to Australia? And could she do that and leave her parents without both eldest son and daughter? 'I always wanted to travel. When I was young I was always asking my parents if we could come and visit you and Peggy, Aunt Meg and Uncle Joe.'

'And now you can,' he assured her. 'If you still want to.'

'I need time,' she murmured. 'Time to consider.'

'All the time in the world,' he insisted. 'There is no hurry.'

Except that time was moving on ever faster and the day was almost on them when Jack and Phoebe would be going home; and the question was, would he return with them?

They turned back as the afternoon drew on, clouds drifting across the low sun. He told her of his life at home in Australia, of the sheep station and of the sheep shearers who in their hundreds rode or walked across the country to shear the millions of sheep which supplied the wool that was sent to England to keep the hungry mills turning.

He told her of the ridge of Blue Mountains which he could see from his window, yet which was inaccessible, except to the Aborigines, and of the birds which Roger would see: the scarlet honeyeater, the red wattlebird with its yellow belly and harsh cry, the dainty fairy-wren, the golden whistlers and coloured finches, the cockatiels and parrots and thousands of budgerigars.

'Roger will love it,' Amelia said. 'He is so looking forward to going.'

'Look, Amelia.' May caught her sister's attention as they entered the drive to the house. 'That's Dr Fowler's carriage. Why would he be here?'

Lily appeared at the door and started to run towards them, her skirts flying, waving her arms at them.

'Oh, Amelia! Thank goodness you're here. Come quickly. Uncle Sam has been taken ill! Roger had to ride like the wind to fetch Dr Fowler and everyone is so distraught, especially Deborah who won't leave Uncle Sam's side!'

'Don't be so dramatic, Lily!' May admonished her sister for her emotional manner.

'What has happened, Lily? Calm down and speak slowly.' Amelia was more disturbed than she appeared. Uncle Sam was never ill. He had the constitution of an ox, though he had seemed quiet lately after Roger had broken the news to him that he was going away.

'I don't know what happened, except that it took four men to carry him into the house.' Lily's face started to crumple. 'He's not going to die is he, Amelia? I couldn't bear it if he did.'

It would be unthinkable. Amelia suddenly felt faint; she had never faced death and Sam was such an integral part of their lives. They had ridden on his broad back when they were small, he had shown them where to gather the best mushrooms, and where there was frogspawn and tiddlers, and he'd allowed them to watch a foal being born, but most of all he took care of Aunt Mary and his half-sister, Deborah, who couldn't look after herself.

She felt Ralph's hand on her elbow and he helped her down from the trap. 'It may be nothing much,' he murmured soothingly. 'Perhaps a fall, he's a big man, he'd fall heavy. Try not to worry.'

'No,' she breathed, clutching his arm. 'Thank you.'

But it wasn't a fall. The door was opened as they approached: Mrs Linton was thanking the doctor as she saw him out. Her face was pale and her eyes were large with unshed tears.

'Sam has suffered a seizure,' she said in a low voice. 'The men brought him in. Roger is with him and is so upset. He says it is all his fault.' Her tears started to fall and she brushed them away. 'Sam has been like a brother to me since I was five years old,' she choked, 'and now he is lying so still and helpless.'

'But – Mama! He isn't – ?' Amelia couldn't bring herself to say the dreaded word.

Her mother shook her head. 'He is still with us. The doctor says he might pull through as he is so strong.'

'He will! He will!' Amelia exclaimed. 'He must.'

'Why does Roger say it is his fault, Mrs Linton?' Ralph asked quietly. 'Was he with him when it happened?'

'No.' Mrs Linton took out a handkerchief and dried her eyes. 'Sam was helping one of the men to bring down a dead tree when apparently he collapsed. They brought him home and Roger rode for the doctor.'

Amelia put her hand up to her mouth and tried to quell her own emotion. Roger had confided in her that Sam was upset about him going away, even though he had assured him that he would come back. Roger is feeling guilty, she pondered, and thinks that the worry has brought on Sam's seizure. Poor Roger, she thought. He won't want to go away now.

Amelia slowly pushed open the sick-room door. Roger and Deborah were by Sam's bedside. Aunt Mary, Sam's mother, had gone to lie down.

'Deborah,' Amelia whispered. 'Mama says will you come now and take some tea? I'll sit with Sam for a little while so that you might rest.'

Deborah shook her head but didn't answer. She held Sam's hand and constantly stroked his fingers.

'She won't leave him,' Roger said quietly. 'She says she's going to look after him until he's better.'

He reached for a handkerchief in his pocket and blew his nose vigorously. 'This is my fault, Amelia. My talk of going away has preyed on his mind.'

'Nonsense,' she whispered tearfully. 'You mustn't say such things.'

'It's true.' Roger turned towards the bed where Sam was lying so still and pale. 'I was being totally selfish anyway, leaving him and Mama to cope.'

'We have a steward and good men,' Amelia began.

'But they can't make decisions can they?' There was disappointment in his voice and a hint of bitterness. 'And neither can Sam. We know that, even though we have always reckoned that he did.'

Amelia nodded. Sam was not aware of his shortcomings. He knew instinctively about farming, but times were changing, machines were coming in, foreign grain was flooding the market and no longer was farming localized. And Sam wanted to continue to farm in the way he had been taught as a boy.

'I won't go now,' Roger said, his eyes on Sam. 'I can't possibly,' and Amelia nodded again in agreement. Of course he couldn't. She would feel exactly the same.

Deborah stayed by Sam's side. A truckle bed was brought into the room so that she might rest, but she spent most of the time sitting or kneeling at the side of his bed. This child-woman who had been cared for by Sam, now cared for him. She mopped his brow, trickled water through his lips and only left the room for calls of nature or when the nurse required to attend to Sam's personal needs.

And when Sam opened his eyes and made his

first murmurings, Deborah was there to hear them and ran to fetch the nurse. 'You see,' she said. 'I said that I would make him better, and I did.'

His speech was slurred and his left arm hung uselessly by his side, but the doctor was convinced that he would recover well. 'You must take things a little easier, Sam,' he admonished him. 'Let some of these other fine young men do the heavy work. You do the advising; but not yet. You must rest now and get your strength back.'

Ralph caught his aunt alone in her study. 'Aunt Emily, can I speak to you?'

She was sitting at her desk in the window. A ledger was open in front of her. 'Of course,' she said, and smiled a little uncertainly. 'Are you coming to tell me that you are taking my daughter away with you?'

He shook his head. 'Amelia and I haven't had a chance to talk since Sam was taken ill. It didn't seem appropriate. But it was of Sam and Roger that I wanted to speak.'

'Roger says that he won't go back with Jack and Phoebe now. That he will go at some other time. But of course he won't. This will be an opportunity that is passed over. Poor Roger,' she sighed softly. 'It was what he wanted more than anything.'

'Then he should go,' Ralph said. 'And I will stay in his place.'

'You will?' she said in astonishment. 'But what

will Joe— your father say? He will surely want you back!'

'Well that's just it, Aunt Emily. Da likes to manage on his own, he never wants me to take the reins. He likes to always be in charge, and I do understand that now, although I didn't before. Da isn't ready to hand over to me, not yet, but he would enjoy showing Roger how the sheep station is run.' He grinned, 'And telling him of how he pulled himself up from the stain of being a convict.'

'Yes,' his aunt agreed. 'He's very proud of that, and rightly so. He wouldn't have had the same opportunities in England. But I don't think Roger would agree,' she added. 'He won't want to leave Sam.'

'I know that I haven't the experience of farming in England,' Ralph persisted. 'But the seasons are not so harsh here as in Australia and with Sam to advise me, when he's feeling better, I'm sure I can manage.' He hesitated. 'Also, Aunt Emily, I do observe as an outsider, and it seems to me that in order to continue successfully you need to take advantage of more modern methods.'

'I know,' she answered. 'But Sam won't hear of it and Roger won't go against him.'

'But Sam might listen to me,' he insisted. 'If I tell him of what is happening in other countries, and that they are sending in natural food products to England much cheaper than England can produce at the present time, then he might agree to change. He thinks of Roger still as a boy,' he said gently. 'He won't think of me in the same way.'

But Sam had ideas of his own. He asked for Roger to come in at the end of one day, and asked Deborah to leave them for a little while. His voice was halting and his speech was slow, but he appeared to have more energy and was propped up on his pillows.

'You look quite perky, Uncle Sam.' Roger sat on the end of the bed. 'Much better than you were yesterday.'

'Yes,' he agreed. 'I am. But I wanted to ask thee about 'oats. How long have I been abed?'

Roger gave a grin. He knew what was coming. Sam knew his oats and always supervised their harvesting. 'Two weeks, Sam.'

'Ah!' Sam sighed and looked thoughtful. 'So we've not heard third *choch* bell?'

'No. Not yet.'

''Cos tha remembers, doesn't tha, how 'old saying goes?'

'Aye, I do,' Roger answered, and said in unison with Sam, 'Tha mun hear *choch* bells ring three times on Sunday afore stooks are lifted into 'stack.'

'I'll make sure we lift the stooks after next Sunday, don't worry. They're almost ready.'

''Stalks not too green?' Sam asked anxiously. 'They'll fire if they are.'

'They're coming along fine. I promise.'

Sam took a deep breath. 'Aye. Tha's a good

412

lad and I mun tell thee summat. I want that tha should go to Australia. We'll manage here all right once I'm up and about.'

'No,' Roger said firmly. 'It was a crazy idea in any case. There's too much to do here.'

Sam shook his head. 'It would be good for thee to go. Your ma would like that, especially for thee to see her brother Joe.' He rubbed the side of his face as if it ached. 'And I reckon that yon young fella, Ralph, might stop here for a bit. He seems a mite sweet on our Amelia.'

'He is,' Roger agreed. 'He wants to marry her.'

'Well, there we are then.' Sam put his head back on the pillow. He seemed tired after all the talking. 'He's a clever young chap. He can help out. I'll show him. He'll soon get 'hang o' things.'

Chapter Thirty-Seven

Mrs Boyle confided to her hostess that she had decided to return to Australia after all.

'It will be hard for you to go back, Mrs Boyle, but I feel sure that you have made the right decision.' Emily Linton's manner to her guest was warm and sympathetic. 'Phoebe will need your support and love. There will be many difficulties ahead for her.'

'I know.' Mrs Boyle sighed. 'And that is why I changed my mind. I realized that I could not abandon her, that my own feelings were of secondary importance.'

'And you will see your son again,' Emily smiled. 'That will bring you great joy.'

'Yes,' she replied a little dubiously. 'But not so often. I received a letter from him yesterday in which he said that he will not be at home when I return; he is to share a house with his friend Marius Nugent. He does not get along with his father, Mrs Linton. He is – of a sensitive nature, and does not share his father's ideals.'

'So you will spend some lonely hours when your husband is away from home?'

'The hours are more lonely when he is *at* home, Mrs Linton,' Mrs Boyle said sadly, but then added optimistically, 'but I intend to make some changes in my life. I am going to endeavour to be as brave as my daughter is. I will not be bowed down by my husband's rules any longer. I will visit Phoebe openly, as I will also visit my dear friend Meg.'

'Tell them of us,' Emily said eagerly, 'and tell them that we think of them constantly.' She hesitated and when she spoke again her voice was husky and full of tears. 'And that we are lending them our dearest son Roger in exchange for theirs, who loves our eldest daughter.'

'Goodbye then, old fellow.' Ralph put out his hand to Jack who grasped it firmly with both of his. 'Think of me sometimes when you are not thinking of your lovely wife.'

'I will think of you often,' Jack replied with feeling. 'I will think of the freedom of our boyhood at Creek Farm when we thought ourselves brothers. And of our struggles as we grew up, when we perceived the prejudices of those who did not understand that we were equals; and I will think of your friendship which never wavered. Now I must stand alone without your support.'

Ralph felt his eyes prickle. 'You will always

have my support, Jack. Know that even though we are miles apart.' He swallowed hard. 'Shall we ever meet again?' he asked softly of his lifelong younger friend, who always seemed wiser than he was.

'We will, brother.' Jack's brown eyes were moist and he put both arms around Ralph and hugged him. 'Never fear. We will meet again.'

Two letters came with a York postmark on them. One was for Ralph. 'It's from Elizabeth,' he said, looking up at Amelia who had received the other. 'She says, "I have heard from two different sources that Edward Scott has left the country. One said that he had gone to Italy, the other said to Germany. Either way he has gone and we may all breathe a sigh of relief that we may never see him again. His house is shuttered and empty, and there is no sign of Dolly either." '

'That is good news!' Amelia held the other letter in her hand. 'No-one will be sorry if he is never heard of again. My letter is also from Elizabeth. She tells me that she has just heard that Moira's mother has died. She has told Moira so that she can grieve, and asks, will I tell Kieran so that he can do the same and know that their mother is at rest.

'Poor Elizabeth,' she murmured. 'She was never able to do that for her mother, not until you came along.' Then she gave a sudden smile. Elizabeth had also said how proud and happy she and Harriet were to have discovered such a brother as Ralph, who was so kind and understanding as well as bold and brave. I will not tell him that, she determined. That will keep for some other time.

'Why are you smiling, Amelia? Did Elizabeth say something more?' he queried.

'No.' She put the letter back in the envelope. 'Nothing else.'

Since Jack and Phoebe, Mrs Boyle and Roger had departed for Australia, Amelia and Ralph had spent less time together and their courtship was deferred, as Ralph introduced himself to the local farmers and estate workers and asked their opinion of farming methods. They talked of ploughs and cultivators, grubbers and drills and of the exodus of farm workers into towns where they could earn more money in factories, if indeed they could find work. He was invited to attend agricultural clubs where he heard the grumbles of the labourers, and the insistence of the landowners that they must move with the times or they would be bankrupt.

He pored over agricultural-machinery catalogues, and Amelia and her mother, with the steward, went over the estate accounts and worked out whether or not what Ralph proposed was feasible.

Sam had finally agreed that buying the sail reaper had been a good investment; now he had to be persuaded that they should buy other machinery.

'A horse mower, Sam,' Ralph suggested enthusiastically. 'It will mean that we can cut when the hay is lush and in full flower and the weather is right. And it also means that *you* can use it.' Sam's movements were restricted since his seizure, though he was now up and walking slowly.

'Nay, I don't know about that,' he said ponderously. 'I'm not used to mechanical things.'

'A boy could use it,' Ralph assured him. 'Let alone an experienced farmer such as yourself.'

'It's all very well.' Sam stared straight at him. 'Spending money on newfangled ironwork. What's going to happen if tha doesn't stop here? What if tha goes back to Australia and teks our Amelia as well? What'll we do then eh? Tell me that!'

Ralph was silenced. Amelia hadn't said yes or no to his proposal. And if she said no, then he couldn't stay, there would be no place here for him. Where would there be a place? Would I settle again in Australia working under Da? he pondered. Would Da give me more responsibility and would I want it if he did? He gave a little shake of his head. Wherever he went, without Amelia, he realized, it wouldn't be home.

He gazed back at Sam. 'It needs some thought, doesn't it, Sam? We need to take our time.'

Sam, who had expected to be persuaded and cajoled, stared at him in surprise. 'Well, not that long!' he said. 'I don't know how long I've got,

418

do I? If we're going to modernize, we've got to get started, so tha'd better let me tek a look at them catalogues.'

I'm afraid: that's the trouble, Amelia finally admitted to herself. All my grand thoughts of travel abroad and when it comes down to it, I don't know if I am brave enough. I enjoyed my time in Switzerland but I always knew I would come back, and when I was a child and always asking Papa to take me on his ships I knew that I would be safe with him. But Australia! It is so very far away.

'Mama,' she appealed to her mother. 'When you were in Australia, did you ever think that you would like to stay?'

Her mother gazed into the faraway past, and shook her head. 'I always wanted to come back,' she said softly. 'I belong here, my roots are well down. But', she said, and looked at her daughter with affection and understanding, 'if your father had wanted to stay, then I would have done so, just to be with him.'

She smiled and said, 'But he knew me so well. He knew that I wanted to come home.'

The next morning, Amelia was about to start breakfast when her mother came in dressed in her green travelling outfit. On her head was a matching hat with a veil. As Amelia looked up to greet her, the trap driven by Ralph went past the window to the door. 'Are you and Ralph going somewhere, Mama?' she asked.

Her mother nodded. 'Yes, and you too, Amelia. I thought the three of us would take a drive. It's short notice, I know, but I had a sudden desire to go somewhere in particular, and I also wanted to show Ralph. That's all right isn't it, Ralph?' she asked, as he came into the breakfast room. 'You haven't anything pressing that you must do today?'

'No, I haven't, Aunt Emily. There's nothing that can't wait a day.'

Hedges were being cut and relaid, the stubble being ploughed and fences repaired ready for winter, and Sam had his head down over the catalogues and could be heard every now and again exclaiming, 'Well I never.'

Amelia hurried upstairs after finishing breakfast to put on a warm jacket over her wool dress. She took a hat from the shelf, a blue beribboned one with a jaunty feather in it, and placed it on her head. Then, looking at herself in the mirror, took it off and put on a plain grey one. 'No.' She looked this way and that at her reflection. 'Today I will be frivolous,' and she took it off and put back the first one, tipping it over her forehead, so that it gave her a rather saucy image.

'I'll drive, Ralph,' Amelia's mother said as they went out into the autumn sunshine. 'You and Amelia can sit back and enjoy the ride!'

Amelia laughed. 'This is very mysterious, Mama, where are we going?'

Her mother shook the reins and they moved

off, the trap jerking so that Ralph and Amelia were thrown against each other. 'We are going', said Emily, as she negotiated the gate at the end of the drive, 'to a place I haven't visited since I was five years old! Sit back,' she repeated. 'It will take us an hour. But,' she added quietly, almost under her breath, 'much longer if we were walking.'

They set off at a spanking pace, but presently the mare eased to a brisk trot and they bowled along the Holderness lanes, between hawthorn hedges glistening with early berries and horse chestnut trees with crisp golden leaves and the last of the nut-brown conkers dropping with a soft thud onto the road below. Rabbits and stoats ran in front of them and pheasants rattled and croaked in the woodland on either side of the meandering road.

They came to a rise and Ralph looked across the Holderness Plain. He could see for miles across acres of harvested stubble of gathered corn, which glowed warm in the morning light, except on those farms where it had been burnt black and gave off the smell of acrid smoke. Along a distant road a plank-sided wagon stacked high with winter wood was being drawn by a pair of draught horses, and on the horizon to the west he could see the shadowy outline of hills and dark copses.

'Is that the Wolds?' He nodded over to the far-off grey rise.

'Yes,' Amelia answered. 'My father's family are

421

from there. It's lovely. Gentle rolling hills and pastureland, a different landscape entirely from Holderness.'

He took hold of her hand and stroked her fingers. 'You're happy here, are you not, Amelia?' His voice was low.

'Yes,' she whispered. 'I am. But that is not to say that I wouldn't be happy elsewhere.'

He smiled then and squeezed her fingers gently, but made no answer.

They came presently to a narrow road which drew past a manor house and Mrs Linton slowed the horse to a walk. 'I remember coming past here with Sam when I was a child,' she said. 'It was the biggest house I had ever seen and Sam touched his cap as we went by,' she laughed. The road continued through a wood where she told Ralph that masses of bluebells and primroses grew in the spring.

'Mama is reminiscing,' Amelia whispered. 'We have visited that house several times since then.'

'Ah, yes.' Her mother overheard her. 'That is true, Amelia. We have visited the house as neighbours, but at the time I am remembering, I was a nobody. Just a poor child leaving home.'

They came eventually to a coach road which led between the town of Hull and the coast, and Mrs Linton drove up it for a little way until they came to a large red brick building. 'The workhouse!' she said softly. 'Where your da grew up, Ralph.'

Ralph sat forward suddenly. 'Da?' His father's

past suddenly confronted him and came alive. 'He lived here?'

'With our mother,' Aunt Emily said quietly. 'She died in poverty here and was buried in a pauper's grave.'

She said no more, but turned the mare's head and drove back the way they had come. Ralph twisted around in his seat and watched as the building disappeared as they dropped down the hill and then up another rise, before coming off that road to enter another set of narrow winding country lanes.

'Mama?' Amelia asked quietly, 'did you and Sam walk all this way?'

'We did. We had no trap, no horse or donkey. We walked from where I am going to take you, almost to the Humber bank, and the cottage which was to become my home for many years until I went into service.'

Ralph and Amelia looked at each other. It was a very long walk for a small child.

They passed a hamlet of half a dozen houses and then the road became just a track. 'We will have to walk from here,' Aunt Emily said and her voice shook. 'It isn't far.'

Ralph helped her down and then Amelia, and tied the mare's reins to a tree. 'Aunt Emily,' he said. 'I can't help thinking that this is upsetting for you.'

'No,' she said. 'I should have done this long ago, but I know now why I have waited. The time wasn't right. But now it is! Come with me.'

She led them down the track which although overgrown was still well used; then she stopped. Ahead of them was a small dwelling, a hovel almost, but someone was living in it for the door was open and the chimney had a curl of smoke coming from it.

'The fire always smoked,' she murmured. 'We always had to open the door.' A tear trickled down her cheek. 'This is where Joe and I were born,' she said in a whisper. 'Your da, Ralph! This is where we lived with our mother and father.'

Ralph felt a sudden rush of emotion and he caught his breath as if in pain. I didn't understand. Whenever Da spoke of his childhood, it was as if he was talking of another world. And now here it is in front of me.

His aunt was speaking. 'And on this very path,' she said, 'as Sam came to collect me to take me away, I saw Joe. He was crying. He was eight years old, and had just been told by the estate foreman that he wasn't wanted for work.' She clutched her throat. 'There was no work for him after the harvest, because he wasn't big enough, and Joe knew, even then, how much he was depended upon, that there was no other money coming into our home. Eight years old!' she repeated. 'Just a child.'

'I didn't know,' Ralph muttered, and felt Amelia's hand steal into his.

'Nor did I,' she murmured. 'And if we had known, would we have understood? We have not known poverty or privation to have any understanding of it.'

Her mother turned to them. 'I want to be alone for a little while and I would like to knock on the cottage door and see who is living there. I'll see you back at the trap.'

She walked away from them down the path to the cottage and Ralph exhaled a deep breath. He felt very strange. It was as if he had been on a long journey and had finally arrived at his destination. He had set off from Australia in search of his family and discovered that they had been with him all his life. That although the blood of his ma and da didn't run through his veins, he was shaped irrevocably by them, and not by the man who had given his seed, or the mother who had given birth to him.

'Ralph!' Amelia said softly, and the feather in her hat fluttered as she looked up at him. She felt her love for him enveloping her as she realized intuitively that his search was ended. 'Ralph! I will marry you, and I will come with you back to your home in Australia.'

He put his hand on her face and gently stroked her cheek. He shook his head and she felt a fleeting pang of dismay. Had she taken too long? Did he no longer want her? But then she saw his eyes crinkle and he gave a pensive smile. 'How could I take you away from here, Amelia? This is where you belong.'

'But—' she began, and he shook his head as he continued. 'Sam showed me,' he said, 'only the other day, how to graft a stem from one rose onto another, so that they shared the same root-stock.'

She wrinkled her brow. She knew that. What did he mean?

'My da – Joe,' he said, and he kissed her on the nose so that she smiled and knew that everything would be all right, after all. 'He was that rootstock, and he and Ma grafted me to them so that I became theirs. Do you understand what I am saying?'

'Yes,' she murmured, not wanting to break the moment, for she could see that he was emotional. 'I do understand.'

He blinked and gave a sudden grin. 'I thought you would. You seem to know me so well!'

She lowered her eyes. She hadn't always. She had been so wrong about him on several occasions. 'So, you will return to Australia? Where you belong?' So be it, she thought. I will go with him if that is what he wants.

'Do you love me, Amelia?' he asked softly.

'Yes,' she replied. 'I do,' and she lifted her lips to his. 'And I will go with you, wherever you choose to go.'

He heaved a sigh and put his arms around her and neither of them saw her mother standing in the cottage doorway watching them, with a shadow of someone behind her.

'We will go back,' he murmured, giving small kisses on her ear, 'to see Ma and Da and Peggy. But not yet, and we will come back. I choose to stay here with you, if you will have me. This is where my roots are and Da and Ma will be happy for me, to know that I have come home.'

He tucked her arm into his and turned her so that they were facing back up the track, away from the cottage. 'Come, Miss Linton,' he smiled. 'Let us not delay. I have a courtship to continue.'

She gave a chuckle. Life would not be dull with such a husband. With her bare hand she pushed aside a bramble that was laid across their path; the berries on the bush were already turning a rich luscious black, and where its tip touched the earth it had rooted, sending down suckers and making a strong loop.

'Look,' he said, as they came out from the track, and pointed upwards into the sky. The very last late swallows of the summer were swooping overhead, wheeling and crying with their high-pitched note.

'They're ready to fly,' she said softly.

He nodded, and bent to kiss her. 'Yes. But they'll be back. They will come home again.'

THE END

EMILY
by Valerie Wood

From shame and imprisonment to a new life . . .

Emily was only five years old when she was sent away
from her Ma and Da and her brother Joe to go and
live with old Granny Edwards. Growing up to be a
loving and hard-working child, she goes into service
at the age of twelve at the house of Roger Francis,
whose connections with Emily's own family prove to
be closer than she could ever have imagined. Roger's
daughter Deborah takes a fancy to Emily, and when
she moves away to another household in Hull Emily
finds that her new employer's son, Hugo, is to marry
Deborah. But Hugo, too, has become obsessed with
Emily; he dishonours her and betrays her, bringing
her to the very depths of ruin.

Imprisoned, tried and transported to Australia, her
life seems finished – until she is reunited with the one
man who can save her from her misery and bring her
wealth and happiness.

0 552 14740 0

THE ROMANY GIRL
by Valerie Wood

Polly Anna could not remember her father, and after her mother died, in poverty, when Polly Anna was just three, the workhouse was the only place for her. Helped by Jonty, a young misfit who became her best friend, she run away with the fairground folk and became a horserider and acrobat – travelling to Bartholomew Fair, Nottingham Goose Fair and Hull Fair. Her friends became the circus people and the gypsies, and her home the caravans and tents of the travellers.

Meanwhile, in a great house in the Yorkshire Wolds, old Mrs Winthrop had never given up hope of finding her daughter, who eloped with a handsome Romany and was never seen again. Her young neighbour Richard Crossley set out to find the missing daughter, and discovered the colourful world of the fairs and the gypsies. He also discovered Polly Anna – once the waif from the workhouse, and now a fully-fledged *Romani Chi* – the Romany girl.

0 552 14640 4

THE DOORSTEP GIRLS
by Valerie Wood

Ruby and Grace had grown up in the slums of Middle Court, the poorest place in Hull. Friends since early childhood, they had supported each other in bad times and good. Ruby's ma, Bess, addicted to the opium which dulled the pain of her miserable existence, tried hard to be a good mother, but without too much success, while Grace's parents, Bob and Lizzie, looked after the girl – as well as their own family – as best they could. But the two families were bound together by more than friendship, and secrets from the past threatened to make their hard lives even more difficult.

The local cotton mill had provided work for Ruby and Grace since they were nine years old, but with the decline of the industry they, like many others, were cast off. Both girls found themselves the object of attention from the mill owner's sons, but as times grew harder and money became even scarcer, Grace became involved in a militant campaign against poverty and injustice, while Ruby was tempted into prostitution. Both girls were searching for something which would take them far away from the slums they had always known.

By the author of *The Hungry Tide*, winner of the Catherine Cookson Prize for fiction, and also *Annie*, *Children of the Tide*, *The Romany Girl*, *Emily*, *Going Home* and *Rosa's Island*.

0 552 15031 2

FAR FROM HOME
by Valerie Wood

When Georgiana and her maid, Kitty, make the long sea-journey from their native East Yorkshire to America, they are seeking a new life of freedom. But in New York, Georgiana encounters an imposter posing as Edward Newmarch, her cousin's womanising husband, who has abandoned his wife and fled to America. Edward himself seems to have vanished.

Meanwhile Edward, having escaped from a disastrous marriage in England, is now running from a bigamous union with the daughter of a wealthy plantation owner. His flight takes him through Mississippi swamps, across arid desert and mountain ranges towards the gold fields of California. As Georgiana and Kitty journey to the hidden valley of gold, and Edward tries to flee his enemies, the dangers and passions of this new country and its people threaten to overwhelm them.

By the author of *The Hungry Tide*, winner of the Catherine Cookson Prize for fiction, and also *Annie*, *Children of the Tide*, *The Romany Girl*, *Emily*, *Going Home*, *Rosa's Island* and *The Doorstep Girls*.

0 552 15032 0

A SELECTED LIST OF FINE NOVELS
AVAILABLE FROM CORGI BOOKS

THE PRICES SHOWN BELOW WERE CORRECT AT THE TIME OF GOING TO
PRESS. HOWEVER TRANSWORLD PUBLISHERS RESERVE THE RIGHT TO
SHOW NEW RETAIL PRICES ON COVERS WHICH MAY DIFFER FROM
THOSE PREVIOUSLY ADVERTISED IN THE TEXT OR ELSEWHERE.

☐ 14058 9	**MIST OVER THE MERSEY**	*Lyn Andrews*	£6.99
☐ 14974 8	**COOKLEY GREEN**	*Margaret Chappell*	£6.99
☐ 14712 5	**ROSIE OF THE RIVER**	*Catherine Cookson*	£5.99
☐ 14452 5	**PARADISE PARK**	*Iris Gower*	£5.99
☐ 15066 5	**TROUBLE IN PARADISE**	*Pip Granger*	£5.99
☐ 14538 6	**A TIME TO DANCE**	*Kathryn Haig*	£5.99
☐ 14906 3	**MATTHEW & SON**	*Ruth Hamilton*	£5.99
☐ 14566 1	**THE DREAM SELLERS**	*Ruth Hamilton*	£5.99
☐ 14686 2	**CITY OF GEMS**	*Caroline Harvey*	£5.99
☐ 14535 1	**THE HELMINGHAM ROSE**	*Joan Hessayon*	£5.99
☐ 14603 X	**THE SHADOW CHILD**	*Judith Lennox*	£5.99
☐ 13910 6	**BLUEBIRDS**	*Margaret Mayhew*	£6.99
☐ 14872 5	**THE SHADOW CATCHER**	*Michelle Paver*	£5.99
☐ 14752 4	**WITHOUT CHARITY**	*Michelle Paver*	£5.99
☐ 12607 1	**DOCTOR ROSE**	*Elvi Rhodes*	£5.99
☐ 15051 7	**A BLESSING IN DISGUISE**	*Elvi Rhodes*	£5.99
☐ 14903 9	**TIME OF ARRIVAL**	*Susan Sallis*	£5.99
☐ 15050 9	**FIVE FARTHINGS**	*Susan Sallis*	£6.99
☐ 15052 5	**SPREADING WINGS**	*Mary Jane Staples*	£5.99
☐ 15138 6	**FAMILY FORTUNES**	*Mary Jane Staples*	£5.99
☐ 14990 X	**DATING GAME**	*Danielle Steel*	£6.99
☐ 14506 8	**JOURNEY**	*Danielle Steel*	£6.99
☐ 14118 6	**THE HUNGRY TIDE**	*Valerie Wood*	£5.99
☐ 14263 8	**ANNIE**	*Valerie Wood*	£5.99
☐ 14476 2	**CHILDREN OF THE TIDE**	*Valerie Wood*	£5.99
☐ 14640 4	**THE ROMANY GIRL**	*Valerie Wood*	£5.99
☐ 14740 0	**EMILY**	*Valerie Wood*	£5.99
☐ 14846 6	**ROSA'S ISLAND**	*Valerie Wood*	£5.99
☐ 15031 2	**THE DOORSTEP GIRLS**	*Valerie Wood*	£5.99
☐ 15032 0	**FAR FROM HOME**	*Valerie Wood*	£5.99

All Transworld titles are available by post from:

Bookpost, P.O. Box 29, Douglas, Isle of Man IM99 1BQ

Credit cards accepted. Please telephone +44(0)1624 836000,
fax +44(0)1624 837033, Internet http://www.bookpost.co.uk or
e-mail: bookshop@enterprise.net for details.

Free postage and packing in the UK.
Overseas customers allow £2 per book (paperbacks) and £3 per book (hardbacks).